DIRTY SECRETS

A STEAMY BILLIONAIRE ROMANCE

SEDONA VENEZ

WANT FREE SEDONA VENEZ BOOKS?

Sign up for Sedona Venez's Newsletter and receive FREE BOOKS. In addition to the free stories, you will also get special pricing, exclusive previews and news of new releases.

GET A FREE SEDONA VENEZ BOOK!

Join Sedona's mailing list to be the first to know of new releases, free books, special prices and other author giveaways.

https://sedonavenez.com/free-book

TWISTED LIES

"It has been said, 'Time heals all wounds.' I do not agree. The wounds remain. In time, the mind, protecting its sanity, covers them with scar tissue, and the pain lessens. But it is never gone."

—Rose Kennedy

PROLOGUE

SINTHIA

Manhattan. Present Day. W.C. (With Core)

How the hell did this shit happen?

I fucking hate him, but I want him.

It was sick and sordid, and I couldn't tell what this really was. I only knew when I was around him, he suffocated me with his twisted lies and dirty secrets, only to cruelly resuscitate me. And shamefully, I loved it.

Core stepped forward, caging me alongside his desk, making sure my body was flush against his. "Ready to fuck, Sin?" he whispered in my ear.

I sucked in a breath as his hard bulge pressed into my stomach. Mesmerized, I watched his hand reach out. His callused fingers slid down my cheek before his thick thumb dragged across my bottom lip and penetrated the barrier of my wet, pouty lips. My body jerked at the sensual intrusion.

Honestly, I wasn't really sure how to process the touch of a man again. It'd been so long I'd forgotten just how good it felt to have a strong hand touching me.

He scowled. "Sin, don't move," he demanded huskily while grabbing the back of my head with his other hand. "Show me how much you want this, how much you want me. Lick it like you want it, darling."

I should stop him before this goes any further.

I knew I should, but my body thought otherwise. I was high off his lies and drunk off his hate. Now there was no way out. On cue, I ran my tongue along the length of his thumb as if it were his shaft. When he growled with pleasure, a tremor pulsed through my body as my cunt contracted.

Jesus, I'm so fucked.

Our mouths were a breath away. The desire and tension were almost more than I could take. Abruptly, he removed his thumb, still cupping the back of my neck, pulling hard on my hair, before his lips settled across my mouth. My breath caught, my mind undecided as to whether I should pull back or allow him to delve further.

Who am I kidding?

There was no allowing. I was Core's possession, and the cocky bastard knew it.

I moaned sensually as his tongue curled around mine, demanding it come out and play. He awakened a need that lay dormant in the pit of my stomach, a need only he could satisfy.

He skated his hand down and squeezed my hip while his eyes were fixed on mine. "I want you. Now," he growled.

My pulse raced, and my body trembled with want. He was crumbling my resolve. Diabolically, he stripped me bare emotionally, leaving me vulnerable and raw to the bone. He was revealing a piece of me that would be better left hidden. The message was clear. He knew what I needed, and he would give it to me if I took the leap of faith.

He smiled like the devil reincarnated as he released me and sat on the leather chair with his legs splayed. My stomach rolled with anxiousness as I leaped into the pits of scorching hell by pushing up the hem of my dress before straddling his legs. I shook my hair slowly as I rotated my hips. He grabbed my ass hard, stilling my movement.

I trailed my fingers over his chest. "Then take me, McKay, until there's nothing left." I leaned in toward him and bit his lower lip.

He gave me a bad-boy smile, causing my stomach to flip-flop like I was on a roller coaster.

"Sinful." He licked my bottom lip slowly. He pulled back with his eyes locked on to me with a power that left me breathless. "Are you mine?" he asked gruffly.

My heart raced with sickening excitement. I knew he was evil, lust, and darkness personified. He should have terrified me, but he didn't because I was just as fucked up in the head as he was.

"Always," I whispered.

"I'm never letting you go, Sin." Tilting my head back, he kissed me hard. "What I claim, I keep."

I was a spider trapped in his web.

"Now get on your knees," he ordered in a brusque tone.

This was it—the moment of truth that would seal my destiny. Self-preservation finally kicked in.

My mind screamed like a banshee, *Run, Sin! Tuck your ass and run!*

My body tightened, preparing to run away as if a horde of paparazzi was nipping at my stilettos.

Core's cold gray eyes narrowed. "I'm a hard-hearted, ruthless motherfucker who doesn't know shit about love or relationships." He pulled me forward, one hand taking a firm hold of my wrists, while his legs forced my knees apart. "And neither do you." His free hand ripped off my panties. "Perfection is complete fantasyland bullshit."

His hand slid against my pussy, and two fingers pushed inside, stretching me open. I moaned as I clenched around those fingers tightly.

"See, darling?" He smiled knowingly. "That's our reality. It's raw, wicked, and wild—a connection on a level very few will ever have or could even dream of."

I didn't have it all figured out. What I did know was Core was no Prince Charming, and I, for damn sure, wasn't a princess. There would be no fairy-tale ending for us. It would be hard work, and more importantly, it would be real. Life couldn't be all about tiaras and knights riding in to save the day.

Damn it! I would rewrite my fucking story and leap into the black abyss on faith alone because I wasn't looking for forever.

I licked his lips, unzipped his pants, and wrapped my hands around his hard cock before squeezing hard. He hissed as he relaxed against the soft leather chair, watching with intensity as I slid to my knees.

This was my give. This was his take.

And there was no going back.

Till death do us part…

CHAPTER 1
SINTHIA

Manhattan. Past. B.C. (Before Core)

I blinked back happy tears. Me, the girl from the other side of the tracks, had been accepted into my dream school. And naysayers like Kyle Fillion—my worthless ex-boyfriend—could kiss my ass.

Even after all this time, I couldn't believe his hateful words still hurt like a motherfucker.

The truth of the matter was I wasn't sure what I was more ashamed of—that I had been so weak back then when we were together, or that he'd proven it so easily when I allowed him to trample my heart and pride without even fighting back.

My heart raced just thinking about that ego-bruising night. *No. That's ancient history, and I'm not that naïve girl anymore.*

I brutally pushed down the emotional pain.

Fuck Kyle, and fuck love!

Horns honked loudly, mercifully jolting my thoughts back from an impending descent into depression. I sucked in a lungful of stale, humid air as the cab driver cursed and hit his own horn. He mumbled under his breath while tapping the steering wheel as we sat in heavy Manhattan traffic.

Damn, I should have just taken the subway.

I bit my bottom lip, staring at the bumper-to-bumper gridlock. I was going to be late for work, again, and Grace was going to lose her shit. I pushed a few wisps of blond hair off my face, then touched my neck.

"Great," I muttered.

The ringing of my cell snapped me from an almost frantic tirade.

"What's up, Jade?" I smiled goofily.

Only Jade could bring me back from the brink of panic.

"What's up?" She paused dramatically. "My girl, Sinthia Michaels, has arrived! That's what's up. I'm so happy for you, Sin. I knew you would get in!" Jade screamed.

Knowing her, she was probably doing her happy dance in the middle of Manhattan. It was so cute how gleeful and excited she was for me.

"Well, I wasn't as sure. Getting into fashion school was a long, frenzied, competitive process," I responded.

Jade laughed. "Please. You worry too damn much. You're a super-talented clothing designer. One day, your hot collection will be parading down the runway during fashion week. And I'll be holding court in the front row, salivating over all the clothes I get to snap up first."

I chuckled. "Well, thank you for being my living mannequin."

I designed most of my clothes using her as my sounding board. She was patient, enthusiastic, and always there for me. She was everything a best friend should be.

What other high school girl would allow a budding designer to create her prom dress? Only Jade would take such a risk, and it had paid off. The dress had been all anyone could talk about at prom. The excitement over my design had given me the extra boost of confidence to pursue my dream.

I wanted to design clothes for a living. According to Grace, it would be a complete waste of fucking time. Just thinking about her constant verbal barbs filled me with anger, pain, and fucking resentment. Her emotional abuse would have broken me by now if it weren't for my dad's love and nurturing.

Damn it! I miss him so much.

I blinked back the tears. It had been nearly a year, and I still couldn't think about him without breaking down in a sobbing fit. Just trying to cope with his death had been rough on me. He had been my rock. Dealing with the psychological bullying from Grace had made coping with his untimely death and the trials of living without his protection nearly impossible.

But I was taking it one day at a time, and thanks to Jade's moral support, I was surviving. Jade had been my best friend and my biggest fan since high school. We complemented each other despite the fact that Jade and I were just so…different.

Jade was the daughter of Ariana Bellisario—a philanthropist, heiress, and successful businesswoman—making Jade a member of the illustrious group of New York socialites whose monthly allowance was more than what most people would make in a year.

I, on the other hand, grew up in a middle-class family. They had been happy as shit when I'd received a scholarship to attend the ultra-elite private high school whose students included the children of celebrities and foreign dignitaries.

Our differences didn't end there. Jade was beautiful and lithe, with shocking apple-green eyes. My olive-colored skin and features were more exotic—or what guys would call sensual. I could live with that description, but it was my tight, curvy body that caused me angst—well, that and the fact that I had more ass and breasts than should be allowed on any woman unless her lifelong ambition was to be a very well-paid stripper.

Jade was my bestie and my partner in crime. When she needed me, I was there just like she'd be for me. It'd been that way from the first day we met as freshmen in high school, and it would always be that way.

Jade jarred me out of my thoughts by screaming at the top of her lungs, "Sin! Are you fucking listening?"

I clutched my pearls. "Shit! Do you have to be so damn loud?" I snapped.

The cab driver scowled at me in the rearview mirror.

"Okay. Grumpy much?" Jade responded dryly.

I sighed. She was right. I should have been bouncing up and down with excitement. It was a huge life goal of mine to attend one of the best fashion schools in the country. I'd worked so hard for this day, and it was finally here.

"Now, how in the hell are you going to break the good news to Grace?" Jade asked.

And there it was, the motherfucking killjoy—my mom. My fingers twitched. Anxiously, I straightened my crisp oxford shirt and then smoothed down my black skirt as if I were somehow being scrutinized by her unforgiving glare.

"I don't know." I bit my bottom lip. "I'm on my way there now. Any suggestions?"

I felt sick to my stomach just from thinking about the inevitable confrontation. Our relationship had never been good. Grace wasn't... well, motherly. Okay, the woman was plain narcissistic. She always had been, and she always would be.

"Number one—don't let her mindfuck you, Sin. Stay true to your plan. You're going to school." Jade's voice hardened. "You've worked too damn hard to let her dash away your dream."

It hurt like hell to admit it, but I'd never gotten the sense that Grace loved me, and I damn sure never could do anything right in her eyes, no matter how hard I tried. And believe me, I'd tried. It was fucking embarrassing how hard I'd worked to be everything she expected me to be—flawless. I'd even dyed my long, naturally auburn hair blond like hers, which looked utterly ridiculous with my olive-colored skin and exotic features. What was worse was the sheer disdain in her eyes when she'd seen it. In comparison to her ethereal, porcelain looks, I wasn't pretty enough or thin enough or smart enough. I just wasn't enough...and, frankly, the truth hurt like a motherfucker.

I sat stiffly, clenching my fingers around my leather handbag. "You're right. I have to be firm with her. I want to go to school. I just haven't quite figured out how in the hell I'm going to pay the tuition."

"Sin, just tell her you earned her help with paying the tuition. You've been busting your ass while assisting her in that overpriced teahouse for months. For fuck's sake, she claimed she couldn't afford to pay you, but then she went out and bought a luxury vehicle with cash." Jade scoffed. "God, that woman is worse than my piece-of-shit father."

My lips pursed just from thinking about how Grace had burned through the money from my dad's life insurance settlement on extravagant purchases. Including a new condo with a homeowner's association fee that was more than what most people paid for their monthly mortgage. To make matters worse, she was living way above the income generated from her new teahouse business.

I ran my fingers through my hair. "Thank you for giving me the swift kick in the ass I needed. You're right. I must take care of me. God knows, if I don't, she damn sure won't."

"That's what friends are for," Jade responded.

I sighed. "I'll call you later."

"Okay. Remember, I have an audition today, but I'll be home right after. I have a feeling this is going to get real ugly, so give me a call, or even better, stop by."

"Shit! I'm sorry. I forgot your big audition is today. Get off the phone. You need to get your mind right. No more talking about my dysfunctional family." I sighed heavily. "Thank you, Jade. I don't know what I would do without you."

Jade laughed huskily. "Shit, you were there for me when I went through my hot-mess phase, and now it's my turn to be there for you. Just call me, no matter what, okay?"

"Okay. Concentrate on getting that part." I hung up, pulling a compact out of my handbag, checking myself in the mirror.

I flipped my hair over my shoulder, touched up my mascara and lip gloss, and then fiddled nervously with my pearl necklace and earrings. They were gifts from Grace for my eighteenth birthday in lieu of the new sewing machine I'd asked for.

My body jerked from the sharp stop in front of Grace's teahouse. After paying the cab fare, I hopped out. My hands trembled while running them along my tight pencil skirt, trying to get out the nonexistent wrinkles. I froze, realizing I was on my way to what Jade called my *level ten panic attack*. Blowing out a breath slowly, I counted to ten before making sure to cover my one act of rebellion—the tattoo that read *Sin* in cursive letters on my wrist. If Grace were to see the tattoo, she would clutch her damn pearls, screaming that proper young ladies —more importantly, her daughter—didn't get tattoos.

My hands clenched and unclenched while I stood in the middle of the busy sidewalk, jostled by irritated New Yorkers. *I can do this. I can go in there and tell her I am fucking done with her shit.* My heart was racing as if I'd just run a marathon. *I need to get my shit together.*

Okay, it's go time.

I straightened my skirt once more. Pushing my shoulders back like Dad taught me, I marched into Grace's over-the-top Victorian teahouse like I was going to war—because I was, and it would be a bloody one.

Immediately, I gagged from the overpowering rose incense in the anteroom as I stared around the packed, twenty-seat establishment. *Great!* Now I would have a full audience when she went ballistic.

I skirted around the guests milling about and admiring the Victorian-style architecture and furnishings that had cost a fortune—and I should know. I had been an unwilling participant in antiquing with Grace on many long Saturdays. She had insisted everything had to be perfect when she opened her teahouse, which was located on the Upper West Side. Moving farther into the parlor designed with dark wood tables, exposed brick, and the white pressed-tin ceiling, I slowed my pace as I took a few minutes to gather my waning strength before proceeding into the dimly lit dining room with the tall, fringed floor lamps.

My stomach clenched when I saw her, and as usual, not one strand of her blond hair was out of place in her tight bun. Her apple figure— large chest, small waist—was encased in a tight black sheath as she strolled between tables, greeting guests with a beauty contestant's smile and a flawless facade. But her frosty blue eyes told the true story. She was drunk…again.

How could a woman so beautiful be such a damn mess?

Between her binge drinking until she blacked out and her disappearing every night before closing and not returning home until the next morning, she had been more erratic and self-destructive than ever. The strange behavior had been going on for weeks, and I was tired of being her free labor. This was her damn business—a business she'd forced Dad to work extra hours to help her attain, a business that had ultimately cost him his life.

Grace tripped, and I grimaced.

Shit!

This was the last thing I needed right now—to go toe-to-toe with her when she was all liquored up. Like a bloodhound, she sniffed out my presence, pinning me to the spot with a glacial stare.

"Good," she snapped loudly. "You're early for once." She pointed impatiently to the tables. "We're short-staffed today. I need you to work the tables. I'm expecting a big crowd." She jammed her hands onto her narrow hips, looking me up and down with undisguised disgust. "And stay away from the pastries. You're busting at the seams in that skirt."

The guests snickered into their dainty teacups.

My mouth dropped open in shock. *What. The. Fuck?*

Effectively dismissing me, Grace returned to flitting among the tables.

I rolled my shoulders to relieve the pressure.

Enough! I wasn't going to let her bully me. There would be no running away in shame or purging everything I'd eaten to compensate for my inadequacies. *The madness stops now.*

"Mom!" I screamed over the clinking of teacups.

Grace's head whipped around. Her lips thinned. "My name is Grace—not Mother, not Mom. How many times do we have to go over this?"

My stance widened. "*Grace*, we need to talk."

Her eyes narrowed. "Be quick about it."

Okay, if she doesn't want to handle this politely, then I'm not going to make it easy for her. "I quit," I snarled. "Is that quick enough for you?"

Her serene mask slipped. "In my office," she hissed before snapping her fingers at me. "Now!" She swayed off toward her office with her stilettos tapping angrily against the wood floor.

By the time we stepped into the white-on-white, expansive space with a silver, glass-topped desk, I was practically grinning, enjoying the fact that her facade had slipped. Now her customers had caught a glimpse of the real monster she was. Grace slammed the door. Photos of her faded beauty queen–contestant era crashed to the floor.

She stalked toward me. "This is my damn business, and you will treat it with respect, young lady!" she screamed while pointing in my face with erratic, jerky motions.

I flinched. She smiled smugly.

Fuck!

The stench of alcohol on her breath made me want to hurl.

"Respect?" I looked at her incredulously. "You belittle me in front of a roomful of strangers, and you want to talk about respect?" My jaw tightened. "I've been accepted into fashion school, and I'm going," I snapped.

Grace crossed her arms. "Well, that's not happening. You will work here until you find someone from the right family to take pity on your ass and marry you." She stared at me coldly.

I couldn't believe that growing up, all I'd wanted—no, all I'd *needed*—was to be loved by her. It was a bitter pill to swallow that she would never love me, but I had to let go.

"No, Grace, I'm not. I'm going to school. It's what I want, and more importantly, it's what Dad would want."

She glared at me with contempt. "Well, he's not here, is he?"

My mouth tightened. "No, he isn't!" I shouted. "Dad died from working himself to death to give you all the superficial bullshit you demanded, like some pampered princess." My mind reeled with distaste at how cavalierly she was acting, as if Dad's death had meant absolutely nothing. Briefly, I closed my eyes to calm down, and then I stared at her pointedly. "Look, I'm not here to ask for your permission. All I ask is that you help me with tuition for the first semester."

She scoffed. "Not happening."

I shook my head, disappointment clear on my face. "Maybe I'm expecting way too much from you. I was hoping for a little happiness or maybe some compassion." Tired, I ran a hand over my forehead. "Fuck, I'm so damn delusional."

Grace was the only family I had left, and even when she cut me down every day with her hurtful words, I would stay. It was a fucked-up dependency. Maybe all the years of her pounding into my head that

I wasn't worth shit had finally taken root, like poison ivy tainting my soul and mind. Maybe I was just too fucked in the head to leave. *I mean, who in their right mind lives and works with someone who doesn't like them—let alone, respect them?*

I sighed heavily. The answer was abundantly clear—me.

I was done being walked on and making sacrifices for a woman who didn't give a shit about me.

Grace's eyes were vacant. "My answer is no, Sin. I'm not giving you a damn dime," she snapped. "Besides, I need you here to help me run the teahouse."

I opened my mouth, closed it, and then repeated the procedure. "You can't be serious?" I glared at her. "I'm not a child, Grace. I'm eighteen years old. I've spent all my life being exactly what you want—good grades, no drugs, and flawless. After Dad died, I helped you build your business. I did it because I love you, but that doesn't mean you get to make my decisions for me or judge me when I don't agree with you or don't want to be your minion."

Her well-groomed eyebrows lifted. "I will not use my money to pay for some bullshit fashion design school. Besides, I've seen your tasteless clothes, and you're not that talented. Believe me, you will *never* make it."

I stared at her, wondering when she became such a hateful, judgmental bitch. "I'm not working here, and I'm going to school," I sneered.

She went stubbornly silent with pinched lips. "Fine. You are no longer welcome in my home. Consider yourself cut off from me."

I swallowed hard. "Since you've never loved me, Grace, there's not much to miss."

Her face went rigid. "You ungrateful little tramp!"

"What the hell should I be grateful for?" I laughed bitterly. "I spent so long putting everything you want and need first that I stopped mattering, even to myself. I'm not even a functioning person. I'm just a shell." I was done with Grace and her verbal abuse. I needed the toxic waste out of my life. It was time to start anew.

"Good-bye, *Mother*."

Her mouth dropped open in shock. "You'll never make it," she screeched. "You'll be back, begging for forgiveness."

My face tightened. "I wouldn't hold my breath if I were you."

I turned on my heel and walked out of the office and back through the teahouse. I was never planning on looking back. Stepping onto the sidewalk, I ripped the pearls off my neck, staring as they bounced and rolled across the pavement and into the gutter, exactly where they belonged. I glanced up at the beautiful clouds as I exhaled. This was my new start, and I wasn't going to waste another damn second thinking about my dark past again.

CHAPTER 2
SINTHIA

Jade fluffed up my hair, determined to glam me up. I rolled my eyes at her. I guessed it wasn't enough that I had on my hottest outfit. She pursed her lips, beholding her masterpiece—me.

"Where's your party face?" Jade asked.

I yawned. "What are you talking about? This is my party face."

"The hell it is. You look like you're about to curl up as if you were some damn cat." She rolled her eyes. "Get your party face on, damn it. We're celebrating. We're going to turn it up tonight. Tabitha, the Iron Dragon, has finally acknowledged how talented you are."

I pumped my fist unenthusiastically before sliding down against the leather back seat. I'd only had a few hours of sleep, and this was all the zeal I could muster. It had been an exhausting day—or rather, it had been an exhausting year. After I'd enrolled in design school, my life had gone through a tornado of events—from moving into Jade's new luxury apartment in Manhattan to interning during the day for Tabitha Thorp, the temperamental and eccentric celebrity fashion designer. All the while, I'd been working a dead-end job at night.

I was mentally and physically drained.

Even with the steady paycheck coming in, I still hadn't been able to keep up with the tuition. It had been heartbreaking when I'd had to drop out of school after only nine months. I'd really thought my dream was over, but surprisingly, Tabitha had thrown me a lifeline, offering me a full-time job. The job offer had turned my life from negative to positive.

Even though Tabitha was a perfectionist and a pain in the ass, I'd learned a lot from her, and I'd eventually gained her trust and formed a strong friendship. Our friendship had forced me to push my creative process and clothing designs to the next level. So today, when she'd called me into her office and told me she was giving me a small space to sell my designs in her upscale SoHo boutique, I'd nearly fainted from excitement.

"Heads up, your stalker, Jaxon, is going to be at the club tonight." Jade dug in her designer handbag, pulled out lip gloss, and handed it to me. "Here, put this on and plump up those gorgeous lips."

I gave her a sidelong look while grabbing the tube. "Jaxon? How does he know I'm going to be there?"

"Because I told him." Jade ran her fingers through her hair. "It's time for you two to stop circling each other with your exhaustive flirting. Get to the damn fucking already."

Kirby, who worked as Jade's chauffeur, chuckled.

I jabbed her in the side. "Will you lower your damn voice?"

"Ouch! What?" she screamed, giving me the evil eye. "Kirby's like family."

"And it's not flirting. It's foreplay, which you know nothing about," I said.

"Foreplay doesn't last for three months. That's as annoying as a guy going down on you for more than fifteen minutes. Enough already." Jade pursed her lips. "It's been months since you've had sex. All that work and no fun has made you one cranky bitch."

I grimaced. "It hasn't been that long."

"Bullshit."

I counted in my head. *Shit. She's right.* Maybe it was time.

I shook my head. "I'm not sure I want to have sex with him."

I twirled my hair, staring out the window at the New York traffic whizzing by. I wasn't opposed to filthy, hard sex with Jaxon, but it would only be on my terms. My terms were nonnegotiable—no attachments and absolutely no relationships. I didn't have time for it. These were my rules of engagement. The knowing gleam I'd seen in Jaxon's eyes told me he was willing to play by my rules. He wanted me. I was his current fixation, the new flavor of the month, and he craved a lick before he moved on to the next woman.

The situation should have been golden, but something about him niggled at me, warning me to stay away. Maybe I was just annoyed that he was what I called a *chameleon*. By night, he would play gigs like some starving musician, and by day, he was the only son of a filthy rich family, who were waiting for him to get his shit together and join their prominent law firm.

Maybe I was just tired of men like him—cocky, wealthy, spoiled, and privileged. Their entire lives had been planned for them, and those lives didn't include getting serious with women like me with no pedigree. Men like Jaxon would only fuck women from the wrong side of the tracks, and when they got bored, they would settle down with the ice-princess socialite women their parents had picked out for them from the day they were born. I'd learned the hard way that relationships, love, and commitment didn't mean shit to affluent, overindulged people like him.

"Okay… Well, maybe some deep-throat action?" Jade asked matter-of-factly.

Kirby swerved.

"Uh…that's still considered sex." I sighed heavily. "I don't know." I arched a brow. "Don't you think it's creepy that he's been showing up at every club I'm at? It's like he's got a damn GPS on my ass."

Jade shrugged. "Creepy? No. Focused? Yes. He wants you—bad. According to his schedule, you should have been checked off on his 'already fucked' bucket list." She lifted a brow. "Would it be so horrific to try him out? You know"—she waggled her eyebrows saucily—"to take the edge off?"

"You do know he's not some car I can take out on a test-drive?"

Jade regarded me, totally perplexed. "Why the hell not?"

I couldn't stop my laughter. "Okay, you're right. I could test-drive him, but… I don't know." I bit my lower lip. "There's something about him I can't put my finger on."

Jade's eyes softened. "Sin, you've got to get over Kyle."

My brows came together in a puzzled frown. "I have."

Jade stared.

My gut started churning in that familiar way when I thought of Kyle. He had been my first everything—first boyfriend, first lover, first mistake. And just like clockwork, the self-loathing began to slither through my veins like poison.

I sighed heavily. "All right, fuck it, I haven't."

I cringed just from thinking about the emotional mess I was after Dad died. I had been weak. Mom had turned her back on me, leaving me searching for something I didn't understand, even now. I was like a junkie, cut off from my next fix of love, and I'd been left to die a slow, emotional death. Adrift, I'd shut down my heart, but Kyle had wanted in, and I'd let him in because my delusional ass thought he was worth it. But A.K.—After Kyle—I decided there was only one way to avoid the pain of love. Close off my heart permanently. It was no longer open for business, and I planned on keeping it that way.

Jade studied me, worried. "There's no shame in admitting it. He was a fucked-up high school crush. We all have one. Shit, I have several."

I rubbed the back of my neck, feeling the tension mounting. "But the difference is you didn't catch some chick fondling your boyfriend's cock."

Jade's lips pursed. "Uh…hello? Did you forget the Justin scandal? Nothing's more fucked up than discovering a selfie of your boyfriend going down on his mom's bestie."

We shuddered. It was an image we'd both wanted to burn from our memories.

I smirked. "Yeah, but you got even by sending the selfie to his parents and the woman's husband."

"Exactly. No one fucks with a Bellisario." She smiled smugly. "It was the biggest divorce scandal that summer." Only Jade could take heartbreak and turn it into a reality show.

"Well, I lost my chance to get revenge on Kyle years ago."

Jade tilted her head and stared at me incredulously. "Are you fucking kidding me? Look at you." She leaned forward and tapped Kirby on his shoulder. "Isn't she gorgeous?"

Kirby winked at me in the rearview mirror. "Absolutely."

"See?" Jade smiled like a Cheshire cat. "You're gorgeous, smart, talented, and still standing tough, like a damn warrior princess. Believe me, that's the greatest revenge against arrogant asswipes like Kyle Fillion. You didn't crumble and blow away like he'd hoped."

"Yeah, but it was real close."

Jade slapped my thigh. "Not on my damn watch."

She was right. I hadn't crumbled or blown away, but I had changed too much after what happened that night. I blinked back the pain, remembering the pivotal night that was still vivid in my mind.

That night had started out with so much happiness and excitement. I was practically giddy when Jade and I pulled up in the driveway of Kyle's parents' enormous redbrick mansion. I had pinched myself for being so lucky. I was Kyle's girlfriend. After months of me crushing on him hard, gorgeous Kyle had finally noticed me and smiled at me one day in chemistry class. He'd taken my breath away. He was the hottest guy in my high school, and it hadn't hurt that his parents were New York City's most influential political couple. Kyle was destined for greatness. Everyone expected it.

We had come from different worlds, but he'd chosen me over all the girls clamoring for him. Those girls had come from the right families and looked the part—blond, lithe, and beautiful. But he hadn't seemed to care, and just like a tornado, he'd swept into my life and validated that I was worthy of love. He'd said all the right things, making me believe I was special, and in turn, I'd given him everything.

I thought we were in love, and I'd even lost my virginity to him, fucking him on his parents' boat on my birthday. That night had turned into Kyle and me fucking like rabbits every weekend. Jade told me not to trust him, but I'd said fuck it and ignored her. I thought he was the one, so he was worth it. I should have listened. All the shit he'd told me was so unoriginal.

I laughed bitterly, remembering how nervous and excited I had been when we headed inside Kyle's pre-graduation bash, the hottest party that night. I couldn't wait to celebrate with Kyle, and like a fool, I'd resolved to shed my fear and utter the words I hadn't said since the day my dad died—I love you. I'd expected to find Kyle holding court, surrounded by his preppy friends, but he wasn't around, so I'd gotten some liquid courage before I set out to find him in the maze of the huge mansion. Just like everything in my damn life, happiness turned to dust the moment I pushed open his bedroom door. Kyle's designer jeans were gathered around his ankles while his cock was being fondled by some chick with perfectly smooth, highlighted blond hair that fell across her shoulders like a gorgeous curtain.

I remembered how I'd just stood there shocked with my mouth gaping open as if it were some sort of mirage. I watched as the girl glided up from kneeling with too much sway in her narrow hips. When she'd given me a smug look before sauntering out of the bedroom, it felt like a dagger to the heart.

"Kyle? How could you do this to me?" I'd rasped with tears streaming unchecked down my cheeks. "I love you." My voice had hitched.

His face had turned into a mask of hate that shocked me to the very core.

"Love?" He'd huffed out an arctic laugh. "Sin, this isn't love. It never was, and it never will be."

I'd flinched, like a punch was launched to my gut. "If this isn't love, then tell me, what the hell is it?" I'd stared at him with narrowed eyes, feeling my heart ice over inch by inch.

"What do you want from me? I haven't promised you anything, Sin!" He'd sneered while unhurriedly buckling his belt.

"We've been dating for months!" I'd yelled.

His jaw tightened. "No, we've been *fucking* for months." He'd walked up and stared at me without a trace of emotion in his beautiful blue eyes. "Sin, I'm going away to college, and you're staying here to work for your mother. It would never work out between us."

He'd reached out to touch my hair, but I smacked his hand away.

He shrugged. "Take it for what it is. We're over."

I'd stood there, feeling stupid that I'd allowed myself to be weakened after my dad's death. I couldn't believe I'd let Kyle into my heart and body. I never would have let him in if I had known he would hurt me and leave me drowning in the deep end.

"Over?" I'd frozen like a deer in headlights, gasping for breath as I sank into the murky waters of an emotional abyss.

Then he'd gone for the ultimate emotional bitch slap.

"Let's keep it real, Sin. What we had was fun but temporary. You and I know there's no way in hell I could bring you home to my parents. You just don't fit into my world."

His parting words had burned, fueling my hate fire.

Everything had clicked into place that night. To people like Kyle, it was perfectly acceptable to fuck a girl like me in secret and then discard me like trash, like a whore.

Jade nudged me, interrupting my disturbing trip down memory lane. "Sin, I'm not saying to forget. I'm saying you need to heal and let that shit go."

Jade was right, but the truth cut like a knife. I couldn't let it go. No matter how hard I tried to distance myself from the past, it was still stuck to me like shit on the bottom of my stiletto. I tried to scrape it off, but the residue and stench remained.

And Kyle Fillion was that stench, the shit that had lingered. He'd sabotaged the chance for any man to break through the thick ice encasing my heart. Many had tried, and all had failed. I wouldn't—no, I couldn't—trust again, not after Kyle had trampled my heart and pride like it didn't mean a thing.

I stared through the window, watching the blur of city lights as Kirby darted in and out of Manhattan traffic. The past didn't matter. Love didn't matter. Perfect love didn't exist. It was a cliché. I understood good, hard, and sweaty no-commitment sex. No emotions were required.

I looked at Jade and winked. "Enough of this sappy stuff. I'm over that shit. Let's get to partying. It's time to turn it up and toast to the end of my dark past."

Kirby pulled up in front of the club and opened the car door. I shivered from the icy blast of air whirling around us as we stepped out of the car. Jade looked every inch the rich diva as she swathed herself in a huge white-and-gray fur coat, which she wore over the top of a tight leather minidress, leaving her long, tanned legs on display. Meanwhile, for a night out on the town, I rocked my own design, a black silk pantsuit and black bustier. It was sexy with a hard edge, and it was a direct reflection of who I was now.

Jade strutted past the crowd freezing their asses off queued behind the red velvet rope. Giving a bored stare to the intimidating bouncer standing atop a set of stairs holding a tablet, she held out her hand. He grunted and stamped it, and the crowd grumbled.

"What does it look like in there tonight?" Jade asked.

"A mixture," he responded.

Then he stamped my hand.

"This is bullshit. How come they don't have to wait in line?" a female in the line complained.

Shifting uncomfortably, I avoided the heated glares of the crowd. I still wasn't completely at ease with bypassing the line outside the club and going right in with VIP status. But Jade had clued me in on how the whole club thing worked. It was a silent business relationship. The clubs liked to pretty up their establishments, and the fact that Jade was rich and came from a famous family was a bonus. She would party at the club, and the club would comp her drinks. If she liked the place, she would invite her rich, beautiful friends, making that club the hottest place to be.

The bouncer stepped aside, and I followed Jade into the trendy New York City nightspot, located in the borough of Brooklyn, that edged a little closer toward bar-with-a-dance-floor territory. I loved this club. It was one of my favorite places to party. The whole scene felt fairly Miami-inspired with mojitos and drinks that came in real coconuts. The crowd was culturally diverse. The club would have DJ nights or live bands that rolled out sets chock-full of rock, salsa, merengue, samba, rumba, reggaeton, calypso, and a smattering of old-school hip-hop.

An eager hostess hurried over to us as we stepped over the threshold, ready to provide us with the VIP treatment. She escorted us to the lush lounge area with VIP seating where we could indulge in superior table service or just sit in the all-black mezzanine lounge.

Minutes later, Jade and I were sipping our drinks while watching some of the upscale crowd walk around like sheep in the same designer clothes. Their clothing was boring, with no originality, which was one of the main reasons I'd decided to move forward with my dream of designing my own clothing line. After losing the monotony battle with my closet, I knew I had to change the rules. If I couldn't find what I wanted to wear, I would make it instead.

Jade stared at me knowingly. "No thinking about business tonight."

She dragged me onto the dance floor. I closed my eyes, enjoying the exuberant energy of the salsa rhythm. My eyes snapped open when I felt a pair of hands wrap around my waist. "What the...?" I snapped before being spun around and finding Jaxon's blue eyes staring down at me.

God, he even smells good. Damn.

Jade smiled naughtily before sauntering away.

Jaxon leaned in, and his lips brushed against my ear. "When am I going to get your number?"

I rolled my eyes. "Uh...I don't give my number to stalkers." I swayed my body to the beat, enjoying the pressure of his hands on my hips a little too much.

"Stalker? Wow! I've never been called that before."

"Don't you think it's fitting for a guy who always ends up at the same club I'm at?"

This wasn't me making idle chitchat. It was a fact. In one way or another, Jaxon and I always seemed to end up at the same parties. Tonight was the first time I actually took the time to study his face. Blond and handsome, he was tall, that was for sure, and his toned, golden body told me he hadn't missed a session with his personal trainer. By his cocky smile, I knew he was all too aware of his good looks.

"Dance with me?" he asked, flashing his teeth, his voice low and sexy.

I arched a brow. "You know how to dance to salsa?"

"Of course," he said into my ear. "One dance."

The beat of the music thumped as he looked at me with a question in his eyes while his hands squeezed my hips.

I shrugged.

His hips pressed sensually against mine as he took my arms and placed them over his shoulders. He slid his hands along my back. Sighing, I allowed my body to caress his lean frame, my hips gyrating to the beat, and my body stirred.

Fuck it.

I grabbed a handful of his hair. It was soft to the touch, like silk running through my fingers. Pulling his face down, I ran my tongue against his lips just to test the chemistry, but when he tugged on my lower lip and kissed me hard, everything went from playful flirting to full-throttle fuck mode.

It wasn't long before my fingers were stroking through his hair as his fingers walked down my back and landed on my backside before squeezing my ass. I tilted my head back, looking at him through my lashes, before leaning forward, the tip of my tongue licking the heated skin of his throat.

The thoughts running through my mind were jumbled, irrational, and downright surprising. I wanted Jaxon more than my next breath. I nibbled and caressed the exposed skin, smiling when he shivered. The control I had over him was absolutely heady.

Jaxon growled as he picked me up and then pushed me against the wall of the club. To feel the desperation of his hands as they caressed me with an edge of trembling neediness was hot as freaking hell. His mouth touched and nipped me like he was a man on a mission. By the time I came up for air, my lips were swollen and my eyes were glazed over.

He didn't smile. In fact, his eyes were the most serious I'd ever seen.

"I could say a lot of pretty words right now, but they wouldn't mean shit. I want you." He slid me down to my feet. "Come home with me tonight."

I couldn't keep my hands off him. Spreading out my fingers across his back, I enjoyed the way the sensual heat of his skin seeped into my fingers.

He stared at me with unwavering focus. "Is that a yes?"

I nodded. "Yes," I whispered.

I could still taste him on my lips. I wanted to have this moment, knowing it would all disappear in the morning. I would walk away then, never to see him again. And that made me want him even more.

Jaxon gestured toward the vigilant hostess who flittered through the club. She practically tripped over her feet trying to get over to him. "Sir?" she asked.

"Tell the valet to bring my car around," he said briskly before pulling me over to the lounge area where Jade was flirting outrageously with some guy.

I passed her my empty coconut and said bluntly, "I'm leaving."

"You treat her good." She stared coldly at Jaxon.

His face tightened. "Always."

Her eyes narrowed. "You better. I know exactly where to find you."

They glared at each other. I rolled my eyes. "Guys. You do realize I'm standing right here?" They stared at me blankly. "I can take care of myself."

"I'm just making sure Jaxon understands you're like family. No one fucks with my family." Jade winked at me. "Call Kirby when you're ready to go home, and he'll be there ASAP to get you."

I nodded before Jaxon and I pushed our way through the crowd, heading for the exit. As we walked out into the cold air, an expensive-looking silver car pulled up. The valet stepped out, handed the key to Jaxon, and then opened my door. After I slid in and sank down into the leather seat, we exchanged no words as we pulled away. When he put his hand on my thigh with the promise of things to come, I shoved it away. I wasn't big on intimate touching.

He frowned. "You okay?"

"Yeah." I smiled slightly. "Just didn't think tonight would end with me going home with you."

He smirked. "Don't worry. I'll still respect you in the morning."

I laughed. "The question is, will I still respect you?"

He looked at me, his eyes traveling over my body. "I guess that depends on how I perform, huh?"

"Pretty much."

He pulled up in front of a building I recognized from multiple photos in magazines. It was where many celebrities lived. He swerved his car into the underground parking garage before pulling into a space. He turned off the ignition, and I waited for him to come around and open my door.

Then he said, "Look, I don't want you to think I'm running a game on you, but I have to say, I've been watching you for a long time."

I smirked. "All confirming my initial stalker assessment."

He gripped the steering wheel and then released it. "Sin, you're not like all the other women I know."

I rolled my eyes. "You mean rich, spoiled, and boring?"

"No. I mean beautiful, independent, and inaccessible." He paused. "I just don't want you to think this is all about me fucking you."

Oh God!

I was going to lose my shit if he started spewing some crazy promise, thinking it would make what we were about to do seem more romantic. I wasn't looking for romance. It didn't fucking exist—at least, not in my world.

"Jaxon, you don't have to promise me anything. In fact, I would prefer if you didn't because I can't give you anything beyond tonight."

"What if I want more than tonight?" His eyes hardened.

I pulled out my cell. "Then I need to call my ride because I can't give that to you."

He placed his hand over mine and squeezed. "I'll take tonight."

He leaned in and kissed me, but I hesitated. Something just felt… wrong. It was almost as if shackles were being slapped around my wrists. I pulled back, but he pressed forward, his tongue coaxing mine.

I broke off the kiss, but he was not deterred.

He nuzzled his face into my hair and then backed away. "Ready?" he asked.

I stared at him. "Tonight only." I wanted to be perfectly clear that's all he would get.

"I hear you, Sin." He ran a finger across my cheek before getting out of the car.

There was something about his response and his blank stare that made me pause. Common sense battled with the heat between my legs, and the shameless need to have sex with Jaxon won.

As we stepped into the elevator, Jaxon grabbed my hand, but I pulled it away. There would be no bonding or cuddle time or whispers of sweet nothings.

This was all about straight-up sex.

Jaxon placed a guiding hand on my back as we walked toward his door, and I tried to calm my uneasiness. Jade was right. Maybe I was too paranoid. Maybe I did overthink things way too much. *Jaxon is cool. He knows this is only a sex proposition.*

I took a calming breath as I strode over the threshold. I stared at all the expensive furniture. The apartment was freaking immaculate.

"This is new—a guy with a spotless apartment."

"Smoke and mirrors." He winked at me. "My mother pays for a cleaning service. She hates my messy habits."

His admission wasn't surprising and only confirmed my initial assessment. He was a spoiled mama's boy.

"That's interesting." I walked around, admiring the beautiful artwork and photos.

As I'd suspected, his parents were blond and beautiful just like him.

My body stiffened when I felt his arms wrap around me possessively. He pulled me around and into him. I forced myself to relax as his lips came crashing down onto mine. I kissed him back eagerly, my tongue entering his mouth and exploring it fervently.

He lowered his hands from my back to my ass. He groaned as he cupped my ass cheeks, pushing me against his erection. "Playtime is over," he growled.

Taking my hand, he pulled me behind him until we were in his bedroom. I didn't resist when he gently pushed me onto the bed, his eyes focused on mine. I was used to this game of seduction. It all ended the same way, with my sexual itch scratched until fulfilled. I stared at him, enjoying the strip show, as he tugged off his black T-shirt, displaying his six-pack. His well-built body looked like he'd spent hours at the gym getting hard and gorgeous.

I started to take off my clothes when he grasped my hand.

"No, let me." He hauled me up and took off my jacket and top. His fingers expertly unhooked my bra before throwing it across the room. "Gorgeous," he mumbled. His eyes were dark and intense as he pressed me back onto the bed. His lips ravaged me as his hands undid my pants.

I lay there in my panties, wanting him more than ever. I shivered as his fingers pulled off my panties before slipping into my pussy and rubbing sensually against my wetness.

"I'll make this good for you, Sin. It'll be so good you'll never want to leave me."

That was where he was wrong. I would leave him in a heartbeat.

Jaxon leaped from the bed and ripped off his jeans along with his black underwear. I reached up and worked my fingers over his rock-hard cock, enjoying my power when he hissed with pleasure.

"Not yet, Sin." He pressed me against the bed before kissing me like a man on the verge of going full fuck mode on me.

I pushed his chest. "Condom," I whispered. "Where's the condom?"

He gave me a perplexed stare. "You're not on the pill?"

I snorted. "Even if I were, I wouldn't sleep with you without a condom. I'm STD-free, and I plan on staying that way."

His body stiffened. "What kind of guy do you think I am?"

I leaned up onto my elbows. "Hopefully, you're a guy who knows that fucking around without protection is fucking stupid."

He narrowed his eyes. "I don't have any STDs, Sin."

I looked at him incredulously. "Uh…that's good to know. Now, where's the condom?"

I sighed with relief when he slid off the bed and opened the drawer of his nightstand. He pulled out a big box of condoms.

I glared. *What the fuck? He has condoms, so why the hell was he making such a big deal about wearing one with me?*

"Now, wasn't that easy?" I asked him.

He rolled onto the bed and kissed me hard. "You're such a smartass."

"I just keep it real, rocker boy."

He stared at me, and I boldly glared right back. In the past, I would have been self-conscious of my curvy, toned body, but months ago, I'd accepted the woman I was. I was perfectly fine with how I looked, and from the hardness of his cock, so was he.

His head fell to my breasts, and his tongue darted out, circling one tight bud. I jerked at the hot, sensual slide of his tongue. Jaxon trailed his big hand across my stomach, pinning me to the bed, while he alternated between my nipples, licking and sucking each one.

"Jaxon, stop being such a fucking tease," I groaned as my hands reached up and tugged on his hair.

Ignoring me, he slipped his fingers into my damp folds. Moaning, I arched up, wiggling to get closer. His thumb circled and played with my clit as his wicked tongue wreaked havoc on my nipples until both turned to hard points.

Jaxon growled while yanking me higher onto the bed. Draping my knees over his shoulders, he dived face first into my pussy. His thick tongue flicked and lapped my clit with such savageness that I went over the edge, screaming his name like a prayer before I knew it.

Pulling back, he stared at me with satisfaction, with me glistening all over his mouth. "Again, Sin."

He pushed his fingers into me. I panted, my hair sweaty and tangled, as my hips gyrated.

"Scream for me again, Sin. I need to hear it. I need to know you crave me as much as I crave you."

He thrust his fingers harder and deeper. My back bucked, and I screamed like a madwoman. My toes curled as his fingers fucked me into another orgasm. By the time I came down from my sexually induced euphoria, Jaxon was right above me. He ripped open the packet and quickly slid the condom over his cock before lowering himself down onto me.

I groaned, wrapping my legs around him. My body hummed with anticipation. I felt the tip of his cock nudge my entrance before he finally slammed in. He moved his hands to either side of my shoulders as he looked down at me with possession stamped all over his face.

"Oh God, yes. Finally…" He groaned as he started to move slowly.

His cock was driving me insane. Thank God the rumors had been right. He did know how to fuck like a damn champion.

"Fuck me, Jaxon," I cried out.

He continued to piston in and out smoothly, his balls bumping against my ass. My eyes closed as the heat blossomed within my center. He pulled out and drilled back in, and with each thrust, he hit the right spot. I scraped my nails across his back as our bodies moved in perfect synchrony.

"No one but me," he said, pushing in farther.

My eyes popped open. "What?"

"No one else but me," he chanted.

He pulled out and sank back in, hitting my G-spot with every thrust.

Lost in my sex-crazed moment, I gasped out, "Fuck me harder!"

"I'll never let go," he growled as he lost control, pounding into me again and again.

My breathing hitched as my body shuddered, nearing explosion. His body convulsed as he roared. I climaxed with an intensity I had never experienced in my life.

Rolling over, he withdrew his cock from me and stared at me with a sexy, lazy smile. "Again. This time, you're on top," he demanded. He slipped the condom off and slid another one onto his still-hard cock.

I lay still, trying to get my breath back as I planned my graceful escape.

He pressed his lips against mine. "Stay, Sin." He nuzzled my neck. "Ride me."

I heard the neediness in his voice, and I hesitated. I couldn't decide whether I should follow my instincts and leave or give Jaxon a chance by pushing my past behind me. My gut clenched as I made a decision that countered anything I'd done in a while.

I swung my leg over his body and smiled. "My pleasure. If there's anything I adore, it's a good, hard ride."

CHAPTER 3
SINTHIA

Leaving Tabitha's boutique, I plowed my way through the chaotic evening crush of New Yorkers rushing to get home. I was exhausted. It had been a really long day, and my mind was still a damn cobweb of random thoughts. One in particular had me reeling.

He loves me? Holy shit!

A week later, I still couldn't believe it. Right in the middle of our early morning, hot-and-heavy fuck session, Jaxon had looked down at me with those gorgeous baby blues and blurted out that he loved me.

He loves me? Is he out of his damn mind?

We'd only hooked up one time. At first, I'd thought I was just hearing things when he said he loved me, but when he'd followed it up by saying he couldn't picture being with anyone but me, I freaked the hell out. I'd scrambled off the bed and pulled on my clothes like hellhounds were nipping at my heels.

I hadn't even called Kirby to pick me up. I'd rushed out of Jaxon's apartment so fast that I didn't remember to grab my favorite designer underwear. When I'd gotten back to Jade's penthouse, I realized I was fucking commando. *Shit!* And I loved those see-through pink panties. I'd stalked them for months until they finally went on sale.

I shook my head. *I need a cup of coffee.*

My cell rang. *Restricted* with no phone number came up on the caller ID, but I answered, knowing what would happen. The person would hang up immediately or hold on for a few seconds to listen to my irate cursing before hanging up. It had been happening for days, and it was fucking maddening.

I shoved my cell into my handbag and kept walking farther into the quiet part of town. The streets were blissfully empty—no traffic and no rude pedestrians pushing and shoving one another. First, I needed coffee, and then I was going straight home to sketch clothing designs.

I stopped at the corner and waited for a taxi to pass before I crossed the street. Halfway across, I nearly swallowed my tongue when a dark car sped out of the darkness, barreling toward me. In the nick of time, I jumped back onto the sidewalk and watched in horror as the car sideswiped a parked one and then kept going.

What the fuck?

Shaken, I stood frozen. My heart raced.

Oh God, is someone trying to kill me?

Stop it, Sin. You're just being paranoid.

I straightened my jacket and started to cross the street again, only to snap my head to my left when that same dark car peeled around the corner with its headlights off. It screeched to a stop three cars away from where I stood frozen with one foot on the curb and the other in the street. The driver revved the engine menacingly. I gritted my teeth, stepping fully into the street to square off with the car, trying to see who was inside, but the tinted windows prevented me from seeing the driver's face.

Fuck this.

I wasn't going to let some crazy person scare me. I started walking toward the car. The driver revved the engine again and then sped toward me.

Oh, hell no!

I hopped back onto the sidewalk, running in the opposite direction, picking up full speed when I heard the roar of the engine. I looked back, and oddly, it had stopped. My heart leaped into my throat. Not hesitating, I turned back around and ran so hard my chest burned from the effort.

I didn't stop running until I got to Jade's building, bypassing the doorman who was talking to a police officer. Huffing and puffing, I stepped into the elevator. I grabbed my knees, trying to catch my breath. The whole ride up, two thoughts raced through my mind—one, *Damn! I need to get in fucking shape*, and two, *Someone is definitely stalking me.*

Walking out of the elevator, I felt my pulse quicken at the sight of Jade's neighbors standing and talking in the hallway. When a police officer came out of the penthouse, I ran in with dread pooling in my stomach. I skidded to a stop when I saw Jade looking around the apartment with a frown.

"What the hell happened?" I croaked.

"The strangest shit ever," she responded, gesturing toward the door. "When I got home, the door was wide open. I know I locked it. I panicked. All I could think about was that all our shit had been stolen."

I looked around. "What was stolen?"

She frowned. "Not a damn thing. That's the strange part. I looked around, and nothing was gone or out of place. I called the police just in case. This type of shit doesn't happen in this neighborhood—let alone this building." She strolled over to the refrigerator and pulled out two bottles of water.

Thirsty, I walked over, grabbed one, and drank it. Pulling my hair away from my face, I grimaced at the dampness on my forehead from the sweat. "What about the security cameras?"

She shrugged. "I checked with security. There's nothing on them." She stared at me. "This is a new look for you. What's going on with the grimy, flustered thing you have happening?"

"Some fucker tried to run me the hell down," I mumbled before taking a large gulp.

Jade choked on her water. "What?"

"Long story, but I think someone is trying to frighten me or, worst-case scenario, kill me." I nibbled on my bottom lip.

Jade came over and hugged me before stepping back. "Are you sure it wasn't just some crazy New York driver?"

"Oh, I'm sure. New York drivers tend to leave the scene of an accident. They don't come back. This car did and fucking terrorized me for blocks." I leaned my hip against the granite counter.

"I don't like this," Jade said.

"You think?" I asked tiredly.

Way too many strange things had happened over the span of a couple of days, and I didn't believe in coincidences.

Jade's eyes clouded over with worry. "I decided to change the locks, and the locksmith should be here shortly. You go take a hot bath and relax. I can wait on my own. You have an early morning."

"Yeah, that's what I need. My nerves are fried right about now." I couldn't even think about working on my sketches.

Walking through the apartment, I started peeling off my jacket. My mind unfocused, I didn't even realize I was in my bedroom until I stepped over the threshold. As I threw my jacket onto the bed, I nearly fainted when I saw something unthinkable lying there. The pair of pink panties I'd left at Jaxon's apartment were wrapped around a long-stemmed white rose.

Just like I'd thought, there was no such thing as a coincidence.

CHAPTER 4
SINTHIA

I loved summer nights in Manhattan. Sultriness lingered in the air as New Yorkers hustled to their Friday night of fun. *But damn, it is hot.* Now I was cursing my decision to walk instead of catching a cab to the club.

I pulled my auburn hair away from my neck. Every muscle in my body was fatigued from working all day on my new fashion collection. My body begged for me to slow down, but my mind raced a mile a minute with lists of things I hadn't completed.

Maybe I bit off more than I can chew. Just the thought made me queasy.

This collection would make me or break me. It was a scary reality, but it was my reality.

When Lily Sanchez, an energetic buyer from a Fifth Avenue luxury goods department store, had walked into my friend Francisco "Cisco" Rodriguez's upscale boutique and fallen instantly in love with my couture clothing that he sold in his store, she'd changed my life forever. Just like that, at twenty-six years old, I'd moved from fledgling darling of the fashion world to having several luxury goods buyers clamoring to carry my edgy Sin Michaels women's wear line in their stores.

Expanding from selling in posh boutiques, including Tabitha's and Cisco's, to going full throttle in department stores was a scary proposition. Frankly, I was comfortable with selling my clothing in small venues and making a name for myself with my signature street-smart style.

But Lily was right. Being *comfortable* wasn't enough anymore. It was time for me to expand, and I was ready—well, almost ready. I needed financing to help me manufacture my new line, or my dream would die. I was slowly digging myself out of a ton of debt, so no bank would ever give me a loan. So I had been floored and excited when Tabitha called me. She'd been practically giddy that one of her business connections would provide financing in exchange for a small percentage of my future profits. The ink hadn't even dried on the business contract when two million dollars was deposited into my business account with the promise of another million in six months.

Can I really make my new line a reality?

I took a deep, cleansing breath, refusing to go down the destructive path of self-doubt. This was a very exciting time in my life. I should be jumping up and down at the lucky turn of events that had changed my life for the better. But instead, I was focused on all the things that could turn it to dust.

I was finally standing outside the nondescript warehouse. It was a tricky place to find on a little street with minimal signage.

Shit, if it weren't for the big, beefy man positioned in front of the entrance, I would have bypassed it completely.

With interest, I watched as a couple practically pawed at each other while strolling up to the bouncer, who promptly turned them away. Frowning, I strutted up to the burly guy blocking the club's entrance.

"Sin Michaels," I said while simultaneously handing him my ID.

He scanned my ID through a device attached to his tablet. He smiled as his eyes focused on my ample breasts.

I snapped my fingers. "Hey! Up here."

He leered in a simply icky way that said he didn't give a shit before glancing down at his tablet. "The rest of your party isn't here yet, but you can go in." He gestured toward my wrist and then placed a black-and-gold wristband around it.

I arched a brow.

He winked. "It lets the guests know you're not interested in playing. As hot as you are, sweetness, you're going to need it just to keep them off you." He stepped aside. "Welcome to the McKay Club."

I snorted. He'd said *the McKay Club* like it was a religious shrine. Everyone knew about the McKay Club. It was part of a chain of private clubs owned by the wealthy New York City recluse and business mogul, Core McKay. According to insiders, all his clubs were invite-only playgrounds for the elite, rich, and kinky to indulge in discreet liaisons, allowing all their freaky fantasies to come true.

Why the fuck would anyone want to have a business meeting in a fetish club?

The rhythm of the music slammed into my body like a sledgehammer as I stepped over the threshold. Each thump felt like a nail sinking into my head, awakening the migraine I was fighting to suppress. All I wanted to do was go home, put on my comfy yoga pants, and pass out from sheer exhaustion.

Scanning the dark corners of the room, I noticed McKay's looked more like a lavish penthouse than a club. The decor was strangely sensual and intimate, with Asian motifs, bamboo screens, and paintings dotting the walls throughout.

My gaze wandered to the bouncer standing guard before an entrance draped with expensive-looking fabric. He stepped aside, giving way to the men and women flashing their ink-black wristbands. It was probably a room where all the off-the-wall sexual debauchery happened. I was so not interested in going inside.

I sighed, deliberately walking up to the bouncer blocking the entrance. He pointed to my wristband. "Sorry. This area is invite only."

I scoffed. "I don't—"

My tirade was interrupted by a tap on my shoulder. Annoyed, I looked over my shoulder, almost biting my tongue when I locked eyes with a gorgeous man staring at me with more than a little interest.

"Are you going in?" he asked in a smooth, baritone voice.

"What?" I croaked before clearing my throat. "No. I'm not."

"Well, that's a shame." He winked at me before showing the bouncer his wrist and pushing aside the fabric. He strode through without a second glance. Curious, I tried to get a glimpse of the area through the slit of the closing curtain.

The bouncer rudely snapped it shut. "Like I said, invite only."

Pursing my lips, I asked, "How do I get to the rooftop bar?"

He pointed over to the discreetly placed elevator, and I made a beeline for it. The trip up to the roof took mere seconds, and the doors slid open to reveal women carrying high-end purses and lots of men in suits and ties. I could almost smell the money wafting through the air. Just when I thought the rooftop was the PG version of downstairs, I saw the semi-nude bodies gyrating and reenacting scenes from a porn movie on the dance floor.

Inching through the crowd, I made my way toward the bar. I just wanted to get this business meeting over with and leave. Ignoring the interested stares from men and women who were more focused on my legs than their drinks, I reached my objective.

I beckoned the bartender, requesting a dry gin martini.

He nodded and walked away.

I scoffed at the smoldering gaze of a pretty boy who looked like he'd stepped out of a fashion magazine. His hair was too perfectly styled, and his clothing had come straight off the runway. I rolled my eyes when he stopped in front of me, smiling with bleached teeth that nearly blinded me. He wasn't remotely close to my type—too sweet-looking. I liked my men hard and edgy, with tattoos decorating every inch of their exposed, muscled bodies.

He glanced down at my bracelet and then up to my breasts, like he wanted to ask them out on a date. "Hello."

I frowned. *Pretty boy was aiming too high.*

Holding up my hand in his face, I said, "No. Just no. Okay?"

Thankfully, he shrugged before walking away, probably deciding I wasn't worth the effort or the embarrassment.

The bartender slid the martini between my fingers. After picking up the glass, I sipped the drink as I watched Tabitha sway toward me, looking as gorgeous as ever in a head-to-toe black ensemble that accented her sensuous body. Beside Jade, Tabitha was my favorite person. She was a talented designer and my mentor. Behind her polished veneer of Tabitha Thorp, celebrity designer, only I knew that she had grown up on the rough streets of Brooklyn, *doing things she wasn't really proud of*—her words, not mine. I wanted to know what those things were, but she wouldn't share the gossip about that part of her life, so I'd just left it alone.

"Hey, Tabi! I can't stop drooling over your outfit," I said cheekily.

Tabitha kissed me on my cheek. "That's precious. The designer is salivating over her own design." She nudged me with her elbow. "Yes, oh, queen of fashion, you are so great. Let's all dance around and bask in your creative hotness."

I smiled. "Okay, yes, I was fishing for compliments. You don't have to rub it in."

Tabitha eyed me. "What the hell are you wearing?"

I batted my eyes innocently. "Huh?"

"You lied. You said it wasn't finished. I want it. Take it off now."

"You like?" I looked at her coyly. "I'm bringing booty back." I nodded toward the crowded dance floor. "Go run and tell them skinny bitches."

The black leather dress was super short in the front and longer in the back, flaring out around my curvy hips. The skintight corset pushed up my ample breasts while cinching my narrow waist.

"I just finished it today, and I wanted to take it for a twirl—you know, show the people what I'm working with." I smiled saucily.

This was my freak-'em dress, and from the way the men's eyes were following me, I hadn't lost it. More importantly, once I added it to my collection, it would fly off the rack.

Tabitha's smirk disappeared. I knew she spotted the shadows under my eyes.

"Sin, you're working too hard. You need to take a break, have a bit of relaxation. How about that vacation you said you and Jade were going on?"

I rolled my eyes. "Any vacation with Jade wouldn't be relaxation. It would be a nonstop party, and I don't have the strength for that right now. Besides, I have a whole collection to design."

Tabitha's pouty lips pursed. "You have to rest, Sin. You're driving yourself into the ground."

My face tightened. "Well, that's cute—advice coming from the president of the workaholic club. No thanks. I have a lot of work to do. Speaking of work, I left early to attend this meeting." I pressed forward. "So, where's my investor?" My lips pursed with displeasure.

I really hated the word *investor*. It was too mysterious, and not in a good way. Knowing the rough crowd she did business with, it was damn near sinister.

"He just called me. He can't make it. He has a business deal to wrap up, but his partner, Ram Steele, will be coming in his place."

I glowered. "He called an emergency meeting and then doesn't show? Sounds like some bullshit to me."

Tabitha shrugged. "He's a very busy man."

Staring at her like she'd lost her mind, I responded, "And I'm not? What's with all this mystery?" I hissed. "Why can't I know his damn name?"

Tabitha's eyes hardened. "Darling, the less you know, the better. Believe me."

My hands tightened around the glass stem. *Shit! That's exactly what I'm afraid of.*

"Sin, I swear to you he's legit. I wouldn't get you involved if he weren't."

I stared at her with disapproval.

Tabitha sighed heavily. "Sin, you can't have it both ways. You asked me to find an investor, and I did. You got the money. Isn't that all that matters now?"

Is it?

Frankly, I didn't know, but what I did know was that I wouldn't be able to complete my collection without this mysterious investor.

My body slowly relaxed. "You're right." I sighed heavily while tapping my fingers against the glass. "I guess I'm anxious about why he wanted to meet me. Shit, it's been several months since he gave me the money, and he hasn't met me once. Why does he want to meet now?" My eyes widened. "Is he concerned about my business being able to make a profit?"

Tabitha shrugged. "Don't know. I didn't ask."

I arched a brow. "You didn't ask?"

"He's not exactly the type of man you question. He orders, and you do it. That's it."

I furrowed my brows with concern. "Oh God." I gulped my drink.

He was a control freak. This was going to be a mess if he wanted to step in now and micromanage the way I ran my business.

Squished by the mounting crowd, Tabitha bumped me with her elbow and hip. I instantly adjusted to make room for her to lean against the bar.

"Look, there's nothing to worry about." She glanced around curiously. "He's pretty much hands-off until he thinks the business isn't going to make a profit. And your business is on the cusp of making a shitload of money. If it weren't, believe me, he wouldn't have given you the money in the first place." She paused. "Be grateful, Sin. It could be worse. My investor is up my ass on every collection. Do you know what that does to the creative process?" She wrapped a hand around my waist and gently squeezed. "Sin, will you relax? Why can't you just enjoy your success without adding drama?"

Nothing about my life had been easy, especially since I'd walked away from my mother, Grace. I'd had to fight, scratch, and crawl to get to where I was today. I knew I'd earned the right to be here, but I couldn't help looking over my shoulder, waiting for the bubble to burst.

I took a calming breath. "God, you're right. I'm worrying for nothing."

Tabitha winked at me. "That's right, baby. Now let's order a round of martinis, toast to the good life, and hope Mr. Steele drags his ass here sooner rather than later, before we both get pissy drunk."

She gestured for the bartender, but he was already heading toward us with two dry gin martinis.

"Dry gin martinis," he said, sliding a drink each toward Tabitha and me.

"We didn't order drinks," I said, tapping my fingers against the bar.

He smiled beautifully. "Courtesy of the gentleman." He nodded toward a dark-haired man leaning against the bar.

His muscles bunching against his crisp white tailored shirt, it was hard not to notice the tall man staring at me. Tilting my head, I glared boldly at him. Even in the room full of gorgeous men, he didn't blend in with the crowd. He was hot—well, hot and scary. He didn't even smile. In fact, he was scowling at me with menace pouring from him like a dark cloud.

Tabitha's doe eyes widened before she cleared her throat. "Well, isn't he yummy?" she growled, looking sideways at me with a smirk. "So are you going to go over there and thank him?"

He looked like trouble waiting to fucking happen. I lifted the martini glass to my lips, continuing to stare at my new sinful fixation.

"Nope. Just like at the zoo, I like to gawk at dangerous and beautiful creatures from afar."

She jabbed me in the side. "For fuck's sake, you're licking the rim of your glass while eye-fucking him."

Shit! My tongue stopped mid-twirl. I hadn't even realized I'd been doing it. *Damn it!*

I scowled at her before draining my glass. I should be at home, sleeping. Instead, I was leering at some man like I was a sex-starved freak. I snatched the drink he'd sent.

"Jesus, what the hell am I doing here?" I mumbled under my breath.

Tabitha hip checked me, wiggling her body to the thumping beat of the music. "It's okay to break out of your vanilla world and walk on the wild side." She raised her eyebrows.

"Uh-huh." I sighed. "Absolutely not. He's off-limits," I responded flatly.

He was gorgeous, just plain fucking gorgeous. His dark hair was shaved short. His searing gray eyes made me seriously horny. His stark features blended well with his chiseled cheekbones and painfully hard jaw. His body was pure rippling muscle, but he was completely not my type. He looked like CEO material, and I was damn sure I wasn't remotely close to his type of woman, especially with my nontraditional clothing and tattoo-covered back.

I deliberately turned and pulled my long auburn hair over my shoulder, giving him a full view of the intricate tattoos covering my back. I was hoping he would just move on to the Barbie-looking women eyeing him with lustful eyes. I looked over my shoulder smugly, but he was still standing there, staring at me.

Shit. Well, this is new.

Running my hands through my hair with trembling fingers, I mumbled, "Tell me again. Why am I doing this shit? I've got a ton of work to do."

Tabitha rolled her eyes. "Like what?"

"I have clients depending on me."

Tabitha choked on her martini. "Sin, you're a clothing designer not a doctor. Besides, you haven't had a date in months. You work nonstop. Just enjoy the interest of a sexy man."

Feeling his scorching gaze, I turned and stared at him. His eyes flashed as he arched his eyebrow at me. There was no smile. It was probably something he didn't know how to do. When he crossed his muscular arms, my eyes traveled up his tall, well-built body, stopping at his piercing, bright gray eyes. My fingers clenched, wanting so badly to run through his blunt-cut, midnight-black hair.

Shit, shit, shit.

It was going to be another long night of pushing Beast, my favorite vibrator, to the breaking point.

Breaking eye contact with the man, I looked over at Tabitha. "I need to stop. I don't want to raise his expectations because I'm damn sure not taking him home tonight." I nudged her. "Why don't you go over and tame him?"

Tabitha pouted playfully. "Well, unfortunately, the gorgeous lion isn't into me. If he were, I would be over there in a heartbeat, ready and willing to take him down as if I were on a safari."

I laughed, nearly choking on my drink. "I've never had a man stare at me with such intensity. It's like I'm a deer he wants to chase down and eat. Don't get me wrong. I'm not opposed to being eaten by a good-looking man." I waggled my eyebrows.

Tabitha swatted me playfully. "You're so naughty, and I love it."

"But what's up with the I-want-to-rip-you-apart stare?"

"Well, go find out," she responded dryly, gently prodding me forward.

I shot her an annoyed scowl, rooting myself to the spot. "Hell to the no."

Tabitha groaned. "What happened to fun Sin?"

I grinned. "She sharpened her his-dick-ain't-worth-the-trouble detector. With this guy, my detector is ringing like a motherfucker." I winked at her. "Beep, beep, beep."

Tabitha laughed. "Girl, you're a hot mess." Her cell rang. "About time. That's Ram calling. I have to go somewhere quiet to hear. I'll be right back." She started to walk off, and then she stopped. "And when I come back, I want all the juicy details on the lion. Now, scoot." She waved good-bye before walking away with her cell pressed to her ear.

I turned and stared at him. His eyebrow lifted, and my own answered.

"Oh, fuck it."

I strode toward him, and as I stopped in front of him, I tossed my long hair over my shoulder while I licked my bottom lip. Awareness strummed through me. I planted my feet firmly, gathering my strength around me until the menace shrouding him like a veil ceased to intimidate me. I forced my gaze to linger over him, and then my eye caught sight of it—the all-seeing eye tattoo on the side of his neck.

Sweet baby Jesus. I'm in big fucking trouble.

"What do you want?" I asked.

Our eyes locked. The power of his demanding stare willed me to lower my eyes, but I forced myself not to do that. His eyebrow lifted, and mine furrowed. His eyes traveled from the top of my head down to my curvy body, seeming to like everything about it. I swallowed hard, trying hard not to squirm under his sensuous stare. He lifted his glass to his crazy-sexy hot lips and sipped his drink. My breasts tingled, and my nipples went rock hard.

Jesus, who the fuck is this man?

"The question is, do you know what you want?" he rasped with his eyes flickering in the twinkling city lights.

Holy shit!

I had to squeeze my thighs together as my sex clenched with need. His face twitched. I pinched back the urge to caress the light jagged scar running across his eyebrow.

"Does that line normally work on women?" I rolled my eyes.

Humor flashed in his eyes, but then it faded, and his gray eyes glinted. For a long couple of minutes, we just stared at each other.

"You tell me." His voice was diamond-hard.

Uncertainty crept up on me. "Can't confirm or deny." I inclined my head, refusing to cower.

He assessed me with his eyes as I waited for him to say something.

"This is not a battle, darling."

His deep drawl had my heart instantly pounding while goose bumps formed along my arms. His magnetism intrigued me, much to my annoyance.

"If it were, you wouldn't have a chance in hell of winning," he said without a trace of warmth reflecting in his cold eyes.

Something about this man made me rise to his unspoken challenge.

"I beg to differ. I tend to fight dirty."

His eyes flashed. There was no humor, just raw steel. Awareness hummed through me.

"We're not fighting, so you can relax. I just saw a beautiful woman and bought her a drink."

His low, gravelly voice strummed over my body, and a vision of him whispering very kinky shit while fucking me flashed through my mind.

Shit!

I couldn't look away from this arrogant ass. My creative streak wouldn't allow it. He was a work of art. He wasn't classically handsome or a pretty boy. He was very attractive in a rugged and dangerous way. He had eyes the color of steel, and I was fascinated by the way he watched me, like he could read my mind and knew exactly what I was thinking. And I was thinking of all sorts of filthy, dirty things that I'd bet he was well versed in doing.

"Is this your first time here at McKay?" One of his dark eyebrows cocked.

I squirmed from the dampness in my panties. "First and last." I ignored my arousal and focused on him.

"Not your type of crowd?" The corner of his mouth twitched with suppressed amusement, but it was gone as soon as it had arrived.

"I don't do kink clubs. I like my sexual exploits to be a little more private," I retorted.

He leaned down and whispered in my ear, "You have no idea what you're missing, darling."

My mouth parted at his words. My pussy clenched so hard my knees almost buckled. This wasn't good. This was going way past the normal snarky-flirt-then-walk-away routine. Something about him intrigued me, and I couldn't figure out what it was.

"Fuck," I blurted, fighting the crazy impulse to lay myself at his feet.

He lifted his damn beautiful brow again, and I forced myself not to freak out from the pure sexiness of this man.

A small smile played on his lips. "Is that an invitation, darling?" He lifted my hand before I could stop him, and then he brushed his hard lips against the backs of my fingers. "Because I'm more than happy to accept."

When I felt the nip of his teeth against my skin, my breathing became shallow and erratic. I quickly pulled my hand back. "It wasn't an invitation. It was a statement." I held up my mostly empty glass to my lips and tilted it, draining the contents for liquid courage. I was horrified and disgusted that my body was responding to this cocky bastard.

He stared at me like a cat playing with a mouse. "Let me get you another."

My heart jumped in panic. "No, not interested," I hastened to say. "Look…" I arched a brow, waiting for his name.

He arched a brow right back.

"Okay…so you buy me a drink but refuse to give me your name?"

He stepped closer. He was so close I could smell the tantalizing fragrance notes of sandalwood, cedar, and rich amber from the cologne he wore. His hand lightly touched my hip, like he was branding me as his possession. I should have moved away, but frankly, I couldn't. My mind was telling me to get my shit together, but my body rebelled and became even more aroused.

"My name is meaningless since you're too afraid to explore anything beyond this drink." As he leaned over, his lips deliberately brushed my lobe while he whispered in my ear, "Such a shame. I was just starting to have fun."

He pulled back and gave me a sly, dark stare that licked my skin, setting me afire. His arrogance should have been irritating, but all I could think was, *How would his callused fingers feel on my bare skin?* Curiosity added to my inner struggle.

"So I guess that makes you the big, bad wolf in this club," I stated flatly.

He shrugged. "No, I'm just a man who recognizes a woman who's bored with men dropping at her knees." He cocked his head. "Your mind and body crave a challenge. You want to know what it would feel like to drop to your knees before a man." He raised his eyebrow. "Do you want to take a walk on the wild side, darling?"

Mesmerized, I watched his hand reach out.

His callused finger slid across my cheek. "Do you want to play with the big, bad wolf?"

My eyelids fluttered at his words. I could almost imagine myself kneeling between his thighs with his huge hands wrapped around the back of my head. I swallowed hard, snapping back from the edge of insanity. This man was definitely a do-not-touch situation. Pulling away, I was determined to put some distance between us.

"I'm not interested." The words tumbled out of my mouth.

He stroked his index finger over my bottom lip. "There is no strength in denial, darling."

My mouth fell open, and then my tongue flicked over the pad of his finger, tasting a hint of scotch and cigar.

"Good girl," he said lazily, watching me with a heavy-lidded gaze.

Fear spiked. *Sweet Jesus, this man makes me want to lower myself at his feet.*

That would defy everything I was—strong, powerful, and in charge. I snapped my head back, and my lips snapped shut, but he caught me firmly by the jaw.

"Calm yourself. Don't run from what your mind and body know you need." He clamped his fingers onto my chin, gently stroking as if he were calming a baby. The peacefulness of his touch contradicted the iciness in his eyes.

My thoughts spiraled. I cleared my throat and swallowed hard. "Get your hand off my face."

It annoyed me that he touched me so casually, so possessively. There was no asking for fucking permission. He acted like I actually belonged to him.

His slightly mocking smile returned, and he dropped his hand from my face. I knew he'd let go because he wanted to, not because I'd demanded. This man was like no man I'd ever encountered. He brought out a submissive side I hadn't been aware I had, but I had no intention of ever exploring. I needed to leave. Playtime was over, and I was grabbing my toys and going home—alone.

"Well, this was entertaining, but I'll pass on the bullshit you're shoveling."

He took my hand with a domineering gleam in his eyes. My breath caught as I felt the slide of warm liquid between my thighs.

"I'll see you again, darling." He caressed my palm with his fingers, revving the scorching connection between our bodies.

My clit throbbed with greediness. His mesmerizing touch stoked the flames of awareness, holding me captive. The dark, sensual promise in his eyes chilled me to the bone. He was trouble with a capital T.

I blinked, snatching my hand back. "Don't count on it."

I stepped around him, and I could feel his eyes everywhere on my body as I eased my way through the crowd. My hands were trembling as if I were a junkie who needed a fix and mystery man was my heroin. By the time I made it out of the club, I was kicking myself for getting sucked in by his games.

What a total waste of damn time.

Pulling out my cell, I dialed Tabitha. "Hey, Tabi! Where the hell are you?"

"At the bar, looking for you. Where did you go? I came back, and you and the lion were both gone. Please tell me you decided to take him home."

Frantically, I waved down a cab. "Oh, hell no. He was too…everything. Look, I've got a raging headache. Give Mr. Steele my apology." I hopped into the cab and gave the driver my address.

Tabitha exhaled loudly. "No need. He couldn't make it. Just go home, and we'll reschedule."

"Later."

I shoved my cell into my bag and watched the blur of lights as the cab whizzed through the city. Finally approaching the treelined street where my townhouse—purchased when prices were low but poised to climb in the revitalized area in Manhattan—was located only a few steps from Central Park, I barely waited for the driver to stop before shoving the money at him and jumping out. Running up the stairs, I skidded to a stop, breaking out into a cold sweat at the sight of a vase of long-stemmed white roses sitting in front of my door.

"Oh God. Shit just got real." I pulled out the card, reading it aloud. "J."

Oh, hell no!

I grabbed the vase, stomped down the stairs, and dumped it into a trash can. I gritted my teeth, trying not to freak out as I went back upstairs and entered my house.

How the hell did Jaxon find me?

My body shivered with disgust, remembering how the utter madness had spiraled out of control after he'd broken in to Jade's apartment and left the rose and my underwear on my bed.

I'd lived through agonizing months of huge, elaborate vases filled with white roses being delivered to me every day with one creepy sentence scribbled on each card—*Love you. J.*

Even now, the mere scent of roses made me queasy to the point of throwing up.

When the roses had mysteriously stopped showing up, I'd thought the madness was over, but of course, I had been wrong. It had just begun. He'd shown up at every party I attended, and he'd chased away any guy who attempted to talk to me. When I confronted him— telling him to leave me alone—that only seemed to enrage him.

Paranoid that he'd been lurking in the shadows, waiting to hurt me, I'd locked myself away in my apartment, only venturing out for work. After weeks and months had passed without incident, I'd breathed a sigh of relief. I'd thought my world was safe again—until it had come crashing down.

I tried to fight the all-too-familiar dread that seeped into my bones. The memories lingered. The fear remained. Nothing could erase that day from my mind.

The day Jaxon had grabbed me, pulling me into a dark alleyway with a knife pressed against my throat. He'd babbled words of love over and over as he'd brutally ripped off my clothes with sick lust in his eyes. In that moment of total hopelessness, I'd known from his crazed stare that he actually thought he owned me. Bitterness had coated my tongue when I realized I was nothing but a piece of property to him, his possession that he had every intention of claiming repeatedly until I broke.

Tears had streamed down my face as I braced for the impending savage violation. Shivering on the cold ground, I'd turned my head away, letting my mind go blank. I'd known I would never be the same after this day. But when a lone homeless man had stumbled upon us, saving me, I'd been thrown a lifeline. Though, I knew Jaxon wasn't finished with me, and that had just been a momentary reprieve. Utter rage had clouded Jaxon's eyes before he'd sliced me across my shoulder.

His gaze had gone flat and hard. "Never forget, you'll always belong to me," he'd hissed before calmly walking away.

My thoughts snapped back to the present while I rubbed the light scar. "Never forget," I whispered, fighting the cold fear running down my spine.

Jaxon was back to claim what he thought was his—me. I was ready to fight as if my life depended on it. Because it did.

CHAPTER 5
SINTHIA

I gulped my coffee, feeling like shit after tossing and turning all night. My thoughts were torn—half fretting over the horror of Jaxon's return, and the other half lingering over the sensual memory of the mystery man from last night. The only thing chasing away the craziness was reading the newspaper article before me.

First page! They put me on the first page.

I still couldn't believe the woman smiling up from the page, displaying pieces from her upcoming clothing line, was me. I was reeling from being interviewed by the most iconic newspaper in New York City when my thoughts were interrupted by my ringing cell.

"What's up, Cisco?"

"Hello, Sin, baby! Congrats on your interview. The phone hasn't stopped ringing all morning. We have lots of new clients booked for today," he stated matter-of-factly.

I loved Cisco, I really did, but he was a pushy pain in the ass. Our friendship worked well, but the business relationship was sorely lacking.

"Cisco, how many times have I asked you not to book clients without checking with me first?"

I could picture the adorable pout on his face when he said, "What would you have me do? They've been clamoring for a private session with you, and I booked them."

I sighed heavily, wavering between the daunting tasks of creating one-of-a-kind pieces for my private clients and finishing my collection.

I was grateful Cisco had given me the opportunity to sell my clothing in his boutique. It allowed me to cultivate my cult following of rich women who had everything—including catwalk queens and Jade, my in-house muse, all of whom thought nothing of splurging on my edgy clothing. My clients kept me well paid and living comfortably, but my unfinished collection was one step closer to my dream. And my dream was so close I could taste it.

"And it has nothing to do with the fact that you get a hefty commission from every new client, huh?" I knew I sounded grumpy, but I couldn't keep up with the rampant pace of new clients and complete my collection at the same time. Something had to give. "Cancel all the appointments, and don't book any clients until I tell you."

"Come on, Sin," he whined. "I need more pieces. I can't keep your clothing on my racks." He huffed. "Besides, you have to come in. Cate wants to discuss some design changes to her wedding gown."

I rolled my eyes. "Again?"

Agreeing to create a wedding gown for Cate, Jade's aunt, had been a big damn mistake, but I'd decided to do it because of my friendship with Jade.

"Cisco, I can't do it. I have to get my collection done."

"You know her. What Cate wants, Cate gets," Cisco responded dryly.

Sadly, it was the truth. Cate Bellisario was the most powerful member of the Bellisario family. She was beautiful, rich, conniving, and bored. She was currently using her status among the New York elite to get her fiancé—Bigsby Calhoune, a wealthy shipping mogul—elected as the next New York City mayor.

When Cate had revealed she wanted to walk down the aisle in a Sin Michaels creation, it hadn't exactly been a jumping-up-and-down moment for me. Every week, like clockwork, Cate would show up, unannounced, at my house to discuss her gown. Over time, those visits had turned into her giving me unsolicited business advice, even recommending I talk to Bigsby about investing in my "little fashion" business. I politely declined. Her slick-looking fiancé made me very uncomfortable, to say the least.

"Cisco, just cancel the appointment." My doorbell rang. "Look, I've got to go. I'll call you later."

I padded over to the door, knowing exactly who it was. Flinging the door open, I saw Jade bouncing up and down as she excitedly waved the newspaper like a flag.

"My Sin is in the newspaper," she squealed, pulling me in for a tight hug.

I stepped back with a wobbly smile as we dashed away the tears of joy. "Oh, don't get all emotional on me, actress extraordinaire."

Jade pouted playfully. "I can't help it. My best friend is on the front page of a major New York City newspaper."

"Yes, it's a change from seeing your gorgeous face staring up from the entertainment section."

It had been quite a year for Jade. She was on fire and was now starring in a smoking-hot television series. Not to mention, she'd been cast in three lead movie roles this year. I was so proud of her.

I pulled her in before closing the door behind her. "What are you doing here anyway? I thought you'd still be shooting that difficult scene you had so much angst about last night."

She smiled. "Nope. I dazzled them as usual, and we wrapped up early."

I walked over to the kitchen counter, picked up my cup, and took a sip of coffee. "Never the modest one," I responded, smirking.

Jade playfully batted her eyes. "What? I'm the star of that damn show, and I'll never let them forget it."

"Uh-huh." I took another sip of coffee. "Help yourself to some."

She shook her head. "No coffee. You and I are going out to celebrate tonight. First, we'll have dinner, and then we'll hit the hookah bar."

I gestured to the mess of fabric scattered around my house that also doubled as my workspace. "I can't. I have to work."

Jade scrunched her nose. "Too much work—that's all you do now. I'm worried about you. You need to rest."

I waggled my eyebrows. "There's no rest for the wicked."

Jade frowned. "I'm not joking, Sin. You're headed for a major burnout."

I lifted my hands in surrender. "Okay. As soon as I launch my collection, I'll take a break. I promise."

"Bullshit. You're obsessed with impressing that pretentious bitch, Tabitha, and she's fixated on outshining you, her protégée." Jade jammed her hands on her hips. "I don't like or trust her."

I rolled my eyes. "You've made that abundantly clear from day one." Leaning over the counter, I pressed my forehead against the cool granite, feeling the migraine approaching.

Listening to Jade's and Tabitha's snide comments about each other was exhausting, and it was even more strenuous trying to keep them apart. Jade hated Tabitha's biting, acidic personality, and Tabitha resented Jade's privileged lifestyle. I was stuck in the middle of a pointless fight.

Why can't they just get along?

Jade drummed her manicured nails on the countertop. "And you're a stubborn ass who refuses to listen. I've seen the way she looks at you. It's creepy, like *The Silence of the Lambs* creepy. It's like she wants to rip off your skin and wear it like a fucking fur coat."

I snapped my head up, refusing to laugh at her joke. "I'm not even talking about this right now, Jade."

"Okay, well, let's talk about the mystery investor she hooked you up with. How did the meeting go last night?"

I hesitated. *Damn! She's got me on this one.* "You won the bet. He didn't show up. He had an emergency meeting."

She looked at me smugly. "Uh-huh. First, let's deal with what I get for winning our bet." She swayed toward the racks of clothing and pulled out the leather dress I'd worn last night. "I'll take this in cream and make it tight. I have a movie premiere next week, and I need to look smoking hot." She winked at me. "Oh, and you're coming as my guest. Feel free to sex it up with your outfit."

I rolled my eyes. "Anything else, Queen Jade?"

"Yes." Her eyes narrowed. "I call bullshit on that meeting last night. Either Tabitha is a fucking liar, or that investor is a shady fucker. I say yes to both."

My fists tightened. I knew exactly where she was going with this, and I didn't like it. "What do you want me to say, Jade? Money and family don't mix, so I couldn't take money from you."

Jade crossed her arms. "Couldn't or wouldn't?"

"Wouldn't. I know it would have been a loan, but it just didn't feel right." I paused, struggling with the words. "You've been right by my side through the shitstorm of my life. I love you for that and for…well, being you. I don't know where I'd be if I didn't have you in my life, kicking me in the ass when I wanted to give the hell up. But sink or swim, I needed to make this deal happen on my own." I bit my bottom lip. "Do you understand where I'm coming from?"

Jade sighed heavily before walking over to me and grabbing my hands. "I understand more than you think. You're a strong woman, Sin. If I weren't around, you would have survived." Tears spilled down her cheeks. "I can't say the same thing for myself. You're my anchor. I wouldn't even be here if you hadn't walked into that restroom that day."

I sniffled. "Shit, now you're going to make me cry ugly tears."

Before that fateful day, I hadn't been a big believer in luck or that stupid fucking saying, "Everything happens for a reason." Then I'd walked into our high school restroom, and I'd seen a girl, Jade, lying on the floor with a needle stuck in her forearm. The EMT had said I saved her life. From that day forward, we'd become unlikely friends, tethered together by tragedy and fate. We pushed each other further. Our friendship tightened, creating a perfect synergy unmatched by any other relationship to date. We were an unstoppable team who stuck by each other no matter how rough the circumstances.

"It's no secret that I had a drug problem," Jade said. "You dragged me from the pits of hell when the lure of drugs had nearly drowned me. I almost died, but you saved me. You're not my best friend, Sin. You're my sister, and what is mine is yours. That's keeping it as real as it gets."

I tugged her hair playfully. "Why can't I stay mad at you?"

She gave me a hundred-watt smile. "Because I'm charismatic and beautiful." She hugged me quickly before pouring herself some coffee. "Tell me what else happened last night at the McKay Club. Did you see anything wickedly dirty that I can add to my sex position to-do list?"

I snorted. "Like you need help with that."

She winked. "I'm a student always willing to learn."

"Nope. I wasn't invited into the grown-up section." Absently, I rubbed the scar on my shoulder. "But something strange did happen when I got home. I think Jaxon's back."

Jade's eyes widened. "I, uh… Shit. This is bad." She fumbled with her mug as she plopped down onto a stool. "Why do you think he's back?"

"I came home to find a vase of white roses and a note with the letter *J* scribbled on it in front of my door."

Jade leaned forward. "I can't believe that bastard is back to stalking you. You need to go to the police."

"He's careful and diabolical. Even if I went to the police, what in the hell would I say?" I arched a brow. "Leaving a vase of roses on my doorstep is hardly grounds for filing a complaint." I sighed. "No, I'm going to have to wait for him to slip up."

"You need to stay with me." Jade's jaw tightened.

"I can protect myself, Jade. Shit, I've been doing a damn good job for twenty-six years."

Jade grabbed my arm. "Don't get all huffy. I'm worried."

I squeezed her arm gently. "I know. I'll be okay, I promise."

I stared off into space, fighting the urge to never leave the safety of my house again, but I'd come too far to ever let that shit happen. Now everything was finally going my way. It had been a hard road to success, but finally, the pain of my past was behind me. I was no longer the broken girl. I was strong and in control, and I refused to let Jaxon win.

CHAPTER 6
SINTHIA

After finally kicking Jade out so I could start my workday, I finished checking my emails, following up with possible buyers and distributors. Normally, during the initial stages of my collection, the majority of my day would be consumed with design work, closing myself off for at least two weeks just to focus on drawing and sorting through everything. But this time, the design work had already come together, and I was starting on a gown Jade would wear for her upcoming gala. The premiere of my gown would have the fashion hags salivating for the release of my collection, and I couldn't wait.

Sitting on the arm of my couch, I stared at the beginnings of the Sin Michaels collection, which were hanging on racks in parts of my four-thousand-square-foot townhouse. I exhaled a frustrated breath. I was going to have a busy day of working on toiles and cutting patterns.

My phone vibrated with a text from Cate.

We need to meet. I have design changes. Call me!

I stared at it with my fingers poised to text her back with two words—*Fuck off.*

I looked over at my sketchbook lying on the coffee table, and I stared at the wedding dress I'd designed for her.

She can kiss my ass.

I wasn't going to change another damn thing.

My temper was on the verge of flaring. I had so much work to do and so little time to let her take me out of my element.

I considered calling Giselle, my talkative intern who helped me most of the time, but then I changed my mind. I was already in a pretty fucked-up mood, and I needed to work in solitude. Turning on some music, I danced over to my workstation, ready to rock through the day, when my cell rang. I stared at the number I didn't recognize. Must be a new client, referred to me by Cisco.

"Sin Michaels," I chirped into the phone.

"Hello, Ms. Michaels. This is Ram Steele. I'm sorry we couldn't meet last night." His voice was smooth and easy.

I fumbled the phone. "Hold on." I ran over to my tablet and turned off the music. "Hello, Mr. Steele. I'm happy you called." I walked back over to my workstation while wiping my now sweaty palm against my jeans. "I wanted to talk to you. I'm not sure what your concerns are, but I assure you Sin Michaels Corporation is doing just fine—well, more than fine." I cleared my throat. "Did you see today's newspaper? I had a whole article giving kudos to my upcoming line."

"Yes, we did," he stated coolly. "But we have some major concerns that will delay us in giving you the additional money you requested."

Fuck. My. Life.

My heart clenched. Without that money, I would be screwed. I'd ordered expensive custom prints from a factory in Asia. One delayed payment could mean the fabric wouldn't arrive in time, halting my whole collection.

My stomach churned.

"What concerns?" I croaked.

"Business concerns that should be discussed in person," he stated calmly.

My fingers tightened around the workstation's edge. "Mr. Steele, can I be blunt?" I tried to calm down, but the more I thought about the impact of his devastating announcement, the more pissed I grew.

"Please do."

"This is bullshit." I paced back and forth. "You gave me two million dollars, and per our agreement, you committed to giving me another million within six months."

"Ms. Michaels, did you actually read the agreement?" He paused. "Because if you did, you would know it contains a clause that entitles us not only to request our two million dollars back, with interest, but also to break the contract altogether."

I nearly swallowed my tongue.

Oh, hell no!

"Are you fucking kidding me? What in the world would make you want to do some dumb shit like that? We had a deal." There was no way that I was going to give up without fighting for my dream. I needed this damn money.

"I do respect your candor, Ms. Michaels." His voice was low and even, almost kind. "But that doesn't change the fact that we need to discuss our concerns in person. We'll meet today at three. Please take down this address."

I scribbled his directions with shaky fingers. "I'll be there at three sharp."

I disconnected and promptly dialed Tabitha.

"You've reached Tabitha Thorp. I'm away on a creative sabbatical. Please leave a message, and I'll get back to you when I return."

I stared at the phone. *Creative sabbatical? What. The. Fuck?*

I'd known her for years, and not once had she taken any sabbaticals.

Damn it!

I didn't know what was going on, but I felt like I was being royally screwed. I released a frustrated growl, and with a sweep of my arm, I knocked everything off my workspace.

CHAPTER 7
CORE

I snapped my head up when my office door opened, and Ram, my business partner, walked in before closing the door behind him with a decisive click.

"That was the most fucked-up thing you've ever asked me to do," Ram snarled.

I arched a brow. "The hell it was." Pushing aside the contract on my desk, I waited for the brewing tirade I knew was on the tip of Ram's tongue.

"Okay, not the most fucked-up thing, but a damn close second." Ram sat down, running a hand over his head. "I still don't get it." He paused. "What the hell is this Sinthia Michaels shit about?"

I remained silent for a few minutes, trying not to lose my patience. No one in the McKay organization would dare question me this way except Ram. Our years of connection as friends and business partners had given him that right.

Ram kicked his feet up onto my desk. "Don't give me that fucking stare, bro. I want to know. What the hell possessed you to give a fashion designer two million dollars?"

I leaned back in my chair. "You should know me by now. I don't give shit away. I invested two million dollars," I snapped.

Ram scoffed. "Well, you invested a shitload of money into a clothing business, and I'm pretty sure that was a dumbass decision. That pussy must be serious."

I shrugged. "Fuck the two million. I spend that much on the upkeep of my house in the south of France. The money is nothing compared to what I stand to gain if my hunch turns out to be right."

I still marveled at the fact that I'd come a long way, going from a vicious criminal thug to a legitimate businessman. Now powerful and rich, I could invest millions in a business that I thought would make a profit for me.

"This is bullshit, Core. You invested in a business you don't give a shit about. Why?"

My temper flared. "You're pushing the boundaries of our friendship, Ram."

Ram leaned forward. "Like I give a shit. We're family, and family asks questions."

I closed my eyes in irritation before snapping them open. "I finally found him—Bigsby Calhoune, the man we've been searching years for. He's been right under our noses."

Ram sucked in a quick breath. "Bigsby Calhoune? The man running for mayor? How did you come to that damn conclusion?" He blinked rapidly, followed by an open stare.

"Remember the charity event you couldn't attend?" I asked with a sharp tone.

CHAPTER 8
CORE

Manhattan. Nights Ago.

Flanked by my enforcers—who roughed up my enemies and kept my business associates in line—brothers, Max and Rocco, I exited my luxury vehicle.

"Wait here," I instructed them. "I'll be in and out of this place in fifteen minutes."

I didn't normally mingle with New York's elite, and I damn sure never did political fundraising events. I'd only accepted tonight's invitation as a courtesy to Mitch Fillion. Mitch had stepped in and provided assistance with the legalities of a complicated and contentious company takeover that had been on the verge of crumbling. Mitch had proven to be more valuable and ruthless than I'd expected. I needed to keep men like Mitch—those who only cared about money, power, and status—in my pocket.

I watched the crazy scene progress. Overflowing into the street, New York's elite were sauntering into the invite-only, fifty-grand-per-plate dinner that was being hosted by Mitch in honor of his newest pet project—mayoral hopeful Bigsby Calhoune.

Adjusting my bow tie, I strode confidently by the frenzied mess of paparazzi, who ignored me in favor of the star-studded elite, preening before the flashing cameras. I hated the press. Unlike most men with my wealth and power who gravitated toward the ego-stroking media, I avoided them like the plague, living my life in anonymity.

I waited impatiently while a white-gloved security staffer politely scanned my body with a handheld metal detector. Entering through the huge front doors, I immediately moved through the room—a cavernous, modern space with large columns and slab granite. The private, formal political party was in full swing as men in tuxedos escorted their diamond-encrusted ladies around the room like arm candy.

Blending smoothly into a throng of foreign dignitaries, business-men, and socialites, I headed for the bar, ordered a drink, and absorbed the high-octane mixture of new oil money and old European wealth before the bartender pushed a glass of scotch between my fingers. The cigar-smoking men talked business as their beautiful flavors of the month looked on with blank faces, casually taking a glass of cham-pagne or a canapé from the passing waiters.

Glittering, sleek women with strikingly sculpted faces smiled provocatively at me while circling around me in hopes of snagging husband number two or three. My eyes roamed over them with disin-terest. They looked like most women I'd fucked over the years during my transition from crime lord to legitimate business mogul. Along with surgically enhanced breasts provided by top plastic surgeons, they all had hard bodies courtesy of hours in the gym with their personal trainers.

I was bored with the selection.

Sipping my scotch, I ignored them. Until now, it hadn't occurred to me that I hadn't fucked anyone who looked remotely like a real woman in a while. Even with a string of women and business successes over the years, I found I actually missed one thing from my days as the ruthless leader of the largest crime empire in New York—a woman with soft curves, pretty, girl-next-door looks, and a sassy, take-no-shit personality. Maybe it was time for a change, but finding a woman who could satisfy my distinct and dark sexual tastes would be nearly impossible.

My thoughts were interrupted by Mitch's loud, animated introduction of the well-matched, beautiful couple—Cate Bellisario and Bigsby Calhoune—to a guest. Bored, I watched Bigsby shake the guest's hand with an exaggerated flourish.

My body tensed.

My mind flared with recognition at the unmistakable glint of diamonds and rubies on Bigsby's middle finger.

Pushing away from the bar with adrenaline coursing through my veins, I walked leisurely through the crowd and toward the trio. The guests shifted, cutting off my view of Mitch and the couple, but I easily found them again and confidently strode up to them.

"Core." Mitch was all smiles as he shook my hand. "I'm glad you could make it tonight."

Bigsby's eyes narrowed on my all-seeing-eye neck tattoo. As Bigsby frowned, his gaze darted to Mitch. He clearly did not approve of my presence at his dinner event.

My expression darkened. "Is there a problem?"

Mitch shot Bigsby an irritated glare before laughing loudly. He clapped me on the back. "Apologies, Core." He gave Bigsby an admonishing stare. "Bigsby is new to the intricacies and important players of our circle, so please excuse his ignorance. I'm still trying to get him up to speed."

Bigsby's body tightened as he ran his hand over his salt-and-pepper hair with agitation.

Mitch looked pointedly at the couple. "This is Core McKay—as in McKay Corporation. He's one of my biggest clients."

Cate's mask of neutrality slipped as her eyes widened. "Well, this night is full of surprises. I get the privilege of putting a face to the renowned name." She smiled. "Congrats on your recent billion-dollar merger."

I inclined my head but remained silent.

Mitch looked at me eagerly. "This is Cate Bellisario."

Cate nodded politely as I swept my gaze over her. From her form-fitting designer dress to her perfectly coiffed hair and artfully applied makeup, she was the very image of New York socialite success. I smirked. I knew her perfection was a facade for the seedy dark side she kept hidden from her fiancé. On several occasions, the smoldering nymph had trolled my sex club, begging Ram to top her. The duality of her flawless persona amused me.

Bigsby cleared his throat. "I'm Bigsby Calhoune." He smiled as he offered his hand to me before shaking it enthusiastically. "I apologize. I thought I knew most of Mitch's friends."

My face was a cold mask, barely hiding my disdain. "Leave the thinking to Mitch and your fiancée. You're way out of your depth, Mr. Calhoune." I stepped back, sipping my scotch.

Bigsby shifted uncomfortably before looking to Mitch for assistance, but none came. I knew Mitch expected Bigsby to grovel and make amends for his slight against me.

Bigsby's smile was forced as he said, "Cate says I'm like a bull in a china shop at these events. Apologies, Mr. McKay."

I tilted my head. "You're from Brooklyn," I stated matter-of-factly.

Bigsby looked visibly startled. "Uh…yes. How did you know?"

I stared at him shrewdly. "You're trying too hard to hide the accent." Effectively dismissing him, I turned to Mitch. "You pulled out the big guns tonight. You must think he's a winner."

Mitch beamed at Bigsby. "You're damn right. If I have anything to do with it, Bigsby will be New York's next mayor."

"I wouldn't start writing acceptance speeches. I know his opponent personally. He's thorough and ruthless." I narrowed my eyes on Bigsby. "And his specialty is unearthing his opponent's skeletons."

Bigsby's grin slipped before his lips curled up into a stiff smile.

I winked at Cate while addressing Bigsby. "I hope your beautiful fiancée has taken care to bury them deep."

Bigsby wrapped a possessive hand around her narrow waist.

I glanced at the chunky gold ruby-and-diamond-encrusted horseshoe ring on Bigsby's middle finger. "That's a unique ring you have there, Calhoune. It's one of a kind, I'm sure."

Bigsby smiled cockily. "Yes, it is. I've had it for over forty years. It's custom-made." He looked over at Cate. "And I'll never take it off."

Cate sighed heavily, looking at the gaudy ring with disgust. "Believe me, I've tried."

Bigsby winked at Cate. "It's my good luck charm. You will have to pry it off my dead body, sweetheart."

She stared back with a simple look and said plainly, "Do I really have to wait that long?"

Bigsby laughed loudly. "You're such a minx."

Mitch waved to someone across the room and then looked over at me apologetically. "Can you excuse us? We need to make the rounds before dinner is served."

"I'm leaving anyway. I have important business to attend to," I responded.

Mitch looked disappointed. "I seated you at our table with Cate and Bigsby, but I understand." He started to usher the couple away. "We'll talk this week."

Exiting the venue, trying hard to contain my building rage, I pulled out my cell and barked, "Kevin, dig up everything you can on Bigsby Calhoune."

~

My mind snapped back to the present. Unclasping my fingers, I said to Ram, "The plan is now in motion. After all these years, we've finally found the ring. What are the odds of that?"

Ram leaned forward. "We've been searching for that shit for years, and it's been right under our noses." He paused. "So what's Sinthia's connection?"

"I don't know. Kevin dug up some interesting intel about Bigsby looking into Sinthia Michaels's business. If he's interested in her and her business, there has to be a pretty damn good reason." I leaned back in my chair, smiling coldly. "Now he has to deal directly with me."

When I'd gotten the call from Kevin about Bigsby's interest in Sinthia, my first question had been, *Who the fuck is Sinthia Michaels?*

It hadn't taken Kevin long to do a thorough investigation, but he hadn't found anything linking Bigsby to her. I had known, though, that if Bigsby was interested in Sinthia, there had to be a sinister motive, which was why I had to acquire Sinthia Michaels's business fast. I'd had Kevin search through her background again, looking for anything that could be used as leverage. Surprisingly, Sinthia was squeaky-clean and free from scandal. Frustrated and running out of time and options, I found a chink in her armor—money.

She needed money, and I had lots of it. But to my frustration, I couldn't find a way to get into Sinthia's small inner circle without raising suspicion or scaring her off.

That was when Kevin had found the game changer—Tabitha Thorp. I had known Tabitha from the old neighborhood. When we were young, we had hung out in the same criminal circles. The only difference was, back then, the now-famous Tabitha had worked as a drug mule for her seedy drug kingpin boyfriend, Ben Vargos. I knew Tabitha. I'd even fucked her several times behind Ben's back. She was a money-hungry whore who could be easily manipulated.

So when I found out the currently successful Tabitha Thorp owed a shitload of money to her unsavory criminal ex-boyfriend, Ben, I swooped in.

One call later, I'd recruited Tabitha to help me get close to Sinthia. Tabitha had convinced Sinthia of the value of getting an investor— specifically, me—to help her expand her business. In exchange, I'd agreed to pay off Tabitha's debt to Ben and send her on a very long vacation.

Bigsby was a dirty criminal underneath his slick, cleaned-up politi- cian veneer. I still couldn't figure out why Bigsby's socialite fiancée, Cate, would marry a lowlife, but she had cleaned Bigsby up like some stray puppy she'd found on the street. She'd gotten Bigsby a well-paid publicist, and she was now helping him run for mayor.

"Bigsby Calhoune might have a new identity and life, but he's still the power-hungry thug who killed my mother and left me to die. He's going to pay for what he did," I hissed.

I had thought of nothing but revenge for years. It consumed me. Just thinking about the night when the unknown assailant had shot both Mom and me fueled my hate fire. Mom had died, but I survived.

I stood up, absently tracing the scar across my brow while staring at the Manhattan skyline. "Bigsby is unfinished business. Business I've been waiting to resolve for far too many years."

"I saw the picture and read the newspaper article about Sinthia Michaels. But what does she really look like?" Ram asked.

I shrugged. "A stunner with curves in all the right fucking places."

"A stunner?" Ram laughed. "I've heard you describe women as fuckable, but never a stunner." He paused. "Interesting."

"There's nothing interesting about it. She's definitely fuckable, but I don't mix business with pleasure, especially not this business."

"I see."

I looked over my shoulder. "It's not that deep, Ram."

Ram snorted. "A fuckable stunner? Well, that's a game changer when it comes to your track record with women."

"I'm going nowhere near Sinthia Michaels. I don't need the complication." Turning back around, I continued to stare at the skyline.

My life was difficult enough, and I didn't need any distractions, particularly now that I'd found Mom's killer. Besides, I wasn't relationship material. I never was and never would be.

Watching Mom getting killed had changed me, shaping me into the man I was today—a sadistic, driven, ruthless, cold, and heartless killer. I was the product of my environment. Growing up in a run-down part of Manhattan and fighting every kid on the block who would talk shit about my young, single mother, who had performed at strip clubs to earn a living, had done that to me.

At a young age, I'd seen and lived through shit most people would only see in movies. Those things were not easily forgotten—like people being gunned down ruthlessly in broad daylight or single mothers giving blow jobs in alleyways so they could pay rent and put food on the table.

I had come a long way from those days and now had more money than I could ever spend, but the fucked-up memories remained. I would never forget where I'd come from or the day when my world had changed forever, leading me to the ultimate task before me— avenging my mother's murder.

Even after all these years, the details of that fateful day were burned into my memory... I had been doing my homework when I heard Mom's blood-curdling scream. I remembered running from the living room into the kitchen where I saw her being pinned against the wall by a big, burly man whose back was facing me while he repeatedly beat Mom's face to a pulp. I charged, jumping onto the man's back while trying to claw his eyes out of his head.

I could still hear the bone-crunching thud Mom's frail body made as the man slammed her to the floor.

The man swung around and yelled at me, "You little bastard, you're dead!" He grabbed me by the neck before throwing me clear across the kitchen.

My head had smashed against the corner of the kitchen counter before my body bounced onto the floor.

Dazed, I slowly reached my hand up to my head. I felt the oozing thickness of gushing blood across my eyebrow, but I refused to give in to the pain. Mom needed me.

My heart had leaped out of my chest when my mother screamed, "Leave my son alone, you fucking bastard. This is between you and me, damn coward."

The man charged at her, pulling a .357 Magnum from his beltline. "Shut the fuck up, whore. You brought this on yourself. I warned you to keep your damn mouth shut!" he yelled while grabbing her by the hair with one hand.

Turning her face away from him, the man had placed the gun to her head. It had seemed like an eternity to me as I stared at the gold ruby-and-diamond-encrusted horseshoe ring on the man's middle finger before he fired the gun, killing Mom. He then stormed over to me with his gun aimed toward me before squeezing off some rounds, and then my world had gone completely dark.

I had been near death when Ram found me choking on my blood on the gore-soaked kitchen floor, but it had been too late for Mom. Ram saved my life, and we made a pact that day. The man who killed my mother would pay with his life.

Young, wild, and ruthless, Ram and I had risen quickly in the world of organized crime, building our empire from the bottom. As the years passed, we never forgot the man without a face, only knowing him by his ruby-and-diamond ring.

Our criminal territory had expanded. Life and money had been good, but we knew we had to get out or we'd end up like so many of our friends—dead or in jail. So it hadn't been a hard choice to decriminalize our business and turn our lives around, but I wouldn't rest until I made the man with the ring pay.

"Sinthia Michaels is all business, and I'm willing to destroy her business in order to take down Bigsby," I retorted.

Ram's face tightened. "You know how I feel about this shit. We've been through hell and back together, so there's no question about me helping you take him down. But this is between you, me, and him. No one else. Cut the Sinthia Michaels chick loose."

My temper flared. "I don't give a shit about her," I snarled.

I needed Sinthia Michaels as bait, and if that meant she might become a casualty in my war against Bigsby, then so be it.

"She's already involved whether she knows it or not, and I have no intention of letting her go until I get what I want—Bigsby." I pulled out a cigar. "Now we've got lots of work to do. We need to call every retailer that we own a major stake in and let them know the Sinthia Michaels deal doesn't happen until we personally approve it."

CHAPTER 9
SINTHIA

Less than three hours later, the cab pulled up in front of the huge building. My stomach was queasy. My head throbbed as I gawked at the structure.

I looked into the rearview mirror, meeting the gaze of the cab driver. "Are you sure this is the right place?"

The driver drummed his fingers against the steering wheel. "Lady, this is the address you gave me." He jabbed a big finger toward the sign. "See that? McKay Corporation."

I frowned. "This can't be right."

"Young lady, if you want to go to another address, tell me where to go. If not, pay the fare."

I bit my lower lip. "No, I'm good." I paid before hopping out.

Pulling damp tendrils of hair away from my neck, I stared at the huge sign, *McKay Corporation*, as if it were a mirage. A shiver of trepidation ran down my spine.

This was all wrong—first the Ram call, then Tabitha's disappearing act, and now this. Someone was fucking with me, and I wanted to know who and why. Pulling myself to my full height, I walked confidently through the glass doors and over to the guest desk.

"I'm here to see Mr. Steele." I tapped my fingers on the counter, hoping the man would say I was in the wrong building.

The guard looked at me blankly. "Ms. Michaels, ID, please."

Shit. I'm at the right building.

Fumbling inside my handbag, I pulled out my driver's license and handed it over. "Here."

He glanced at it briefly. Then he scanned my license through a device on his tablet before smoothly tapping the on-screen keyboard.

I frowned. "What are you doing with my information?"

"Just a security precaution, Ms. Michaels. We record the information of everyone who enters this building." He nodded toward the elevator as he returned my license. "Top floor."

The elevator ride up to Steele's office was the longest one I'd ever taken. I wasn't sure what was going on, but I didn't like it one bit. If Mr. Steele thought he could just screw me on this deal without a fight, he was damn mistaken. I was prepared to do battle.

The elevator dinged, and I stepped out into the palatial suite decorated with ornate, eighteenth-century furniture. My eyes immediately went to the office door guarded by two well-dressed, armed men.

"Is this an office or a high-security prison?" I mumbled under my breath.

I walked down a long hallway, passing by a massive glass conference room. My sway became deliberately more sensual when I noticed a striking woman sitting behind a large desk, scrutinizing me with frank disapproval. She scanned my outfit of skintight leather leggings paired with a black T-shirt and tailored jacket. I didn't give a shit. I had plenty of appropriate business attire, but I'd promised myself years ago that I wouldn't dress or act a certain way to please anyone but myself. I kept it real. If Mr. Steele didn't like it, he could kiss my ass.

I stopped before her desk. "I'm here to see Ram Steele."

"Have a seat, Ms. Michaels," she responded with a British accent.

Giving her a cold smile, I responded with, "Thanks, but I'll stand."

"Your prerogative," she huffed.

Just to get under her skin, I swayed over to the cushy chairs, making sure that my ridiculously high stilettos tapped loudly on the marble floor.

"Shh!" she snapped with an admonishing glare.

I snickered. *What an uptight wench.* I could just imagine what Mr. Steele was like. He was probably some uptight billionaire who was so old his bones cracked when he walked.

I turned my head in the direction of the huge office door that had just opened. My eyes widened at the sight of the tall, lean, and exceedingly handsome man striding toward me.

Jesus, he's hot enough to make panties melt.

He tilted his head curiously as he greeted me coldly. "Please come in, Ms. Michaels. Mr. McKay is waiting."

I recognized his voice—Ram Steele. I quirked a brow. "What's going on?"

Silently, he motioned me to enter the office.

"I asked you a question, Mr. Steele," I snapped.

Mr. Steele heaved a long-suffering sigh before pressing a gentle hand against the middle of my back, nudging me into the office. "Ms. Michaels, a word of advice—if I were you, I would play nice with him. He's in a real fucked-up mood today," he said, his voice clipped, before closing the door behind him with a decisive click.

Play nice?

Not a damn chance.

I was ready for a fight. Squaring my shoulders, I found my eyes drawn to a man in a tailored business suit, standing with his hands clasped behind his back as he looked out the window. His large, muscular frame would have intimidated anyone, but I refused to be cowed by him. Taking a deep, calming breath, I walked toward the middle of the room and stopped.

"Sinthia Michaels," he said in a low-pitched voice that sent delicious chills down my spine. "Have you brought my money?" he asked in a gravelly voice that sounded vaguely familiar.

My mouth opened and shut, not believing what he'd just asked. "Money? What money?"

He turned from the window and looked straight at me. I nearly swallowed my tongue. It was the man from last night.

"You're Core McKay?" I took a step forward, compelled by the invisible string drawing me to him.

His gaze was intimidating and unrelenting. "Good to see you again, Ms. Michaels." His booming deep voice resonated throughout the office. "Have a seat. We have a lot to discuss."

His eyes traveled all the way down my body. His predatory stare made me feel like a mouse beneath the bloodthirsty gaze of a cat. In the light of day, he was even more fucking menacing. His body was pure, rippling muscle—not workout-five-days-a-week-at-the-gym buff, but more like mixed martial arts, fucking-kick-motherfucker's-asses-just-for-the-fun-of-it buff. But it was his searing gray eyes that told the real story.

Core McKay was not a man to fuck with.

I hesitated, but I needed to get my bearings before I passed out from stress. "Fine," I conceded, taking a seat. "Listen, I'm going to cut to the fucking chase," I said. "Why the fuck am I here?"

He regarded me for a long time and then sat in the chair behind his mammoth desk. He smoothed the sleeves of his tailored shirt before running a hand across his blunt-cut, midnight-black hair. "Unfortunately, some disturbing information has recently come to my attention, and it makes me question your ability to make me a profit." His words were civil, but his eyes were hard as granite.

Oh, hell no! There is no way in hell I'm going to let him punk me like I'm some prison-yard bitch.

In a gesture of defiance, I raised my chin and met his gaze. "No offense, Mr. McKay, but my business deal is with MK Partners."

He actually smirked like he found me mildly amusing.

My eyes widened when it dawned on me. *Motherfucker!*

"Yes, Ms. Michaels, MK Partners is my investment company," he drawled.

I shook my head. *Oh shit. Please say it's not true.* My throat went completely dry as I felt like the walls were closing in around me. Still, I refused to roll over and surrender. I was a damn fighter.

"While that might be true, our agreement was not a loan. I would never take a loan from a man like you."

His eyes hardened.

Well, it was true. I had been hard up for an investor, but even I hadn't been that desperate—or stupid. I knew about the McKay

Corporation and the rumors circulating about the mysterious and eccentric owner, Core McKay. He'd built his billion-dollar empire using drug trafficking, money laundering, and prostitution, and that was only to mention a few of the criminally speculated trades.

His jaw tightened. He was pissed, and it was damn scary.

"In your desperation to finance your business, you obviously lowered your fucking highbrow standards," he ground out. "Now the only thing I don't own is your company name. Other than that, I own ninety-seven percent of your precious enterprise."

My breath stuck in my throat. The silence stretched between us. My failure to look over the fine print of the contract was coming back to bite me in the ass. *Shit.*

"Impossible," I denied.

He gestured to the neatly stacked paperwork on his desk. "The impossible became possible, Ms. Michaels." His eyes flashed before he crossed his muscular arms, his biceps bulging.

He reminded me of a tiger patiently stalking its prey, and in his case, that was me.

I squared my shoulders before snatching the stack off the desk. I scanned the paperwork slowly, stopping at the fine print. *Shit, it is a loan. How the fuck did I miss this?*

My gaze stopped on the name right next to my signature—*Core McKay.*

My stomach rolled. "This is a huge mistake. This wasn't supposed to be a loan. It was a deal for seven percent of my future earnings." I shook my head.

"Sinthia," he said my name as if testing it on his tongue. "Is that your signature?"

I tightened my lips, fighting back the impending flood of tears. "I swear, this was not what I thought I was agreeing to."

He inclined his head slightly. "Let this be a lesson. Read things thoroughly before you sign."

This just didn't make sense. *Why didn't Tabitha tell me my investor was McKay?*

I bit my lip, thinking about that day she'd brought me the contract. My stomach dropped when I remembered she'd seemed entirely too happy. In fact, come to think of it, she had been practically giddy that she'd found me the deal I needed to solve all my business problems.

He looked at me coldly. "Can you pay back my two million dollars plus interest today?"

Now he was toying with me.

He knew damn well I didn't have the money, and I sure as hell couldn't get it.

In desperation mode, I shifted my thoughts immediately to Jade, but I couldn't borrow the money from her because her assets were tied up in a big business venture to take the script she wrote and independently produce the film version.

I sputtered, "What the fuck do you want, McKay? Because—" I stopped mid-sentence, feeling warm and tingly as he stared at me with hooded eyes.

His physical magnetism was palpable. I swallowed hard, trying not to squirm under his sensuous stare.

Bastard. He wants me to beg. Well, that shit isn't happening.

Our eyes locked.

"I know you don't expect me to fuck you so you'll forget about this whole loan thing?"

He actually laughed at me as if I'd just told a joke. The sly sound ruffled my nerves.

"Do you really think I have to pay to get fucked?" he replied.

Such an arrogant ass.

I ground my teeth. "Then what do you want?"

"Not a damn thing but my money plus interest." He narrowed his eyes. "I'm not sure you're able to produce a profit, darling. My sources tell me your retailers are getting cold feet about the viability of your collection. They're pulling out of your deals."

I flinched like he'd physically slapped me. "Bullshit! I have concrete agreements with each of them."

"You really don't know shit about contracts. Nothing in business is concrete. That's what loopholes and a shitload of well-paid lawyers are for." He shot me an irritated glare. "I can tell you don't believe the shit I'm saying, so call Lily Sanchez."

I narrowed my eyes. "How do you know Lily?" I asked with disbelief ringing in my voice.

He shrugged. "Just call her." He cocked his head. "She'll confirm the gravity of your situation."

I pulled out my cell. My fingers trembled, but I willed them to stop. I would not break down in front of this prick. I called her.

"Hello, Sin. How are you?" Lily asked.

"Shitty. Look, is everything good to go with my collection deal?"

Lily cleared her throat. My stomach dropped.

"I was going to call you, Sin. I don't know what the hell is going on, but the financial planners are seriously discussing backing out of your deal."

I jumped up, turning my back on Core. "What the hell happened?" I whispered.

"Don't know. I'm still trying to find out. All I know is this is bigger than you or me."

My shoulders slumped. Her store was my biggest account.

"I'm two million in, Lily. My collection is almost complete. That's months of work. Do you understand me? Set up a meeting with the financial planners," I snapped.

"I'm sorry, Sin. My hands are tied. Give me a couple days to figure this out."

I stood there in shock after our call ended.

How in the world could my life have turned from rosy to shitty in a matter of hours?

I could feel Core's heated stare scorching through my clothes. I gathered my strength and turned around, feeling the noose tightening. It was time to make a deal with the devil. But before I did, I just had one question.

I lifted my chin. "How do you know Tabitha?"

He gave me a hard smile.

My eyes widened. "Oh, I see. You're one of her many fuck buddies." My voice was tight with accusation.

He straightened to his full, intimidating height. "Let's cut to the chase, shall we? I've known Tabitha for years in various...capacities. That's why she came to me when you had financing issues. She knew I was in the market for another lucrative investment." He pulled out a cigar. "I did some extensive investigation of you and your company, and you are very talented." He lit his cigar. "But obviously, you're very naïve when it comes to business."

I tightened my fists.

I am going to fucking cunt-punch Tabitha when I find her.

"So you know where she is?" I hissed.

His lips twitched into a mockery of a smile. "Don't know, and I don't care. But when you find her, give her my regards." He paused, looking at me coolly. "Sinthia, you're tougher than I thought. I like that." He took a puff of the cigar. "I've come to a decision." He blew a ring of smoke before placing the cigar in the ashtray.

"What decision?" I barked. "You already made a decision when you gave me the two million dollars. Now you're making another decision?" I sneered.

"I will make it really simple for you." He crossed his arms and widened his stance. "I've invested two million into your business, and I intend on getting it back plus a hefty profit. I will retain full control of your company."

I nearly choked on my own breath. "This is bullshit! This is my business," I protested.

His eyes were ice-cold and distant when he continued, "Kevin, my accountant, will take care of all financial matters, including providing the money to continue your line. In addition, I will make some calls to my contacts to see if we can get your retailers back on board."

I licked my lips. His eyes fell to my mouth.

"And all of this is coming at what price?" My back stiffened and my eyes narrowed. "I will not use my company as a front for illegal business dealings."

His gray eyes narrowed. "What the fuck are you talking about?"

I closed my eyes tightly to block the sight of his hateful presence. "I worked too fucking hard to have my business and my name tied to anything illegal." I forced myself to look at him again.

He stalked over to me, his gaze blatantly ogling my body. "What a beautiful hypocrite. There was no thought about where the money was coming from when you took it. Now you're looking at me like I'm the fucking scum of the earth?"

He regarded me silently. It irritated me that he could unnerve me with just one look.

"I'm just calling it like I see it, Mr. McKay. I will not use my business for anything illegal."

He scowled. "Many years ago, I might have used you for that…and more. But now I'm a legitimate businessman."

My stomach twisted into knots. I was between a rock and a hard place, and legally, there was nothing I could do.

"What else do you want, McKay?" I asked.

I licked my bottom lip anxiously at the strange surges of energy rolling off him in waves.

His eyes roamed from my face to my body and then back again. "Oh, darling, I can't begin to tell you all the things I want from you. They would send your gorgeous ass running from this room. But the question is, what do you want, Ms. Michaels?"

Is he out of his damn mind?

As hot as he was, I wouldn't fuck him even if his cock were made of solid gold.

"I want you to let me out of this fucking deal," I grumbled.

McKay laughed coldly. "Not going to happen. Next," he all but sneered.

"If you wanted to, you could," I responded.

His expression revealed nothing. "I'm in the business of making money, not losing it. The deal remains." There was a tight note in his voice.

Lifting my chin, I continued to hold his stare. For several minutes, I didn't say anything as he continued to watch me.

"This is fucking ridiculous," I snapped. "It might be illegal too."

"Even you don't really believe that shit." The hardness of his voice sent chills down my spine.

I bit back the expletive hovering on my tongue. I knew I would be tied to him forever. Judging by his focused gaze, that was exactly what he wanted.

"And how long is this business arrangement going to last?"

"Until I determine the debt has been paid in full," he bit out letting his words sink in for a few seconds.

My blood froze in my veins. "Fuck you! You might own the company, but you don't own me."

His hands clenched and unclenched before he caught me by the arm and pressed me against the wall. In one swift move, he pinned my arms above my head. His tongue swept into my mouth while his other hand grabbed the back of my head with unleashed fury.

The last shreds of my ironclad control disintegrated as his mouth devoured and stroked me with a restrained sensuality that made my cunt clench from emptiness.

I opened my mouth wider, and I pushed my tongue into his. I groaned, tasting the hint of coffee and cigar. My head spun out of control as I kissed him back with all the pent-up anger, passion, and the most damning attraction that I had been denying.

Shamefully, I wanted him like no other.

My stomach plummeted with the sudden realization that this man would be my undoing.

As if he could read my mind, he broke off the kiss abruptly and stared at me with knowing, hard eyes. "I might not own you now, but I will," he responded with a steely voice before stepping back from me.

I stood there against the wall, trembling like a fool, as I watched him turn around and stride over to his wall of floor-to-ceiling windows.

"Now you may go, Ms. Michaels," he hissed, effectively dismissing me.

For several minutes, I just stared at his wide back in shock. Finally, I gathered what was left of my pride and walked out of the room.

On shaky legs, I stepped into the elevator and pressed my head against the wall as my mind clouded over with confusion.

I swallowed hard as the door slid closed.

Just when I thought I'd made peace with the universe and success was within my reach, fate had thrown me the ultimate middle finger.

Tears rolled down my cheeks as regret and dread washed over me.

I just made a deal with the fucking devil.

TWISTED LIES 2

"Oh, what a tangled web we weave. When first we practice to deceive!"
—**Sir Walter Scott**

CHAPTER 1
CORE

I absently traced the scar across my brow while staring at the Manhattan skyline. Mom's killer was New York City's mayoral hopeful Bigsby Calhoune—and I wanted him dead.

But killing him fast would be too easy. I planned to ruin him, stripping away everything he held dear—his wealth, his trophy fiancée Cate, his political career, and his freedom.

Bigsby was a dirty criminal underneath his slick, cleaned-up politician veneer. He might have a new identity and lifestyle, but he was still the power-hungry thug who had killed my mother and left me to die.

"He's going to pay for what he did," I hissed.

Bigsby was unfinished business, business I'd been waiting to resolve for far too many years.

I had thought of nothing but revenge. It'd consumed me, just thinking about the night when the unknown assailant wearing a gold, ruby-and-diamond-encrusted horseshoe ring had shot Mom and me. Mom had died, but I survived.

I'd finally found the owner of the ring—Bigsby. *What are the odds of that?* I had been searching for that ring for years, and it was right under my nose.

But what's Sinthia's connection to Bigsby?

It was something I was determined to find out. It hadn't taken Kevin long to do a thorough investigation, but he hadn't found anything linking Bigsby to her. However, Kevin had dug up some interesting intel about Bigsby looking into Sinthia Michaels's business. If Bigsby was interested in Sinthia, there had to be a sinister motive, which was why I needed to acquire her business fast. Kevin had searched through her background again, looking for anything that could be used as leverage. Surprisingly, Sinthia was squeaky-clean and free of scandal. Frustrated and running out of time and options, I had found a chink in her armor—money.

She required money, and I had lots of it.

That was when I'd swooped in with the assistance of her friend Tabitha Thorp, who had helped me get close to Sinthia. Tabitha had convinced Sinthia of the value of getting an investor—specifically, me —to help her expand her business.

I leaned back in my chair, smiling coldly. Now Bigsby would have to deal directly with me.

My jaw tightened as I glanced impatiently at the watch adorning my wrist.

What the hell is taking her so damn long? Sinthia should have arrived fifteen minutes ago.

I'd give her five more minutes before hopping into my car and driving over to her house to lay down my number one ground rule. When I called, she'd drop whatever the fuck she was doing and haul her sexy ass to my designated destination, or there would be hell to pay.

Ram, my business partner and friend, opened my door and stepped into the office. "Security just informed Zuri that Sinthia Michaels is on her way up." He strode in, closing the door behind him.

I sat forward. "She was supposed to be here fifteen minutes ago!" The words rushed from my mouth like an angry roar.

Ram arched one dark eyebrow. "What the fuck is up with you?" Sitting down in a chair, he propped his feet on my desk, much to my chagrin. "You need to relax, Core. If you bark at her like that, you'll send her ass running out of here, fucking up our plans."

"Do I look like I give a shit?" I retorted, eyeing him coolly.

Ram looked at me as if hinting at something. "Yes, you do," he replied so calmly it raised my ire.

My temper flared. "I don't give a shit about her," I snarled.

Ram grinned like the idiot he was. "Yeah, okay."

I pressed on the bridge of my nose and took a deep breath, pissed that I'd been intrigued by her since we'd met last night at my club. I'd spent the last couple of hours semi-aroused, and it was fucking with my head. This morning I'd woken to a raging hard-on with her name on my damn lips.

It was a real fucked-up predicament. I had no business thinking that way about a woman I was using as bait.

Sinthia was an addictive distraction.

Ram cleared his throat loudly. "Kevin showed me a photo of her. Damn, she's smoking hot." He grinned, leaning back in the chair. "Tell you what. I'm more than willing to take her into my office and show her we mean business…kinky business." He waggled his brows suggestively. "I wonder if she's into handcuffs." He pursed his lips. "Shit, I would love to bend her over my desk, cuff her, and frisk that ass like she's under—"

I put my hand over my face, sighing loudly, and Ram stopped.

But when I looked up again, I had a wicked smile on my face. "You're fucking crazy." I laughed. "But you always know how to calm me down."

"That's what friends do," Ram said.

Ram was more than my best friend. He was the brother I'd never had and the only one I trusted other than a small group of trusted employees. Max and Rocco, my enforcers, roughed up my enemies and kept my business associates in line. Kevin handled the financing and accounting for all of my businesses and my private intelligence-gathering efforts. And Zuri, who was my personal assistant and the little sister I'd always wanted. Ram and I had been through hell and back together. Rising quickly in the world of organized crime, we'd built our empire from the bottom. There were times when I'd thought we'd never make it out alive, but we had. We'd decriminalized our business and turned our lives around.

"Okay, so how do you want to handle this meeting? Good cop/bad cop scenario?" Ram asked quietly.

I took a deep breath and let it out. "No, I'm going solo with this meeting."

Ram gaped at me. "What the fuck do you mean, *solo*?"

For the first time in my life, I opened my mouth, and nothing came out.

Ram's eyes widened. "You want to fuck her?" he asked, shaking his head. "I can't believe it."

I grimaced as the knots in my stomach grew. It took me a good minute or two before I finally managed to get my thoughts together. I gritted my teeth. "Sinthia Michaels is all business, and I'm willing to destroy her business in order to take down Bigsby," I retorted.

I needed Sinthia Michaels as bait, and if that meant she might become a casualty in my war against Bigsby, then so be it.

"Uh-huh." Ram's gaze held a hint of amusement. "We've been friends for a long time. I've learned to read you like a book. You want her."

I leaned back. "I don't need the complication." My life was difficult enough, and I didn't need any distractions, especially now that I'd found my mother's killer. Besides, I wasn't relationship material, and I never would be. I'd fuck women and then show them the door.

Ram's lips twitched. "Yeah, well, that's a damn relief." He looked at me pointedly. "I would hate to have you complicate this mission by fucking her."

Damn. Little did Ram know, shit was already complicated between Sinthia and me.

The phone on my desk rang twice, signaling that Sinthia was waiting to be guided into my office. Excitement raced through my veins as if I were some high schooler waiting for my prom date.

Damn. What the hell is wrong with me?

Annoyed, I glared at him, my patience gone. "Just escort her in."

Shooting to his feet, Ram gave me a mock salute. "Aye-aye, fearless leader. Let me get my game face on, showing Ms. Michaels that I—" He grinned slightly. "I mean *we* mean business."

I snorted before turning my swivel chair around to face the

window. I stood up and clasped my hands behind my back, staring at the Manhattan skyline again.

I heard the huge office door open.

Ram greeted Sinthia formally. "Please come in, Ms. Michaels. Mr. McKay is waiting."

"What's going on?" she asked.

There was utter silence.

"I asked you a question, Mr. Steele," she snapped.

Ram heaved a long-suffering sigh. "Ms. Michaels, a word of advice —if I were you, I would play nice with him. He's in a real fucked-up mood today," he said, his voice clipped, before closing the door with a decisive click.

The soft tapping of heels against the Carrera marble floor alerted me to her approach.

"Sinthia Michaels," I said in a low-pitched voice, "have you brought my money?"

There was a slight pause before she responded, "Money? What money?"

I turned from the window and looked straight at her. My mouth went dry. Lust slithered through my body. Sinthia Michaels was sexy as hell, wearing skintight leather leggings that accentuated her voluptuous curves and a body-hugging black T-shirt that dipped in the front to reveal her tempting full cleavage. My hands could probably span her tiny waist.

Sinthia squared her shoulders as if daring me to say something negative about her attire. She wouldn't get any flak from me. I thought she looked smoking hot.

"You're Core McKay?" She took a step forward, her eyes blazing with rage.

My stare was unrelenting. Sinthia was absolutely gorgeous. She wore her hair pulled back into a tight ponytail, emphasizing her high cheekbones, bow-shaped full lips, and tip-tilted nose. I felt a strange stab of longing deep inside, a strong magnetic pull I hadn't felt about anyone since Maya's death. That loss had devastated me both mentally and emotionally, and it was the reason I'd stayed single and kept my relationships brief with no strings attached.

"Good to see you again, Ms. Michaels." My deep, booming voice resonated throughout the office. "Have a seat. We have a lot to discuss." I pointed to the chair nestled in front of my desk.

She bit her lip as my eyes traveled from the top of her head down her curvy body. Sinthia hesitated, her gaze locking with mine. For a moment, I believed she'd stand her ground, but in an abrupt movement, she conceded, taking a seat.

"Fine." She lifted her shoulders in a shrug. "Listen, I'm going to cut to the fucking chase," she said. "Why the fuck am I here?"

I regarded her for a long time and then sat in the chair behind my mammoth desk. Sinthia shifted, and her jasmine scent wafted into my nostrils, making me want to bury my face against her neck. My cock stirred and stiffened against my pants.

Shit. I had to get over my undeniable attraction to her—and fast.

I smoothed the sleeves of my tailored shirt before running a hand through my hair. "Unfortunately, some disturbing information has recently come to my attention, and it makes me question your ability to make me a profit." My words were civil, but my eyes were hard as granite, letting her know right away that I was in charge.

In a gesture of defiance, she raised her chin and met my eyes. "No offense, Mr. McKay, but my business deal is with MK Partners." Fire flashed from the depths of her hazel eyes.

If looks could kill, I was sure I'd be dead.

I smirked. Just like I'd thought, Sinthia was a fighter, but she was sadly mistaken if she thought she'd win against me. No one did.

Her eyes widened, her mouth forming a perfect O, when the reality of the situation dawned on her.

"Yes, Ms. Michaels, MK Partners is my investment company," I drawled.

She shook her head. "While that might be true, our agreement was not a loan. I would never take a loan from a man like you."

What the fuck? A man like me?

My jaw tightened. "In your desperation to finance your business, you obviously lowered your fucking highbrow standards," I ground out. I was disappointed she'd been so judgmental without even digging deeply into the kind of man I really was. "Now, the only thing

I don't own is your company name. Other than that, I own ninety-seven percent of your precious company."

Sinthia went completely still, her eyes locking with mine. "Impossible," she denied, giving me a suspicious look.

I gestured to the neatly stacked paperwork on my desk. "The impossible became possible, Ms. Michaels." I crossed my arms as I waited patiently for her to comprehend that I had her exactly where I wanted her—under my thumb.

She squared her shoulders before snatching the stack off the desk. Folding my hands in front of me, I projected an air of nonchalance I didn't feel as she slowly scanned the paperwork.

A thrill of excitement raced through my body. Sinthia Michaels was all mine.

Come on, darling. Get with the program and recognize the game is over. Checkmate.

She raised her chin once again. "This is a huge mistake. This wasn't supposed to be a loan. It was a deal for seven percent of my future earnings." She shook her head.

I knitted my brows. "Sinthia"—I tested her name on my tongue—"is that your signature?"

Her mouth tightened. "I swear, this is not what I thought I was agreeing to."

I inclined my head slightly. "Let this be a lesson. Read things thoroughly before you sign." I looked at her coldly. Her mistake was my gain. "Can you pay back my two million dollars plus interest today?"

Kevin had given me a detailed report on her finances. She was living within her means while digging herself out of debt. There was no chance in hell she could raise the money to pay me back.

She sputtered, "What the fuck do you want, McKay? Because—" She stopped mid-sentence as I stared at her with hooded eyes.

She swallowed hard while I allowed my gaze to rake quite intimately over her. Our eyes locked. My groin stirred.

Damn, I love her sexy toughness. It made me want to fuck her senseless.

"You don't expect me to fuck you so you'll forget about this whole loan thing, do you?" Sinthia asked, watching me with disgust.

My lips tilted into a brief small smile. As much as I'd enjoy finding out if she was a hellcat in bed, that wasn't on the agenda—today.

"Do you really think I have to pay to get fucked?" I replied.

She ground her teeth. "Then what do you want?"

Sinthia was trying to bait me, but I wouldn't let her.

"Not a damn thing but my money plus interest," I countered. "I'm not sure you'll be able to produce a profit, darling. My sources tell me your retailers are getting cold feet about the viability of your collection, and they're pulling out of your deals."

She flinched as if I'd physically slapped her. "Bullshit! I have concrete agreements with each of them."

"You really don't know shit about contracts. Nothing in business is concrete. That's what loopholes and a shitload of well-paid lawyers are for." I shot her an irritated glare. "I can tell you don't believe the shit I'm saying, so call Lily Sanchez." I pushed away from my desk and stood up.

"How do you know Lily?" she asked, disbelief ringing in her voice.

I bit back a snort.

Lily was a pawn to maneuver any way I wanted, and she was insignificant in the food chain of New York City power. Lily had been blindsided when her bosses abruptly decided to pull out of Sinthia's deal. Just one phone call to my shadowy connections—who were wealthy, deadly, and ruthless—had killed the agreement.

I'd built alliances while doing things like blackmail, coercion, and extortion, and that had made me one of the wealthiest and most feared men in New York City. Billionaires would quake in their custom-made shoes in fear of being exposed by the cache of intelligence I had about their shady business dealings and sordid sexual tastes. That information would ruin them if I chose to reveal it. I was the puppet master pulling the strings and making CEOs, politicians, and the very affluent dance for my amusement.

I shrugged. "Just call her." I cocked my head. "She'll confirm the gravity of your situation."

She pulled out her cell. Her fingers trembled as she dialed Lily. "Lily, is everything good to go with my collection deal?" Sinthia asked.

There was a slight pause before she jumped up, turning her back on me. "What the hell happened?" she whispered. Her shoulders slumped. "I'm two million dollars in, Lily. My collection is almost complete. That's months of work. Do you understand me? Set up a meeting with the financial planners," she snapped before ending the call.

She turned around with her chin lifted. "How do you know Tabitha?"

Raising a brow, I met her angry gaze.

Her eyes widened. "Oh, I see. You're one of her many fuck buddies." Her voice was tight with accusation.

Interesting. Was that a tinge of jealousy I detected in her voice?

"Let's cut to the chase, shall we? I've known Tabitha for years…in various capacities. She knew I was in the market for another lucrative investment, and that's why she came to me when you had financing issues." I pulled out a cigar and a long wooden match. "I had you and your company extensively investigated and found you are very talented." Placing the cigar between my lips, I struck the match and then held it at the end of the cigar. "But, obviously, you're naïve when it comes to business." A surge of flame shot out from the tip of the cigar, and a puff of smoke came from my mouth.

"So do you know where she is?" she rasped.

My lips twitched into a mockery of a smile. "Don't know, and I don't care. But when you find her, give her my regards." I paused, looking at her coolly. "Sinthia, you're tougher than I thought. I like that." I blew a ring of smoke before placing the cigar in the ashtray. "I've come to a decision."

"What decision?" she barked. "You already made a decision when you gave me two million dollars. Now you're making another decision?" She sneered.

So I've hit a nerve. Interesting. I stared, wondering how many more buttons I could push.

"I will make it really simple for you." I crossed my arms and widened my stance. "I've invested two million into your business, and I intend on getting it back plus a hefty profit, so I will retain full control of your company."

She stared at me in astonishment. "This is bullshit! This is my business!" she shouted.

"You mean it *was* your business, Sinthia. Now, it's mine," I replied. "Kevin, my accountant, will take care of all the financial matters, including providing the money to continue your line. In addition, I will make some calls to my contacts to see if we can get your retailers back on board."

My eyes fell to her full lips as she licked them. *Damn, they are absolutely sinful.* My mind roamed to the vision of my manhood sinking deep into her pouty mouth. *Fuck.*

"And all of this is coming at what price?" Her back stiffened. "I will not use my company as a front for illegal business dealings."

I blinked, and then my expression hardened. *Is she out of her damn mind?*

My eyes narrowed. "What the fuck are you talking about?"

She closed her eyes tightly as if she wanted to block the sight of me from her presence. "I've worked too fucking hard to have my business and name tied to anything illegal." She opened her eyes to look at me again.

I stalked over to her, letting my gaze blatantly roam over her sensual body. "What a beautiful hypocrite. There was no thought about where the money was coming from when you took it." I let out a snort of contempt. "Now, you're looking at me like I'm the fucking scum of the earth."

I regarded her silently.

"I'm just calling it like I see it, Mr. McKay. I will not use my business for shady activities." She spat out the words.

I met her frown with a cool look. "Many years ago, I might have used you for that and more. But now, I'm a legitimate businessman." *With dark and twisted connections.*

"What else do you want, McKay?" she asked before licking her bottom lip.

My eyes traveled from her face to her body and then back again. "Oh, darling, I can't begin to tell you all the things I want from you. That would send your gorgeous ass running from this room. But the question is, what do you want, Ms. Michaels?"

"I want you to let me out of this fucking deal," she bellowed.

I laughed without humor. "Not going to happen. Next." I all but sneered.

"If you wanted to, you could," she responded sullenly.

"I'm in the business of making money, not losing it. The deal remains."

Lifting her chin and holding my stare for several minutes, she didn't say anything as I continued to watch her.

She folded her arms across her chest. "This is fucking ridiculous," she roared. "It might be unlawful too."

"Even you don't really believe that shit," I responded with a hard voice.

"And how long is this business arrangement going to last?"

"Until I determine the debt has been paid in full," I bit out, letting my words sink in for a few seconds.

"Fuck you! You might own the company, but you don't own me." She curled her lip in scorn.

The challenge in her eyes filled me with a need I'd never even known I possessed. My hands tightened and unclenched before I caught her by the arm and pressed her against the wall. In one swift move, I pressed my lips against hers. Moving my mouth on hers, I forced her lips open and I plundered inside, one hand tightening on her waist and drawing her even closer. My tongue swept into her mouth while my other hand released her arm, reaching up to wrap itself in her hair, tilting her head back.

Her hands fisting my shirt, she leaned up into me. My mouth devoured and stroked her with a controlled sensuality that made my cock jump to life, straining against my pants to break free. I growled when her mouth widened, and she pushed her tongue into my mouth. I groaned, tasting a hint of mint and coffee.

My head spun out of control as she kissed me back with unleashed anger and passion. The ache within my throbbing balls grew. I knew I wouldn't last much longer until I needed to bury myself inside her cunt.

Sinthia's breath caught as my hands went around her, pulling her away from the wall and flush against me. My fingers traced over her buttocks. She tried to remain motionless, her ass cheeks tensing in reaction. Blood raced to my cock, stiffening it to near pain as I imagined her tight, voluptuous ass clamping down on my cock as I fucked her from behind.

Damn, I burn to have her.

Lifting my head, I broke off the kiss abruptly and stared down at her with hard eyes. "I might not own you now, but I will," I responded with a steely voice before stepping back from her.

Sinthia lowered her head, but not before she seared me with a furious glare. A perverse need for her to acknowledge I was in control overtook me. With slow deliberation, I turned around and strode over to my wall of floor-to-ceiling windows.

"Now you may go, Ms. Michaels." I kept my voice low and soft but left no room for doubt that I'd issued a command.

For several minutes, I waited until I heard the tap-tap of her heels and the soft click of the door closing before I relaxed.

Now that I knew what it could be like between us, one taste wasn't enough. I had to have her. The thought of making her whimper and beg while I took her from behind aroused me more than I would have believed, filling me with the kind of anticipation I'd thought was long behind me.

I wanted her, and that put a completely new spin on everything. My cock jumped as I imagined the possibilities and the challenges of making this work. I needed to banish my ridiculous fixation on her.

Folding my arms, I mumbled aloud, "This shit is about to get really complicated."

CHAPTER 2
CORE

DAYS LATER

I pulled up in my low-slung Porsche and stepped out. "I fucking hate Newark," I mumbled, looking around the dirty warehouse.

Ram hopped out of the passenger side, and before slamming the door, he said, "Who doesn't?"

We both headed to the warehouse, slipping into the dark building. Our motorcycle boots sounded like trumpets as they slapped against the hard-concrete floors in the dark, cavernous space.

Rats almost the size of kittens ran across the floor to hide. The air was stale and cloying. Total silence reigned as Ram and I made our way down the metal stairs and through the corridor. Tense and focused, we recognized the importance of this moment. We were one step closer to bringing Lexis, Ram's baby sister, home.

"We're going to find her," I stated through gritted teeth.

"She's been missing for almost a year," Ram grumbled with bleak eyes.

Ram had been blaming himself for her disappearance, for not step-ping in when Lexis had gushed about the perfect guy she'd met at a party near her college campus. The guy, Jeff Barolo, had become Lexis's boyfriend after dating her for only two weeks.

Ram had grown suspicious when Lexis refused to introduce Jeff to him, so Ram had driven to her Ivy League school in Massachusetts, only to find out from her friends that Lexis had dropped out of college and run away with Jeff. After a background check, we'd found out Jeff was some preppy wannabe pimp who had a track record for luring pretty college freshmen girls into a life of human trafficking, selling their bodies for sex. It had been hell trying to find any information on the whereabouts of Lexis, because the human trafficking world was dirty and secretive.

One tip after another had led us to dead ends. Every time we'd gotten close to finding Lexis, Jeff would transport her from state to state, changing their location and leaving no trace.

The last hot lead we'd gotten was that she'd been traded between traffickers across the country. After months of attempting to infiltrate the seedy traffickers' world, playing cat-and-mouse games while trying to find her, we'd finally gotten a solid clue from one of the girls with whom Lexis had worked who had escaped Jeff's clutches. She had given us one name. The name, a flashback from our criminal past, was Ben Vargos.

"Where did they find him?" I snapped.

"He's set up shop in the Bronx with some butcher shop as a front." Ram gritted his teeth.

We stood before the door in deadly hunt mode with adrenaline coursing through our veins. This was a slippery slope for ruthless men like us. It had taken us years to leave our criminal lives behind, ones filled with the constant chaos of brutality, most of it perpetrated by us. Now, we were right back where we had started—a life of violence.

Ram grabbed the doorknob.

I clamped my hand on his shoulder. "Let me do this, Ram. You're in a real fucked-up mood right now. You might end up killing him before we even get any information."

His body stiffened as he turned to look at me. Our eyes locked in battle.

"Core, I can do this without fucking it up."

"You can't, not like this." I narrowed my eyes. "Trust me."

Ram blew out roughly before nodding.

Grinding my teeth together, I stepped into the damp-smelling cell. My eyes quickly adjusted to the darkness as we strode in. Ram closed the door with a decisive click. I nodded curtly to Max and Rocco before my eyes locked on the man in his mid-thirties who was bound to the metal chair sitting between them.

Ben Vargos was unshaven, and his clothes looked slept in.

I sighed heavily. What I was about to do would drag me right back into the criminal world I'd left behind. But we had to get Lexis back, and there was nothing I wasn't willing to do to accomplish that.

Ben's eyes widened. "McKay?" he squawked. His eyes turned to look at Ram. "Ram?"

My nostrils flared slightly before I responded, "Hello, Ben."

Ben glanced around furtively.

The room was silent, except for the low whir of the air conditioner. Ram moved toward the table smack dab in the middle of the room. He snatched up a pair of black latex gloves and impatiently snapped them on.

Ben bucked against the rope binding him to the chair. "Untie me!"

Max growled, slapping Ben on the back of his head. "I will snap your damn neck. Shut the fuck up." Max's voice was flat.

Ben's face contorted with pain. "Core? What the fuck is this shit about?" he squeaked while watching me move unhurriedly toward the narrow table. "I haven't seen your ass in years, and you send your men into my business to drag me out like some punk." He struggled uselessly against the rope.

I ignored him while taking off my leather jacket, folding it, and then laying it over the table ever so carefully. Cracking my knuckles before slipping on my own pair of black latex gloves, I stared blankly at Ben.

His eyes darted toward Ram. "Ram? Come on. We go way back. Talk to Core." Beads of sweat dripped down his forehead.

Ram sneered but remained eerily silent as he moved to sit on the edge of the table.

"Come on, man. This is totally fucked up!" Ben yelled.

I fixed him with a cold stare. "He's not going to save your ass, Ben."

"This is bullshit!" Ben's panic was distinct.

I smiled unemotionally as I rolled up my sleeves, displaying my tattooed forearms. "This is how it's going down. I'm going to ask you some questions, and I want straight answers."

"Fuck you, McKay!" Ben screamed.

I nodded toward the tub of water. Rocco shoved Ben forward, ruthlessly slamming his head under the surface of the water. Ben struggled, but Rocco didn't relent. Ben struggled more frantically until Rocco whipped his head up. Ben gasped for air.

I twirled a chair around, and I sat in front of him. "This is about unfinished business." My eyes were cold, my voice flat. "I hear you've moved up in the world, Ben." I leaned forward. "No more selling underage girls on the corner. You've upgraded to sex trafficking."

Ben licked his lips nervously. "What? No." He shook his head in denial, but the truth was written on his face. "Don't know what you're talking about, man."

Ram's body tensed. "You don't know what he's talking about? You piece of shit!"

He stalked toward Ben before hitting him hard across the face. I watched with disinterest.

"You pimp out underage girls, and when you're done with them, you sell them to other traffickers," Ram accused as he studied Ben with murderous eyes.

Ben grunted in pain. "Not everyone can go straight like you two."

"I'm going to cut to the chase, Ben." My face remained emotionless. "I know you're part of a sex-trafficking ring that's making a lot of money pimping out college women. I'm looking for one of your buddies, Jeff Barolo."

Ben squirmed. "I don't know him."

I arched a brow. "Our informant says you do. We need to have a little talk with Barolo. And given your precarious predicament, I think you need to be quick about snitching on his whereabouts."

Ben's face tightened. "I'm not saying shit."

Ram shouted, seething with anger, "Where is he?"

I had to move quickly before Ram completely lost it. I bolted to my feet, upending my chair, before shoving Ben forward and bending him over the tub of water. I was done playing around with him.

My voice dropped to a lethal, low whisper. "You either give me the info I want, or I'm going to torture your ass with no mercy."

Ben's whole body trembled. "If I tell you, they'll kill me."

"And if you don't tell me, I'll kill you. So it sounds like you're in a real fucked-up position. But the difference between them and me is I'll make sure you stay alive for five long, agonizing days until you bleed out completely." I smiled cruelly. "Your choice."

"Fuck you, McKay," he spat.

His bravado amused me. "No. Fuck you."

I plunged Ben's head back into the water. He struggled, but not as much as before. I pulled his head back out, and Ben gasped, but I gave him no time before I pushed him back under. Again and again, I forced Ben down. The water stilled. Ben was under, but he'd stopped struggling. When I pulled him out, he didn't gasp for air. His head lolled back, and he was barely coherent. His brow was gashed and raw.

"I know your lungs are burning." I stepped back, drying my hand on a black towel. "I can see the panic in your eyes. You want this to end, and I promise, I will end it. Just tell me what I want to know. Where's Jeff?"

"I don't know." Ben coughed. "Jeff was recruiting women for me, and then I would bring them to my loaded connection to pimp them out to his rolling-in-it friends." He shrugged. "But Jeff got smart. He cut me out of the deal and went straight to my contact, Bigsby Calhoune. He's Bigsby's errand boy now."

"Holy shit," Max mumbled.

My mouth tightened. "Bigsby Calhoune? The politician running for New York City mayor?"

"Yes," Ben responded.

"Bullshit!" Ram barked.

Ben jumped apprehensively. "I'm telling you the truth." His Adam's apple bobbed. "Think about it. Why can't you find Barolo?" He looked around with uneasy eyes. "He's protected by Bigsby. There's a huge demand from his rich friends who think nothing about paying to fuck fresh, untrained women any way and anywhere they want."

Ram snarled, "You fucking bastard."

I grabbed Ram's hand, stopping him from killing Ben. "Go on."

"Jeff fucking me over like he did should have earned him a dirt nap, but I'm not about to make waves with Bigsby since he's helping us clean lots of dough."

Ram's fists tightened at his sides. "Who the hell is *us*?"

Ben gulped. "A bunch of us traffickers got smart. For a huge fee, Bigsby arranged to help us clean our money through his shell company called Pomtonic International. On top of that fee, we're also pumping a hell of a lot of money into UF-Star."

My mind spun with this new information. UF-Star was a super PAC. The independent political action committee had been spending a ton of money to advocate for Bigsby as New York City's new mayor.

I couldn't believe it. After all these years, fate had finally thrown me a bone. I was one step closer to bringing down the man who'd killed my mother. I'd be avenging her death *and* helping Ram get Lexis back in one fell swoop.

"Why the hell are you contributing to UF-Star?" I hissed.

Ben tried to bite back a response. Rocco grabbed the back of his neck and squeezed.

"Once Bigsby gets elected, he'll turn a blind eye to all our illegal activities for a percentage of our profits. That's all I know. I swear." Ben's eyes pleaded. "Look, I told you what you wanted to know. Now let me go."

I leaned forward menacingly while pulling off my gloves before putting them into a black garbage bag. "You actually think I would let a piece of shit like you back on the street?"

Ram smiled coldly before nodding over to Rocco.

Rocco slammed Ben's head into the water. Eventually, the water stilled. He was under, but he'd stopped struggling. When he was pulled up, he didn't gasp for air. His eyes rolled back into his head, and he dropped to the floor. He didn't move.

Ram pulled off his gloves while looking over at Max and Rocco.

"Bury him somewhere he won't be found and then clean this place and get rid of all the evidence."

They both nodded.

I pulled out my cell, quickly swiping my finger across it. "Kevin, pull up everything you can on UF-Star and Pomtonic International."

"Will do," Kevin responded before disconnecting.

"I have a feeling once Bigsby finds out we're digging into UF-Star and Pomtonic International, he'll be more than happy to shove Jeff out of hiding and put him right on our doorstep." I looked over at Ram while grabbing my jacket. "Let's go. We have lots of work to do."

CHAPTER 3
SINTHIA

I snapped my eyes open to the sound of my cell phone ringing. Grumbling, I rolled over to grab it off the nightstand. "Yes?" I answered.

"Sinthia Michaels?" the man drawled.

Groaning, I sat up in bed gingerly, putting my cell on speaker. "Yes?"

"My name is Kevin Rawley. I've been calling you for days." Kevin's voice sounded annoyed.

I swung my legs over the bed and leaned forward, putting my elbows on my knees and clutching my head. I was exhausted from working on my collection late into the night.

"I left you several voice messages and sent multiple emails."

I could hear the exasperation in his voice.

"And?" I snapped.

"I work for Core McKay. I'm his accountant, and by virtue of your contract with him, I'm now yours too."

Sighing, I sat up before scrubbing my hands over my face. "How can I help you, Kevin?" I stood and decided to get a cup of coffee before taking a nice cold shower.

"Why the fuck do I deal with this shit?" he muttered under his breath. "Like I said on all the messages I left for you, I need access to your business records—more specifically, your invoices."

"No," I responded bluntly while putting on my handpainted silk kimono robe before going downstairs. "If McKay wants my records, tell him to man up, call me, and demand them," I countered.

I stepped into my gourmet kitchen, pressed the button on the espresso machine, and placed a cup beneath the brew head to capture the wonderful stream of black liquid gold.

I was chilled to the bone at the thought of how many things had gone wrong in the last couple months. I had gone from being the sole proprietor of a thriving fashion business—one that had been ready to go live in a matter of months with my highly anticipated Sin Michaels women's wear collection in luxury goods department stores—to none of the retailers willing to return my calls.

Moreover, the most frustrating part of it all was Core McKay, the gorgeous but major asshole, now owned ninety-seven percent of my business. Either I had some pretty fucked-up karma, or fate was just playing a bad joke on me. Either way, I was royally screwed.

"You know what you're doing doesn't make sense," Kevin stated flatly.

"I'm still the designer, and he won't make a damn dime if I decide to sit on my ass and do nothing." When sufficient coffee had flowed into the cup, I lifted it to my lips and took a small sip, savoring the much-needed awakening.

It wasn't about playing games. It was about respect. I wasn't going to stand for McKay sending his minions every time he wanted something from me. And I didn't give a shit that he now owned ninety-seven percent of my business. I wasn't about to bend down and grab my fucking ankles every time the king of bullshit bellowed from his damn iron throne.

"Ms. Michaels, he's going to get what he wants. Fuck it. Let's be blunt. He already has what he wants—ninety-seven percent of your business."

"A valid point. However, I won't be treated like a prison yard bitch."

When he chuckled, I jumped.

"I love your spirit. I truly do, but I'm sure you can't be happy that all your retailers have pulled out of the deal to distribute your collection."

Heat flushed through my body. "No, I'm not."

"And your bills? How are they being paid?" Kevin asked acerbically.

I put down my cup and crossed my arms, staring at my unfinished Sin Michaels collection, which was hanging on racks in parts of my four-thousand-square-foot townhouse.

I sighed heavily.

There was no working around the missing custom fabric I'd ordered. I had no hope in hell of getting it until I paid the overdue bill, which should have been cleared days ago.

"They're not," I muttered.

I didn't feel good about dodging calls from Nia, the president of the fabric distribution company. Moving around some of my assets to make the payment would get the bill paid, but it would also leave me living off next to nothing until my collection hit the high-end retail stores. In theory, that would have worked if they hadn't all pulled out of their agreements to carry my line.

"Play this smart, Ms. Michaels. I've seen the newspaper article that touted you as the next big fashion maven. Don't let your pride dictate your future."

With an aggrieved sigh, I pulled out my notepad. "What's your email address?"

He reeled off his address. I jotted it down before saying, "Check your email in five minutes. I'll send you a link giving you access to all my online business documents and then a separate email with the password." I paused. "Look, I have a massive five-figure bill for custom fabric I ordered. I'm in a real jam, and I can't finish my collection without it. If you could just handle that first, it would be helpful."

"All payments have to be approved by Mr. McKay, so I'd advise you to give him a call," Kevin stated.

"Why can't you just deal with it?" I countered in a sharp tone.

"Because I'm just the accountant. He's the boss. So you need to call him."

"I'll think about it."

"No thinking. Just do it. Let me give you his number," he grumbled.

I rolled my eyes heavenward.

"Sinthia, I'm trying to help."

"Go."

Kevin gave me McKay's number, and I took it down.

"And, Sinthia, stop fucking around. Just call him." Abruptly, he ended our call.

"It was nice talking to you too, Kevin," I replied sarcastically, slamming my cell onto the counter.

CHAPTER 4
SINTHIA

Hours later, after sketching until my fingers hurt, I'd had enough of being cooped up in the house. I had a couple of hours to burn before heading over to my scheduled appointment at my friend Francisco "Cisco" Rodriguez's upscale boutique. It was just enough time to partake in some much-needed window-shopping.

Stuffing my cell into my pocket, I grabbed my handbag and stepped out of my townhouse, sighing as the fresh air caressed my face. I loved this time of year. It was right after Labor Day, but the air was still sultry with summer temperatures refusing to go away quietly to make room for fall.

Glancing around my tree-lined neighborhood only a few steps from Central Park, I ran down the stairs before skidding to a stop in the middle of the sidewalk. I shivered from the eerie feeling of being watched.

The more I tried to ignore the feeling, the more creeped out I became. I was paranoid, my eyes darting around as I expected to see my stalker, Jaxon, emerging from the shadows. But there was nothing, only harried New Yorkers hurrying home after work.

"I'm totally losing it," I mumbled.

Deciding to walk instead of taking a cab, I quickened my steps, pushing my way through the Manhattan foot traffic. I loved the energy of New York City. I could meander for hours, but today, I had things to do.

Grabbing a cup of coffee from the coffee cart, I sipped on it while strolling through the heavy pedestrian gridlock. Finally, I arrived at one of my favorite upscale department stores.

I was giddy when I stepped through the double brass doors that kept out the hustle of Manhattan, leaving customers to shop in peace. Like a kid in a candy store, I practically skipped past the chic cosmetic counters. Some people would go to yoga class to relax. My vices were grandiose department stores. I loved to stroll through them, imagining the day my collection would be prettily featured for women to drool over and buy. Even though I had clients to see today, I needed this— just a little me time to dream.

My heart raced with excitement as I wandered through the store, stopping occasionally to touch a garment that caught my eye, before heading to my destination—couture heaven. Riding up the escalator, I arrived at my goal, the prime high-traffic spot on the floor where another trendy designer's clothing line was presented like delicious eye candy.

"Someday," I whispered.

I was so close yet so far. My collection was almost finished, but with my horrible luck, I would be standing at the door, looking in with no entry allowed. The only person who had the power to give me access was Core McKay. One little call—that was what he wanted. Then my business could resume. He would give me the rest of the money. It was stupid and illogical not to swallow my pride and call him, but I knew the call would be a first step down a slippery slope.

Core McKay had thrown down the gauntlet. He was in control, and he wanted me to submit. Just the thought of rolling over in obedience left a bad taste in my mouth.

I was jolted out of my thoughts by the cold drawl of a woman saying, "Still dreaming, huh?"

I recognized the voice. My body tightened. It had been years since I'd heard her hateful, icy tone.

Pivoting on my heels, I turned around to see the one woman I'd never wanted to see again—my narcissistic, alcoholic mother.

"Hello, Grace."

As usual, not one strand of Grace's blond hair was out of place in her tight bun. Her hourglass figure—large chest, small waist, slender thighs—was encased in skintight designer jeans and an expensive-looking silk blouse that showed way too much cleavage. In essence, she looked like a woman desperately trying to look young. It was an epic fail.

"Sin," Grace bit out, wobbling forward.

I scrunched up my nose when I smelled the alcohol seeping from her pores. Grace was drunk, which was nothing new. I'd spent my entire childhood suffering under her drunken tirades and mood swings.

The woman who had given birth to me was still beautiful on the outside. But from the derisive twisted sneer of her lips as she looked me up and down with distaste, she was still a hateful, ugly mess inside.

Grace's frosty blue eyes zeroed in on my body. "I see you're still working on losing those last few stubborn pounds." She smiled. "A personal trainer should fix that right up."

In other words, Grace thought I looked fat.

I smiled coolly. I was far from fat. I was curvy. But from experience, I knew this was Grace's desperate attempt to chip away at my self-esteem to feed her insatiable ego.

That shit is not happening.

When I was a teenager, I'd wilt at her constant digs about my weight. I would run to the bathroom and purge all my food, punishing myself for not being a size six like her. But not anymore. Now, I was a confident woman who'd worked years to heal myself after a lifetime of emotional and mental abuse by Grace. There was no fucking way she could break me...ever again.

I looked back at her with just as much venom. Then I nodded to the multiple shopping bags she had clutched in her hands. "And I see you're still living a life of champagne dreams on a beer budget," I said disdainfully.

Grace's face hardened.

I smirked. I'd heard through the gossip hags that Grace's teahouse was nearly bankrupt, and she'd been looking for husband number two to keep her in the lifestyle she thought she deserved.

"I'm doing well, you disrespectful wench. Can't say the same for you. After all, you're standing here, lusting after things you obviously can't afford."

I made a face. The woman didn't know shit about me.

"Excuse me, ladies," said a man with a slightly hoarse-sounding deep voice.

I looked up to see him smiling down at me. I stared right back with just as much appreciation. *Dude is hot as hell.* He wasn't too manicured or metrosexual. He was well-groomed with that I'm-not-trying-too-hard look.

Jesus. Yes, please.

"Hello," he said.

He was staring at me, but it was Grace who purred, "Hello." Immediately standing straight while dropping her bags, she ran her pale fingers over her blond hair.

His eyes skated across her with disinterest before returning to rest on me with warmth. A nasty frown crossed Grace's face. For the first time in my life, I noticed the jealous gleam in her eyes. She was looking at me all *Silence of the Lambs*-like, as if she wanted to rip off my skin and wear it like some fucking fur coat.

He smiled wider. "Sinthia Michaels?"

I turned to face him. "Yes?" I answered.

He stuck out his hand. "I'm Nathaniel Butler, merchandising manager for women's clothing. Lily Sanchez reports to me."

I remembered Lily—the energetic buyer from this Fifth Avenue luxury goods department store—had gushed about her hot boss. Well, now I could see why.

I shook his hand before saying, "Nice to meet you, Nathaniel. How's Lily?"

I was distracted when Nathaniel turned our handshake into a half-handshake and half-caress thing before I had the wits to pull my hand away. Disgust was clear on Grace's face as she absorbed our exchange.

He shook his head. "Hell to work with since your deal fell through."

I smiled, knowing Lily's headstrong personality. She'd probably staged a one-woman protest. After all, she was the one who'd pushed for my deal from day one. When Lily had walked into Cisco's boutique and fallen instantly in love with my couture clothing he sold in his store, she'd changed my life forever. In the blink of an eye, at twenty-six years old, I'd moved from fledgling darling of the fashion world to having several luxury goods buyers clamoring to carry my edgy Sin Michaels women's wear line in their stores. But when the stores mysteriously backed away from my deal, Lily had been just as pissed and puzzled as I was.

"At least I have one person who still believes in my collection," I responded.

He smiled. "Two. I wouldn't have backed her idea of bringing your collection to our store if I didn't believe in you." He touched my shoulder. "But all of that is water under the bridge now that your deal is back on the table."

My mouth fell open then closed. "What?"

Nathaniel replied, "It was unfortunate you missed the great conference call we had this morning, but your new business partner, Core McKay, explained you had a meeting conflict. He smoothed over all of the management's concerns over the viability of carrying your collection in our store, and he assured us your clothing line would be delivered on time. It's a relief to be doing business with you once again, Sinthia."

I balled up my fists by my sides. "I'm confused. There was a conference call about my business and my collection this morning?" I swallowed over the lump in my throat. "And your store has agreed to carry my collection again?" I was excited yet pissed about the new predicament. Why didn't McKay inform me about this meeting?

Nathaniel looked uncomfortable as he cleared his throat. "Yes. We're back on board with carrying your collection." He frowned. "Mr. McKay didn't inform you?"

"No, he didn't." My nostrils flared.

Confusion clouded his gaze before it disappeared. "Wait, I get it.

He did say you'd be dealing strictly with the creative end of the business, and he'd be handling all the business decisions."

What in the world is going on?

"Excuse me?" My mouth compressed into a thin line.

"I'm sorry. Maybe I misspoke." He looked at his watch. "Anyway, I'm late for a meeting. It was nice seeing you, Ms. Michaels."

He rushed away, leaving me staring at his back.

Grace leaned in with a spiteful mask. "So…having business problems? I'm hiring a hostess at my teahouse. You could always apply."

Her tone ignited my temper.

"You can't afford me," I delivered from between drawn-together teeth. "However, I heard your teahouse is about to be shut down, so you should worry about your own damn self." I smiled coldly. "I think management is taking applications for clerks upstairs. Run along now and apply."

I flipped my hair and walked away with a smile on my face, swaying my hips even though anger was burning in the pit of my stomach.

How dare McKay just take over my business as if he owned it!

I couldn't even see past the rage to the rational side of what he'd done. He'd smoothed things over with at least one retailer. All I could focus on was he hadn't had the respect to tell me about the conference call and his high-handed move of telling the retailer that he was now the decision-maker. This shit would not do.

I stepped out of the store and ran smack into the middle of a throng of pushy New Yorkers when my cell rang. I dug it out of my pocket and immediately recognized the number.

"Hi, Nia," I greeted while navigating my way to Cisco's boutique.

"Hi, Sin," Nia responded. "I've been trying to reach you for days. It's about the shipment of the custom fabric you ordered."

"I apologize, but things have been hectic lately." I pinched the bridge of my nose. Any delay in shipment of the expensive custom prints I'd ordered from Nia's factory in Asia meant the fabric wouldn't arrive in time, halting my whole collection. "I'll get the money by the end of the week. Look, I—"

Nia cut me off, "Sin, what are you talking about? The bill was just paid by your partner, Core McKay. Since it's such a big order, I just wanted to confirm the delivery date so you'd be available to receive it."

I skidded to a stop. A man bumped into me from behind, and he shot me an annoyed glare while grumbling for me to move the hell out of the way. I shot him the bird before walking over to the edge of the sidewalk near a parking meter.

"What the hell are you talking about, Nia?"

Nia cleared her throat. "I spoke to Mr. McKay personally, and he made the payment on your order."

I paused to calm my wildly racing heart. "Please schedule the delivery for Tuesday. Thank you." I hung up, swearing under my breath.

Staring up at the sky, I knew with every twist of fate, the noose was tightening. Whether I liked it or not, Core McKay was making it a point to let me know he was repairing my business, one major fuck-up at a time.

CHAPTER 5
SINTHIA

Stepping off the elevator, I scanned the studio that had been designed with a contemporary look in mind. I loved the ambiance of Cisco's boutique. The space was sleek, modern, and very glam. The walls were painted black, which allowed the rich colors of my designs on display to pop against the beautiful darkness. Those dark walls also perfectly contrasted with the plush velvet furniture and natural light.

Pulling my tablet from my leather handbag, I quickly took a couple photos of my pieces before flipping through the photos I'd already saved of the gowns I had designed for my bestie Jade Bellisario, her mother Ariana Bellisario, and my new client Erika Watson to wear to Bigsby Calhoune's fundraising gala scheduled for tomorrow night.

I needed to make sure their gowns were perfect. Tonight was the last of three fittings, and I was hoping to get everything wrapped up in time to put the finishing touches on my own gown.

I sighed. *This is going to be a very long night.*

Distracted by my thoughts, I was startled when I heard a squeal.

Then a lilting voice said, "My favorite person."

I didn't even have time to put away my tablet before the petite dynamo rushed up, wrapping her arms around me.

"Hi, Summer." I hugged her and then stepped back with a wide smile. "How's the family?"

She gave me an impish smile. "Crazy," she replied.

I propped my hands on my hips. "You mean *you're* making them crazy."

She waved her hand dramatically. "Me, them—all the same thing." She chuckled. "I completed the alterations on the gowns, and they're waiting for you upstairs." She swung her handbag onto her shoulder. "I have to go and clean up the chaos and mayhem waiting for me at home. Tony's howling like a big bear, wanting to know when I'm coming home. He tries, but God help him, he lets the babies run circles around him."

I snickered because Summer had Tony wrapped around her finger. It was good to see her content after finally finding Tony. She complained about him, but I knew my friend was joyfully grappling with the tornado her adorable newborn twins had unleashed on her home and her big, burly, but lovable husband. I was happy for her but also a little forlorn. I had a small circle of friends, and the circle was getting smaller and smaller every day. They were either in serious relationships, settling down, or getting married.

"Thank you so much for coming in to put the last-minute touches on the gowns. I couldn't have finished in time without you." I really meant it. I hated to take time away from her babies, but Summer was a top-notch seamstress and the only one I trusted to work on my designs.

"I would do anything for my girl Sinthia." She squeezed my hand while smiling warmly. "I doubt you'll need any additional alterations, but call me if you do." She turned on her heel and rushed out.

"Sin, baby!" Cisco exclaimed, rolling his hands about in emphasis. "I haven't seen you in ages."

As usual, he was crackling with energy. Dressed in black jeans, a crisp blue shirt, and his signature old Rolex, he barely paused before closing the space between us and yanking me into his arms. I hugged him back without any hesitation.

"I've been crazy busy trying to get my collection finished."

He pulled away and clasped my hands. His eyes swept over me from head to toe. At thirty-six, he still looked boyish, but he had intense dark eyebrows that conveyed his seriousness. "Too busy, I see, by the shadows under your eyes."

I scrunched my nose. Cisco was observant and brutally honest.

"I'm exhausted," I snapped, snatching my hands away.

"Mm-hmm."

I rolled my eyes heavenward. "Okay, I'm in a fucked-up mood," I complained.

"Clearly," he responded dryly. He caressed my cheek. "I'm just worried about my Sin. Don't get fucking snarly about it."

I saw the concern flash across his eyes. Instantly, I felt ashamed. Cisco was worried about me like a mother hen.

I softened a little. "I apologize." Wrapping my arm around his lean waist, I dragged him along with me toward the stairs, which led to the dressing lounge.

He draped one arm around my shoulders. "Apology accepted, Sin baby. So any word on Tabitha's whereabouts?"

"Don't get me started. I'm so fucking pissed off right now."

The fact that Tabitha had disappeared without a trace was still confusing. Her cell number was now disconnected, and her boutique had shut down.

I frowned. "She just up and left everything. Who does that?"

Cisco stopped and scowled. "She's a backstabbing skanky bitch. I can't believe she lied to you like that."

"Me either. It just doesn't make sense."

The whole craziness of Tabitha's deception nagged at me. *Why didn't she tell me my investor was McKay?* I felt sick just thinking about her betrayal. When she'd brought me the contract, she'd seemed entirely too happy that she'd found me the deal I needed to solve all my business problems.

Granted, I'd been desperate for financing to help me manufacture my new clothing line, and no bank would have given me a loan until I could dig myself out of the ton of debt I'd accumulated over the years. Tabitha had been my salvation. She'd used her business connections to find me a secret investor who would be willing to provide financing in exchange for a small percentage of my future profits. I'd been practically giddy when I signed the contract with the secret investor and felt the same again when two million dollars had been deposited into my business account with the promise of another million in six months. I'd quickly spent every last dime, paying outstanding business expenses to keep my company running.

My biggest mistake had been not looking over the fine print of the contract or taking the time to find out who the secret investor was. It was a mistake I was still kicking myself in the ass for to this day. But desperation could make you do some fucked-up things, and desperation had introduced the mysterious and eccentric owner of investment company MK Partners into my life.

"I never trusted her. Never," Cisco snapped.

"Let's be clear. I'm not blaming her for my stupidity in signing the damn contract without looking at the fine print." I pointed to myself. "That fucked-up move is all me. But, damn, I trusted her as my friend. She could have been straight with me and told me Core McKay was the investor. She owed me that much."

Her betrayal had stung the most. Tabitha had been my mentor, and I'd thought she was my friend.

"But to leave her successful business and disappear? That shit is crazy," I said flatly.

His eyebrows shot up. "Successful? Her business was only making money from the pieces of your collection you'd allowed her to sell there."

"She had a little creative dry spell."

"God, how can you still defend that bitch?"

I shot him an annoyed glare. "I'm not defending her. I'm just stating a fact."

"And I told you months ago about the rumors circulating regarding her money problems."

"Tabitha always had money problems. Her income could never support her lifestyle."

Even after a lengthy stint as the go-to designer for several celebrities, Tabitha's extravagant lifestyle and years of partying and jet-setting more than she was designing had taken a toll on her business. But she'd still managed to stay afloat—or so I'd thought.

"Exactly," Cisco responded.

"I don't want to talk about Tabitha." I grabbed his hand and pulled him along, deciding I needed to change the topic fast. "So how's your newest acquisition?"

"Young and hung." He laughed huskily. "Jesus, he does this thing with his tongue and my ass that makes my toes curl." He waggled his eyebrows. "Oh, and did I mention he's also a master at—"

I skidded to a stop, holding up my hand. "Don't you dare say it, Cisco."

His eyes widened with fake innocence. "But—"

I slapped my hand over his mouth. "Don't. I get it. He's gifted. Stop trying to make me jealous."

He started talking, but thankfully, it was muffled by my hand. I removed it.

He smiled in his simply gorgeous way. "Only if you promise to have lunch with me this week. I miss hanging out with you."

I grabbed his face and kissed him soundly on both cheeks. "I will."

"Good. Now hurry your sexy ass upstairs to the lounge. The fitting rooms have been set up. Yell if you need anything."

I stepped away, waving my hand over my shoulder. I hurried off, dashing up the stairs and into the cream-colored lounge. A champagne bottle was open, glasses waiting. Dropping my bag, I checked each fitting room to see which one had whose gown before pouring myself a flute of champagne. Kicking back, I flipped through my designs on my tablet.

Jade sauntered in, and she flopped down beside me.

"Rough day?" I handed her my glass before pouring another for myself.

She guzzled her champagne like water. "Erika was a real hag today. She made me do a zillion takes just to flex her I'm-the-producer-of-this-damn-show muscle."

"I don't blame her. She's frantic because you're going to be away for months in New Zealand on your movie shoot."

I was very proud that Jade was finally making her dream come true. She was taking the script she'd written and was independently producing a movie.

"So she makes me shoot longer scenes as punishment." She sulked playfully. "I'm not just a pretty face, you know. It's emotionally draining, running the gamut of gut-wrenching scenes."

"Oh, poor baby. Starring in a smoking-hot television series is so much work." I pointed to the dressing room. "Now get your ass in there and change. I have lots of shit to do tonight, actress extraordinaire."

Jade's apple-green eyes narrowed. "Come on. Give me a minute." She plopped her feet onto my lap. "I'm exhausted."

I pushed them off. "The gala is tomorrow night, and this is your last fitting. Go. I can't have you looking like a hot mess in my creation."

Jade stood up and swayed away, mumbling under her breath about my lack of respect for her craft.

"Oh my goodness, Sin," she squealed from inside the dressing room. She peeped out, grinning from ear to ear. "It's beautiful."

I grinned right back and said, "Change, Jade."

The two-piece ensemble was risqué, but as usual, Jade wasn't afraid to let the fashion take the lead, which was one of the many things I loved about her.

"And the designer can't accept compliments," she grumbled before popping her head back in.

Two glasses of champagne later, I yelled, "Jade!" There was total silence. "I know you're dressed and taking selfies. Get your skinny butt out here. Now."

"You're so bossy today."

She sauntered out, looking every bit one of Hollywood's most beautiful actresses as she flaunted her perfect body in my couture design of a midriff-baring white crop top with a flowing skirt. She turned around, examining her ass in the floor-to-ceiling mirror, doing a perfect imitation of a dog chasing its tail.

"Sin! Fix my skirt. It's hanging funny around my ass."

Leaning back against the soft, comfy gray couch, I sipped champagne, watching with amusement. "What do you want me to do about it?"

"You designed it. Fix it." She frowned.

"God, you're such a whiny baby," I huffed before getting up and walking over.

Jade spun around in the mirror. "I'm your bestie, so I'm entitled. Fix it. My ass looks unspectacular."

"That's because it requires more ass." I smiled saucily before twisting the skirt until it lay perfectly.

I stepped back, examining her in the white gown. The two pieces accented her lean body. She was the best walking commercial for my clothing line.

She laughed huskily. "Not everyone is blessed with a sexy ass like you." She grabbed my glass before taking a sip.

I smiled. "What can I tell you? Ass is in, and I'm riding the mother-fucking bootylicious wave, baby." I reached in and hugged her. "And thank you for wearing my dress to the gala."

Just the press coverage of Jade, the most desired and in-demand actress right now, would be enough to keep the fashion hags talking for days.

She fanned me away. "Please. You make me look sexy. Besides, if you made a dress out of plastic bags, I would proudly wear that shit." She winked.

That was why I loved her so much. Despite the money and fame, she remained humble and real.

Jade shook her long black hair. "So how did your day go?"

"Sugar and spice," I said. "I spoke to my new accountant today, Kevin…McKay's minion."

She fluffed up her hair. "What do you think? Up or down?"

"Up." I walked behind her, twisting her hair up into a high, loose knot. "Like this but less messy."

She preened in the mirror. "Up it is." She shook out her hair, letting it cascade over her shoulders and down her back. "So what was Kevin the accountant like?"

I tightened my mouth. "He seemed like an okay guy. Just a little pushy. He kept going on and on about me calling McKay, and he gave me his number." Stalling, I flicked at the nonexistent dust on her shoulder. "Oh, and I found out McKay paid my outstanding bill for the custom fabric I ordered."

Her mouth dropped open. "That bill was five figures." Her eyes narrowed at my frown. "That's a good thing, right?"

I shrugged. "I guess. I also found out he got one retailer back on board with carrying my collection."

"Okay. So what's with the sour face? You should be jumping up and down with joy—or at the very least, planning a scorching hot lap dance for Mr. McKay."

I shook my head. "You do realize a lap dance isn't exactly the solution to every girl's problems?"

Jade screwed up her mouth. "Says who?"

I groaned. "Moving on because it's just too exhausting to debate about your theory right now."

"Well, it seems to me McKay is doing all the right things by you."

"I beg to differ. He had a conference call with the retailer this morning and didn't bother to invite me."

She jammed her hands on her hips. "Uh-huh. And why does that matter?"

My eyes widened. "Because I'm a part of this business. I'm not just the hired help."

"There could be a plausible reason for his oversight."

I walked toward the settee before sitting down. "Like what?"

She rolled her eyes heavenward. "Like why don't you fucking ask him? This shit is ridiculous. Woman up. Pick up the phone and call him."

"Negative on that idea." I rolled my shoulders to relieve the tension. "Do you think I'm cursed? Because it feels like it."

"Cursed? Blessed is more like it. He paid off your fabric distributor bill and smoothed things over with at least one retailer." Jade blinked her eyes humorously. "Holy shit! Yes. He's a damn monster," she finished mockingly.

"He didn't do it because he's a saint."

She strolled over to the sofa and sat down with a loud sigh. "You're damn right. He did it because, guess what? He's a businessman. Has it even crossed your mind that your approach to your predicament is all wrong?"

I sat straight up. "Oh, hell no! Don't go all Zen bananas on me."

She held up her hand. "Don't get mad. Just listen to me. I know men."

I frowned. "And I don't? I haven't fucked in a while, but that doesn't mean I'm hopelessly out of commission."

"I'm going to ignore that statement because it's just too much work to go into why it's just…well, all wrong." She gave a quick shake of her head. "Jesus. Have you learned nothing from me all these years?"

"Oh, I've learned plenty from your too-much-information recaps of your sexual escapades. Lesson number one"—I counted off on my fingers—"breathe through your nose, not your mouth, when trying to take a cock to the back of your throat without gagging. Number two, a Dirty Sanchez isn't for the fainthearted. Oh, and the most important lesson"—I batted my eyelashes almost comically—"have lots of painkillers on standby after getting fisted." I smiled saucily. "All good lessons. Thank you."

Jade winked at me. "Well, you know me. I'm willing to do all the hot, sweaty research for the betterment of your fuck game."

"I haven't had any complaints yet."

"Because of me doing all the damn legwork." She slapped my thigh. "But let's not get distracted. Back to McKay."

I reclined. "No. I'm tired of talking about him."

"All I'm saying is you're fighting fire with fire and getting absolutely nowhere with him. Honey is what's needed." She fluttered her eyelashes, tossing her hair dramatically. "Like that. But with you, you've got to spread it on thick and wear something low-cut when you're doing it."

I looked at her like she'd lost her ever-loving mind. "Not going to be able to do it."

"Okay. Your choice, but he's holding all the cards."

I scoffed. "He's a prick." *Gorgeous and smoldering, but undeniably, he's a bona fide asshole.*

"Grasshopper, that shit doesn't matter. All that matters is you're making yourself miserable over a deal you're stuck with until he chooses to end it. Do you know how many deals I've made that suck ass? Too many to fucking count, but I made them because I had to give a little so those Hollywood movie executive pricks would even consider me for prime roles."

"He took ninety-seven percent of my business."

"He's the bank, and you're the creator. You both need each other."

"But—"

Jade interrupted me. "It doesn't matter why this shit happened, but it did. He gave you two million dollars and an accountant. Use this opportunity to learn what makes him tick, and work the man until you can flip this deal and change the business stake on paper."

I groaned painfully. "I know I should, but I can't."

She shook her head. "I love you, but you're driving me crazy with your stubbornness." She arched a brow. "Let's keep it real. You're a talented designer, but keeping the books isn't your forte. You can barely balance your fucking checkbook. I think it makes perfectly good business sense to have someone manage your finances. It's no biggie. If McKay wants to pay all your expenses, let him."

I exhaled loudly. I hated that she'd picked the most inopportune time to be logical.

"Sin, I'm telling you to play nice with him. Now, put on your big-girl panties and then call him and thank him…nicely."

"I can't."

"Why?"

My body tensed. "Because that's exactly what he wants me to do."

"You mean that's what you want to do, and it scares the shit out of you."

Damn it!

I couldn't hide shit from Jade. It'd been that way since the first day we met as freshmen in high school, and it would always be that way.

"Yes, it does." My fascination with McKay was fucking strange and sordid. I'd been masturbating almost every night since my last meeting with him. My vibrator, Beast, simply couldn't handle the pressure. "On a business level, I get him. He's all about money and work. It's the personal side that scares me because I can't read him." *Or trust myself when I'm around him.* "One minute, he looks like he wants to devour me. The next, he looks like he wants to kill me. He's crazy."

"Excuses. It's not complicated, Sin. You're tearing yourself up for nothing." Jade arched a well-manicured brow. "Just swallow—"

I cut her off. "I will not give him a blow job."

"Uh…" She smiled. "I was going to say swallow your pride and call him. But I'm all for you taking the blow-job approach."

I scoffed. "I'll just call him."

Jade was right. I had to call him. Things between McKay and me couldn't go on the way they had been. Maybe I was building this friction thing between us to be a bigger thing than it was.

I jumped up, pulling my cell out of my pocket as I braced myself to make the call I'd been dreading for days.

This madness between McKay and me had to stop.

Her face dropped with disappointment. "Okay. You could do that, but the BJ is much more fun and creative."

My mind raced while I paced. On one hand, I disliked him. On the other, I wanted to fuck him. I was on the verge of snapping like a twig from the stress.

She rolled onto her stomach on the sofa, propping her chin on her hands.

I stormed over to her and slapped her arm. "What are you doing? You're rolling around in a couture evening gown."

She fanned me away. "Stop stalling. And don't forget to put it on speaker. I want to hear it all."

I plopped down next to her, scrolling down my contact list, and touched his number, automatically calling it. I pointed at her, putting it on speakerphone. "I'm going to cunt-punt you down the stairs if you make a sound," I whispered.

She made the zipping motion across her mouth.

"Hello?" he rasped in a gravelly voice.

My heart thumped at the allure of his voice. *Get it together, Sin.*

She whacked my arm and mouthed, *Oh my God!*

I jabbed her in the side and mouthed, *Shut up!*

"It's Sinthia Michaels," I croaked, suddenly feeling like an insecure high school girl. I counted to ten before saying, "I wanted to say thank you for calling the retailer and for paying my distributor."

He took so long to reply I thought the line had disconnected.

"Are you still there?" I asked impatiently.

"I'm only cleaning up the shit you got yourself into."

I straightened my back. "What did you just say?"

"I've reviewed your business records, and I found the steady decrease in your income. I also noticed the few business deals you've made are ridiculously unprofitable."

I wanted to claw his damn eyes out.

He continued, "I will not lose money on this business deal. I'll give you free rein to steer this business creatively, but I'll make all the strategic decisions from this point on."

I jumped up and marched up and down, feeling my frustration mount. "This is my company, and I will not be relegated to some corner while you run *my* business," I hissed. "You might have a major stake in my company, but there is no Sin Michaels collection without me. So this is how it's going to go, McKay. Regardless of what's on that fucking contract, you will treat me as an equal partner."

The phone was silent.

"Hello?" I shouted.

"Ms. Michaels, don't ever give me an ultimatum," he said in a brisk tone. "You might have creative control, but that doesn't mean shit without my fucking money." Without another word, he ended our call.

I gaped at the phone in shock. "He hung up on me." I stared at Jade. "He's an asshole."

She smiled. "I disagree. He's just not putting up with your shit. He's alpha delicious." She moaned like a porn star. "The man is sex on a stick, and he's ready to blow your back out, girl."

I sat down beside her. "You sound like a lunatic. That shit is not happening."

"Yet." She smiled smugly.

"Ever," I snapped.

McKay might have my livelihood in his hands, but now I was determined to find a way out of his clutches—the sooner, the better.

Jade scooted to sit up. "I know that look, Sin. Your mouth says no, but your mind and body are saying completely the opposite." She waggled her eyebrows.

I gave her the evil eye. "Are you trying to make me shank you?"

Ariana breezed in with her new bestie, Erika Watson, walking beside her.

"Cate, enough!" Ariana screamed into the cell pressed against her ear.

"Hello, Erika," I said.

Erika kissed me on the cheek before dropping her outrageously expensive designer bag onto the sofa like it was a sack of greasy fast food. "All the way over here, they've been at it on the phone." She rolled her eyes. "If I wanted to hear that shit, I could have stayed at work and listened to the overpaid divas bitch about who has more lines."

"Are you talking about Jade?" I winked at her.

I loved Erika. She was remarkably laid-back for a woman who'd achieved so much so fast. She was an award-winning writer and producer who created hit TV shows. She was also the first African-American woman to create and executive produce a top ten network series, a series starring Jade.

Erika smirked. "I refuse to confirm or deny that shit." She looked Jade up and down. "I love you in that gown." Erika grinned at me. "Are you ready for me to get all sexy?" She poured a glass of champagne.

"You're set up in the second room," I responded.

"I'm done with this conversation, Cate," Ariana growled into the phone.

"Thank God." Erika grimaced, eyeing Ariana. "Ariana and Cate are like two pit bulls in skirts." She swayed toward the fitting room before slamming the door behind her.

"Good-bye. Yes, I'm hanging up, Cate," Ariana barked before tossing her cell into her handbag. "I'm going to kill her."

Jade arched a brow. "So what's the self-appointed queen bee of the Bellisario clan bitching about now?"

Jade was the daughter of Ariana Bellisario—a philanthropist, heiress, and successful businesswoman—making Jade a member of the illustrious group of New York socialites. Her aunt, Cate Bellisario, was older than Ariana by a couple years. To some, that made Cate the most powerful member of the Bellisario family. She was using that status among the city's elite to get her fiancé, Bigsby Calhoune, a wealthy shipping mogul, elected as New York City's mayor.

"Anything and everything." Ariana flopped down next to me and smiled. "How are you, darling?"

"Better than you, I gather," I said.

"Mom?" Jade asked.

Ariana sighed. "She's micromanaging the shit out of this fundraising gala." She rolled her eyes heavenward. "Bigsby arranged a family photo opportunity at the gala with a major magazine. *Arrive early,*" she mocked Cate's whiny voice.

I laughed because it'd sounded exactly like Cate. New York City's queen socialite bitch Cate had handpicked the rich elite and A-listers for the fundraising gala, and they had been granted the opportunity to get all gussied up in honor of her fiancé. The gala was the biggest event on the high-end social calendar. The ten-thousand-dollars-per-ticket gala was meant to raise funds for Bigsby's mayoral race, but in reality, it was just an excuse for a self-celebratory orgy of red-carpet posing.

"Blah, blah, blah. God, I hate that fucker Bigsby," Ariana hissed.

"Exactly!" Jade chimed in. "He reminds me of some two-bit used car salesman."

I shuddered. "He just gives me the creeps."

He did. He always seemed to be leering at me like some perverted slimeball.

Ariana pointed at me. "Exactly. You hit the nail right on the head. He's creepy. That's why I hired a private investigator. I'll be damned if I let my sister marry that sleazy bastard."

I gave Jade a sidelong stare. "Does Cate know?"

Jade nodded. "Hell yes. We're the last members of the Bellisario dynasty and each worth millions. If you want to date a Bellisario, you get investigated thoroughly. Most guys just bow out ungracefully because they can't deal with Irvin, the investigative proctologist."

I arched a brow. "He's that thorough?"

Ariana pursed her lips while pouring champagne. "Yes, but surprisingly, he didn't find shit on Bigsby."

"That's a good thing, right?" I inquired.

Ariana's eyes narrowed. "No, not when it comes to Bigsby. Irvin is suspicious. He says Bigsby's records were too squeaky-clean. Irvin's still digging. If there's something to find, he will find it. Believe me."

"See, Sin? This is the shit rich people have to resort to. We don't know the meaning of trust because everyone has a side game. At least with McKay, he's keeping it real."

I shot Jade a warning stare. "Shut up."

She shrugged. "Don't shoot the messenger."

"What's going on with you two?" Ariana looked at me and then Jade.

Jade nodded in my direction.

I sipped my champagne, avoiding eye contact with Ariana.

"Sin?" Ariana queried.

I looked at her sheepishly.

She pursed her lips. "Jade?"

Jade looked at me pointedly and whispered loudly, "She wants to have sex with a banging hot billionaire."

I gave her the one-finger salute. "I hate you so much right now."

Jade blew me a kiss.

Ariana swatted at Jade. "Leave her alone."

"Hello? I'm trying to help," Jade responded.

I frowned. "So annoying."

Ariana patted my hand. "I know, sweetie. She can be like that piece of corn you can't quite get out of your teeth. Annoying." Ariana smiled sweetly, too sweetly, at Jade.

"I love you too, Mom," Jade mumbled under her breath.

Ariana eyed me. "Now are you going to tell me who's the lucky man and why you look so pissed off about him?"

"I'm angrier at myself." I had to take responsibility for my actions. I hadn't looked at the fine print on the contract. It was a total idiot move. "Stupidly, I signed a business deal with the devil, giving him my soul and ninety-seven percent control of my business in exchange for financing," I blurted out in one breath.

Ariana sat straight up, spilling her champagne. "Ninety-seven percent? Who's the lucky devil?"

"Core McKay," I responded.

She shot me an incredulous stare. "Billionaire Core McKay?"

"Yep, that's the devil incarnate."

Ariana scowled. "If you needed financing, why didn't you come to Jade or me for the money?"

"Don't blame her, Mom. She couldn't borrow the money from me because my assets were tied up in my indie movie project."

Ariana pursed her lips. "Okay. What about me?"

I sighed heavily. "I love you, but I can't go running to you and Jade every time I have money problems." I grabbed her hand when I saw the flash of sadness in her eyes. "I wanted to do this on my own."

She squeezed my hand back. "You're not on your own. You're like my daughter, and if I can help, I'll do it, no questions asked." She nudged me playfully with her elbow. "But I get it. You want to be independent. There's nothing wrong with that, but be independent *and* smart."

I leaned my head on her shoulder. I loved Ariana because she was beautiful inside and out.

When Dad died and Mom disowned me, Ariana had taken me into her family, treating me like I was her daughter. Yes, I knew Ariana would have loaned me the money, but that was a line I would never cross. Family and business did not mix. I'd learned that the hard way with Grace.

"I had it under control—or at least, I thought I did."

Ariana and Jade scowled at me.

"Okay. Fine. I'm stubborn and irrational. I know this. I'm paying for my flaws right now."

I kissed Ariana's cheek, and that seemed to pacify her.

"Next time I get into a jam, I'll at least call you to get advice before I proceed."

Ariana hugged me. "See? That wasn't so hard." She sat back, settling in like she had nothing but time.

My eyes widened. "Oh no, you don't. Can you please get in there and get dressed?"

She smiled, putting up her hands. "Okay, I'm going." She grabbed her glass. "Which room?"

I pointed to the last dressing room on the left, and she happily swayed off.

Jade slid off the couch and stood on wobbly legs, most likely from way too much champagne. "I've got to get out of here. I have a hair appointment," she said before rushing over to the dressing room.

Hours later, I was elated to have some peace and quiet. Jade and Ariana had already left, and Erika was getting dressed. This allowed me to sit on the couch, sipping the last of the last bottle of champagne, while finishing up business.

Erika came out, fully dressed in her street clothes. Smiling at me, she grabbed her bag and handed over a check.

I gave her a questioning look. "This isn't the price we agreed on. You overpaid by three thousand dollars. I can't take it."

She waved away my objection. "It's for all your help and for rearranging your schedule to make my gown for tomorrow night." She looked at me shrewdly. "I hope you don't get offended, but I overheard your conversation with Jade and Ariana about your contract issues."

"I'm not remotely close to giving up designing for a job at a fastfood restaurant."

"I know, but money means nothing to me these days, and if I can help in any way, I will. It sounds like you need help and fast," Erika drawled. "I have an excellent attorney whom I trust implicitly—Mitch Fillion, my husband."

My eyes widened. *How did I not know she was married to him?*

Erika dug into her ridiculously expensive designer bag before passing me a business card. "He's the best damn attorney in New York City, if I do say so myself."

I eyed her. "You're married to Mitch Fillion?"

"Recently married. We're still newlyweds." She waved her fingers, displaying the large, sparkling diamond engagement ring coupled with the diamond-encrusted wedding band. "I'm wife number two." She pursed her lips. "Wait, is it number three?" She laughed huskily. "Shit, it doesn't matter because that man is a genius in the bedroom." She shivered deliciously.

Why do my clients insist on oversharing?

Most people would be surprised at how much personal information my wealthy and famous clients shared with me. From the benign tidbits about who just got cosmetic surgery and butt implants, to steamy shit like who was fucking whose husband, to lovers fucking lovers, to who was caught at the McKay Club in the private kink room, to wives fucking employees, to husbands fucking butlers, and three-somes and foursomes—it was all one big fuckfest in the world of the rich and privileged. None of the gossip I really cared about, but with all the information, I could make a shitload of money by writing a scandalous tell-all book that would cause fucking chaos.

I shook my head and said, "Thanks, but no thanks. There is no way I'm calling him."

Her eyes widened. "Why?"

I swallowed over the pain and embarrassment, which still stung to this day. "Because his son Kyle is my old high school boyfriend and a prick. Frankly speaking, the apple doesn't fall too far from the tree."

Erika's face tensed. "Kyle really hurt you." She reached out and grabbed my hand.

"It's more how I made a fool out of myself for him."

Her grip tightened. Normally, I wasn't a touchy-feely woman with strangers, but her rich chocolate eyes that reminded me so much of Dad's, combined with the warmth and comfort of her touch, put me surprisingly at ease.

"I know you blame Mitch, but believe me, he had nothing to do with how that arrogant, spoiled prick turned out. That's all Mitch's ex-wife's doing." She sighed. "That woman is a real piece of work. She's fucking nutty." Erika quickly pulled her hand away as if she'd just realized she was still clutching mine. "Please just call Mitch. He's not like you think he is. He's a good man. Plus, like I said, he's the best damn attorney in New York City."

Maybe that was what I needed. A devious, ruthless fuck would be necessary to get me out of the contract with McKay.

I shoved the card into my handbag. "I'll think about it."

"Wise decision. Sometimes, we have to align ourselves with people who will help us get to our ultimate goal, and there's no shame in that." She winked at me before walking away. "See you tomorrow night."

CHAPTER 6
SINTHIA

I paced back and forth, my mind spinning. I stopped and stared at his business card. *How bad can he be if he's married to a woman like Erika?*

My mind spun around the fact that my life had turned full circle. I was seeking help from the man whose son had destroyed my self-confidence for years. I knew I shouldn't lump all assholes together, but it was hard not to.

I blew out heavily before quickly tapping the phone number shown on the card into my phone.

"Mitch Fillion," he clipped out.

I licked my lips, which had gone desert dry. "Hello, Mr. Fillion. My name is Sinthia Michaels. I was referred to you by Erika."

I was a little relieved when his voice held a softer edge as he said, "How can I help you?"

"I have a business issue. I need help with a contract."

"You need me to look over a contract?"

I wiped my now sweaty palm over the leg of my jeans. "No. I need you to help me break it."

"Who is the contract with?"

I exhaled slowly. "MK Partners."

The silence on the line lasted so long that I thought our call had gotten disconnected.

"Hello?" I asked.

He cleared his throat. "I'm sorry, Ms. Michaels, but Mr. McKay has me on retainer."

I squeezed my eyes shut. *Shit.*

"Well, this is awkward," I mumbled while my mind whirled around one question. *Will Fillion tell McKay I called him about breaking our contract?*

I clenched my fists.

There was no doubt in my mind the answer to that was yes. *Damn! McKay is going to be fucking pissed.*

He didn't seem like a man who would take kindly to the fact that I was trying to outmaneuver him.

"Since my wife referred you to me, she must hold you in high regard, so I can recommend an excellent attorney who might be able to help you."

"Sure. Thank you." I went over to my workstation, grabbed a notepad, and scribbled the name and number he gave me. "Thank you, Mr. Fillion," I said before clicking off.

Jesus. I am so screwed.

Dressed and sitting on the arm of my love seat, I swirled the red wine in the glass as I stared at the clock. Jade was late again. I was already disgruntled about agreeing to go to this ridiculous gala in honor of the one man, Bigsby Calhoune, whom I did not intend to vote for as mayor. But I'd agreed to be Jade's plus-one, and I didn't renege on promises to friends, no matter how badly I wanted to.

My cell rang. It was a private number. "Hello?" I answered.

No one responded, so I hung up.

The cell rang again with a private number. I said, "Hello?"

Nothing.

"Who the fuck is this?"

Heavy breathing.

"Fuck off, pervert." I swiped my finger across the screen, ending the call.

The doorbell rang. I walked toward the entry. Peering through the peephole, I saw Jade standing on my stairs, looking annoyed but strikingly beautiful. Opening the door, I stared at her features highlighted with smoky eye shadow, a smidge of blush, and a slick touch of rose-pink lip gloss. Her nails, painted a bright shade of red, tapped against the doorframe.

"You're late," I snapped.

She held up her hand. "Don't even start with getting all anal about me being late," she responded while crossing the threshold.

I slammed the door behind her.

Rudely, she snatched my glass of wine out of my hand and took a sip.

"Uh, you take my Jesus juice without so much as a hello?" I asked.

"I'm sorry." She kissed my cheek before guzzling more of the wine. "I swear this gala is going to be the death of me." She swallowed another gulp of wine. "I lost precious brain cells while mediating another argument between my mother and Cate over the fact that Mom and I refuse to take part in the special photo op Bigsby arranged at the gala."

I strolled over to the kitchen, grabbed another glass, and poured wine into it. "Sounds like rich people's drama," I said in a singsong voice.

"Yeah, yeah, I know. People are dying of hunger while my family's number one concern is with whom we will or will not take a photo. Trifling but true." Jade drained her glass and stared at me. "On a lighter note, you look absolutely gorgeous, Sin."

I spun around, showing off the backless part of the sleeveless beaded gown with a revealing plunging neckline that barely hid my belly button. The only thing keeping my full breasts from falling out was the discreet beaded hook right below each. I twerked my ass, calling attention to the back of the gown that was cut low to show off my back tattoos.

I turned around to face her and asked, "So what do you think?"

"First, did you just twerk? I think you've been watching way too many music videos." Jade's lips curled up into a smile. "Second, wow, I love the vintage vibe of your gown. How you've managed to pull off a look that's elegant and includes a little butt crack is beyond me." She tapped her bottom lip. "But you're missing something. Don't you have some vintage jewelry to wear?"

"My diamond cuff bracelet. I could throw that on."

She frowned. "No. Not retro enough. Wait. I got it. Remember that Victorian-looking silver bracelet your father gave you for your birthday? Wear it."

My heart thudded. "Yeah, um…" I licked my lips anxiously. "I don't want to wear it. Way too many sad memories." It was stupid and pathetic, but I'd compartmentalized all my memories of Dad years ago, stowing them in a trunk I'd shoved into my guest bedroom. Out of sight and out of mind was my goal.

She glared at me. "Sin, where did you hide it?"

I swallowed a large mouthful of wine. "Trunk in my spare bedroom." I rolled my eyes. "Don't give me that look. I haven't had many opportunities to wear it." Well, that part was true, but the most important reason was the bracelet caused too many emotions to surface—happy and sad.

She sighed heavily. "You can't continue to blame yourself for his death, Sin. You were young. You argued with him, but you didn't cause that reckless driver to slam into him."

I blinked back the tears and fought the impending guilt. "He was driving around that night, looking for me." The memory of that morning and the shouting match I'd had with Dad still made my heart heavy with emotion.

It was my birthday, and I was so excited Kyle was going to take me out for lunch after school. I bounced into the kitchen, intending to grab a yogurt before heading out, only to stop at the sight of Dad flipping pancakes at the stove.

"Dad? What are you doing here?" I was happy to see him.

Normally, he'd leave for work before I got up in the morning, and he'd come in late at night after I was already in bed.

He turned, grinning at me. "I'm going in late. I couldn't miss making a birthday breakfast for my little girl."

I rolled my eyes heavenward. "Not little. I'm seventeen today," I boasted before eyeing the small box wrapped in pink-and-green paper on the table.

He smiled indulgently. "Yes, it's for you."

Snatching up the box, I ripped off the paper and then pulled off the top. Nestled inside was an agate silver bracelet. "Oh, Dad, I love it." Running over to him, I hugged him. "Thank you so much."

He kissed my forehead. "Give me your wrist."

I could barely stand still from excitement as he clasped the unusual bracelet around my wrist.

He grabbed my face softly. "Sin, this bracelet is very special. It's an heirloom which belonged to my Scottish great-grandmother. It's the only piece of our heritage our family has left." His eyes clouded over with emotion. "Promise me you'll cherish it."

"Always, Dad."

"Good." He nodded before stepping back and picking up a plate stacked with pancakes. "Sit down. The pancakes are getting cold," he ordered before resting the plate on the table.

Plopping down at the kitchen table, I gave him a wobbly smile. Dad looked tired. Dark shadows were under his eyes. His tall frame looked gaunt. I tightened my fists, hating Mom for forcing him to work longer hours so she could live the lifestyle of the elite.

He sat down, and I tucked into my pancakes.

"You're not eating?" I asked in between bites.

He pointed to his cup of coffee. "This is the breakfast of champions." He frowned down at his cup, twirling it around in a circle.

I arched a brow. "So what's really going on, Dad?"

He cleared his throat. "Sin, I found this great job out in Arizona." He smiled stiffly. "It's a promotion with more money. I can't pass up this opportunity."

Just like that, I lost my appetite. I slammed my fork down before pushing away my plate.

"I'm not moving again, Dad. When I started high school, you promised we wouldn't move again."

His mouth tightened. "Things change."

I crossed my arms. "Well, I'm not moving. I'm happy here. For the first time in my life, I have a best friend and a potential boyfriend."

"This is not debatable, Sin. I delayed this as long as I could. We're moving at the end of the month."

"At the end of the month?" I swallowed around the lump in my throat. "I like him, Dad, and he actually likes me too."

He sighed. "Sin, don't make this more difficult than it already is. We're moving."

I flinched. "I'm going to be late for school." Standing stiffly, I grabbed my backpack and tossed it over my shoulder.

"This conversation isn't over, young lady." He crossed his arms. "After school, you'll come straight home."

My eyes widened. "No, I'm not. I'm going out with Kyle for my birthday."

He stood up. "Sin, you live in my house, so you'll abide by my rules."

My fists clenched and unclenched. "I hate you."

The color drained from this face. "Like I said, my house, my damn rules."

"Whatever," I said before storming out of the kitchen.

I didn't give a shit about what he'd said or what he wanted. And I was determined to show him I was no longer his little girl.

After school, I disobeyed my dad and went out with Kyle.

After hanging out with him all night and coming in after curfew, I went home to find a cop car pulling away. Racing up the front stairs, I slammed into the house to find Grace sitting on the stairs with a drink in her hand, reeking of alcohol.

"Why were the cops here?" I asked, my heart pounding.

"Where the hell were you?" Grace slurred as she wobbled to her feet.

"Where's Dad?"

Grace ignored me while she straightened her disheveled clothing.

"Grace?"

"He went out looking for you." Guzzling her drink, she looked at me with bloodshot eyes that lacked focus. "A car slammed into his, sending him off the bridge. He's...dead."

Tears streamed down my face. Lurching forward, I sought her comfort for once in my life. Grace sloshed her drink, warding me off. With a flushed face, she tightened her mouth before she turned on her heel and staggered up the stairs.

Jade's voice jerked me out of the past. "Sin? Are you okay?"

"I miss him so damn much." Tears filled my eyes, making me feel like that broken girl once again. I wiped away my teardrops, hating I was still racked with so much guilt and self-loathing about that day.

Instead of telling him, *I hate you*, I wished all I had said was, *I love you, Dad.*

She walked toward me with her arms wide open. "Come here."

I swatted her arms, but she pulled me into a hug anyway. I quickly hugged her before stepping back.

Her eyes softened. "Let it go. Forgive yourself and remember how much he loved you." She stepped forward, smoothing my hair. "Honor his love for you and wear the bracelet."

It was time to let go of the guilt. I couldn't bring him back, and pretending I didn't miss him almost every day was disrespectful to his memory. "Yeah, you're right," I said. "You know you're the bestest friend ever?"

She sidled up beside me, hip checking me. "Yes, I am, and don't you forget it."

I yanked her hair before strolling out of the kitchen and through the living room with her on my heels. Stopping in my guest bedroom, I went to the pile of fabric stacked on top of the trunk. Pushing aside the folded remnants, I stared at the old, worn trunk that used to be my father's. Running my fingers along the aged leather, I smiled. Dad had dragged the ratty trunk around the country to every place we moved. The scratched surface was so worn and dirty that I couldn't tell the original color.

Unlatching the lock, I lifted the top. Pulling out a stack of photos and sorting through them, I blinked when I saw one of Dad and me, taken on the beach. He was smiling, and I was sticking out my tongue at the camera.

I missed him. I fucking missed him every day.

How abruptly I had lost him hurt. It had changed me, leaving me vulnerable and scared to let any new people into my life for fear of losing them.

"Sin?"

I cleared my throat. "God, I haven't seen this stuff in years," I muttered, continuing to sift through the photos. I stopped at a photo of a blond-haired version of myself hugging Jade.

She snatched the photo. "Ew, it's blond Sin. Promise me you'll never ever dye your hair again."

"You don't have to worry about that," I mumbled. I dug into the bottom of the trunk before pulling out the small silk bundle containing the bracelet. Unwrapping the fabric, I saw the impressive agate silver piece was still in excellent condition. I ran my fingers along the stones set into the silver. Holding it up, I examined each of the panels in between the stones, hand-engraved with patterns from scrolls to flowers to cross-hatching plaids. Turning it over to the backside, I noticed the small, very faint but readable lettering, "To my love Aubrey." It was strange that this was the first time I'd actually noticed the engraving. *Who is Aubrey? My Scottish great-grandmother?* For some strange reason, Dad never talked about his family, only saying that he had no family left. After clasping the bracelet around my wrist, I started to close the trunk, when something odd caught my eye.

I blinked and then blinked again. "What's this?"

I yanked at the piece of red leather peeking out of the broken bottom of the trunk. No, it wasn't broken. I hit the bottom. With the thump of my palm, a secret compartment shifted completely, and a plume of dust rose, revealing a well-worn leather ledger.

"What is that?" Jade asked impatiently, looking up from admiring the photos.

"Some weird journal was buried in the bottom of my dad's trunk." I lifted the cover and flipped through the thin paper. It crackled against my fingertips.

"What's in it? Dirty secrets?" Jade asked.

The first several pages were a collection of names. This was not my father's handwriting. The initials G.L.C. were scrawled in red ink at the bottom of every page. Next came numbers and phone numbers. All the pages had codes running along the margins.

"Nothing I understand."

The ledger had been deliberately concealed in the false bottom. *Why did Dad hide this?*

My dad had been the most transparent person I knew, and if he'd hidden it, there had to be a good reason.

I pushed the journal back into the false bottom, banged the base back into place, and then dumped everything I'd pulled out back on top of it, promising myself to further investigate the ledger over the weekend.

CHAPTER 7
SINTHIA

Jade and I walked out of my townhouse and down the stairs toward Kirby, Jade's chauffeur.

He was leaning against the expensive luxury SUV. He pushed away, tilting his head toward us. "You look lovely, Miss Michaels."

"Thank you, Kirby." I smiled impishly at him. "How's my favorite man?"

He smiled. "Still way too old for you."

I winked at him. "Age is nothing but a number."

I loved messing with Kirby. He was an older version of James Bond —gray but still hot and dangerous.

Jade rolled her eyes. "Will you get in?"

He chuckled while opening the door, and then he helped us maneuver our gowns into the SUV. He strolled around to the driver's side and slid in while we fastened our seat belts.

Kirby fastened his own seat belt before turning the key and revving the engine. He smoothly pulled into the Manhattan traffic before zipping in and out of the snarl of taxicabs and buses.

Jade pulled out her cell, pressing her cheek against mine. "Selfie time," she chirped. "Smile, Sin." She pouted prettily.

I scowled. "Nothing to smile about," I responded dryly.

"Got it." She took the photo. "And posted." She kissed my cheek. "And next time, you'd better smile because I assure you that grimace will be torn apart by my followers." She threw the cell in her clutch.

"Nice. More critics. That's exactly what I need right now." I rubbed my temple, feeling a wicked headache approaching. "Why am I doing this again?" I mumbled under my breath while frowning at the grid-locked New York City traffic.

She leaned her head on my shoulder. "Because there's a special place in hell for people who don't support their besties."

"I hate these types of events with rich people parading down the red carpet like racehorses."

"Hey"—she gave me a fake pout—"rich person here."

I petted her silky black hair like a horse's mane. "And you're my favorite rich person," I cooed.

"So rude." Jade swatted my hand.

I laughed. "Come on. You know what I mean. I hate these things. Red carpets are so fucking intimidating," I explained. "Not that the paparazzi will be remotely interested in me, but I do have to walk down the thing in order to get into the gala." I winked at her. "And more importantly, the open bar."

"The red carpet is scary, even for me, but you can do this." She squeezed my hand reassuringly. "I've seen you give a lecture on fashion design in front of hundreds of sarcastic, know-it-all young fashion students. You can do this." She leaned forward and tapped on Kirby's shoulder. "Don't you agree?"

"Miss Michaels is tough as nails." Kirby winked at me in the rearview mirror.

All too soon, we slowed, and I could see flickers of light up the road. We were in line to be dropped off. Kirby pulled up to the venue and stopped.

I stared at the flashing cameras in shock. "Why the hell do you do this?"

I sat there, stuck, trying to get mentally prepared to step out in front of the paparazzi's cameras. It was sensory overload. The bright side of this whole fiasco was the media coverage I would get from the Bellisarios wearing my couture gowns tonight.

Kirby got out of the SUV, opened the door, and helped Jade out.

"Jade! Jade!" the paparazzi screamed.

Jade was undoubtedly one of Hollywood's most beautiful actresses, and the media was obsessed with her glam style and beauty. But I knew she was more than just good looks. She was genuine and smart.

Kirby reached for me.

I took a deep breath and hesitated. "Well, all righty, time to make tonight my bitch," I grumbled.

Kirby smiled at me, and I grabbed his hand. I put on my I-don't-give-a-shit face as I stepped out of the SUV. I wasn't as comfortable as Jade standing in front of hundreds of photographers, so I had to go somewhere else in my mind and pretend I was a confident person in front of a horde of people.

When my feet hit the carpet, the lights exploded everywhere. I lifted the train of my gown and tried to walk around Jade.

The paparazzi screamed questions, coming at me from all directions.

"Sinthia Michaels! Can you pose for a photo?"

"Are you wearing a gown from your upcoming collection?"

"Can you comment on the rumors that you and Core McKay are now business partners?"

I looked at Jade uncomfortably before trying to hurry up the stairs.

"Go, go, go!" the paparazzi said, actually moving to chase me.

Jade wrapped an arm around my waist and whispered, "Relax."

"This is new. I didn't realize I was a celebrity," I muttered.

I plastered a frozen smile on my face as we posed for photos.

"Enjoy it, sweetheart. You deserve it." She stepped aside, allowing me to have additional photos taken by myself.

The flashing lights started to freak me out. I sighed gratefully when Jade looped an arm through mine, leading me away from the cameras.

We ascended the red-carpeted staircase lined with camera crews, photographers, reporters, and other gawkers. Tonight's gala was a tribute to all the wealthy A-listers congregating at the venue.

I surveyed the scene upon entering the mansion. A giant chandelier made from hundreds of red and white roses hung conspicuously above the information desk. The desk was completely covered with red roses rising five feet high.

Jade and I handed over our invitations for inspection, and then we waited patiently while a white-gloved security staffer politely scanned our bodies with a handheld metal detector.

Walking farther into the mansion, we strolled up the main staircase bordered by walls covered in pristine white roses. At the top of the staircase, Cate and Bigsby stood regally as if they were a royal couple and greeted arriving guests. Millions of dollars were at stake tonight, money that could be added to Bigsby's political war chest by wealthy patrons. Cate had corralled and badgered donors to death. No one said no to her unless they wanted to feel her wrath. She was a ruthless, conniving bitch who would think nothing about taking down the most powerful people unless they played nice. All those traits made her an excellent match for Bigsby.

Bigsby adjusted his bow tie, looking ultra-sharp in his black tuxedo with a white silk cummerbund. He advanced forward, offering his hand to me. "Sinthia, it's great to see you."

I shook his hand. Bigsby lingered a second or so too long on the handshake. I quickly pulled my hand away, barely suppressing the urge to wipe my palm on my gown to remove any trace of his touch.

Cate swayed frontward. Her mask of neutrality slipped as she eyed the deep-V neckline plunging to my belly button. Her lips pressed into a thin line. Then she said, "Thank you for coming, Sinthia."

My irritation swelled. Cate was an uptight, judgmental witch. I was at ease with who I was. It had taken me too many years to get comfortable in my skin.

My gaze swept over her gown. It wasn't my design, but I could admit Cate oozed glamour, from her elegant updo to her white-and-black couture ball gown and the pair of white gloves she'd donned.

"I was dragged here," I responded stiffly, nodding over at Jade, "by your arm-twisting niece."

Cate inclined her head with her eyes locked on Jade. "You're late," she snapped.

Jade's lips pursed. "I'm not in the mood to argue tonight. Just be happy I came to this circus."

They faced off tensely.

Cate's eyes narrowed, disapproval turning down the corners of her mouth. She bit out, "Jade, a minute in private." She smiled warmly at Bigsby. "Darling, I'll just be right back." She turned on her heel, walking toward the corner of the room.

Jade swiveled to me and said, "Sin, I'll be right back," and then she followed Cate.

The top of the staircase opened to a huge space. My eyes flickered over the room. The stunning venue had been transformed for the occasion with light-gray sofas and flowers placed throughout. It was amazing and hard to take in the splendor all at once. My gaze paused on Erika and Ariana, who were huddled together and whispering while giving the guests sly glances.

"What a beautiful bracelet. Where did you get it?"

My head snapped to look at Bigsby, only to find his eyes locked on my wrist.

"A gift." I kept my answer short.

"Scottish?"

I arched a brow. "What?"

A muscle twitched beneath Bigsby's left eye. "The bracelet is Victorian Scottish."

"How do you know that?"

Bigsby held up his hand, displaying a chunky gold ruby-and-diamond-encrusted horseshoe ring on his middle finger. "I have a distinct taste for jewelry."

I eyed him suspiciously. He tried to look innocent but failed. I absolutely didn't like something about Bigsby, and my dislike had grown when he launched a bid for New York City mayor as an independent candidate.

"We have something in common—Scottish family roots." His eyes narrowed. "But curiously, your last name isn't Scottish. Why is that?"

I was just about to tell him it was none of his fucking business when a couple I recognized from television sauntered up to him. Bigsby's body tightened as he ran his hand over his salt-and-pepper hair in agitation.

"We'll definitely continue this conversation later." He reached to touch my elbow.

I stepped back, avoiding his caress. His eyes went cold before turning away, promptly dismissing me to greet the couple.

I turned and made a beeline toward Ariana and Erika.

Ariana kissed my cheek before twirling around in the Swarovski crystal-covered halter jersey column dress I had designed. "Go ahead. Tell me how hot I look."

"Ariana, you look beautiful, but trouble is on the horizon, and I need you to rescue my bestie." I pointed my finger over to the corner where Cate had Jade hemmed in while jabbing her bony finger in Jade's face. "Like, right now."

Ariana's face turned thunderous. "I'll be right back," she said before charging over to Cate and Jade.

I smiled at Erika. "So how do you feel in your first Sin Michaels design?"

Erika was stunning. The dark richness of her skin contrasted beautifully against the formfitting pale-yellow silk gown that featured a neckline composed of silver crystal embroidery.

She air-kissed me. "Gorgeous, sexy, perfect. All of the above."

"Good. That's what I like to hear"—I pursed my lips dramatically—"because I'm really sensitive about my shit."

I wasn't kidding. I'd dealt with difficult clients who rejected all my sketches, asked me to try other options, and then ended up picking the first sketch I'd shown them, wasting my precious time. But Erika was the opposite of all my notoriously difficult clients. When I'd shown her several sketches, she'd loved them all. She'd said she wouldn't pick, and she'd wear whatever I designed for her. That had shocked the shit out of me. I'd been in design heaven when she gave me complete creative control.

Erika looped an arm through mine. We walked toward the thick of the gala patrons milling around. "My husband has been drooling over me, and that's worth the price of admission, darling." She grinned at me. "Oh, speak of the handsome devil."

A tall blond man walked over to us and kissed Erika's cheek with a twinkle in his eyes.

"Darling, this is Sinthia, the designer I told you about. Sinthia, this is my husband, Mitch Fillion."

I never met Mitch while dating Kyle. I noted he looked nothing like Kyle, except for his blond hair.

Mitch stepped forward and shook my hand. "Erika was talking about you nonstop on the limo ride over here." He smiled at Erika. "It takes a lot to impress my wife."

Erika leaned forward and whispered, "I've got a girl crush."

He chuckled. "Should I be worried?"

She smiled up at him. "Nope. My girl-on-girl phase disintegrated when I graduated from college. I'm all yours."

I could tell they were in love.

Mitch wrapped his arm around her. "After our energetic limo action, I'm not complaining." He kissed her ear.

I almost swallowed my tongue when the Television Producer Voted Most Likely to Bitch-Slap an Actor giggled like a damn schoolgirl.

Erika pinched his ass.

I cleared my throat loudly and said, "Right here, guys. I'm right here."

Normally, couple PDA made me uncomfortable, but they were cute.

Erika inclined her head, peering around the room, when her eyes narrowed. I turned to look at what had caught her eye. It was Kyle and a blonde barreling through the crowd toward us.

My breathing picked up. I was baffled as to why I had a lump in my throat while my stomach churned. Maybe it was because I hadn't seen him since the night I caught him cheating. The heartbreaking memory of his jeans bunched around his ankles and a blonde preparing to deep-throat him hit me. Kyle had ripped my heart out and stomped on it until it was a bloody pulp. Yet, here he was, heading for me with a ridiculously big smile on his handsome face, staring at me as if we were long-lost friends. As abruptly as the feelings had appeared, they disappeared.

"Mitch, you'd better do something." Erika's heated stare bore into Mitch. "I swear if he says anything to embarrass Sinthia, I'll castrate him."

Erika's vehemence broke the tension, and I bit back a laugh. I could tell Erika wasn't bluffing from the way her fingers clenched and unclenched as if she were actually squeezing the shit out of Kyle's balls.

"Calm down, Erika." Mitch patted her arm. "He won't. I warned him I wouldn't tolerate his rude behavior." He looked at me. "Sinthia, Erika didn't go into detail, but she did make it very clear that Kyle was less than kind to you in high school." He sighed heavily. "The long and short of it is I wasn't the greatest father when his mother and I were married. Kyle went through a rebellious asshole phase, and I pretended not to notice."

I smiled, liking his brutal honesty.

He touched my elbow. "I can't make amends for anything he's done in the past, but I can hold him accountable for his behavior tonight. Trust me on this."

"It's okay, Mitch. I'm fine." Surprisingly, I was. There was no pang of unrequited love. There was nothing—no emotions, no desire. Just fucking nothing for Kyle.

Kyle dragged along the beautiful blond woman clinging to him like arm candy. "Sinthia, wow. It's so good to see you," he said, leering at me as if he wanted to eat me alive. "You look really great!"

The blonde's fingers tightened possessively around his arm. Frankly, she was captivatingly beautiful, so I had no idea why she would be insecure in my presence.

I coolly eyed him. "Kyle," I responded.

I really wished I could laugh at the fact that time had not been good to Kyle, but that was far from the truth. He looked the same. Tall and blond, he was gorgeous, with a cocksure smirk that made me want to smack him senseless.

Erika growled, "Oh, for fuck's sake, Kyle, stop staring at Sinthia with your mouth hanging open. Introduce your *wife*." Her hands went to her hips, accentuating her small waist.

"Oh, Kyle." Mitch covered his face with his hand.

He shot Mitch an annoyed stare before looking back to me. "Sin, this is—"

I cut him off. "It's Sinthia, not Sin. Only friends call me Sin."

His smile slipped. "Sinthia, this is my wife, Claire," he muttered under his breath.

I nodded at her politely. She nodded right back.

Thankfully, Jade materialized by my side, looping her arm around mine. "I'm sure you'll be happy to know my family crisis was averted, and no Bellisario was killed in the making of the reality show starring Cate." She turned to smile at Erika and Mitch. "Hello, guys." She pursed her lips at Kyle. "Oh, look, it's Kyle, the prick."

Kyle glared at her, and she glared right back.

A giggle slipped out of Claire's mouth before she slapped a hand over it. Kyle looked at her coolly, and her face went back to a blank mask.

Shit, she was like some marionette being manipulated by her puppet master.

Jade smiled widely at Mitch and Erika. "We'll see you two later. There's a bar calling our names."

I barely had time to wave good-bye to Erika and Mitch before Jade smoothly maneuvered me away.

I glanced over my shoulder to see Kyle leering at me. From the determined glint in his eyes, I knew his mission was to pursue me like a stalker.

"Damn, that was fucking uncomfortable," I whispered.

"He's an idiot. I swear, he was sporting a hard-on while he was drooling over you."

Seeing Kyle again had been that heart-stopping moment I'd dreaded for years. Frankly, it hadn't had quite the drama and anxiety I'd anticipated. I'd felt absolutely nothing—no pitter-patter of my heart, no I-wish-he-were-mine-again angst. I said a thankful prayer to the universe that the conceited, egotistical douchebag was someone else's problem.

"Let's head to the bar. I'm going to need something stronger than champagne to get through this shit of a night," I said.

We strolled amiably among the glittering, star-studded men and women as we each casually snagged a glass of whiskey and a canapé from the passing waiters. Celebrities preened for the photographer floating through the crowd.

Shrewdly, Cate had ensured that only her richest friends were invited, and every one of them was competing for social media clicks and likes. The conversations were punctuated with, "Oh," "Hey," and, "Sorry," as heels landed on long skirts.

Attending enough of these events had taught me how to move in a roomful of vultures. I snickered when men's eyes followed me with blatant interest and their dates clutched on to them tensely while shooting daggers at me. My tattoo-covered back and stripper strut ensured I didn't blend with the affluent crowd, even in my couture gown.

Reaching the venue's midpoint, I glanced across the room, only to see McKay holding court with Ram by the bar. My eyes locked with McKay's, and then the crowd shifted, cutting off our view of each other.

"Damn. Shit just got real," I muttered under my breath.

The throng moved again. McKay was checking me out with unveiled interest.

I tried to calm my beating heart to no avail. Biting my bottom lip, I drank him in. *Jesus.* He looked smoking hot. If you looked up *fuckable* in the dictionary, McKay's photo would be right there next to it. He sizzled in a shawl-collared tuxedo paired with a crisp tailored white shirt, black silk bow tie, black leather shoes, and a Panerai watch. Ram was looking flawless in a white tuxedo. It was masculinity at its finest.

McKay's eyes flashed as he arched his eyebrow at me. I stopped and turned so I was facing Jade and my back was toward McKay.

Jade looked at me curiously. "What's up?"

"Don't look. That's McKay by the bar," I hissed.

Of course, Jade did the exact opposite of what I'd asked and stared boldly in his direction.

I wanted to choke her. "Really? What part of 'don't look' was unclear?"

Staring over my shoulder, Jade whispered loudly, "Which one?"

"In the black tux with the black silk bow tie. He's staring at me like I owe him money," I responded. "Because I do."

"Damn! Look at that face." Jade blinked and then blinked again. "He's crazy hot."

"No. He's just crazy." I turned back around, glaring at him. Okay, he was hot, but I'd be damned if I acknowledged the way my cunt pulsed under his scrutiny.

He appeared hard, domineering, in control. The disdain in his eyes as he glared at the spoiled-rich patrons said he didn't like them. He barely tolerated them. At least he and I had that much in common. He just didn't fit into their world despite his ultra-expensive suit and shoes. I could tell he didn't want to by the tattoo etched across his neck. People in this world didn't have tattoos. They looked down their noses at people like him and me. I guessed he and I did have a little in common.

Jade grinned at me. "Oh my! He's definitely a suck-and-swallow situation."

"If you don't lower your voice, I'm going to cunt-punt your skinny ass across this room. Now calm down and act like a lady for once."

"I am a lady—a freaky lady." She winked before eyeballing McKay. "Jesus. He's big all over. I'd bet you he's packing big time."

I swallowed anxiously because I was way too interested in finding out. "I don't doubt it. Damn! He probably has women lining up for a chance to find out."

She arched a brow. "Including you?"

My pulse accelerated at her question. *Yes.* There was no doubt in my mind that he was bound to be my next mistake.

"Not even touching that question, Jade."

A smile curved her lips. "Scared, huh?"

I sighed. "Not in the least. My bad history with men has taught me to stay away from shiny, sharp objects."

She waggled her eyebrows. "Shit. I'd let him cuff me and spank me, and I'd call him Daddy."

An elderly woman looked at Jade with disdain.

Jade eyed her right back. "Move along, lady. Nothing to see here."

I slapped my hands over my mouth to stop the laughter. "I can see you're planning on making trouble tonight."

"What's new? Besides, you need a little trouble in your life." She looked at me knowingly. "Now, let's get back to McKay. His hot side-kick in the white tux looks promising. Who is he?"

I smiled snidely. "His lover."

Completely mystified, she stared at him. "Really?" She twirled her hair. "After arguing with Cate, I don't have the strength for a sexual conversion."

I laughed, shaking my head. "No. It's his business partner, Ram Steele."

Her eyes narrowed with interest. "Fascinating." She looped her arm through mine and pulled. "We must go over and bask in their hotness."

I didn't budge. "Nope. We're not doing that," I said simply.

Jade smiled widely. "Yes, we are." She paused. "But if you want me to make a scene and call them over, I can do that too. It's your choice, sweetness."

I growled. Jade had the finesse of a bull in a china shop. I knew she would take pleasure in making a scene for a multitude of reasons.

"Fine. Let's go."

She looked at me smugly. "I knew you'd see it my way." She pulled me through the crowd toward McKay and Ram.

McKay's eyes traveled from the top of my head down my curvy body. His wolfish glare made me feel like a mouse beneath the blood-thirsty stare of a cat.

"Lick them," Jade muttered.

I almost tripped. "What?"

"Lick your damn lips," she hissed.

I scoffed, raising my chin in a gesture of defiance.

"Do it. He's checking you out, all marauder-like."

And he was checking me out. His smoldering gaze slowly perused my length in a deliberate way. I went breathless right to the pit of my stomach. I didn't understand how he had the power to make me feel excited, giddy, and turned-on all at the same time.

His mouth curved in that secret way that said he knew how much I wanted him.

Damn it. This is not good.

I wanted to walk in the opposite direction, fleeing from his disturbing, heated focus. But McKay was a beast of prey, and any sign of fear would be my doom and his victory.

I sighed with relief when Bigsby ambled over to McKay and said something to him. McKay nodded to Ram before stalking away from the bar with Bigsby at his heels.

Jade stopped, looking at me incredulously. "Where the hell are they going?"

I tried to quash the glimmer of disappointment as I watched McKay navigate through the crowd and up the staircase.

"Hopefully home," I said while grabbing a champagne flute from a passing tray before downing it like water.

CHAPTER 8
SINTHIA

The night was turning out exactly as I'd envisioned it—boring. Between Kyle stalking me from the perimeter of the room and no sign of McKay, I drank more alcohol than should have been allowed.

It was like a fucking circus. Botoxed and siliconed-to-death women were trying to catch the attention of the hired photographer roaming with a camera around his neck as he playfully snapped shots of celebrities. Cate and her fiancé Bigsby made the rounds. Erika and Mitch meandered about. And I was drinking solo while Jade did her Bellisario duty by circulating among the boring guests.

I had many moments of wanting to pull my hair out from sheer boredom or wanting to leave to get some much-needed sleep. I would have, but I'd promised Jade I would stick it out until the end of the event.

Damn. This night was turning out to be one big epic fail. I thought it couldn't get worse—until I saw Kyle's wife making a beeline toward me.

I sighed loudly. *Let the drama begin.*

"Hello," Claire said, standing in front of me while twitching nervously.

Her designer gown clung to her slender frame. She looked as

though she'd blow away if I breathed too hard in her direction. There was one thing for certain. Kyle's wife was drop-dead gorgeous. By her whole aura, I could also tell she was well-bred and came from lots of money.

I arched a brow. "Hello." Nonchalantly, I continued sipping my drink.

I bit back a laugh, fascinated by the antsy flutter of Claire's eyes as they discreetly darted around as if she expected Kyle to fly into a rage at seeing her talking to me.

Her mouth tilted into a brief, small smile. "I love the gown you created for Erika. You have a keen sense of design."

Raising a dark brow, I said, "Thank you."

"This conversation is…awkward, isn't it?" She chewed on her lower lip in consternation.

My lips twisted into a smirk. "Yes, very."

A smile curved her lips. "Exactly."

I shrugged. "But I get it. You're stuck at a gala with your husband's ex. It's natural to be curious."

"When did you two date?" she demanded in a low tone.

I sipped my drink, looking at her pointedly. "He was my high school crush," I responded. I left out the fact that Kyle was my introduction to fucking like horny rabbits in every position and place we could find—his parents' boat, under the high school bleachers, the back of his expensive convertible.

Claire couldn't hide her incredulity. "High school?" she inquired, her eyes wide. "He just seemed so…happy and elated to see you."

I shrugged. "What can I say? I'm an enchanting kind of chick." I kept my tone conversational.

She bit her bottom lip with a worried look in her baby-blue eyes.

"Look, Claire, Kyle and I have been over for years. I have no interest in him whatsoever." I drained my glass.

"Kyle and I have an open marriage." She cleared her throat. "Well, the open part is something he wants. From the way he's been watching you tonight, I just assumed you and he were sleeping with each other." Confusion clouded her gaze.

Watching? Kyle was eye-fucking me from across the room.

With an aggravated sigh, I said, "Absolutely not. He's not my type." I paused. "Anymore."

"He's rich and handsome. He's everyone's type."

I rolled my eyes. "I don't give a shit what you think, Claire. You came over to me, asking questions, and I'm answering even though I don't fucking have to."

I stared, contemplating where I wanted to go with this conversation since Claire was being very polite. I just couldn't even muster up the strength to be a bitch and dislike her.

"So how did you meet Kyle?"

Years ago, I'd learned that, for some reason, the super-rich loved talking about their personal lives.

"We grew up together," she offered tentatively.

I scrutinized her. "It figures," I muttered under my breath.

Claire actually smiled. "I know. It's pathetic."

I smiled back. "I'm trying not to judge…too hard."

"I heard Mitch warning him to stay away from you." She frowned. "I was curious because of the way Kyle sounded when mentioning your name." She bit her bottom lip, looking at me apologetically. "So I asked around about you." She eyed me sheepishly.

I stiffened. "Invading my privacy? That's a pretty fucked-up thing to do."

She held up her hand. "I'm sorry, but I had to know."

I frowned. "Had to know what?"

"Who my competition is."

There it is. The claws are finally out.

I laughed, looking her up and down with disdain. "Sweetie, from where I'm standing, there is no competition."

She licked her lips. "You're taking this the wrong way. I'm not trying to fight. I'm telling you to stay away from my husband."

I frowned. "Shouldn't you be telling your husband to stay away from me?"

"I have."

I shrugged. "Okay. Well, problem solved. Are we done?"

She stared at me tensely.

I sighed loudly. "What makes you think Kyle's interested in me?"

Her mouth tightened. "Because you're exactly his type."

I choked and then cleared my throat loudly. *No, she didn't say I was Kyle's type.* "That's funny because when he broke up with me, he made it abundantly clear I could never be his type." It was a fact that still stung to this day.

She tapped her glass anxiously, but the look in her eyes was icy and conniving. "I didn't mean to upset you, Sinthia. I just—"

I blinked. *What's up with this passive-aggressive bitch?*

One minute, Claire had been timid and nervous, and the next, she was ready to rip out my throat.

I cut her off. "For the last time, I'm not interested in fucking your husband." I placed my glass on the bar. I was so done with this conversation.

"Sinthia, I'm really sorry for…" Claire blinked as if she were ready to cry.

Bullshit. She wasn't sorry. She was a manipulative wench, putting on a show to garner sympathy from the guests, acting like I was a whore who was trying to steal her husband.

Not giving her a chance to finish, I pinned her under a hard look. "Nice meeting you, Claire," I said before calmly walking away.

"Bitch," Claire mumbled.

"I heard that," I responded without bothering to turn around. Weaving through the crowd, I stopped a passing waiter. "Where's access to the rooftop?" I needed air and space to get away from the bullshit.

He pointed to the spiral staircase. "Top of the stairs and toward the left."

"Thanks," I responded before making my way up the grand staircase to the top floor.

I froze when I felt something brush against my ass. Whirling around so fast, I almost stumbled down the stairs before firm hands gripped and steadied me. They were Kyle's. The idiot was holding on to me with a fucking stupid look on his face.

I pulled away from him, stepping securely onto the landing. "Did you just touch my ass?" I snapped, pointing in his face.

He stepped closer, spreading his hand across my hip. I promptly knocked it off.

"I couldn't help myself. Damn, you are so tempting."

I refused to let him intimidate me. With my chin tilted stubbornly, I held my ground. "Touch me again, and I will fuck you up. I don't care who's watching, including your wife," I said, my voice flat.

He held up his hands in front of him in fake surrender. "Whoa." He laughed. "I'm not a fighter. I'm a lover."

I was done with his stupid ass. "Why are you stalking me, Kyle?"

"Seeing you stirred up old memories"—he licked his lips and studied me—"like memories of how good we were together in bed."

I scoffed. "First, you're married. Second, you're fucking married," I said with a sneer.

"My wife and I have an understanding. I'm free to see and sleep with whomever I want."

"What you're suggesting is—"

His lips twisted into a mockery of a smile. "A no-strings, no-promises night of hot, sweaty sex." His voice held a cocky confidence.

I scrunched up my nose. He was truly a worthless piece of shit.

I pasted a smile on my face and delivered my next line in a saccharine tone. "I wouldn't fuck you even if you had a thousand-dollar bill stuck to your limp cock."

His smile slipped. "Liar," he accused. "I saw the way you were staring at me."

The dude was fucking delusional. I couldn't believe I'd let him steal my chances for a normal relationship with every single guy I met after him. Well, no more. He wasn't worth it.

I balled up my fist, stepping toward him. "That was a gaze of disgust. Get a damn clue, Kyle."

"Are you seeing someone?"

I scrutinized him as if he'd lost his mind.

"You didn't answer, so that means no." He grinned like he'd won the fucking lottery.

My nostrils flared. "I didn't answer because it's none of your fucking business, Kyle."

I wasn't about to divulge that I hadn't had someone in my life for years. Yes, I'd occasionally had sex with a man when I missed the sensual touch of a lover, but I hadn't formed any relationships. I was too emotionally detached for that.

"We can make this work, Sinthia."

"Fuck off." I smiled icily.

Rage twisted Kyle's face, but just for an instant. Turning on my heel, I walked away.

"This is far from over, Sinthia. I'll be seeing you." His dark tone rang with deadly promise.

"Not if I see you first, idiot," I said in a singsong voice, swaying with a grin. There was nothing better than closing the book on an asshole ex.

I veered off to the left, only to see two hulking men leaning on each side of the entryway to the rooftop. I watched Bigsby as he exited the rooftop, storming past the men guarding it.

Shit. He's heading my way.

I'd avoided the prick all night. I wasn't about to have a long, boring conversation that involved him leering at me like some sex object. I dipped into the empty ladies' restroom and waited for him to walk past it. I could hear his footsteps approaching the restroom. Then they stopped, and he walked away.

Taking an extra precaution, I waited a beat before stepping out. I breathed a sigh of relief that Bigsby was gone, but the two men were still standing guard at the entrance. Biting my bottom lip, I debated whether I wanted to mess with the two MMA-looking men or just go back downstairs to the gala. Without a doubt, I knew either Bigsby or Kyle would be waiting to pounce as soon as I stepped into the party. I sighed. That left only one choice—onward toward the rooftop. I swayed down the hallway, stopping before the two men leaning up against the wall with their thick arms crossed. Each one was built like a fucking tank and each just shy of six feet tall.

I smiled winningly at them. "Is the President of the United States out there on the rooftop?"

They didn't crack a smile.

Wow. Tough crowd.

"As gorgeous"—I winked at them—"and intimidating as you two obviously are, I'm going to have to ask you both to get the fuck out of my way. I need fresh air and lots of it. So if the president isn't out there, having some kind of clandestine meeting about saving the world, then I'm going to the rooftop."

I stepped forward, and they swiftly closed ranks. Irritated, I tried to push them out of the way, but it was like pushing a brick wall.

"Whoa. Now, hang on a minute, sweet cheeks," said the one with sandy hair, holding his palms out to ward me off.

I impishly swayed back and forth. "Come on now. Are you really going to make me kick your ass in my pretty dress?"

They both grinned before the one with sandy hair, looking strong as an ox, said, "Sorry. Not going to be able to let you on the rooftop, sugar."

I surged forward again. "Bullshit. I'm not just going to stand here."

The one with sandy hair widened his stance.

"Move out of my way."

The other man with a blond buzz cut and a maniacal glint in his eyes said, "It's reserved, but come back later, and I'll arrange something real private."

He gave me an adorably rakish grin, and his eyes flicked to mine flirtatiously. I bit back a smile. He was hot, but I wasn't interested.

"Private? With you?" I pursed my lips. "Not going to happen." I crossed my arms over my chest. "Move," I huffed impatiently.

A deep voice rumbled from the rooftop. "Let her through."

They cleared the entrance, allowing me to walk to the lighted rooftop with its medieval architecture and vines hugging the bricks.

I skidded to a stop when one of them said, "Wicked tattoos, sugar."

I turned around to find them both staring at me with sly grins.

The one with the buzz cut winked at me.

"I give him two weeks," the one with sandy hair said to the other one.

They stepped back to flank the entrance.

Two weeks for what?

I turned around to find Core McKay staring at me with no smile.

He was standing under the bright moonlight, looking delicious, dangerous, and just plain fucking gorgeous.

"Making trouble everywhere you go," he drawled in that ridiculously gruff tone.

My cunt clenched like it recognized its master's voice.

"What can I say? I'm a very bad girl." I batted my eyelashes almost comically before sashaying toward him.

Stopping before him, I tilted my head, and my eyes traveled up his tall, well-built body. He had discarded the tuxedo jacket he wore earlier. Muscles bunched against his white shirt, and his rolled-up sleeves displayed the tattoos on his forearms. His collar was unbuttoned, and all I could focus on was the all-seeing eye tattoo on his neck.

Damn. This didn't bode well for me. I was a sucker for men with tattoos.

He crossed his muscular arms. "Hmm...that happens to be my favorite type of woman."

He was sexy—well, hot and scary. His dark hair was cut short on the sides, but it was stylishly longer on top. His searing steel-gray eyes made me visualize seriously wicked, naughty things.

Shit. Shit. Shit. Sin, focus.

As the cool air whirled around us, I sauntered past him to take in the beautiful views of both downtown and uptown Manhattan as well as the Hudson River.

Feeling his intense gaze, I sighed before turning and leaning a hip against the ornate railing. I glared coolly at him. Nothing about him was pretty-boy like or classically handsome. He was just very attractive in a rugged and dangerous way.

He regarded me for a long time before smoothing a hand across his blunt-cut midnight-black hair. And just like that, he smiled an actual bad-boy smirk that made my pulse race and sex clench as I imagined all the sexy, kinky possibilities.

McKay was lethal. I shook my head, feeling possessed by his presence. With one look, the man could turn my brain into mush every single time.

"So I heard Kyle Fillion is following you around like a lost puppy. Are you two fucking?" McKay asked boldly.

"Not even close." I sighed heavily. "We dated in high school. He was a fuck-repeat-and-fuck-again fling."

His eyes flashed as he arched his eyebrow at me. "High school?" His lips twitched into a mockery of a smile. "He's chasing you around like you two fucked yesterday. That shit is pathetic."

I tilted my head, kind of enjoying the sarcastic ruthlessness of McKay's demeanor. "What can I say? Obviously, what's between my legs is really memorable."

McKay laughed, and it was a full-on sexy sound, which sent a zing to my cunt.

"Apparently." He eyed me silently.

I squared my shoulders and took a deep breath. "Why are you gawking at me like that?"

He shrugged one massive shoulder. "Just trying to figure you out."

I knew he was toying with me, but I was in no mood for games.

"There's no riddle to me, McKay."

"I beg to differ." His lips tilted into a brief, small smile.

I pasted a smile on my face and delivered my next line in a saccharine tone. "So are you going to continue to eye-fuck me?"

"Maybe."

He smirked, and my heart skipped a beat.

I started to fidget, and then I forced myself to stand still. This man was fucking unnerving.

McKay reached up to run his fingers over my hair.

My jaw dropped. "McKay."

Ignoring me, he expertly pulled my hair from its updo, sending the strands cascading around my shoulders. "You should always wear your hair down," he said simply.

In seconds, I'd gone from wanting to claw his eyes out to full-blown lust. *Damn.* I wanted to let him touch me and screw me in ways I'd let no other man before.

He reached out, grazing the side of my cheek with the back of his hand. "It makes you look...sinful."

My clit pulsed, and my knees nearly buckled from the sultriness of his voice.

I cleared my throat. "Well, this has been…interesting." *And fucking scary.* "Nice seeing you, McKay," I mumbled, stepping forward to make a hasty exit.

McKay placed a possessive hand on my hip, and my body froze.

"I didn't dismiss you," he said with a hard voice.

I pressed my lips into a thin line. "I don't need permission, McKay." I looked down pointedly at his hand. "You want that?"

He spread his fingers across my hip, firmly guiding me to him. His eyes lingered on my lips. "Yes. More than I should."

I swallowed hard. Everything that had come out of his mouth was served with a hot side of dirty sex.

"I'm still not interested."

He bent down close. "Liar," he breathed huskily in my ear, his mouth skirting around the lobe.

"I don't mix sex and business." I pursed my lips. "And more importantly, I don't like you."

He edged forward slightly, squeezing my hip. "Another lie." He pulled away from my ear and winked at me. "Besides, what does liking me have to do with us fucking?" He actually smirked as if he found me mildly amusing. "Angry sex is the best type of fucking, sweetness."

I swatted his hand. "Behave, McKay."

His muscular arm encircled my waist, bringing our upper bodies together. His hand threaded through my long hair. "I don't know shit about behaving."

I struggled to break his embrace. "Don't," I said shakily.

He held my face while staring at me intently. "Why are you afraid of me?"

"Let go of me," I snapped.

He released his hold—not because I'd asked him to, but because he wanted to. Gathering my composure, I walked away, and then I stopped, turning to stare at him. I knew I should have kept going, but it wasn't in my nature to tuck my tail and run, even when it was in my best interest.

"Just for the record, I'm not afraid of you, McKay."

His confident smile called me a liar.

I was done with the cloak-and-dagger routine and decided to lay my cards on the table. "I'm cautious about your motivation. Nothing about you is straightforward. Everything is smoke and mirrors." With my heart pumping, I was raring for a fight. "Yes, I'm attracted to you, but it doesn't mean I'm going to rip off my panties and yell, 'Come and get it.' You're going to have to work fucking hard for that shit to happen."

McKay leveled his gaze on me.

I resumed. "You're an arrogant prick. I get it. You're a sexier-than-thou chick magnet, but it doesn't mean you have to be so cold about our business quagmire either."

He arched a brow. "Meaning?"

"One, you hung up on me yesterday, all rude-like. Two, you keep flexing your muscles as though I'm your minion."

The vein along his jaw pulsed. "Exactly what do you want from me, Sinthia?"

My fists tightened. "I want out of our contract."

His eyes were blazing, and he pressed his lips into a thin line. It was a look of fury I'd never seen on his face before.

"Try again," he said.

I refused to let him intimidate me. With my chin angled stubbornly, I held my ground. "Everything is negotiable, so let's negotiate."

Raising a black brow, he stated, "You have nothing to negotiate with."

I sensed his anger simmering just below the surface.

"I'm the talent and the designer, so I have plenty to negotiate with. If I walk, you're left with nothing."

"I call bullshit on that threat. You'd never walk."

Damn, he called me on my bluff.

I turned my head, unable to meet his taunting gray gaze.

He continued. "And if you do, I won't even think twice about destroying your ass and taking everything you have, including your name. Next."

Fucking asshole.

I forced myself to look at him again. "Next, what?"

"What else are you willing to negotiate with?" He looked me up and down sensually.

My breath caught in my throat as I blinked hard. "Not going to happen. I'm not a whore."

"Never said you were."

I closed my eyes tightly to block the sight of his hateful presence. "You didn't have to say shit. That crazy, wild look in your eyes says it all, McKay."

"I make you uneasy," he stated matter-of-factly.

I opened my eyes. *Hell yes.* "Not even close," I lied.

He was the only man I'd met who could make me jumpy like some high school virgin, and I didn't know why. I knew men. I collected them like trophies and threw them away, but McKay wasn't a man I could play with like a Ken doll and toss aside. He was the mother-fucking rugged and raw real deal. I couldn't manipulate him with the flutter of my eyelashes, and that made me fucking uncomfortable.

He gave me a calculating look. "Come here." He kept his voice low and soft but left no room to doubt that he'd issued a command.

I placed my fingers on my hips. "I'm not a dog. Don't bark at me like that."

McKay watched me with those devastating gray eyes, his expression giving away nothing. "If you're scared, it's understandable." He widened his stance. "But I don't bite."

An image of me stripped down with him nipping and biting my inner thighs flashed through my head. He smiled as if he knew exactly what I was thinking.

"Unless you enjoy getting bitten." His lips twisted into a smirk. "Then I'm so down with that, darling."

Between clenched teeth, I said, "Why does everything that comes out of your mouth sound so scandalous and dirty?" I bit my bottom lip. "You're nothing like those stiff, smelly old moneybags downstairs."

He stiffened.

No. He was nothing like them. He was an enigma I needed to solve in order to get the upper hand. Even after scouring the internet for additional information I could use as leverage against him, I'd found nothing—no photos, no scandals. I'd only discovered speculation and gossip about his alleged ties to the criminal world—his billion-dollar empire having been built using drug trafficking, money laundering, prostitution, and a few other criminally speculated trades. The only bit of information that did pop up over and over was his ownership of the McKay Club, a chain of private invite-only clubs that were essentially playgrounds for the powerful, rich, and kinky to indulge in discreet liaisons to allow all their freaky fantasies to come true.

"Because I'm not. I've earned my money the hard way, darling."

I scrunched up my nose. "Yes, I've heard. Crime—the unpretty, messy side of Core McKay."

"I'm not afraid to get my hands dirty, Sinthia," he spoke with quiet menace. "That's the big difference between me and all those pretty people downstairs. I fucking earned every dime I have. No one gave me shit. There was no trust fund, no job at some fucking law firm, no Ivy League college. I grew up on the streets, and what I am is nothing compared to those elitist pricks down there. I'm better." He smiled. "You're better. And don't let that attorney boy, Kyle Fillion, make you think otherwise."

Against my better judgment, I walked toward him. "I don't care about him or anyone else." I licked my bottom lip. "I am who I am. Anyone who can't accept me can kiss my ass," I finished, standing before him.

"And just for the record—" he leaned down, and his tongue swirled over the delicate folds of my ear "—I'd love to kiss and lick every inch of your beautiful ass."

Holy shit. My breath came more raggedly. My nipples tightened, and warmth pooled between my thighs. What I wouldn't give to ride him hard and fast.

He trailed a thick finger across my collarbone. My heartbeat pounded in my chest. My knees almost buckled when he pushed down my dress strap. He brushed a hand against my breast, and my nipples stiffened immediately.

The sensations of his touch, his clean, masculine scent mingling with the crisp air, and the heat emanating from his body made me heady. He arched down, and his breath skittered along my shoulder before his tongue traced the scar running across it. Losing all sense of self-preservation, I reached up and ran my fingers along the back of his head, sinking my nails into the silky softness of his hair with my fingers splayed against his scalp. I closed my eyes, bowing into him. Our embrace was oddly sensual and too comforting.

This wasn't right. My eyes opened. Breaking the surreal moment, I released my grip on his head and swallowed nervously. Abruptly, his head snapped up, and gray eyes locked on to mine.

Tracing a callused digit over my scar, he asked, "What happened?"

Feeling a little self-conscious, I gave him a stiff smile. "I ran into a stalker with a knife. He won round one. He's gone. I'm here. So it's over." At least, I hoped it was.

McKay frowned as he snaked an arm around my waist, pulling me flush against him. "If it's not, let me know. I can take care of him for you." The smooth proffer of violence in his sophisticated tone was a cold reminder that underneath his expensive tuxedo was a deadly predator.

"Thanks, but I can take care of myself."

The way he looked at me told me he begged to differ. I pulled away, straightening my dress. I didn't need him to run my personal life. No man was going to come in and save the day.

"What you think is going to happen between us will not happen," I said calmly.

He caught my chin, and his gaze bored into mine. "It already has."

His words sent a shiver through me, but I smiled and tried to make light of my surging emotions. "You wouldn't know what to do with me, McKay, because I guarantee you, I'm nothing like any woman you've ever met." I was broken and cranky, but right now, I was also confused and horny.

I gasped when he wrapped my hair around his powerful wrist, tugging my head back so our lips almost but not quite touched.

"You mean a woman who hides behind her pain with snarls and quips?"

I tried to pull back, but my hair was still tightly wound about his wrist. He continued to hold me.

"Let me go, McKay."

He ignored my request and said, "I can see the pain behind your eyes. Let me help you unlock it."

It took several moments before I could compose myself enough to reply. "You don't know shit about me."

"Liar. You're like an open book to me." He nipped my bottom lip. "And when you're ready to get on your knees and beg me to fuck you hard and dirty, I'm going to read you from cover to cover."

In seconds, I'd gone from anger to arousal. I wanted him to touch and fuck me in ways I'd only dreamed about. Then I knew. I was no match for him. He would consume me, fuck me, and spit me out without a backward glance.

He whispered against my lips, "And I have a lot of dirty little things planned for you, Sinthia."

My pulse accelerated. My fingers curled and fisted the fabric of his crisp white shirt. His physical magnetism was palpable. I swallowed hard, trying to resist the urge to lick the all-seeing eye tattoo on the side of his neck.

"I want to strip you naked and lay you on my bed." There was a pause before he said, "I want to tie your legs wide open, so I can see your glistening cunt." His voice was low and rough when he growled, "I will work you with my tongue until you're begging and screaming."

It was so easy to imagine his tongue lapping my womanhood with desire that a deep shiver shook my body.

I tried to get away from his grasp, but he held me close.

"Then I will kiss you." He cradled the back of my head, easing my mouth to his. The kiss was slow, methodical, and scorching hot. He drew my bottom lip into his mouth, sucking softly, until my insides were quivering with need.

He eased back, and his bright gray eyes searched my face. He gave me one last swipe of his tongue before he bit my lower lip and retreated. "Letting you taste yourself on my lips."

The truth of McKay's pull irritated me to no end. Everything about him was overpowering. His touch, voice, and mere presence demanded surrender—my surrender. It was as if he'd known his dirty talk would be my kryptonite.

"I never mix business and sex," I said with way more bravado than I actually felt. "It would just create a wickedly bad scene when I decide to dump your ass."

With any man, it would, but McKay wouldn't give me a second thought. That was the part that made it so humbling.

"Tough words." He reached up to run his fingers over my hair, rubbing a strand between his thumb and forefinger. "That only confirms that you want to fuck me just as badly as I want to fuck you." Steel laced his tone.

"What can I say? I could never resist a man with a big dick and swagger," I responded before reluctantly stepping out of his grip, "until today."

His face twitched. I pinched back the urge to caress the faint jagged scar running across his eyebrow. At that moment, I knew McKay would be my undoing. No matter how hard I fought the inevitable, I would end up right where he wanted—in his bed.

"I see right through you, McKay, and I have no interest in being the fucktoy you'll discard when you get bored."

He narrowed his eyes. "Maybe you see right through me because we have a lot in common." He reached down, trailing a finger along my scar. "Like the fact that neither one of us gives a shit about attachments." He leaned downward, kissing my scar. "Sounds like a match made in heaven," he mumbled against my skin.

I reached to push his head away, but somehow, my fingers decided to make a home in his thick hair.

In a sadistic way, he was right. He and I were an ideal match. We didn't give a shit about relationships or playing house. We had an itch, and we both needed to scratch it. But something in the back of my mind warned me that going down this road with McKay would be disastrous for me emotionally.

From my past mistakes, I'd learned to pay heed to my inner voice. And this smoldering lust between us was already out of control. I was playing with fire, and I knew it. He was a strictly do-not-touch proposition, yet I was dancing near the flames, enjoying the fire as it burned my cheeks.

Any chance of disguising my need was shot to hell when he trailed his finger across the cleavage displayed by my low-cut dress. Splaying his hand across my breast, he flicked open the beaded hook holding my dress closed with his thumb.

My full breasts spilled out. Immediately, my hands went to jerk it shut.

"Don't," he ordered, his voice low and rough.

I dropped my hands. Strangely, everything about this man made me want to please and obey.

A smile curved his lips. My heart skipped a beat as I tried to remember how to breathe. He covered my breast with his big hand, moving his palm back and forth over my bare skin.

Willing my mind to function, I stared up at him, blinking. "Oh God," I breathed. My breasts felt swollen. Desire coiled low in my belly, causing my insides to spasm with need.

"I can't wait to fuck you and make you mine."

"I can't do this, McKay." But I wanted to.

"You will—sooner rather than later. It's inevitable," McKay said, never taking his eyes off me for a second. "And when you do, I'm going balls deep in you."

I swallowed hard and bit my bottom lip to hide the emotion that had it trembling. It was too easy to imagine being naked with him, and my pussy flexed in anticipation.

His nostrils flared, and every muscle in his body seemed to tense, straining against his shirt. "But only if you say please." In one smooth motion, McKay released me. He eased back, and his steel-gray eyes searched my face.

Still reeling from McKay's erotic words, I couldn't wrap my brain around losing myself to him. My hands shook while fastening the front of my gown closed.

This was the first time in my life I was scared to death—not of him, but of how out of control his mere presence made me feel. The dirty, naughty things he made me want to do, like fall to my knees and deep-throat him right here in the open.

Not giving me a chance to recover, he pinned me under a hard look. "Go, Sinthia, before I change my mind and order you to get on your knees and suck me dry." There was hardness in his soft words, daring me to disobey his order.

I raised my chin in a gesture of defiance and met his gaze. "Goodbye, McKay," I muttered under my breath before turning on my heel. I walked away, ignoring the hole he was likely boring into my back with his gaze. And like a coward, I picked up speed and ran off the rooftop.

CHAPTER 9
CORE

Ignoring Max's and Rocco's knowing stares, I paced back and forth on the rooftop.

Sinthia Michaels was trouble, and she was just my type of woman. Now all I could think about was fucking her so hard she would taste my cock in the back of her throat.

Shit. How the hell did I let it go so far?

I'd known I was fucked when I watched her strolling into the gala. Her body moved like a panther—sexy, determined, and confident. She was tall and voluptuous with curves that cried out to be caressed. In a matter of minutes, she'd shattered my control. It had taken every bit of self-restraint not to back her into a dark corner, pull up her dress, and fuck the shit out of her.

I'd been obsessed with her bombshell body since our meeting at my office. She was one of the most stunning women I'd laid eyes on. I'd memorized her every feature from her rich, olive-colored skin, bow-shaped full lips, and tilted nose. Her long hair cascaded around her shoulders like a sheet of fine silk. It was all confirmation that I was losing sight of my goal to use Sinthia to get to Bigsby. I'd had to remind myself several times that she was just a pawn to be played to trap him.

But when she'd swayed onto the rooftop, I'd seen the fire and determination in her eyes, and my cock had gotten hard.

Damn. I loved it.

Not many women or men had the nerve to go toe-to-toe with me. It was a shame Sinthia and I hadn't met under different circumstances, but I was playing to win. And Bigsby Calhoune was my game.

Max looked at me hesitantly. "Core? Are you ready to go, bro?"

"I'll meet you two downstairs. I need a minute to cool off."

"I bet you do," Rocco mumbled.

Max and Rocco nodded, and then they turned and left.

I clenched and unclenched my hands by my sides as I took a deep breath. My body was on edge with the need to find Sinthia and finish what we'd started. I was aroused at the mere thought. I couldn't remember the last time I'd wanted someone with the intensity I felt for Sinthia, but I knew I'd have to get over it fast.

My mind raced out of control. *Why the fuck did I have to meet her under such fucked-up circumstances?*

Running my hand through my hair, I stopped short and then slammed my fist against the wall.

Fuck it.

I'd wanted to bend her over the balcony rail and shove my cock so far up her cunt that I wouldn't know where she ended and I began.

It didn't help matters that she was exactly the type of woman I was attracted to.

Shit, she'd looked fucking gorgeous when she welcomed my touch. Her beautiful hazel eyes had glazed over with lust. Her full, pouty lips had turned up at the corners as if begging me to delve further. It was sensual the way her face had glowed, and more importantly, her body had reacted to my touch like a woman tuned to my fingers. All the while, her head had tipped to the side as if taunting me to break her, to make her beg.

Little had she known that her lack of submission was like waving a red flag in front of a bull. My sadistic streak had pushed to the forefront with the burning urge to make Sinthia mine—well, at least temporarily. Eventually, I would tire of her, as I had with all women. My life wasn't conducive to any attachments, even a momentary one.

My lips curved up. It hadn't even bothered me when Mitch told me she'd called him about helping her break our contract. Mitch had thought I would be angry, but it was quite the opposite. I loved a woman who was willing to fight, willing to get her hands dirty, because that was what it would take to stand against me. Going against me was like bringing a knife to a gunfight. It would be a bloody slaughter. I would crush her to get what I wanted, and I wouldn't lose a bit of sleep about it.

I was ruthless, cold, and sadistic. That was how my enemies had described me. But I hadn't gone from street thug to self-made international business mogul by making friends and kissing asses. I did what was necessary. What most people couldn't or shouldn't, I would do that and more. That was how I had accomplished about ninety-nine percent of the things I'd done in my life, and Sinthia Michaels wasn't going to be an exception.

I waited for the inevitable. *What will be her next move? Will she offer her body in exchange for getting out of the contract?* No. She didn't seem like that type of woman. Besides, that wouldn't work. I'd just fuck her and still crush her. But I loved a challenge.

I'd been tempted to tell Mitch to take her on as a client. It would be fun to play around with her like a cat with a mouse, but that would be a waste of my time and hers. Our agreement was ironclad. But, damn, just anticipating her next move was fun. I had no doubt she would continue trying to wiggle her way out of our contract.

Ram came strolling up to me. "So what did Bigsby say?"

"What?" I asked in a low tone.

In exasperation, he threw his arms up in the air. "What the fuck is wrong with you?"

"Nothing." I shot him an irritated stare. "He did a song and dance, apologizing for his behavior toward me at his fundraiser a couple weeks ago."

I shrugged, but it still irked me, remembering how the asshole's eyes had scrutinized the tattoo on my neck. He had clearly not approved of my presence at his dinner event until Mitch had admonished him by pointing out I was Core McKay—as in McKay Corporation, one of Mitch's biggest clients.

"But I knew he was trying to feel me out about the Sin Michaels deal. He'll be calling me soon. I guarantee you." Bigsby was a pompous asshole, and I had no mercy for idiots. My nostrils flared. "We'll wait for his next move. I saw the desperation in his eyes. It won't be long. Trust me."

As if shit couldn't get worse, dipshit Kyle Fillion appeared on the rooftop, decked out in his preppy designer tuxedo. His carefully coiffed blond hair gleamed, and his face was tanned and clean-shaven. I could practically smell the money on him as he walked up to Ram and me.

"Hey, Core. Have you seen a gorgeous brunette with a beautiful ass on the rooftop?" he asked, fixing me with a toothpaste-ad grin.

My fingers curled into fists as I struggled to hold on to my temper. "Excuse me?" I asked, taking a menacing step forward.

I despised Kyle. He was the kind of snob who used to look down on me when I'd been just a poor kid from the projects with a single mom who worked hard by stripping to put food on the table. I was far from poor now, but I'd never forget how it'd felt to be treated like dirt by guys like him.

Kyle ran a hand through his hair. "Sinthia Michaels. Bigsby said he saw her up here." He grinned. "Damn! I can't believe how good she looks. If I'd known she would turn out so hot, I wouldn't have dumped her ass." A wistful expression crossed his face.

I angled my face in a silent warning, never letting my eyes drop from Kyle's. "She's not interested in you," I delivered between clenched teeth, not bothering to hide the fury building within me.

Confusion clouded his gaze. "Wait. Are you fucking her?"

I closed my eyes, trying to bottle the rage bubbling to the surface. I wanted to punch this smug, rich motherfucker in the face and break every damn bone in his body. My eyes snapped open.

He clapped me on the back. "Never mind. It doesn't matter. A woman like her wouldn't think twice about fucking both of us." He winked at me. "I don't mind sharing." A smile curved his lips.

"She's mine," I said to Kyle in a calm but icy tone, grabbing him by the throat. I rammed him against the wall effortlessly, ignoring his yelp of outrage.

"How dare you touch me!" Kyle screeched. He tried to get away from my grasp, but I held him close. "I'll fucking sue you."

"You must have a death wish, Kyle." Anger coursed through my veins as I squeezed.

Kyle sputtered and clawed. The more he struggled, the tighter I constricted. The urge to extinguish his worthless life burned like a fire through my blood until I felt strong hands trying to pull me off of him.

"Core? What the hell?" Ram barked.

I released Kyle.

"Are you insane! I'll…" Kyle huffed and puffed as he quickly tried to straighten his jacket.

My temper and general take-no-shit attitude were known far and wide among both my enemies and peers. I had no damn clue why Kyle hadn't gotten the message.

"You'll what?" I scowled, stepping forward and leveling an ice-cold glower at him. "You want to dance, big boy?" I hissed.

Kyle gave Ram a stricken look. "Ram, this is bullshit. He's out of control."

"Don't fucking look at Ram. Look at me, you sniveling wimp." My tone demanded attention. "He can't fucking protect you. I'm the one you should be worried about."

Kyle dusted off his tuxedo jacket. "I'm not afraid of you, Core."

I stepped into his space, staring him down. "You should be." Cold dismissal hung off every word. I shoved him away. "Now get the fuck out of my face," I spoke with quiet menace.

He held up his hand before storming off.

"What's wrong with you?" Ram asked in a careful tone. His eyes widened. "Fuck! Sinthia Michaels? Are you actually thinking about tapping that ass?"

"And what if I was?" My irritation swelled. I really didn't want to talk about this shit.

"She's hot. I get it." Ram shook his head, annoyance etched on every line of his face. "But you can't fuck her, Core, for multiple reasons. Most importantly, it would be fucking messy."

"What if I don't give a shit about messy?" Challenge dripped off the words.

Common sense told me to walk away from this clusterfuck. That had been my plan until I walked into the gala and she looked at me with that bad-girl stare mixed with a side of trouble. There wasn't anything contrived about the sway of her hips as she'd walked toward me with an impish smile. It had been wicked and real, which said she wasn't the type to run from several rounds of hard fucking.

Ram actually shook his head, and disapproval turned down the corners of his mouth. "Core, don't do this. You're thinking with your fucking cock."

I leveled him with a glare. "I don't need a lecture from you, Ram. I got this."

With a snort, he cut his hand through the air. "I give up. Have it your way."

I rolled my shoulders. "I always do," I snapped before striding past him.

I would be damned if I admitted Ram was right. This was the first time in my life that I was thinking with my cock like some oversexed teenager.

Basic, raw hunger surged through me, beating at my self-control. Sinthia was everything I wanted in a woman—strong and feisty. I was becoming painfully hard. The idea of fighting to have Sinthia submit to me had my cock throbbing and my balls aching. *Damn.* I had no doubt she'd battle me like a hellcat, and I couldn't wait to find out how hard she'd fight.

CHAPTER 10
CORE

Infuriated by my encounter at the gala with Sinthia, I plopped down on my bed. The playful, curvaceous woman always seemed to be one step ahead. Her tenacity made me crave her even more. My attraction to her was trouble and distracting.

I had to stay focused on the mission—the destruction of Bigsby Calhoune. Tucking my hands behind my head, I thought back to the night Bigsby had changed my life by killing my mother.

~

Manhattan. Twenty-Six Years Ago

Mom grabbed my chin. "Look at that mug." She shook her head, dark red hair swirling around her. "What did I tell you about fighting?" She eyed the bruises and cuts on my face.

I pulled away. "Leave me alone." Lowering my head, I waited for her to leave. When I didn't hear the sound of her retreating feet, I roared, "They called you a whore!" I tried to keep the bitterness from seeping into my voice, but as I thought of her stripping in front of drunken men night after night, I found the task even more difficult with each passing moment.

She gasped, her mouth opening and then shutting, as if she couldn't believe what she was hearing. "Core, I dance for a living to put food on the table. I don't give a shit what those snotty-nosed boys from the neighborhood think." She stared at me. "Do you?"

I shook my head, but I did. By now, I should have been used to hearing the horrible names the kids from the building called her, but it hurt as bad as it had the first time. "I hate it here. Why can't we move?" I despised everything about living in our cramped one-bedroom apartment in the crime-ridden, drug-infested project—from the pungent aromas of fish and burned meat that wafted through the air to the piles of garbage lining the dirty sidewalks.

She sighed heavily. "I'm working on it, baby. Real soon I'll have the money to move us out of here. We'll have a fresh start." She ruffled my hair. "You'll see."

I knew she was trying to make a better life for us. Nothing had been easy for her while raising me alone. I despised the fact that my biological father had abandoned us, leaving her before I was born. All I'd ever been told was that he and Mom had a one-night stand, and he'd wanted Mom to have an abortion. When she'd backed out at the last minute, he dumped her and told her he didn't want anything to do with me.

"You promise?" I asked.

She beamed, brushing my hair away from my forehead. "I promise, baby." The doorbell rang, and her face tensed. "That's my friend. He's going to help me with my money problem. I'll be right back."

I frowned. "What friend?"

Mom didn't have any friends. She'd said the women from work were too catty and manipulative.

"That's none of your business, Core. Just stay in your room and do your homework, okay?"

"Okay," I responded grudgingly. She walked through the bedroom door, and I cracked open my math book, dreading doing my homework. When I heard my mother's bloodcurdling scream, adrenaline coursed through my veins, and I ran out of my bedroom, through the living room, into the kitchen, where I saw her being pinned against the wall by a huge, burly man whose back was facing me.

My hands trembled as I watched helplessly in horror while the man repeat-edly beat her face to a pulp.

"I warned you to keep your big fucking mouth shut, but you didn't listen," the man rasped. "Now you're going to end up like Cruickshank —dead."

Mom struggled to breathe. "Please. I'm sorry. I promise. I won't say anything."

"It's too late for begging," the man said with menace while punching her face.

I charged, jumping onto the man's back while trying to claw his eyes out of his head.

I could still hear the bone-crunching thud Mom's frail body made as the man slammed her to the floor.

The man swung around and yelled at me, "You little bastard, you're dead!" He grabbed me by the neck before throwing me clear across the kitchen.

My head smashed against the corner of the kitchen counter before my body bounced onto the floor.

Dazed, I slowly reached my hand up to my head. I felt the oozing thickness of gushing blood across my eyebrow, but I refused to give in to the pain. Mom needed me.

My heart had leaped out of my chest when my mother screamed, "Leave my son alone, you fucking bastard. This is between you and me, damn coward."

The man charged at her, pulling a .357 Magnum from his beltline. "Shut the fuck up, whore. You brought this on yourself. I warned you to keep your damn mouth shut!" he yelled while grabbing her by the hair with one hand.

Turning her face away from him, the man placed the gun to her head. It seemed like an eternity to me as I stared at the gold ruby-and-diamond-encrusted horseshoe ring on the man's middle finger before he fired the gun, killing Mom. He then stormed over to me with his gun aimed toward me before squeezing off some rounds, and then my world went completely dark.

～

Manhattan. Present Day

. . .

I jerked straight up in bed, drenched in sweat and my heart racing. The nightmares every night were the first clue that something wasn't right with my recollection of Mom's death. Events of that mind-numbing night replayed in excruciating detail like a horrible horror movie, revealing details I'd long forgotten.

Running my hands through my hair, I swung my legs over the bed. I leaned forward, putting my elbows on my knees and my face in my hands. There were too many pieces to the puzzle, and none of them fit together perfectly. I couldn't shake the feeling that I was overlooking a key connection between Bigsby and Mom's death.

Sighing, I sat up, scrubbing my hands over my face. I stood, deciding against taking a shower. I needed to burn off some frustration in my home gym this morning. I put on sweats and a T-shirt, and I went downstairs to find the morning ritual of the team gathering in my kitchen for breakfast in full swing.

Immediately going to the coffeepot, I grumbled under my breath, "Just one damn morning to myself—that's all I fucking ask."

Despite the fact that each team member had his own luxury apartment, it never failed that command central was always my penthouse. I didn't know how, but over the years, our living quarters had turned into a quasi-fraternity house with the one elevator giving us unlimited access to each other's spaces. It was a good thing none of us had a special woman in our lives. God knew no woman would be able to cope with the lack of privacy due to the team running through our penthouses unannounced.

I poured a cup of coffee before glancing around the kitchen again, taking stock of my team. Ram was at my kitchen table, frowning into his coffee mug. Max was shoveling bacon and eggs into his mouth like he hadn't eaten in days. Rocco was cooking while jamming to some hard rock pouring from his tablet. Kevin was pacing back and forth with his cell pressed against his ear.

Even with the lack of solitude, these four men were my family, closer than flesh and blood. I'd take a bullet for any one of them, and I knew they'd do the same for me.

There was Ram, of course—my best friend and partner. Then Max and Rocco, brothers and my enforcers, handled all my dirty work.

They'd knock the heads that needed knocking together, roughing up all my enemies and keeping my business associates in line—not because I forced them to do it, but because the sick bastards loved the hell out of inflicting blood and carnage. Kevin took care of the financing and accounting for all my businesses. He was also a tech genius with connections to people in high and low places, making him a highly skilled intelligence asset. Everyone played their part. For years, we'd tightened up my operations along the East Coast, making us all filthy rich because of it.

We'd all made hard sacrifices to get to where we were today, including loving and losing people we'd cared about. Losing the love of my life, Maya, had cut me deep, sending me to a dark and wild place. I'd sunk into the abyss of violence and crime, abandoning Maya's and my dream of leaving the criminal world behind and starting anew.

Only Ram's friendship had pulled me back from the brink of despair and death. We'd focused on a way to go legit. Real estate had been the fastest way out. We hadn't been fazed by the fact that the close-knit world of real estate wasn't about to let thugs like us through the doors. So we'd used bribes, violence, and our connections in the criminal world to fuel our ascent. When we'd broken ground on our first building, I'd known it was just a prelude to the legitimate money to come, fulfilling Maya's dream.

I smiled. She would be so proud of me if she were still alive. Many people underestimated me, but she hadn't. I'd beaten the odds by working long, hard hours to build my empire from the ground up. What I hadn't known about real estate, I'd figured out through trial and error. Now I was part owner of a multibillion-dollar real estate development and investment company with offices in New York and Miami, including a portfolio of condo projects, hotels, and office buildings.

I stared at Ram. "Rough night?"

Ram looked up and nodded.

Max bit off a piece of bacon savagely. "Yeah, right. After the gala, he was banging the shit out of that socialite chick, Cate Bellisario."

I smirked. "Did she tell you anything we can use against Bigsby?"

We were ruthless. I didn't mind taking a hell of a lot of pride in that.

Ram stood up and stretched. "How could she? She had my cock down her throat for half the night." He groaned, walking toward the refrigerator. "I'd thought I was into some freaky shit, but damn, the weird shit she begged me to do to her made me a little uncomfortable." He pulled out a bottle of water and then leveled me with a glare. "The things I do for the job."

Rocco looked over his shoulder and snorted. "Poor baby. Fucking a hot chick is just such sweaty, hard work."

Ram punched him in the shoulder. "Shut the fuck up."

I leaned against the granite countertop, gulping my coffee. "I didn't tell you to fuck her. I said to use her obsession with you to get more leverage on Bigsby."

"You know me." Ram grinned as he twisted open the bottle. "I don't mind going real deep in the name of work."

My lips tilted into a brief, small smile. "I bet you don't," I replied.

Max and Rocco chuckled.

Cate was a frequent patron at the McKay Club. She had a seedy dark side she kept well hidden from her fiancé Bigsby. I'd known, with a little nudge from Ram, Cate would jump at the chance to fuck him. She was our ace in the hole. It would be just a matter of time before she was so strung out on Ram that she would do or say anything to keep getting fucked.

Kevin talked rapidly into his cell. "Are you sure? Okay… Yes. Keep digging. Talk to you later." His brows knitted, his bewilderment evident, as he strode around the counter, shoving his cell into his pocket. Opening the refrigerator, he grabbed a bottle of water.

"What's on the agenda for today?" Rocco turned from the stove with his plate piled high. He sat down before shoveling food into his mouth.

"We need to work on our leads." I drained my coffee cup and refilled it.

"Which ones?" Max asked.

"All of them," I responded.

Kevin choked on his water. "All of them?"

"Every damn one of them. The trail on Lexis was getting cold, but now that we know Jeff Barolo and Bigsby are linked, we need to work that lead and find out where Jeff's hiding. The Sinthia and Bigsby connection is still hot. We need to work that angle ASAP." I crossed my arms, looking at Kevin as he plopped down. "So what else do we have on him?"

Kevin raked a hand over his face. "Nothing new. I couldn't find any ties between Bigsby and Ben. Are you sure Ben was telling the truth about Bigsby cleaning Ben's money through his company Pomtonic International?"

"Yes," I responded.

Kevin frowned. "I don't have any information verifying that yet. And UF-Star, the independent political action committee spending money to champion Bigsby for mayor, is squeaky-clean."

"And the Jeff Barolo lead?" I asked.

"It's going nowhere. I can't locate him. He's off the fucking grid."

Ram's stoic expression turned grim. "So we have nothing? Why the hell are we paying all this money for intel if you can't produce shit?"

"What the hell is wrong with you? You didn't let me finish," Kevin snapped back.

"Go ahead," Ram responded grudgingly.

Kevin slumped down in his seat. "Bits and pieces of information about Jeff's past are surfacing. He's bad news, and he's had some assault charges. Plus, he's on probation. Eventually, he has to check in with his probation officer. So we've got that covered. The Bigsby and Sinthia angle is dry, and what little information I have, I haven't quite put together, but I will." He crossed his arms.

"What about Sinthia's background? Any skeletons in her closet?" I asked.

"Nothing scandalous. She moved around a lot up until she was seventeen. Her parents seem pretty straitlaced. Her father, Ian Michaels, died years ago in some freak car accident. Her mother, Grace Michaels, owns some overpriced teahouse in Manhattan." Kevin frowned. "But I did find something very interesting. Sinthia has two birth certificates."

I whistled as I rocked back on my heels. "Two? How did you find them?"

"I started with her DMV record." Kevin's voice was calm and easy. "Once I had that, it wasn't hard to trace her birth certificate. I just wasn't counting on finding out she had two."

My lips tightened. "What else did you find?"

"She has two names on record—Sinthia Cruickshank and Sinthia Michaels," Kevin responded.

My shoulders bunched, but I kept my face expressionless. "Cruickshank?" I bit back the expletive hovering on my tongue.

What the hell?

Cruickshank was the person Bigsby had bragged about to Mom.

I started to mention what I knew, but then I stopped. I needed hard information, not remnants from dreams that didn't make a bit of sense. I decided to wait until Kevin could dig up more info before coming to a sound conclusion about what this all meant.

"Yes, Cruickshank," Kevin replied.

Ram inclined his head toward me. "What do you think? Does she know?"

I scowled. "Do I look like a fucking mind reader? I haven't spent enough time feeling her out to know anything concrete about her."

"Oh, you did a hell of a lot of feeling her out," Max said. "I saw the way Sinthia looked after you were done with her on the rooftop. The woman seemed well tousled."

Max and Rocco chuckled.

I shot them a dirty look. "Yeah, okay. Laugh it up, idiots."

Kevin smirked. "What I do know is someone tried real hard to hide her birth certificates, but they weren't counting on the fact that I'm really good at what I do—unearthing shit they'd paid a boatload of money to bury." He smiled smugly. "The first birth certificate has her father listed as Ian Michaels and her mother as Grace Michaels. The second certificate has her father listed as Greer Lorne Cruickshank and her mother as Aubrey Cruickshank."

"Find out if the Cruickshanks are still alive." I rubbed my chin. "Put a tap on Bigsby's cell and follow up with your Fed contacts to see if they know anything about Bigsby. If he's laundering money, he has to be on someone's radar."

Rocco leaned back in his chair, raising a brow. "Okay, I have one word to describe that idea—insane. An unauthorized cell tap on a mayoral candidate?"

My jaw clenched. "So the fuck what?" I countered. "We do that shit all the time." I looked at Kevin. "Just put the tap on." Then I glared at Max. "I need you to put a tail on Sinthia. Follow her discreetly. I want to know everything she does, everywhere she goes, who she interacts with. I even want to know who she's fucking."

Max threw back his head and roared with laughter.

"I told you," Kevin said smoothly, nodding at Ram with a knowing look. "I won the bet. Now pay up, Ram."

Ram threw his arms up in the air in exasperation before taking out his wallet. He pulled out a crisp hundred-dollar bill and slid it over to Kevin.

Kevin picked up the bill before loudly snapping it with a wide smile. "I just love taking your money."

I stiffened. "What bet?"

"I bet Ram you'd crack and order Max to follow her. Ram said you wouldn't," Kevin said, smiling slyly at me.

I couldn't hide my incredulity. "You motherfuckers are taking bets on me? What else are you betting on?"

"How long before you fuck her," Rocco admitted.

Totally deadpan, Max added, "Four thousand dollars on the line, and given how long you and Sinthia were on that rooftop last night, I might just win this bet."

Kevin frowned. "Hey! Why didn't anyone tell me about that bet?"

"Because, Mr. Genius, we knew you'd win," Ram said to Kevin. Then he looked at me. "I can't believe you ordered Max to follow her. Damn it. She's not who you should be following. That should be Bigsby."

"That's for damn sure," Max mumbled as he got up. He put his plate and utensils into the dishwasher.

"Don't tell me what I should be fucking doing. I have millions invested in her. I have a vested interest in keeping tabs on her," I responded coolly.

Ram shook his head. "Bullshit! If you care so much about her company, then give me the okay to contact the other retailers so I can give them the thumbs-up to resume business with her."

My jaw twitched. It'd been a while since I'd wanted to take Ram's head off so badly. "Why do you give a shit?" I asked, not bothering to hide the rage building within me. "You interested in fucking her?" In an instant, my hackles rose as my eyes locked on to Ram accusingly, and I slammed my empty cup on the counter.

Ram's mouth turned up into a smile. "She's hot, but I'm not a blocker. No matter how much you deny it, I know you. You'll be fucking her by the end of the month."

I wanted to deny it. Everything about Sinthia Michaels was complicated, too complicated, but I wanted her in my bed. I knew she wanted to be there too, but for some reason, she was hesitant and damn skittish. I needed time to work her a little more. I wanted no doubts to be in her mind when we fucked.

"Given what I know about her, I'm going to have to take it slow until I figure out what's going on between her and Bigsby," I clipped out.

Leaning up against the wall with his thick arms crossed, Max sent me a you-are-so-full-of-shit look. "Uh-huh. I call bullshit on that, Core."

A smile twitched across Rocco's lips. "Me too. Shit. Every time anyone mentions her name, you get that look, bro."

My irritation swelled. "What look?"

Ram took a large swallow of water before responding, "The look you get when we're about to take over a company—predatory, focused, and possessive."

Ram knew me well. He was right. From the minute Sinthia had stepped onto that rooftop, I'd known it was time for a change, and she would be the woman who could satisfy my distinct and dark sexual tastes. I wanted her despite the fact that there were a million reasons I shouldn't.

It didn't hurt that I loved her point of view about sex and me, because she pulled no punches. She was a welcome change from both the women who threw themselves at me because of my money and those I slept with to sate my sexual cravings. None of it was real, and all of it was exhausting.

"Are you fucking with me right now?" Kevin stared at us with an incredulous look on his face. "I can't believe you guys are cosigning on Core going cock deep into her. It's illogical." His voice was rough and serious as usual.

Ram's lips curled up into a smile. "Logic has nothing to do with this shit." That faint smile was still on his lips when he pointed his finger at me. "He's in fuck-and-destroy mode. I say let them fuck it out so he can get her out of his system." He looked at me pointedly. "Besides, I kind of like her. Her take-no-shit attitude reminds me a lot of Maya," he said quietly.

Even after all these years, it was still hard to hear her name. "She's nothing like Maya."

No woman could ever compare to Maya. Maya was the first woman who had loved me for me, who had stood by me when I was poor, and who had grounded me when the money started rolling in and I got lost in fast cars and fast cash.

Maya had been my balance, my rock. The major reason I'd decided to turn my back on my criminal empire was for fear of losing her and my unborn child. But I'd lost her anyway, and my world had shattered into a million pieces. Just one tragic moment, and she'd been taken away, leaving me emotionally void.

Ram stared at me knowingly. "If you ask me, I think it's past time to move on." He cocked his brow at me.

I bit back a growl of frustration, wishing my friend would just shut the fuck up. "I didn't ask you," I grated, "so keep your damn opinions to yourself."

He wanted me to let go of the memories of the love of my life as if she'd meant nothing. If it were so easy, I would have done that years ago, but the loss still hurt like a motherfucker.

Ram's brow furrowed. "I'm just keeping it real. You're thirty-six now. It's been fucking years."

Contrary to his belief, time had not healed old wounds for me. It'd only made the loneliness worse. I longed for her to still be here to enjoy the life I'd built, one that had been in the making when she was by my side. When she'd died, I'd gone on a violent rampage, lashing out at everyone around me, including my friends.

Without her, my life was cold, and I wasn't alive.

My body tensed as the recollections of that fateful day echoed through my mind. Those memories of fire engulfing my SUV, taking Maya with it, had haunted me for years. Making matters worse, I'd never found the person responsible for the car bomb.

～

Manhattan. Thirteen Years Ago

Maya's hand curled around mine. Her eyes were wide and filled with excitement as I ushered her along the sidewalk toward my waiting SUV.

She stopped, reaching up to grab my face between her hands. "Have I told you how much I love you?"

"Not in the last hour." I bit her lower lip. "Let me hear it." I hugged her.

"I love you, Core." She wrapped her arms around my waist, burying her face in my chest.

I'd never believed in love until I had hers. She was everything I didn't deserve—kind, loving, tough. And she was mine. She was the first person I woke up to every morning, and I wouldn't have it any other way.

"I love you too." I ran my hand through her hair as she peppered me with kisses. "Don't tempt me, woman, or I'll take you back upstairs and give you round two of slow and steady fucking."

She tipped back her head and smiled at me. "Promises." She paused. "You know I'd rather be upstairs, being fucked by you, than sitting in floor seats at some basketball game." She frowned, biting her lower lip. "Besides, the tickets cost too much."

And that was one of many things I loved about her. She didn't care about the trappings—money, cars, or the lavish lifestyle—that my illegal deeds had brought me. She loved me for me and embraced me for the man I was—hard and broken.

I grabbed her chin. "Nothing is too much for you. You know that."

She was my kind of perfect.

"Stop spoiling me, Core. I don't care about the money or cars. I just want you—" she stepped back and pressed her palm against her round stomach "—and our baby." Her face pinched with pain, and then she smiled.

"Are you okay?" I asked, looking her over anxiously.

"The baby kicked." She kissed me. "You worry too much. If it were up to you, I would be swathed in bubble wrap."

"You're damn right. I need you and my baby safe." I frowned. "There's just too much shit going on right now."

The tension and violence between my team and a rival gang had been ramping up over territory and money. There was no way around it. Someone was going to get hurt. This was more of an incentive for me to leave the criminal world behind.

"I trust you to protect us, Core." Her smile widened. "Oh, the baby kicked again."

She snatched my hand before placing it on her stomach. I rubbed my hand over the swell of her belly and smiled at the answering movement from my little one.

"See? The baby just said, 'Hell yeah, Daddy.'"

I continued to caress her growing stomach with reverence. I thanked my lucky stars that she wanted a family with me. Bending down, I brushed my lips against hers, and she caught her breath.

"How did a beast like me get such a beauty?"

"What can I say? A big cock and a smile get me every time." She winked at me.

I swatted her ass. "Come on, woman. Let's go to the game and get back home so I can thoroughly ravage you."

With our hands clasped together, we strolled down the sidewalk. I opened the SUV's door, allowing her to get in. Closing the door, I walked around to the driver's side and hopped in.

I glanced over at her while putting the keys in the ignition. "Do you have the tickets?"

She rolled her eyes. "Yes."

I arched a brow. She was prone to forgetfulness.

She dug into her handbag and then looked over at me sheepishly. "Shit. No." She shook her head. "I left them on the kitchen table."

I sighed, killing the engine. "Really?"

"Don't give me that look, Core." She crossed her arms. "A girl can get a little distracted when she's getting fucked on top of the kitchen counter."

I lifted a brow. "Did you enjoy it?"

"Immensely." She smiled impishly.

"Well then, the distraction was well worth it." I winked at her. "I'll get the tickets." I kissed her hard on the lips. "You just stay here and look gorgeous."

"Like this?" She licked her glossy lips, a move that always turned me on.

"Perfect." I leaned forward and licked her bottom lip. Pulling back, I yanked the key out of the ignition before sliding out of my seat and shutting the door behind me.

I turned away and headed for the building.

"Uh, Core?"

I glanced back at her.

"It's cold in here." She pouted playfully. "I need the key."

Sliding the apartment key off the ring, I handed her the key ring before hurrying away.

The next instant, I heard an explosion. The force of the blast threw me back. I yelled as I slammed into the sidewalk. My breath rushed out, and shock froze my body.

A crowd was gathering on the street. Dazed, I reached up, feeling blood oozing from the gash across my cheek. My eyes were on the burning SUV—or what was left of it. My heart slammed into my chest, and tears streamed down my cheeks.

Maya and my baby were dead.

I knew one thing for certain. No woman could replace Maya in my heart, not even the smoldering siren Sinthia.

But I did want her in my bed.

I rubbed my chin, wondering how her dark tresses would look arranged against my pillow. My cock grew hard at the notion.

My thoughts were interrupted by Kevin's loud, animated voice.

"Okay, so what happens if she finds out you're using her as a pawn to bring down Bigsby?"

To annoy him, I just stared at him.

"Well?" he asked, perturbed by the silence as he usually was.

"She won't," I said in a voice sharper than I'd meant it to be. The reminder that I was breaking my number one rule of never mixing business with pleasure was fucking with my mind—big-time. My obsession with her was crazy and fucking reckless, but I found myself shaken by my need to possess her.

Kevin scoffed, "There's a high probability she will."

I slid him a withering glare. "If it happens, I'll deal with it." I wasn't worried about Sinthia finding out.

I'm Core McKay, a billionaire, and I'm always in control.

Once I got her into my bed, she wouldn't be leaving until I was thoroughly sated.

"What I'm more concerned about is Bigsby's interest in her." I frowned, remembering the covetous glint in Bigsby's eyes while he'd eye-fucked Sinthia at the gala. "I have a sneaking suspicion Bigsby's interest in Sinthia is more personal than business." A grim smile curled my lips. "And the faster I can get to the bottom of their connection, the sooner I can get Sinthia into my bed." I stared at Kevin. "So, keep digging."

Kevin took one look at my face and then snorted. "How far do you want me to dig?"

My face hardened, and I drew up to my intimidating full height. I asked icily, "How far do the gates of hell go?"

TWISTED LIES 3

"Love all, trust a few, do wrong to none."
—William Shakespeare

CHAPTER 1
CORE

My long strides covered the short distance from the curb to the entrance. Reaching for the door, I swung it open and entered the expansive lobby of my pet project, the McKay Club. Employees scampered about, efficiently cleaning and scrutinizing every aspect of the interior in preparation for tomorrow night's opening.

"Hello, Mr. McKay," they greeted in unison before resuming their tasks.

The rich and famous were notoriously hard to please, and I made sure the McKay Club over-delivered with a one-of-a-kind kinky spectacle. It was what kept the voracious patrons coming back for more. From upper crust to celebrities, all would clamor to get on the waiting list just to party on the rooftop terrace of the club. But the real lure of the McKay Club was the Noire lounge—a private, members-only playground where the well-heeled indulged in discreet sexual fantasies.

After walking across the lobby, I pulled back the expensive fabric draped over Noire's entrance, stepping over the threshold. Advancing down the mirror-ceilinged staircase leading to the lounge, I smiled just thinking about how close I was to finally destroying Bigsby Calhoune by stripping away everything he held dear—his wealth, freedom, political career, and trophy fiancée, Cate.

But why is the taste of revenge suddenly so bittersweet on my tongue?

The vision of Sinthia's eyes dilated with lust flashed in my mind. Basic, raw hunger surged through me, beating at my self-control. Sin was everything I wanted in a woman—strong and feisty. The idea of fighting to have Sin submit to me had my cock throbbing and my balls aching.

Damn. My fixation on her was annoying, cloying, and a complication I didn't need. Sin was bait, a casualty in my war against Bigsby.

But I knew I was fucked the moment she swayed onto the rooftop. I'd seen the fire and determination in her eyes, and my cock had gotten hard.

Damn, I loved it.

Her body had moved like a panther—sexy, driven, and confident. She was tall and voluptuous with curves that cried out to be caressed. In a matter of minutes, she'd shattered my control. It had taken every bit of self-restraint not to pull up her dress and fuck the shit out of her.

Shit. How the hell did I let it go so far?

The smoldering lust between us was already out of control. I wanted her in my bed so I could fuck her in every dirty position possible.

My cell rang, interrupting my dark thoughts. I didn't recognize the number.

"Yes?" I answered gruffly.

"Core, it's Tabitha."

What the fuck? I stopped mid-stride. "How did you get my private number?" I snapped. "You know what? I don't give a shit. Lose it." I was seconds away from disconnecting.

"Wait! Don't hang up. I need more money," she shouted urgently.

"Hell no," I barked.

"You don't get to say no."

The muscles in my shoulders bunched. "Are you threatening me?"

I didn't respond well to threats, especially from a money-hungry whore like Tabitha Thorp, who had served her purpose when I recruited her to help me get close to Sin. Tabitha had convinced Sin of the value of getting an investor—specifically, me—to help her expand her business. In exchange, I'd agreed to pay off Tabitha's debt to Ben Vargos, her unsavory criminal ex-boyfriend, and send her on a very long vacation.

"It's not a threat. Just a statement. You owe me," she snapped.

My lips flattened. "I don't owe you shit. I paid you five figures in cash to make the Sin deal happen."

"It wasn't enough!" she exclaimed in a rushed tone. "I ran into a few bumps, and now I'm broke. You're the only person I can turn to right now."

"Go fuck yourself, Tabitha. Our business was done the moment you took my money."

I knew Tabitha from the old neighborhood. When we were young, we hung out in the same criminal circles. The only difference was, back then, the now-famous Tabitha had worked as a drug mule for her seedy kingpin boyfriend, Ben. I'd even fucked her several times behind Ben's back.

"One call to Sin and…" Tabitha trailed off deliberately.

I replied with deadly intent. "If you even think about—"

She sputtered with a whiny voice, "I'm not one of your whores. I'll tell her you blackmailed me into betraying her."

"I didn't twist your arm to take the money. And the recording of our business arrangement will surely enlighten Sin." I continued moving toward the elevator.

Tabitha gasped. "What recording?"

My nostrils flared. "Do you think I would ever make a deal with the devil's spawn without a backup plan?"

"You're an asshole," she shrilled.

"I've been called worse by a better class of people." I pressed the face of my watch against the security pad next to the elevator. "Come on, Tabitha. This is not my first rodeo. By the way, if you're recording our conversation right now, don't waste your fucking time. I have so much dirt on your shady dealings with Vargos that by the time I'm done snitching you out to the authorities, you'll end up in jail, designing uniforms for the entire prison."

"If you think this is done…well, you're sadly mistaken."

"It's done because I said it's done," I drawled while watching the green light flash quickly before the elevator door slid open. "Now slither back under the rock you came from." I hit the power button, and the call terminated before I marched onto the elevator, the door closing behind me.

One quick ride and the elevator door shifted open. I stepped out to find Zuri, my personal assistant. A curvy redhead, she was well dressed in a skintight cream dress, leaning against the wall while swiping her finger across the tablet in her other hand. She glanced up and smiled before pushing away from the wall and swaying toward me.

"Max," I voice-dialed.

I didn't break my step, and Zuri naturally kept pace as I strode farther into my soundproofed VIP lounge. It had been built to overlook Noire and provide me with the intimacy and comfort of a sanctuary away from the chaotic, sexually charged energy below.

"Hey, bro," Max answered.

"Anything interesting going on with Sin?"

Max, my friend and enforcer, had been staking out Sin's townhouse for days, and so far, there were no signs of anything. More importantly, there had been no male visitors.

"Nothing. What's up?"

"I just got a call from Tabitha, asking for more money. I need you to find her and shut her up. But don't kill her. I just want to make a statement that I can find her anytime, anyplace. Call me when it's done." Shoving my cell into my pocket, I marched over to my mahogany desk and sank into the leather chair tucked behind it.

"Calhoune just called. He's on his way," Zuri informed me.

"When he arrives, make him wait. I can't have him feeling too confident about our meeting."

Zuri handed over the tablet. "Here's Friday's guest list."

"When Bigsby shows, I want you to give him some of your smoldering Southern hospitality. Let's see how committed he is to his meal ticket, Cate Bellisario."

There was no doubt in my mind that Zuri would have Bigsby's

dick harder than a rock with just one bat of her eyelashes. And when he took the bait, it would be more leverage that could be used to destroy him.

Men were enamored of Zuri's stunning beauty. She was feminine, delicate, and beguilingly innocent. Politicians, celebrities, businessmen —it didn't matter. All fell hard for her Lolita ways. That was what made her more than my assistant. She was an integral part of my team.

Zuri flipped her long, thick, red hair. "I'll make him feel real welcome, ya hear," she responded, switching seamlessly from her native New York accent to a deep Southern drawl.

I was constantly amazed by her gift for assuming cover identities. It was a skill she'd been taught at a young age to worm her way into the hearts of lonely men while her family of nomadic African travelers and thieves ruthlessly drained their victims' bank accounts.

"Good. Now take your Southern belle ass out of my sight. I have work to do." Effectively dismissing her, I scanned the guest list on the tablet.

I released a sigh when I didn't hear the click of her retreating heels, signaling her exit. I glanced up to find her staring at me with pursed lips.

I arched a brow. "Yes?"

Making herself comfortable in the chair in front of my desk, she let out a loud sigh and exclaimed, "These heels are killing me!"

"Zuri, that wasn't an invitation. I'm busy," I grumbled.

"Shit. Do you always have to be such a disgruntled ass?"

Sometimes I wished Zuri wasn't so open with her thoughts. I guessed years of friendship had given her that right.

I rubbed the side of my forehead where the throbbing had started. "I'm not fucking disgruntled. I'm working." My eyes narrowed. "Exactly what I'm paying you to do."

She smiled winningly. "Well, that's just plain rude. I do lots of work. It's not easy being the only ray of sunshine on a team of mean assholes."

Tilting my head to the ceiling, I let out a heavy sigh.

Zuri cleared her throat loudly.

I scrutinized her. "What do you want, Zuri?" Knowing her, she wouldn't shut up until she expressed her opinion.

She arched her brow. "You've been unusually distracted lately."

"What's your point?"

"I've been patient, but it's been weeks." She paused dramatically. "Are you ever going to mention the incident?"

I scowled at her. "What incident?"

"Rocco and Max told me about the 'rooftop incident'"—she made air quotes—"with Sin Michaels."

That was the other downside of working on a close-knit team. It was like a fucking high school. "Not that it's any of your damn business, but just for the record, there was no *incident*."

She blinked. "Sure there wasn't."

No matter how hard I glowered, as usual, she didn't seem a bit worried.

She smiled sweetly, too sweetly. "So the rumors were true."

"What rumors?"

"That you're about to fuck her like you're a recently released prisoner." She crossed her arms over her chest. "If it's true, that's a real bad idea."

"Go on." I was interested to see where her crazy line of logic would take her.

Uncrossing her arms, her eyes flashed angrily. "You're using her to get to Bigsby." She leaned forward. "This is wrong. You're mixing business with sex."

The reminder that I was breaking my number one rule of never mixing business with pleasure was fucking with my mind—big-time. My obsession with Sin was crazy and fucking reckless, but I found myself shaken by my need to possess her.

I shrugged. "I got this."

Zuri snorted. "You got this? Men. Can't live with them. Can't kill them," she spat, eyeballing me. "I've never seen you act like this over any other woman. You always catch and release. What makes her so different?"

To annoy her, I just stared at her.

"Well?" she asked, perturbed by the silence as she usually was.

I slid her a withering glare. "This is none of your business, Zuri."

Zuri gave me that tight smile of hers, the one that told me she was losing her patience. "I'm making it my business, because when she finds out she's been used like a whore, this is not going to end well—for you." She eyed me. "Believe me, hell hath no fury like a woman fucked over."

I smirked. "Oh, that's precious. You have a soft spot for Sin."

She blinked. "Give me a break with that bullshit. I just don't want your johnson getting in the way of business."

I'm Core McKay, a billionaire, and I'm always in control.

"Have I ever let a woman get in the way of business?" I grilled her.

"No. And that's what's got me worried about this Michaels chick. I know you. You want her. If you need to work off some of that sexual energy, let me arrange for Brenda to come out to Noire tomorrow night." She waggled her eyebrows. "She's been dying for you to play with her."

I blew out a noisy breath. Zuri knew me well, too well. I was a man with one simple vice—fucking. That was why I'd opened the McKay Club. It was my only indulgence, giving me unfettered access to beautiful women interested in uncommitted, hard-core sex. But lately, I'd been bored with all of them. My body and mind craved something different.

Sin…different.

"No. Brenda is too damn clingy." I ran my fingers through my hair in frustration. "I'm interested in playing with someone far more tempting." I rubbed my chin, wondering how Sin's dark tresses would look arranged against my pillow. My cock grew hard at the notion.

My thoughts were interrupted by Zuri's loud, animated voice.

"Oh God, you've already decided to fuck her." Zuri splayed her fingers out in a fan against her breastbone. "Whatever." She threw her hands up in the air. "I'm done trying to talk sense into you. I'll just sit back and watch the fireworks when she finds out you've manipulated her."

"If it happens, I'll deal with it." I wasn't worried about Sin finding out. Once I got her into my bed, she wouldn't be leaving until I was thoroughly sated.

Zuri inspected me with a small frown on her face, as though both disappointed in and surprised by me. "Yeah, okay. You keep telling yourself that, Core."

The tightness in my chest bore witness to the effect Zuri's words had on me, even though I wasn't ready to admit it, not even to myself.

CHAPTER 2
SINTHIA

My muscles tightened in readiness as I slung my leather backpack over my shoulder. Then I locked my townhouse front door. Inhaling deeply through my nose and then exhaling through my mouth, I jogged down the steps toward Jade, who was leaning against her expensive red convertible.

"There she is, my marathon-running bestie," Jade greeted with a smirk on her face, pushing away from her car. Dramatically, she morphed her face into a mask of sheer terror as she jumped up and down while pointing down the block. "Oh, shit. Run, Sin. Run. I think I see Core coming this way. And look, he's swinging his big, bad cock." She threw her head back in a bray of laughter.

"Oh, shut the hell up, Jade." I stuck up my middle finger, trying to keep a straight face but failing. "It takes so little to amuse you." I chuckled.

It had been a couple weeks, but Jade hadn't let up on poking fun at me. Nope, not since I'd given her a synopsis of my embarrassing flight from Core after our rooftop foreplay session at Bigsby's charity gala.

"You said absolutely nothing about Core being little." Jade wiggled her pinkie with an impish smile before pulling me in for a big hug.

I hugged her back hard, giving her a slight squeeze at the end before pulling away. "That's because he wasn't." I pinched her cheek playfully.

"Hot damn." Jade's apple-green eyes widened. "Was it wrist-wide?"

Turning away, I burst out in laughter. "All I'm saying is I swore an anaconda was pressing against my stomach." I grinned sassily before opening the passenger door and sliding in.

Jade laughed huskily. "You're a naughty girl," she stated before sauntering around to the driver's side.

"The naughtiest," I quipped as I slammed the door shut. Not wanting my hair to be whipped into a tangled bird's nest from the top-down convertible, I pulled it into a ponytail.

Jade got into the car, fastening her seat belt before turning the key and revving the engine. "Are you sure you want to do this?" she asked while pulling out of the parking space.

I sighed heavily, fastening my seat belt with angry, jerky movements. "You don't have to come, Jade. I can do this myself." That was something I'd repeated several times after I told her about our friend Francisco "Cisco" Rodriguez's call an hour ago.

He'd been practically giddy about the Manhattan gossip mill running rampant with breaking news that Tabitha, my former mentor and longtime friend, was back in town and frantically calling around, begging friends for money. Instantly, I'd dropped everything in my haste to go over to her house and confront her.

"Hell no!" Jade ripped her gaze away from the road long enough to give me the evil eye before turning back to concentrate on weaving through Manhattan traffic. "This is my chance to take part in a real-life, action-packed girl fight."

I shook my head. "You know this isn't some blockbuster movie, right?"

"No, it's going to be way better. I get to see you cunt-punt that backstabbing whore."

I mashed my lips together. "It makes me feel like shit that you're taking so much enjoyment in my Tabitha debacle." The debacle was that Tabitha had deliberately hidden the truth about the secret investor —aka Core McKay.

Jade jutted out her chin. "You mean it makes you feel like shit that she betrayed you, Sin." She reached one hand over and patted my leg in comfort. "Stop blaming yourself for something that wasn't your fault."

I tilted up my head, sighing dejectedly. "I should have known her brokered business deal was way too good to be true."

Good things never just happened to me. Shit, from the day I was born, I'd had to scratch and fight for every damn thing I wanted in life. So when Tabitha had called me out of the blue, all excited about one of her business connections willing to provide financing in exchange for a small percentage of my future profits, I was skeptical but desperate for funding to expand my business and start my new clothing line.

"So now you're kicking yourself for being ambitious?" Jade's tone was sharp.

I blew out a noisy breath. "No, I'm kicking myself for not asking questions."

I wanted to bang my head against the dashboard at how quickly I'd just blissfully signed the contract. The ink hadn't even dried on the business document when two million dollars were deposited into my business account with the promise of another million in six months. Little had I known that the investor was the one and only Core McKay or that I had stupidly given away ninety-seven percent of my business.

Frankly, that wasn't the part that hurt the most. It was that my trusted mentor and friend, Tabitha Thorp, had betrayed me by deliberately hiding the fact that my business investor was Core. My jaw tensed. Even worse, I had a damn sneaking suspicion that Tabitha and Core's relationship went deeper than business.

With disinterest, I glanced at the sleek concrete buildings as we raced over the Manhattan Bridge into Brooklyn.

But do I really want to know how deep?

Heat flushed through my body.

I took a cleansing breath. *It doesn't matter, not now.*

A bitter tang coated my mouth. What did matter was the fact that Tabitha had steered me into a deal that she knew I wouldn't have taken if I had known it involved Core. And given our long-standing friendship, in my eyes, that was a really fucked-up thing to do.

CHAPTER 3
SINTHIA

Jade pulled onto Tabitha's quiet residential block before parking in front of her brownstone. Jade drummed her fingers against the steering wheel. "So, what's the plan?"

"We wait to see if she's in there." My heart pounded as I eyed her home.

The normally vibrant flowers on the stairs were dead. Tabitha, if nothing else, was a stickler for order and appearances.

"Fuck it. I'm going in." Unbuckling my seat belt, I threw open the door.

Jade's eyes widened as she grabbed my arm. "Going in where?"

Shaking her off, I snapped, "Inside," before rushing out of the car.

Jade scrambled out, following me. "You're breaking in?" she squeaked, skirting around the car and jogging to catch up with me.

"No." I reached into my jeans pocket, pulling out a key. "I still have the spare key she gave me in case of an emergency while she was on vacation."

Her mouth slackened. "Sin, stop. This is fucking crazy."

I held up my hand. "I got this," I replied, scanning the neighborhood. I knew I wouldn't arouse any suspicion from the neighbors since, in the past, I'd been a frequent visitor to Tabitha's brownstone.

"I'm not letting you go in by yourself."

I whirled around to face her and whispered, "You can't come in with me. I need you out here, keeping watch, just in case shit goes south. So keep your finger on your cell and get ready to call your family's well-paid attorney, because I, for damn sure, don't want to end up in jail as Big Bertha's bitch."

Jade ran a jerky hand through her hair. "Okay, but I'm giving you fifteen minutes. If you're not back, I'm coming in."

"Deal," I muttered before turning on my heel and sprinting up the stairs.

Bouncing on my toes, I stuck the key into the lock and entered Tabitha's house. Holding my breath, I punched the code on the alarm, hoping Tabitha hadn't changed it. The alarm deactivated, and I sagged against the wall with relief. The pounding of my heart slowed down.

"Thank God," I mumbled, shoving the key back into my pocket.

I nearly swallowed my tongue when I finally got my shit together enough to scan her house.

The space was completely cleared out.

"What the hell?" I murmured with a heavy feeling in my stomach.

My heartbeat raced as I rushed around the empty house. "What in the world is going on?" I jogged upstairs. It was empty too. "I can't believe this." I felt a fluttering in my belly as I ran back downstairs.

There was nothing to see here. I secured the alarm and door before stomping down the stairs.

A flood of adrenaline still tingled through my body as I slid into the convertible.

Jade's eyebrows furrowed and then released. "So, no Tabitha?"

"Nope. She cleaned out her house. It's as if she never existed."

"Shit." Jade peeled away. Then she drove onto Flatbush Avenue, racing toward the Manhattan Bridge. "I don't get it."

I threw up my hands. "Welcome to my world."

I really didn't understand what was going on. The whole ride back from Brooklyn into Manhattan was a blur of chaotic questions. *Where is Tabitha? Why did she abruptly pull up roots? Is she dead?*

It seemed Jade's mind was also racing. Suddenly, she murmured, "This shit is crazy as hell, even for dragon lady Tabitha."

I arched a brow. "You think? Just a couple weeks ago, we were at the McKay Club, laughing and drinking. Now her brownstone is cleared out, with no trace of her." I undid my ponytail and shook out my hair. "I need a drink." Slipping off my sneakers, I pulled my stilettos from my designer leather backpack before putting them on.

"I second that. Our favorite place?"

"You know it." I swiped on lip gloss while staring out at the New York City night traffic as we whizzed through the city.

It didn't take long for us to arrive at our favorite Tribeca dinner place. Jade relinquished the convertible to the overeager valet. We took a few quick steps toward the inconspicuous doorman, who opened the creepy-looking black door, allowing Jade and me to step into the trendy speakeasy.

At the entrance, the willowy hostess with large breasts on display approached us with a huge smile. "Hello, ladies. Welcome back. Please come this way." Using her high-pitched voice, she directed us to follow.

Jade and I were escorted through a private entrance into the retro-styled, closet-sized monochrome space. It was bat cave-level murky, barely letting us see the waiters and waitresses, but that was the point. It wasn't a place to be seen or to see.

We paraded past the banquettes and small tables in the L-shaped portion of the room and private booths, and we went right up to the dark and narrow bar. It possessed the same caliber and quality that came with a five-star restaurant, without the fussiness of a dining room. We loved hanging out at the bar and eating small portions we could share, making it more of a communal meal with a casual vibe. Besides, it was the best seat in the house because it was within arm's reach of the bartender.

Settling down, I was determined to make the best of the evening, and I focused on enjoying a well-deserved girls' night out.

Jade's eyes widened with interest when a lanky bartender with floppy curls and a disarming smile edged close to us. "Well, look what we have here," Jade remarked while sinking down onto a chair. "A new bartender."

He beamed at us. "Ladies, how may I serve you?"

"Let me see…" Jade twirled her jet-black hair, smiling coyly at him. "How about—"

I elbowed her in the side, hard. "Really?"

"What?" Her eyes widened playfully. "He asked, and I have needs. Lots of wicked, dirty needs." She displayed a wide grin.

I rolled my eyes heavenward before glancing at the red-faced but interested bartender. "Two shots of vodka," I responded.

He chuckled before roaming away, and he returned minutes later with two small silver cups, placing them before us. "You two look like you're up to trouble tonight. What's the celebration?" he inquired.

I nodded toward Jade. "Troublemaker is off to New Zealand on a movie shoot."

"Wow. Congrats." He blinked rapidly and then stared openly at Jade. "What would you lovely ladies like for your next round?"

There were no cocktail menus. It was a simple process. We'd let the bartender know what type of alcohol and flavors we longed for, and then he would return with his creations.

Jade's tongue darted out to touch her lips. "Surprise us," she drawled.

He got a little flustered, not unusual for most men in Jade's presence. "Got it," he stammered before plodding away.

"To Team Us," we toasted before smelling the vodka while swirling it in our glasses.

Taking a small sip, I let the flavor rest on my palate for a few seconds before swallowing it, savoring the aftertaste.

"Why do you like them so young?" I needled.

"Because they're so pliable," Jade moaned. "And eager to learn."

"You mean, you like the control." It was a statement, not a question.

Jade snorted. "Like you don't. Knowing you, you orchestrate every move in bed." She mimicked my voice as she said, "Move your mouth here. Um…no, no, no. More tongue, less teeth. Wait. Are you done already?"

I choked out a laugh because she was spot-on. "I can't help it that I have high expectations no man has yet to live up to."

"Uh-huh. Says the woman who hasn't been fucked in months. Shit.

You just gave up trying."

"I'll have you know I had mind-numbing, toe-curling sex with Beast last night." I left out the part that the toe-curling was courtesy of dirty thoughts of Core going down on me.

I shivered deliciously. *Jesus, I bet his tongue game is absolutely spectacular.*

"Beast is your vibrator. It doesn't count," Jade interjected.

"Hells yeah, it does. Beast is way better than any man." I ticked off my points. "He follows directions. He stays hard for hours. And he doesn't bitch and moan or beg to stay when I kick him the fuck out of my bed."

Jade groaned. "I'm going to have to get you laid fast before you decide to marry Beast."

A waiter with a handlebar mustache drifted over to us with menus. "Hello, ladies. The same? Or would you like to try something new?"

"The same," we agreed in unison.

The waiter retreated. We watched with fascination as the pretty-boy bartender worked. He was like a mad scientist of booze.

I nudged her with my elbow. "So, are you excited about your trip?"

I was elated yet sad that Jade was flying out to New Zealand tomorrow morning to begin production on her first directorial feature. She was going to be away on the shoot for months, and I was going to miss her something fierce.

"More like scared," Jade confessed with a hint of a smile. "I can't believe I'm about to step behind the camera with my own script. It was fun just blithely writing whatever I wished without having to worry about whether the movie studios would buy my script. Now I'm terrified about the reality of production. The success or failure of my movie is all on me."

I rubbed her hand comfortingly. "I read your script, and it's really good. You'll make it work."

Jade smiled. "And that's why I love you so much. You believe in me without a doubt."

I grinned at her. "That's how besties roll."

The waiter came back with small sharing plates of beef tenderloin skewers with chimichurri salsa, truffle mac and cheese, parmesan truffle fries, and a trio of bar snacks. We dug in hungrily. The bartender reappeared with our drinks, set them down, and jaunted away. I sipped the drink that tasted of several delicious flavors—rum, lemon, maple syrup, and hellfire bitters.

"Sin." Jade twirled her glass. "Why don't you come to New Zealand with me? Get away for a little bit since your collection is almost completed." She smiled cheekily. "Meet yourself a man. You know what they say. What happens in New Zealand stays in New Zealand."

I choked on my drink. "What happens in New Zealand stays in New Zealand?"

"That's what I heard," she boasted.

I snorted. "First, fucking no one says that shit…like ever. Second, I can't relax until my collection is done." I worriedly bit my bottom lip, contemplating the reality that I might never be able to relax.

"You mean, you won't. There's a big difference," Jade stated. "Sin, things between you and Core are fabulous. Stop looking for a fire where there isn't one."

I sighed heavily. Maybe Jade was right. I should be ecstatic about the fact that, due to Core's arm-twisting, I had received confirmation from all retailers that they were back on board with carrying my collection. Now I was working around the clock to complete my pieces, and Core was handling all the business and financial matters. It was a perfect partnership—maybe too perfect.

With an elbow on the bar, Jade rested her chin on her palm and fixed her eyes on me. "So what really happened between you and Core at the gala? And I want details."

It had been such a busy couple of weeks, with Jade wrapping up shooting for her television show and me frantically trying to finish my collection, that we hadn't managed much communication, except for brief calls and texts.

"Hmm?" I asked before popping a forkful of mac and cheese into my mouth.

"Don't *hmm* me. Why did you run from Core?"

"He scared the shit out of me," I confessed. "No other man has ever made me feel so utterly consumed and possessed."

It was ridiculous how much I'd let my hot foreplay session with Core rattle me. The way his lips had devoured mine, the roughness of his callused fingers against my skin, and the overwhelming urge to fall to my knees, begging him to take me in any position he saw fit, had spurred a surprising fight-or-flight response.

I'd chosen flight, which was terrifying and humiliating.

When I'd weaved my way back into the gala, my palms had been sweaty and my heart had been beating so fast I seriously had thought I was one step away from having a heart attack. Not wanting to spend another minute at the gala, I'd faked a migraine and told Jade I needed to leave early. Thankfully, Kirby, Jade's chauffeur had dropped me at home, leaving Jade to ride home with her mother. And later that night, I'd crawled into bed with Core's name on my lips and my fingers playing with my womanhood.

"I'm going to need a lot more slutty details," Jade demanded in a singsong voice.

"Okay." I covered my eyes. "I almost hiked up my gown and fucked him right there on the rooftop." I peeked through my fingers. "I'm a slut, right?"

Jade blinked twice, hard. "Uh…no."

I frowned at her. "There was hesitation in your response."

Her eyes were filled with laughter. "Because I just don't get it. If you want to have sex with him, go ahead and do it. You're a sensual woman. He's a smoking-hot billionaire. You're both obviously attracted to each other. Just fuck him and walk away." She shrugged. "No biggie."

If only it were that simple…

The memory of his touch, taste, and voice was already imprinted on my body and mind. Just the thought of the emotional damage he could inflict once I let him into my body made my mouth taste like sawdust.

The smiling waiter meandered up to us.

"So? Are you going to fuck him or not?" Jade demanded.

The waiter swallowed hard, watching us with wide eyes. "Anything else?" he croaked.

"No, we're good," I replied unblinkingly.

He hurried away like he couldn't move fast enough.

I turned to Jade. "No, I'm not going to have sex with Core."

"Uh-huh," Jade responded before taking a sip of her drink, peering at me over the rim.

I pursed my lips. "Don't stare at me like that."

"You're lying to yourself. I saw how you were eye-banging Core at the gala."

"I want him. That's a fact." I sighed. "But business and hot sex don't mix."

"Since when?"

My mind yelled, *Since Core!*

Taking a sip of my drink, I remained silent.

Jade continued, undeterred. "What would it hurt if you just saw where this thing with him might go?"

I shook my head. "Given my bad luck with men, it will be disastrous." *Both emotionally and financially.*

"Such a drama queen." Jade rolled her eyes heavenward. "Admit it. You're scared of getting hooked on his hot ass."

The truth of her words made my stomach plummet.

I twirled my glass. "What happens if I do and things get really weird with our business relationship?"

Jade raised her eyebrow. "Cross that bridge when you get there. Are you going to have sex with him?"

"Yes," slipped out. "I mean no," I snapped. But my sex-deprived body yelled, *Hells yes!*

"Yes?" Jade pursed her lips. "No?" She pulled on a strand of my hair. "Which is it?"

I scowled at her defiantly. "It's complicated."

I drained what was left in my glass before motioning the bartender over. I didn't even have to ask. He already had two drinks in his hands. He expertly removed the empty glasses before pushing fresh drinks within our fingertips' reach. I took a sip. It was a gin gimlet with just the right amount of tart and tangy. It was quite refreshing and delicious.

Jade regarded me, wide-eyed, over her glass. "Hmm…complicated. So what you're really saying is if you'd met him under different circumstances, you would?" She popped another appetizer into her mouth while examining me like a specimen under a microscope.

My eye twitched. "Why are we even talking about this?" I grabbed another appetizer.

She leaned closer. "Why are you getting so agitated?"

My eyes narrowed. "I didn't intend for any of this shit to happen. I had a pretty damn good plan." I always lived my life by well-conceived plans. It kept things…well, orderly. "Take the money from the secret investor, complete my collection, get it into the retailers, work that bad boy until I made a profit, and give the investor back the money." I chewed my bottom lip. "Now I feel totally stuck, because without him and his money, my collection will never see the light of day." I didn't have to add that my obligation to Core had been adding up, sending me further and further into his debt.

Core was the spider, and I was the fly caught in his web. My gut twisted—and not in the I'm-scared way. It was more like the I'm-fucking-turned-on way. That was how sick and demented I was.

Jade squealed dramatically. "Oh shit! Your eyes just dilated." She pointed at me. "Admit it. His bad-boy swagger has your lady bits all in a quiver."

My lips pressed together in a slight grimace. "I'm not confirming or denying."

We both knew I loved bad boys, and I had a habit of attracting and collecting them like Ken dolls. It was a gift and a curse. Thus far, the mysterious and eccentric Core McKay was the baddest boy I'd encountered. Yet there was so much I didn't really know about him, except for what the gossip hags whispered about—that he'd built his billion-dollar empire through drug trafficking, money laundering, and prostitution, and that was only to mention a few of the criminally speculated trades.

Jade started loudly humming the "Bad Boys" song.

"I'm not doing another bad boy ever." I took a large gulp of my drink. "Remember Kyle?"

Jade narrowed her eyes into slits. "Are you kidding me? Core and Kyle seem nothing alike. Core is alpha-delicious. Kyle is a cheating prick." Her eyes softened. "Sin, you've got to get over Kyle."

My brows came together in a puzzled frown. "I have."

Jade stared.

"It's true. Seeing Kyle again at Bigsby's gala was not the heart-stopping train wreck I'd dreaded for years. I felt absolutely nothing—no pitter-patter of my heart, no I-wish-he-were-mine-again angst. Shit, I said a silent thankful prayer to the universe that the conceited, egotistical douchebag was someone else's problem."

"All of that might be true, but every man you've met after him has paid the price for the Kyle clusterfuck."

She was right. For so many years, I had allowed my bitter past with Kyle to steal my chances for a normal relationship with every single guy I met after him.

"That's the truth. But what's even more pathetic is that Kyle was never even worth the heartache." I shrugged. "But I was young and naïve. Catching him cheating in such a fucked-up manner tainted my notion of trust and relationships." I cringed just thinking about the night of happiness that had turned into dust the minute I pushed open his bedroom door.

Kyle stood with his designer jeans gathered around his ankles while his cock was being fondled by some chick with perfectly smooth, highlighted blond hair that fell across her shoulders like a gorgeous curtain.

I froze, shocked, with my mouth gaping open, as if it were some sort of mirage. I watched as the chick glided up with too much sway in her narrow hips. Then she gave me a smug look before sauntering out of the bedroom, and it felt like a dagger to the heart.

"Kyle? How could you do this to me?" I rasped, unchecked tears streaming down my cheeks. "I love you." My voice hitched.

His face turned into a mask of hate that shocked me to my very core. "Love?" He huffed out an arctic laugh. "Sin, this isn't love. It never was, and it never will be."

I flinched like a punch had been launched to my gut. "If this isn't love, then tell me, what the hell is it?" I stared at him with narrowed eyes, feeling my heart ice over inch by inch.

"What do you want from me? I haven't promised you anything, Sin," he sneered while unhurriedly buckling his belt.

"We've been dating for months!" I yelled.

His jaw tightened. "No, we've been fucking for months." He walked up and stared at me without a trace of emotion in his beautiful blue eyes. "Sin, I'm going away to college, and you're staying here to work for your mother. It would never work out between us."

He reached out to touch my hair, but I smacked his hand away.

He shrugged. "Take it for what it was. We're over."

I stood there feeling stupid that I'd allowed myself to be weakened after my dad's death. I couldn't believe I'd let Kyle into my heart and body. I never would have let him in if I had known he would hurt me and leave me drowning in the deep end.

"Over?" I froze like a deer in headlights.

Gasping for breath, I sank into the murky waters of an emotional abyss.

Then he went for the ultimate emotional bitch slap. "Let's keep it real, Sin. What we had was fun but temporary. You and I know there's no way in hell I could bring you home to my parents. You just don't fit into my world." His parting words burned, fueling my hate fire.

Jade nudged me, interrupting my disturbing trip down memory lane. "Sin, I'm not saying to forget. I'm saying you need to heal and let that shit go."

"Let it go? I've done that, but the healing part takes a willingness to open up my heart to a man who's worthy. I've met men who are losers, liars, users, and looking for another heart to break, but I haven't met anyone worthy." I pursed my lips. "But that's the story of my fucked-up life. Always finding Mr. Wrong."

"I refuse to give up just because we've both kissed more than our share of frogs. That shit doesn't mean Mr. Love Me Right isn't out there."

I looked at her like she'd lost her damn mind. "Are you kidding me?"

Jade regarded me with a pained expression before waving over the pretty-boy bartender. "We're going to need more drinks over here."

Already anticipating our need, he brought over two more drinks, and then he moseyed away. Jade sat up, peering over the bar.

I snapped my fingers in her face. "Will you take your eyes off his ass?" I admonished, even though it really was an awe-inspiring butt.

As if sensing Jade's heated stare, he grinned over his shoulder at her.

Jade bit her lower lip. "Damn. He's yummy but absolutely not 'the one.'" She made air quotes. "I've done more guys like him than I care to count. Gorgeous but dullsville in bed."

I raised my glass in a mock salute. "Cheers to the few women in Manhattan who are crazy enough to take one for Team Single and Desperately Seeking a Good Fuck."

Jade choked with laughter. "Finding a halfway decent man to fuck is like wading through a cesspool. It's disgusting and leaves you smelling like shit."

I gave her a playful nudge. "Exactly."

To prove my point about the bleakness of the dating game, I quickly scanned the space. "Okay, prime example over there."

I nodded in the direction of a table with flickering candlelight and a beautiful blond woman who was staring blankly at her date—a hot-looking guy with an artfully messy fauxhawk, probably thanks to gallons of hair gel. He was boasting loudly about rubbing elbows with celebrities, business moguls, and politicians during his recent trip to St. Thomas on his newly purchased yacht.

"See her blank-faced stare? I bet she's contemplating which fake orgasm moan, high-pitched or low and throaty, she'll use while he's fucking her tonight."

I nodded over to the end of the bar at the middle-aged man dressed like he'd just stepped off the red carpet for the teen awards. He draped his arm around a busty young brunette. Then he winked at me while licking the rim of his glass in an icky, sexually suggestive manner. "And Mr. Midlife Crisis over there is having some delusional fantasy about a threesome with me and that brunette pasted to his side." I shuddered with distaste. "Hard pass on that shit."

Jade smacked the bar. "True that. The problem is men are clueless about what women really want—foreplay and oral sex."

I snorted. "Hence, the problem. Men wouldn't know how to go

down on a woman even if she wrote step-by-step instructions, taped them to her cunt, and shone a flashlight on them."

Jade chuckled. "Exactly. That's why I've been doing some serious thinking."

Uh-oh. Not good.

She continued. "Don't you ever wonder about what's next in your life?"

"Are you fucking with me right now? Or are you running your lines for your movie?" I popped another appetizer into my mouth, chewing happily.

"Neither." She shrugged. "Ever since my mom started getting serious with that lawyer Erika hooked her up with—"

I choked on a mouthful of food. "They're serious?"

Ariana Bellisario, Jade's mother, was worse than both of us when it came to men. After her nasty divorce, she'd kept men at a distance, but that wouldn't stop her from taking an occasional lover when it suited her.

"Yep, very."

My mouth fell open. "Wow!"

"If she can change, maybe there's still hope for us."

There was a hardening in my stomach. "I doubt it."

Jade's mouth twisted into a grimace. "Have you ever thought about where we would be today if we weren't so emotionally fucked up?"

The bartender lingered while removing our glasses and presenting two fresh drinks.

Pointedly, I eyed him, urging him to keep it moving. He grinned sheepishly.

Turning my head back to Jade, I replied, "Excuse me? I'm not emotionally fucked up. You are."

She snorted. "Okay, so now you're delusional. Our idea of a perfect date is fucking a guy until we pass out and then kicking him out before daylight."

The bartender choked.

Jade winked at him coyly. "Interested?"

His pupils dilated. "Sounds like a match made in heaven," he responded before striding away.

I glowered at his retreating back and then looked back at Jade. "All confirming my original assessment. You're the one who's emotionally challenged, not me."

"I'm about to turn twenty-seven." She looked off into the distance for a moment, and then she scrutinized me. "And I think it's time for a change."

I propped my elbow on the bar, placing my chin into my palm. "I've only known one good man in my entire life, and that was my dad. He was way more man than Grace deserved."

"Your mother is a nutjob." Jade curled her upper lip in disdain. "And my sperm donor screwed me over big time. Now, every time I meet a guy, I can't help questioning whether he wants me for my fame, money, family name, or all of it. That's a really fucked-up way to think."

I took a sip of my drink. "Really, I'm good with my life, Jade. I have a best friend who's like my sister, Ariana, who's the mother that I never had, a beautiful home, and a successful career. I'm damn happy."

Jade tilted her head to the side. "Are you?"

I put down my drink. "Am I what?"

"Happy?"

I formed my fingers into a steeple, considering the question. "Yes." I scowled at my almost empty glass and then gazed over at her. "Have I thought about what it would be like to roll over and bump into a warm body instead of a cold, empty bed? The thought has crossed my mind." I left out the word *lately*. "But honestly, I don't think I'm built for that level of commitment."

Jade sighed. "I think that's what we've been telling ourselves for so long that we actually believe it. This much I know. Someday, I want kids and stability. Don't you want children one day?"

My mouth went dry. "No," I answered firmly. "I don't trust myself not to turn into a monster, cruel and unloving, like Grace. I would never do that to a child."

My life growing up had been an emotional roller coaster, all due to my mother, Grace. Dad had done the best he could to shield me from her verbal and emotional abuse, but still, it just hadn't been enough.

"Grace is a bitch. You're nothing like her."

"I hope not." My pulse sped up. "She never loved me or my dad, and it changed us for the worse. We both morphed into people who lived just to please her—hoping if we changed, if we could be everything she wanted, she would love us. It took me years to learn loving myself was good enough. I don't need a man to validate me—not now, not ever."

"Fuck validation. I'm talking about having the right man to love you for who you are. A partnership of equals."

I let out a sigh of despair. "There's no damn happily ever after when it comes to men and relationships. That's a fairy tale. Reality is way bleaker and darker." I nudged her playfully. "Now, enough of this serious stuff. Tonight is about having fun and celebrating. I think a call to Kirby is in order, because we're about to get fucked up tonight."

Jade swiped her finger across her cell, tapped out a text, and shoved it into her bag. "Done. Our chariot will be waiting outside when we roll out, all liquored up." She winked at the bartender, her index finger gesturing for him to bring his fine ass over. "Keep them coming, baby, because we can go all night."

With an open gaze, he met Jade's eyes directly. "So can I," he responded.

"Really?" Jade asked, licking her lips.

"Yep." He winked at her before roaming away.

"Holy shit." Jade fanned herself. "I think there's movement in my vajayjay, an honest-to-goodness tingly sensation."

I sputtered, "Are you sure that's not the aftereffect from the Brazilian wax job you got today?"

Jade slapped my arm.

I laughed. "Please don't fuck him. I actually love this place and his drinks. If you have sex with him, he'll get all mad and pouty when he realizes it's a one-time bang extravaganza."

Jade shooed me. "He's a big boy." She waggled her eyebrows. "Hopefully, a very big boy."

I shook my head with fake dismay. "And this conversation is officially over."

CHAPTER 4
CORE

Bigsby sauntered across my expansive VIP lounge with a determined swagger. His confidence quickly dissipated as I deliberately said nothing, letting the cooling sound of silence speak volumes.

He stood before my desk and nodded at Ram, my business partner, then at Rocco, my enforcer who handled all my dirty work along with his brother, Max. Both were my family, closer than flesh and blood. I'd take a bullet for any one of them, and I knew they'd do the same for me.

Standing to my left, Rocco crossed his arms and widened his stance. And to my right, Ram stared at Bigsby with a pinched face until Bigsby broke eye contact first by glancing away.

Bigsby cleared his throat before offering his hand to me. "Hello, McKay."

I ignored his outstretched hand as my expression darkened at the unmistakable glint of diamonds and rubies on Bigsby's middle finger. It was like a bullet through the heart. This man standing before me was a cold-blooded killer…who had murdered my mother. Rage surged through my body like a dark, violent thunderstorm, and all the bitter memories came flooding back.

My heart leaped out of my chest when my mother screamed, "Leave my son alone, you fucking asshole. This is between you and me, you damn coward."

The man pulled a .357 Magnum from his beltline. "Shut the fuck up, whore. You brought this on yourself. I warned you to keep your damn mouth shut!" he yelled while grabbing her by the hair with one hand.

Turning her face away from him, the man placed the gun to her head. It seemed like an eternity to me as I memorized the gold ruby-and-diamond-encrusted horseshoe ring on his middle finger.

"McKay?" Bigsby's voice pierced through the recollection of my mother's death.

My lips flattened.

Bigsby's smug-cat smile slipped before he dropped his hand.

Tilting my head, I still had my gaze fixed on his ring. "As I mentioned at your political fundraising event a couple weeks ago, I still cannot get over how unique that ring is. Where did you get it?"

Bigsby smiled cockily, letting himself settle into the chair directly in front of my desk with exaggerated casualness. "I had it made in the eighties. There's only one of its kind."

My face was a cold mask, hiding my bitter hatred. "Interesting."

I studied him for a few minutes. Bigsby shifted nervously, his hands clamped over the armrests of the chair.

Bigsby's smile seemed forced. "Thank you for accepting my request to meet, McKay."

"How can I help you, Calhoune?"

Bigsby's facial muscles twitched before he shook his head in dismay. "Damn, the rumors are true. You really like to get straight down to business."

"Because everyone knows it's all I give a shit about."

"Well, that's great." Bigsby sat forward. "Because I have a big moneymaking venture you'll love."

I gave a halfhearted shrug. "There's nothing you can offer me that I don't already have, Bigsby."

Bigsby crossed and uncrossed his leg. "How about the Port District?"

"I'm listening," I replied in a sharp tone.

His jaw tightened. "As you know, I'll be New York City's next mayor."

"That statement is highly debatable, but continue," I muttered.

"When I'm mayor"—anger flashed across Bigsby's eyes—"I will own the city, including the port."

Shit just got very interesting. The Port District of New York and New Jersey encompassed part of seventeen counties in the region.

"Keep going," I ordered tonelessly.

Bigsby's posture stiffened. "I need your overseas connections for a little matter on my end." He cleared his throat loudly. "I understand from my sources that you're a minor stakeholder in Sin Michaels Corporation."

I chuckled darkly. Bigsby was fishing for information. He'd have to work fucking harder to get anything from me.

"Minor? I own the business. And her," I replied calmly. "Cut to the chase, Calhoune. What do you want?"

Bigsby's body tightened as he ran his hand over his salt-and-pepper hair with agitation. "I've also been informed you're set to manufacture in Thailand, and your first run to the United States will be in weeks."

"And?" I inclined my head for him to continue.

Bigsby cleared his throat. "I just need a small area within your cargo shipment to put my merchandise. If you agree, I'll ensure there are no issues at the port when your shipment arrives."

"I see. So, if I don't agree, you'll make it complicated and expensive to get my merchandise into New York?" The final words were furious and guttural.

The chunky gold ruby-and-diamond-encrusted horseshoe ring on Bigsby's middle finger glinted as he nervously adjusted his cuff. "That could be a real possibility."

Glancing up from his ring, I asked, "What type of merchandise?"

"Does it matter?" He pressed his lips together.

My nostrils flared. "I'm not going to blindly ship merchandise without knowing exactly what it is, especially if it's illegal."

"My informants tell me you don't have issues with getting your hands dirty." He cleared his throat and leaned forward in emphasis. "That's why I'm coming to you with this sensitive matter."

"Sensitive matter? I guess that's code for pimping out girls to your rich friends," I stated matter-of-factly.

Bigsby's mouth hung open. "How did you—" He sputtered over the words.

I cut him off. "My connections love to talk." I left out the fact that the majority of my information came from a now-dead Ben Vargos. "Especially when they're paying a shitload of money to fuck pretty college girls in any way and anywhere they want." I paused for a moment. "Let's cut to the chase, shall we? I know you're running women," I stated bluntly. "I don't deal in sex trafficking. So my response to your business offer is fuck no."

The vein along Bigsby's jaw pulsed rapidly. "I'll give you a thirty-percent cut. That's a deal worth five hundred million dollars."

"I'm accepting all the risk. I want a fifty-fifty split." I scrutinized Bigsby, assessing his level of desperation.

He gawked at me, speechless, before breaking eye contact and then glaring at me. "Deal."

I smirked. He was desperate to accept my throat-cutting deal.

Bigsby stood up, fidgeting. "Will there be an issue with Ms. Michaels?"

"As I told you, I own both the company and her," I stated without any emotion.

Bigsby smiled, but it didn't quite reach his eyes. "Excellent. We'll be talking, McKay," he added before marching out.

I waited for the elevator ding, the signal that Bigsby was gone. "I should have known what that piece of shit was up to." I slapped my palm down on the desk with a resounding noise.

Now Bigsby's interest in Sin's business made more sense. No one would ever suspect a naïve designer would be part of a sex-trafficking ring. Frankly, Bigsby's plan was brilliant.

Ram trudged over to the bar. He poured a drink, a very strong one, and gulped it. "I seriously wanted to rip out his windpipe. That unscrupulous fuck is hiding Jeff's location." He squeezed the glass in his hand. "I swear, if Jeff killed my sister, I'll…" His eyes took on a steely glint.

Ram had been blaming himself for her disappearance, for not stepping in when Lexis had gushed about the perfect guy she'd met at a party near campus. The guy, Jeff Barolo, had become Lexis's boyfriend after dating her for only two weeks.

I tightened my fists. "Don't even fucking think it."

It was hard as hell to watch my level-headed friend slowly becoming emotionally unhinged. We both knew the odds of Lexis being alive were slim, but I was still optimistic. It didn't matter that Lexis had made a lot of fucked-up decisions—dropping out of college and running away with Jeff. She didn't deserve to die.

I strode from my leather chair to the bar, pouring myself a scotch. "We're getting closer to finding Lexis—alive."

Rocco chimed in with his brows knitted. "The sooner we find her, the better, bro."

Kevin, my tech genius, burst into the room. "Listen to this. Bigsby just made a call," he exclaimed excitedly, holding his laptop in one hand.

Ram's eyes grew wide. "How the hell did you record it so fast?"

Kevin's forehead creased into a frown. "I set up a fake cell phone tower, allowing me to spy on him," he stated nonchalantly.

Rocco's stoic expression turned grim. "We're all going to fucking jail."

Kevin squinted. "Only idiots get caught."

"Will you two just shut the hell up?" I snapped. "Kevin, play it."

Kevin pressed a key on his laptop.

Bigsby's voice began. "Jeff, good news. I just made a deal with that bastard McKay."

"Good. I'm tired of clients whining about needing new girls," Jeff remarked.

"I'll make arrangements to move the goods, but there's only one loose end. I need you to break in to Sin's house by tomorrow night and find that damn ledger. It's the only leverage I still have on this city," Bigsby finished.

"No problem. But what do you want me to do about Sin if she's home?" Jeff asked.

"If she gets in the way, rough her up a little, but don't kill her. I still need her alive," Bigsby warned before disconnecting.

What the hell? Rough her up? Oh, fuck no.

I eyed Kevin. "I need answers now. What's the connection between Sin and Bigsby?"

"I'm waiting for my informant to get back to me," Kevin replied.

"You've been working on getting information for days. What's the fucking holdup?" I mashed my lips together. "Call your connection. Triple the amount of money for a solid lead."

Kevin's mouth gaped open. "Shit. Triple?"

"Do it," I responded in a deadly voice.

Kevin pulled out his cell and tapped it. "I need that info I requested *now*," he demanded to the person on the phone. "No more time. I don't give a shit what you're working on." He peered at me, holding up four fingers.

His greedy informant was asking for quadruple the standard rate. I nodded in agreement.

"You got it," Kevin told the informant. "Now get me the fucking info." He paced back and forth with his cell pressed against his ear. "Like I give a shit what you're in the middle of. Move it."

Pinching the bridge of my nose, I waited while Kevin continued to gather intel.

Kevin's face stilled. "Holy shit! Are you sure?" He frowned. "Okay. Yes." He paused. "Yes, I got it. But I want you to keep working that angle." He knitted his brows, his bewilderment evident, as he shoved his cell into his pocket.

I crossed my arms, looking at Kevin as he plopped down on the edge of the desk.

"So?"

Kevin raked a hand over his face. "In the eighties, Bigsby ran a prostitution ring out of his strip joint."

I glared at him. "That's it?"

Kevin held up his hand. "I'm not finished."

"That's a relief, because your intel is straight-up garbage," Ram muttered.

Kevin shot him a nasty glare. "Anyway, this is where things get interesting. Bigsby started rolling with some powerful NYC players. I'm talking about politicians, judges, and Wall Street executives."

"That doesn't make sense." Rocco interrupted. "There's no way in hell a thug like Bigsby could get in good with rich guys."

"He could if he was supplying them with girls for sex," I rebutted.

As the son of a stripper, I'd learned fast about the underbelly of strip clubs. Bitterness filled my mouth as I thought about the nights when Mom would bring me into work because she was too broke to pay for a babysitter. My nose wrinkled with distaste as the faces of the women she'd worked with flashed through my head—young, reeking of alcohol, junkies with eyes glazed over. I'd caught them on their knees, giving blow jobs to customers in dark corners or hallways.

"That's exactly what Bigsby was doing, and he was raking in tons of money. Then, for some unknown reason, he and his business partner went their separate ways." Kevin regarded me smugly. "Guess who his partner was?"

"Sin's father," I snapped.

Ram arched a brow. "Which one?"

I sighed heavily.

Kevin's previous investigation into Sin's family background unearthed that she had two birth certificates, each one showing a different set of parents. The first birth certificate had her father listed as Ian Michaels and her mother as Grace Michaels. The second certificate had her father listed as Greer Lorne Cruickshank and her mother as Aubrey Cruickshank.

"Greer Lorne Cruickshank," Kevin replied. "After Greer and Bigsby dissolved their business partnership, Greer was found dead in an apartment fire."

I bunched my shoulders, but I kept my face expressionless. "Cruickshank?" I bit back the expletive hovering on my tongue.

What the hell?

Cruickshank was the person Bigsby had bragged about to Mom before killing her.

Ram's brows drew together. "What are the circumstances of the fire?"

"Arson," Kevin replied flatly. "Bigsby mysteriously disappeared after that."

I stiffened my shoulders. "Now he's back, and the fucker reinvented himself."

Rocco scratched his chin. "I don't get it. Why would Bigsby run for mayor and risk his past being dredged up? That's political suicide."

"What past?" Kevin's brows furrowed. "Do you know how hard it was for me just to get this much information on him?" He shook his head. "It took a shitload of money and power to clean his record. Now, he looks like some fucking altar boy."

"And he seems untouchable." I tapped my fingers against the desk while contemplating the situation. "The ledger must be the only evidence linking him to his former life."

Knowing what I knew so far about Bigsby, I knew he had come too far to let his new life disintegrate, which meant Sin's safety was in serious jeopardy if she had the ledger.

"I want that damn ledger," I hissed before glancing over at Rocco. "You and Max stake out Sin's house. No need for us to get our hands dirty on this one. Just wait for that idiot Jeff to break in and find the ledger. Snatch him when you see it in his hand."

Ram inclined his head toward me. "And what are you going to do about Sin?"

My face hardened, and I drew up to my full, intimidating height. "Let me worry about that."

CHAPTER 5
SINTHIA

After sculpting and draping the fabric directly onto the mannequin, I stepped back with a critical eye. "Not bad," I mumbled under my breath.

Normally, I'd sculpt directly onto my body while sitting in front of a mirror and ask my intern, Giselle, to take a picture of me to capture the shape when it was pinned to me. Draping was almost as good but a tad bit slower.

Turning around, I threw a stray piece of fabric into a wooden box with rattan trim. I couldn't help smiling at the clothes hanging on the rows of racks in part of my four-thousand-square-foot townhouse. I was practically giddy from seeing my designs come to life right in front of my eyes.

Damn! I can't believe my collection is almost complete.

Rubbing my stiff neck with my fingers, I longed for a soak in a hot tub of lavender-scented bath salts, which was unlikely to happen tonight. I had been working nonstop for days. It had been both exciting and exhausting. There were moments when the stress from pushing myself so hard had driven me to near breaking point, but I'd continued. It had been a challenge, but it was my dream. It was make-or-break time, and I had no intention of failing.

I had designed around twenty different outfits, ranging from shredded organza dresses with flowers at the hem, cobweb gowns fluttering from neck to floor, crystal tank tops over short sequined skirts, to peacock-print silk dresses tumbling off one shoulder. But there were five more over-the-top pieces to go.

Shit.

I needed to work faster, but I was getting sidetracked by all the small details, like checking email, making phone calls, and keeping track of upcoming meetings.

Picking up my cell, I scrolled through my contacts, stopping on my as-needed intern. She was a whiz at helping me get as organized as possible.

"Hi, Sin. Great to hear from you. What's up?"

"Help! I'm up to my elbows in fabric."

Giselle laughed. "Whatever you need. I've been waiting for your call."

I sighed. "Things have gotten really complicated recently. The good news is I just got the thumbs-up from my business partner to hire extra help."

"When do you need me?" Giselle posed.

I flicked through the calendar on my tablet. "Today's already Friday. I'll give you the weekend to rest up and get ready to start working your ass off on Monday. We'll be working twenty-four seven, so be prepared to spend the night when needed. I have five more pieces I need to complete before I sit down with the buying and marketing teams to decide which designs will make the final cut." I made it sound simple, but eliminating designs would be a tiring process, involving fitting sessions and making alterations to clothes when needed.

But I eagerly anticipated the final stage—when my collection would go on sale.

"I'm so excited," Giselle squealed. "See you on Monday."

I sat down at my workstation. "Thanks, Giselle."

One more task was checked off my mounting to-do list, but it seemed like the more I accomplished, the more I added.

Trying to calm the anxious ball of energy bouncing around in my gut, I took a deep, cleansing breath. It didn't help. I jumped up, pulling my hair into a tight ponytail while pacing back and forth.

What the hell is wrong with me?

Things were going exactly the way I wanted. Finally.

Then a scary thought flashed through my head. I knew exactly what was wrong.

Core McKay.

Dammit.

Something had to give before I lost my ever-loving mind.

I had been masturbating nonstop, like a raging hormonal high schooler, but it still hadn't been enough to sate the palpable desire to fuck him senseless. Maybe Jade was right. I should just concede to my base urges and have sex with him. Yep, one hard round of hot and sweaty fucking would be enough to extinguish this insane fixation.

My cell buzzed.

"Hello?" I answered.

"Hello, Sin," Core responded in that wickedly sexy voice that always seemed to make my cunt clench, hard.

I cleared my throat. "What do you want, Core?"

"You on my bed with my face between your gorgeous legs."

The words, the sheer certainty in his rich voice, sent heat stabbing through me. *Shit. I'm seriously in lust with this man.*

"Not going to happen, Core."

He laughed. "Yet."

There was a fluttering in my stomach. "Ever," I finished.

"And just when things were going so well between us, you have to turn this into a fight."

"I'm working," I snapped with way more harshness than intended.

"I'm sending over a surprise for you."

My body stilled. "I don't like surprises." My pounding heartbeat grew loud in my ears.

He laughed huskily. "Liar."

I grimaced. "You know you're an ass, right?"

My doorbell rang.

"So I've been told," he responded dryly. "Go answer the door."

The line went dead.

Prowling over to the door with anxiousness and anticipation curled up in the pit of my stomach, I peered through the peephole. Standing at my door was a woman with sleek, flaming-red tresses left loose around her shoulders. Opening the door, I was stunned by her striking facial features—her dark autumn skin tone contrasted with her red hair, giving her an exotic vibe. Her eyes were shielded by aviators.

"Yes?" I asked, shaking myself out of my blossoming girl crush.

The woman whipped off her sunglasses, smiling impishly. "Sin Michaels?"

I cocked my head to the side. "Uh-huh."

Her almond-shaped black eyes lit with a twinkle of mischief. "I must say, you're even more gorgeous in person."

Arching a brow, I said, "Thank you?"

She stuck out her hand. "I'm Zuri, Core McKay's well-paid minion."

"Okay." Backing away, I eyed her hand like it was a snake.

Zuri shrugged before letting it drop.

"So what does my lord and master want now? A pint of blood? My firstborn?"

Zuri responded with a husky laugh. "Nope. Just your undying obedience to the king."

"Ain't happening."

"Wow. I think you and I are going to be besties. Can I come in?" she pleaded huskily.

I ran my eyes over her while rubbing an ear.

"Pretty please?" Zuri pouted playfully.

I gestured her in. "Sure."

A genuine smile lit up her face before she strutted past me, working skintight jeans and an off-the-shoulder black top. Her outfit was teamed with a mini top-handle bag, a small black shopping bag, and chic ankle boots. Essentially, she resembled a celebrity who had just jetted in from London. And I looked like death warmed over with my scrubbed-clean face and dark circles under my eyes.

She sucked in a quick breath. "Wow, beautiful place, Sin." Arching down, she brushed her fingers across the old worn trunk positioned next to my workstation like an accent piece. "Vintage?"

"No." I laughed. "Just some ratty old trunk that used to belong to my father."

Zuri stood up. "Things of sentimental value are always the most treasured pieces. Reminds you of where you've come from."

I smiled slightly. "So true."

Dad's trunk used to evoke all the sad memories associated with losing him so suddenly. But after years of mourning his loss, I'd decided to celebrate his life by pulling it out of hiding from the closet in my guest bedroom. Now, I admired it every day. It was a source of inspiration to never give up on my dream of making my collection a reality. Dad would have wanted me to be happy and successful, both in life and in business. His trunk was that constant reminder.

"My dad's trunk had more of an interesting life than most people I know. It was dragged around the country to every place we moved to."

The scratched leather was so worn and dirty that I couldn't tell the original color.

"Sounds like happy family memories. I wish we all could be that lucky," Zuri remarked in a monotone voice. Suddenly, she swayed over to the racks of hanging clothes. "Sin," she squealed dramatically. "You're the fucking Michelangelo of fashion." She touched the red cable-knit dress with a bustle and swath of chiffon peeking naughtily from its backside. "I've never seen anything this spectacular." She twirled to face me with a wide smile. "I can't wait to buy every damn piece."

"Thanks." Warmth radiated throughout my body. My collection was an homage to my twisted sensibility and willful disregard of conventional fashion. They were pieces designed by a woman, not a man's fantasy of women.

With raised eyebrows, she asked, "Is your collection complete?"

"Nope. I have five more pieces to go," I replied before padding over to the kitchen and grabbing a bottle of sparkling water from the refrigerator. "Would you like one?"

"No, thanks." Zuri moved away from my work area, surveying my townhouse. Without invitation, she sank down onto my favorite chaise, crossing her long legs and making herself at home.

I leaned a hip against the kitchen counter, and Zuri and I watched each other silently. Strangely, it wasn't a tense and awkward moment. It was more of a should-I-like-you analysis. Grudgingly, I concluded that I liked her so far. She nodded and smiled as if she'd also come to the same conclusion about me.

"So, Zuri, why are you here?"

"Honestly?" She pursed her bright-red pouty lips. "I just had to meet the woman who has Core all grumpy and sexually frustrated."

I strode over, sitting down in the plush chair directly across from her. "I'm pretty sure that fucker is always grumpy." I curled my feet under me. "And sexually frustrated? I highly doubt it. He looks like he gets knee-deep in pussy on a pretty regular basis."

"Fucker?" Zuri burst out laughing. "Wait till I tell the team Core has a new nickname." She chortled so hard a tear trickled at the corner of her eye.

I shrugged. "Just call it as I see it."

She sobered up. "But the knee-deep in sex part is totally off base. Well, at least recently." Her eyes twinkled. She snapped her fingers. "Oh, I almost forgot the real reason for my visit. Over there."

She gestured to the bag next to my chair. It was a small black shopping bag from an expensive and exclusive boutique in SoHo that catered to ultra-rich socialites and edgy celebrities. It wasn't unusual to see clothes from there on the red carpet. It was also a boutique I absolutely loved.

"It's a gift from Core."

"What type of gift?" My chest tightened.

Zuri's eyes gleamed. "Open it and find out."

The interior of my mouth went dry as I grabbed the bag. Reaching in, I pulled out an entirely translucent dress. I gasped. It was the dress I had drooled over when I first saw it in my favorite fashion magazine. I just couldn't rationalize paying the exorbitant price tag. Standing up, I held the knee-length backless mesh ensemble against my body. The dress was a little bit scandalous. Just fishnet and crystals and a couple of fingers crossed. I loved everything about it.

"Is it the correct size?" Zuri leaned forward.

Peeking at the tag, my pulse raced. "Surprisingly, yes, but how did you—"

"Me? No," she interrupted. "Core picked out the dress."

As I traced my fingers over the dress, there was a lightness in my chest. "I'm not sure—"

Zuri sighed heavily. "Girl, please don't say you're refusing that dress of absolute perfection."

"Oh, I'm accepting it." I laughed throatily. "I'm not fucking crazy. I've been stalking this dress for a while. What I meant was I'm just not sure why Core sent it." It was the truth. I had no intention of sending the dress back. I wanted it. Badly.

"There's a note inside the bag."

Digging inside the bag and pulling out the stark-white card, I read it aloud, "My driver will be at your house tonight at 10:30 p.m. sharp. C.M." Snorting, I tossed the card back inside the bag. "Well, what he wants and what he'll get are two different damn things."

"What Core wants, Core gets. Believe me." She smiled devilishly. "Must be that alpha-crazy thing he's got going on."

I drummed my foot against the floor. "And exactly where is Core taking me?"

"You've been cordially invited to the McKay Club's private playground, Noire."

Adrenaline rushed through my body. "A fancy name for the anything-goes section."

She winked at me. "More like anything you want."

"So I've heard from the gossip hags."

"Sweetie, the gossip is nowhere near the reality of Noire. It's total sexual chaos." Her cell beeped. She pulled it out of her handbag, gazing at it with a frown before she tapped out a text. "I've got to go." She stood up, flipping her hair over her shoulder. "I'll see you tonight."

"Wait a minute." My voice wavered. "I didn't say I was going."

A knowing smile curved Zuri's full lips. "Sin, that twinkle of excitement in your eyes says it all." She winked at me. "See you tonight," she finished before gliding away.

CHAPTER 6
SINTHIA

I mumbled aloud, "I'm just going to play nice with Core, but absolutely no sex."

Leaning against my vanity with my fingers trembling, I finished my makeup with a bold red lip and eyes decorated in catlike flicks. And just when I thought I'd actually convinced myself about my no-sex rule, a vision of Core's hands snaking up my thighs and spreading them wide flashed through my mind.

"Dammit." I slammed my palm against the cold granite.

Who am I fooling?

I was most definitely going to have sex with him tonight—but just one round of toe-curling sex, nothing more. I couldn't allow myself to hope for more. I had been down that road before, picking up the pieces from hurt and heartache. I gritted my teeth. I had no intention of living through that car wreck ever again.

Stepping back, I smiled prettily at the mirror while clasping the silver bracelet Dad gave me for my birthday around my wrist before marching into my bedroom. I eyed the gorgeous dress lying across the bed. It was most definitely a dress picked out by a lover. The thought of Core selecting the dress with my body in mind made the liquid heat rage between my thighs.

After slipping on my flesh-toned thong, I skipped wearing a bra. It would stick out like a sore thumb in this barely there slinky, sheer number. Thank God the bodice of the dress was designed to pull up the voluptuous swell of my breasts, similar to the support of a bra. I slid the dress over my head, and it glided down my body like heavy silk. Giving myself a once-over in the mirror, I fell in love with the dress all over again. It was sexy and naughty, and it embodied the persona I needed tonight.

Seductress on the prowl.

Man-eater.

Woman ready to take Core by the balls…literally.

I strode out of my townhouse and down the stairs toward the driver waiting patiently while leaning against a sleek black limo.

He pushed away, tilting his head toward me. "Good evening, Ms. Michaels." He studied at me from head to toe with an appreciative gleam in his eyes while opening the back door.

"Thank you," I replied, maneuvering into the limo.

Shutting the door, he scampered around to the driver's side before sliding in.

"My name is Ace," he offered before turning the key and revving the engine.

"Hi, Ace," I returned before staring through the window, watching him drive smoothly into the Manhattan traffic.

After a few minutes of zipping in and out of the snarl of taxicabs and buses, Ace pulled up in front of the McKay Club.

Anxiously, I smoothed out the nonexistent wrinkles in my dress, waiting for Ace to open my door. Stepping out, I bit my bottom lip while staring at the nondescript warehouse that didn't have any of the fanfare of other clubs of this caliber. No lines were queued up behind the red velvet rope.

"Have a good time, Ms. Michaels."

"Thanks, Ace," I said before strutting up to a man wearing smart business attire and a clear Secret Service earpiece.

"Welcome to the McKay Club, Ms. Michaels." He greeted me as if he'd been waiting all night to see me. "When you step into the lobby, you'll find our door host stationed directly in front of the entrance to Noire." He gestured toward my wrist and then placed a black wristband around it before stepping aside.

"Thank you," I responded before entering the club.

I surveyed the scene, which was a little different from the last time I'd visited. The lobby was lit with what must have been thousands of candles. My gaze wandered to the man standing guard before an entrance draped with expensive-looking fabric as a guest flashed a black-and-gold wristband.

The door host shook his head. "Sorry. This area is members only."

Advancing across the space, the door host glanced down at my ink-black wristband and promptly stepped aside with a, "Noire is down the stairs." He pulled aside the fabric, allowing me entry.

The softly lit corridor with a sloped, mirrored ceiling and dark brick walls was different from anything I'd seen.

My stomach fluttered with anticipation as I thought of what lay ahead. With my sky-high heels tapping down the mirror-lined staircase, it didn't take me long to reach the Noire lounge. Immediately, I was attracted to the dazzling bar that encircled an illuminated champagne tower, and I decided to head toward it.

Once firmly planted in front of it, I beckoned the bartender. "Moscato and vodka."

He nodded before scampering away.

Tapping my foot to the music, I glanced around, stopping at the DJ tucked artfully in the corner. The dance floor was crowded with barely dressed bodies gyrating to the hard-hitting beat. Guests on the catwalk and semi-private second-floor mezzanine seating area eyed the partiers below. The multilevel space was like eye candy. Scantily dressed servers flittered around the edges of the dance floor, holding trays of champagne, mints, and condoms. I scanned around to my right, and nestled around the perimeter of the main level were harem-like tented booths draped with luxurious heavy silk fabric.

My breath hitched when I saw a blond woman I recognized from a popular television show leading a half-naked buff man by the hand into one of the tents. Normally, I would have felt like a total pervert watching the couple, but I knew this was the whole point of Noire—to watch and be watched. So like a deer in headlights, I gawked as the curvy blonde motioned him to his knees. Balancing on one leg, she flipped her other leg over his shoulder while he wrapped an arm around her waist to steady her, and then he leaned forward, devouring her center like he hadn't eaten in days.

"Holy shit," I mumbled under my breath.

So engrossed in the sexual antics, I hadn't even noticed Zuri's approach until she was standing directly in my path with a champagne flute in her hand. Leggy Zuri had donned a patterned cutout leather dress and teamed it with cerulean shoes.

Letting out a loud breath, I gestured for her to move aside. "Zuri, you're interrupting the best sex show ever."

Zuri scooted to my side. "So I see you're enjoying the sexcapade."

The couple had closed the tent.

"I was."

Not that I was into public sex-play myself, but I respected the boldness of others who got off on it.

I felt a soft tap on my shoulder. Peeping over it, I saw the bartender staring at me.

"Your drink." He smiled at Zuri. "Hi, Zuri."

"Hey, Scott. This is Sin. She's Core's guest. Give her anything her heart desires."

"Got it," Scott replied before hustling over to a beckoning guest.

Picking up my drink, I pressed my back against the bar. I didn't want to miss a single thing. Sipping the contents in my glass, I eyed Zuri, who was swaying seductively to the music with her cloud of shiny red hair floating around her.

"By the way, welcome to Noire." She gave me an impish grin. "I'm loving that dress on you."

"What can I say? Core does know the way to my heart. A fuck-me dress gets me every time."

Sipping my drink, I glanced around the club, pretending not to be searching for Core. My body pulsed with arousal when I found him making his way through the crowd. Biting my bottom lip, I gave him a slow once-over.

"Damn, he sure knows how to make cunts wet without even trying," I blurted.

Even among the gorgeous men littering the room, Core didn't blend. He stood out like a sexy marauding Viking, ready to conquer, destroy, and fuck any woman in his path.

I ached to be that woman.

"That he does," Zuri responded.

And as if he felt me eye-fucking him, he pivoted, staring at me, his eyes smoldering with intensity. Shamelessly, I drank in the magnificence of Core like a thirsty woman in a desert. My heart was beating like I'd just run fifty miles in thirty seconds while Core observed me.

Damn, I want to lick every inch of him.

Three words described Core—hotness and dripping sex. From his black tailored slacks that molded over his sculptured thighs to the crisp black shirt that fit across his magnificent, broad chest, I knew without a doubt there would be no denying him, no running away from the inevitable. I was going to fuck Core. My panties soaked and nipples hard as rocks, with deliberate effort, I broke eye contact with him.

Zuri stared at me. "Jesus, you do like him."

I eyed her right back. "No comment."

"There's no shame in admitting it. He's hot but a little rough around the edges." She pursed her full lips.

"A little?" I arched a brow. "You mean a lot."

Zuri shrugged. "He's not perfect, but none of us is."

I took a sip of my drink. "So how long have you been…working for him?"

Zuri snorted. "Is that your polite way of asking me if I've ever fucked him?"

I arched a brow. "Yep."

"We've never had sex. Truth be told, I've never thought of him that way. And he considers me to be a pain-in-the-ass baby sister."

Glancing back at him, I bit my lower lip, pondering why I gave a shit who he'd fucked. Then a horrible thought flashed through my head. *Exactly how many women has Core sent invitations and dresses to?* "Lots of women," I muttered, my stomach hardening.

Zuri eyed me shrewdly. "I know what you're thinking, and it's not like that. Core is very picky."

I wasn't quite sure if I believed that, but so far, Zuri had been straight up with me. Butterflies fluttered in my stomach. Needing all the liquid courage I could muster, I drained my glass and waited for his approach. But then the unthinkable happened. Core strode away.

My breath hitched before turning to Zuri. "Where the fuck is he going?"

Zuri's grin flickered so quickly I almost didn't see it. "It seems like Core wants you to come over and play." It was a statement more than a question.

My heart raced with excitement at the thought of pursuing Core like most men I'd desired. The problem was he wasn't most men. He wouldn't allow me to use him like a one-night stand or fucktoy. No, the rules of engagement between Core and me would be way different.

I flushed angrily. "There is no way I'm fucking him in public. I like my sexual encounters to be private."

Zuri chuckled. "So does he."

I pressed my lips together in a slight grimace. "That's surprising." I watched for any signs of deceit before laying my cards on the table. "Let's cut to the chase, Zuri. You know him way better than I do, and frankly, I'm way out of my depth right now, so—"

Zuri tilted her head. "You're asking for advice?"

"Yes."

"It's simple." Zuri shrugged. "If you want him, then hightail your sexy ass over there and get him."

"Seems deceptively simple," I responded with a weighted sigh.

Core was a predator, an alpha, savvy and calculating in everything he did, but it was too fucking late for me to walk away. Our fates had been sealed from the first moment we met.

Core and I were inevitable.

She offered a bemused smile. "Most things worth having are."

I licked my bottom lip, contemplating my next move while watching Core slice through the Noire crowd. He stopped to speak to several people. A woman boldly touched his arm. He ignored her, making a beeline through the elite crowd and stepping toward the waiting elevator guarded by two men. He said something to one, who eyed me and nodded before Core disappeared inside the closing elevator.

Zuri smiled. "Go on. He'll be waiting for you up in his VIP suite."

"What does he like?" I asked bluntly.

Zuri sipped her champagne. "Results."

CHAPTER 7
SINTHIA

With no further words, I placed my glass on the bar and weaved my way across the dance floor. The sultriness of the air was palpable as bodies pressed against each other in unabashed lust and hedonism. Threesomes, women kissing women, men licking and sucking men, nude bodies slick from the heat of the pulsating energy surrounding them—it was sexual indulgence with no judgment.

Continuing my trek, I stood before the two highly visible men stationed by the elevator.

"Hello, Ms. Michaels," they greeted in unison. One gently ushered me into the elevator, while the other pressed a button on the control panel. "Upstairs is McKay's VIP suite. Just step out of the elevator. The entire suite is all one level."

The sound of music was silenced by the closing door. The ride to Core's suite was short, and the door slid open with a ding. I stepped off the elevator and landed in the opulent area before proceeding farther. I sucked in several deep breaths to calm myself when I saw Core sitting on the edge of a huge desk. His sleeves were rolled up, displaying his well-defined, tattooed forearms. My knees almost buckled from his sheer perfection.

Shit, no man should exude so much sex appeal.

Core was dark, hard, deadly, and absolutely yummy. A strange tingling sensation gripped my body like a vise as I fantasized about Core with his clothes off, my wrists pinned down by his big, powerful hands, and my legs curved around his waist while he fucked me until I blacked out.

God, I can't wait to see him completely nude.

He widened his long legs, giving me a once-over. "You're so fucking beautiful." His voice rumbled.

My body quivered with a desire I'd never felt before. "I've been called many things—exotic, hot, sexy—but never beautiful."

He slowly appraised my body. "Real beauty is quiet. The women I find most beautiful are the ones who aren't trying."

My stomach flip-flopped from the deepness of his words. They were both raw and sincere.

Damn, Core is a side of sexy trouble.

"And you in that dress is simply perfection. Now all I can think about is pulling it up and slipping my cock into your wet cunt."

My mouth dropped open as I took in a harsh breath. The vision of me naked, spread-eagled on his bed, his sexy gray eyes glazed over with lust made my folds warm and moist.

"Fuck, that's hot." My breathless response slipped out before I could stop it.

Silently, Core examined me but made no attempt to move from the edge of the desk. He was like a tiger stalking his prey, and for the first time in my life, I felt uncomfortable and undecided about my next move.

Embarrassingly, most of my previous sexual encounters had been fast and hard with no foreplay required. Pretty much wham, bam, thank you, ma'am. But I suspected Core expected a lot more from me.

I squeezed my eyes shut, trying to channel the anxiety out of my body. When that didn't work, I swayed over to the floor-to-ceiling window. Peering through the glass, I realized the vantage point gave me an excellent view of everything in Noire. It was Core's very own peep show. My eyes darted to the catwalk and then did a double take at the lone couple standing on it. Their bodies were wrapped around each other, and mouths were licking and sucking in the most erotic kiss I'd ever seen.

"Can they see in here?" I inquired.

"It's custom glass. We can see out, but they cannot see in." There was a long pause. "Having second thoughts, darling?"

"None," I replied before feeling the heat from Core's body behind me.

"If you decide to stay, either you're a hundred percent in, or you're out."

He was dark and all-consuming. He was everything I shouldn't want in a man, but damn, I craved him.

"Unlike our business arrangement, this partnership will be fifty-fifty, Core."

"Deal," he hissed against my ear before strong hands gripped my hips, yanking me against his chest. His alluring scent of amber and sandalwood engulfed me.

Biting my lip, I forced myself to focus on the passionate couple. The man pulled away from the woman. He reached for his belt, and he opened it frantically. Reaching inside, he pulled his arousal free as the woman's knees hit the ground. His hips thrust forward, and his cock pushed between her lips.

Core shifted his stance. His thighs spread wide on either side of my legs. "Do you like watching, Sin?" His lips kissed my neck, and his sharp teeth nipped the sensitive skin.

My mind whispered, *Yes.*

But it wasn't just the act of watching. It was Core's presence and the way his hard body felt pressed against mine. My head arched back, resting against his hard chest. A wave of arousal washed over me when his hands squeezed my hips. His firm male heat nudged against the small of my back.

"You see how she's enjoying having him in her mouth? There's no force. He's letting her take what she needs." Slowly, he moved one hand from my hip, using it to trace a finger across my wet lips. "Has your mouth ever been taken?"

A delicious shiver of arousal ran down my spine. "Yes," I whispered before my tongue darted out to lick the pad of his callused finger.

He slid his finger between my lips, moving it in and out. "But with me, your mouth will be a virgin." His finger stilled before falling away. "Watch them, Sin," Core commanded.

I pushed my head back up, and through slitted eyes, I centered on the woman sensually deep-throating her lover. A moan escaped my lips as Core grabbed both my hands, spreading them against the cool glass like it was a stickup.

"Do you want to suck my cock, Sin?"

His seductive words made me inhale sharply. His touch, his smell, his voice were driving me toward the edge of sheer sensual insanity. Bit by bit, I was losing control to him.

"Yes," I hissed. Moisture trickled between my legs. My hips surged forward and then back.

He chuckled wickedly, dropping his hand from on top of mine. I bit back a whimper of lust as Core's hand traced my areolae and taut nipples, trailing his fingers back and forth over the peaks, pinching them hard. His every touch felt hardwired to my core. I wanted to come right on the spot. I'd never had anyone do something so erotic to me.

My hips rolled as I neared orgasm.

"Beg to suck my cock, Sin." The command in his voice was obvious.

Lust and fear curled into my stomach. It sent ripples of desire rushing through my body. Effortlessly, Core was dominating me.

"I can't think—" My voice was barely over a whisper.

Dropping his hand from my breast, he burrowed his fingers into my hair, yanking my head back. "Listen to your body," he growled into my ear.

My sex flexed as his grip tightened. Sexual desire coiled so hard that my stomach spasmed.

His breath caressed my neck. "I want you to crave the feel of my hard cock fucking your mouth."

The power of his words literally made my knees buckle. Core

rotated me to face him. I shivered from the coolness of the glass pressed against my back.

My breath stopped at the intense hunger in his eyes as he stroked a finger down my cheek, trailing to my bottom lip. I jerked at the contact.

"Don't move," he ordered. "I will give you what you need, not what you want."

He slid his hands to my jaw, and he tilted his head before settling his lips across my mouth. My breath caught. His grip on my jaw contracted. He slid his tongue between my teeth. His kiss was long, slow, and deep—the stamp of his possession. No one had ever kissed me like this.

Jesus, I'm so fucked.

He sucked my tongue into his mouth. My stomach contracted as a rush of heat flooded my entire body. My hands wrapped tightly around his lean waist. Lust curled deep into my damp, moist, needy place. Core was slowly crumbling my resolve to remain emotionally detached.

He pulled his lips away from mine but kept his hand firmly controlling my head. He smiled like the devil reincarnated. In one sinuous motion, he released his hold and tugged up the hem of my dress, clutching both of my ass cheeks.

I leaned up, my teeth grazing his throat, before I inched back ever so slightly. Releasing one hand from his waist, I grazed his face with the backs of my fingers, moving from his cheek to his full lips. As I caressed his chiseled mouth with my fingers, he opened his lips and licked my knuckle with just a quick flick of his warm tongue. A feeling of excitement fluttered like butterflies in the pit of my stomach. The sensation ratcheted up my emotions like a kid on a roller coaster.

He fastened his mouth on mine. My womanhood was drenched, with everything inside me shattering from his kiss. I desperately clutched his shoulders with my hand to anchor myself. My soft lips were on his hard ones. A stinging nip of his teeth made me open my mouth, and he plunged in, his tongue stroking mine.

There was no gentleness in Core. That trait should have sent me stampeding away, but instead, like a junkie, it heightened my insatiable need to submit to him. I dug my nails into his muscular shoulder as the searing need burned between my legs.

Nudging my legs apart, he moved between them. With his hands on my ass, he slid me closer until my sex rubbed across the aching bulge in his pants. Our kiss deepened. I rubbed against his hard-on with a slow and steady motion.

Dropping his hold on me, he said, "Sin, get on your knees." His voice was deep and caressing, sliding across my skin like silk.

My stomach rolled with anxiousness as I leaped into the pits of scorching hell and slid to my knees. With trembling fingers, I unbuckled his belt and unzipped his pants.

Sweet Jesus, no underwear.

He stared at me with his penetrating gaze. "Release my cock."

I shivered as I touched his hardness. He was long and beautifully thick. When he was all out, I stroked him gently.

"Damn," I whispered.

He was the epitome of fucking masculine perfection. His engorged, thick manhood stretched taut, almost past his navel. The thick, round crown glistened with a small drop of moisture. His balls were tight with arousal.

My cunt tingled, and my peaks puckered as I craved the salty taste of him. Aggressively, I grabbed his manhood with both hands, feeling the hardness swell. Massaging the smooth, hot column of flesh between my fingers, I leaned forward to take the swollen head into my greedy mouth when he grasped my hair, snatching my head back.

Our eyes locked.

"Ask for permission." He kept his voice low and soft but left no room for doubt that he'd issued an order.

My jaw dropped. "What?"

"You heard me."

I tried to get away from his grasp, but his fingers tightened.

"Ask politely, Sin." His voice was more of a drawl with a definite hint of seduction at the end.

I raised my chin in a gesture of defiance. "No."

"Sin, let's not play games." His voice was deep and held just a tinge of irritation. "Beg for it. Out loud. I want your utter surrender."

I pasted a smile on my face and delivered my next line in a saccharine-sweet tone, "No matter how spectacular your cock is"—*and it was*—"that shit is not happening."

His mouth compressed into a hard line. "We'll go no further if you don't trust me to give you what you need." His eyes narrowed and his nostrils flared.

My body shivered at his words. *Can he really give me what I've been too jaded to believe existed?* A man who understood my needs behind closed doors and would satisfy all the dark cravings I'd kept buried. Deep down, I knew he was that man, but I couldn't quite push past the fear of surrendering to him.

"I can't," I whispered.

He cocked a brow at me. "Can't? Or won't?"

My pulse accelerated at his question, and my eyes narrowed as he did the unthinkable. He stepped back and started stroking his engorged manhood tauntingly.

Dammit! What a cunt tease.

It was straight-up torture as I watched the way he touched himself. Nothing screamed confidence more than a man not afraid of tantalizing his sensual side. My breath became more ragged. Warmth pooled between my thighs. I was so close to the edge that I wasn't above begging for his shaft. And from the smoldering calculation in his gray eyes, Core knew it.

Stubbornly, I ran through multiple scenarios in my head. *One, tell him to go fuck himself, go home, and finish myself off with my trusty and reliable vibrator, Beast. Or two, beg for the privilege of taking him down my throat.* Option one would never satisfy me now that I'd had a glimpse of his hard flesh. Option two... *Oh, hell no.* I'd never had to beg to take a man into my mouth in my entire life.

His stroke became more sensual, slower and methodical.

Shit. He's trying to drive me insane.

I blew out a breath. "Please, Core." I bit my lip and quickly added, "May I suck your cock?"

His stoic expression turned grim. "No." Steel laced his tone.

I stiffened at his response. *Motherfucker!* I swiveled my head, unable to meet his tauntingly hot gaze.

"But you may lick it. Slowly." His voice was full of authority.

I forced myself to gaze at him again. I tightened my fists.

His lips twitched into a mockery of a smile.

I squared my shoulders and took a deep breath. I grabbed his girth, feathering my tongue over him, swirling the salty precome from the tip of his crown, savoring the earthy taste of him. Cupping his balls, I rolled my fingers over his tight sac. My other hand firmly gripping him, I explored the peaked ridge just under the head of his shaft with my tongue.

"Enough." His rough command drew me to a halt.

I let out a strangled cry. My chest heaved as I rested my head against his hard thigh.

His hand ventured to the back of my head. He tugged my hair with his fingers, forcing my gaze upward. "Let me show you how I want my cock sucked." His tone was edgy. "Open your mouth."

His command made my insides tingle. No man had ever talked to me that way. He was pushing my limits, breaking me down, taking everything I'd worked so hard to maintain…to control.

I embraced his length with both hands before my lips greedily slid over the head of his arousal. Core's hands threaded through my hair, as though savoring the feel of it. The low groans coming from him spurred me on.

He tightened his hand, jerking my hair. He grew bigger in my mouth as I bobbed my head up and down over his wide shaft. The more I tasted, the more I hungered. With every flick of my tongue, the hard grip of his fingers against my head seemed to turn me on even more. I fed him into my throat, taking it all. His hard shaft was thick and broad, like him. My lips stretched around his man flesh.

He spread his knees wider. "That's it. Suck me good."

I hummed as he started a slow slide in and out between my lips.

A fog of desire clouded my vision. All I could think of was bringing him pleasure.

His groan deepened, becoming more of a growl, charging the erotic tension even more. "More tongue. Suck harder," he hissed.

His dark words sent me spiraling to the edge of a lust-induced frenzy. My body quivered with a fire I'd never felt before. I didn't give a shit about how wild he was making me or my running mascara or smudged lipstick.

I didn't think. I just felt liberated and bizarrely in control of Core.

I closed my eyes briefly, letting out a strangled sound. My tongue stroked every bump and ridge of his flesh. Moving up and down on him, I sucked him harder. I was thrilled when his hands moved to my head again, positioning me over his member.

"Wider." He tightened his fists even more in my hair. "Open your mouth wider."

I did, and he shoved his staff until he was lodged against the back of my throat. He was huge, the size of my wrist, but I didn't back away or struggle. Holding still, I relaxed my throat to keep from gagging. My tongue slid along his length as I breathed through my nose and swallowed around him.

"Fuck. Do that again." His voice was hoarse and thick with arousal.

Heady with power, I swallowed around him. The sound of his harsh breath filled the room. It drove me on as he thrust into me with a slow rhythm that was rough and primal. His tangled fingers in my hair held my head still for his deep thrusts.

Class was in session, and he was teaching me what he demanded. And like a good little student, I was eager to learn.

My lips danced over him. My hips swayed in tandem.

"Sinful," he whispered.

Moisture pooled between my legs, loving that he called me "sinful" when we got this nasty.

All too soon, a guttural groan erupted from his carnal mouth. "Swallow it all," he commanded a second before he shot into the sweet depths of my mouth.

I continued to suck, swallow, and lick him with gentle strokes until he gradually softened in my mouth.

After inching from between my lips with a heartfelt sigh, in one smooth motion, he helped me stand. My legs were trembling under me, and he cradled me against his chest with unexpected tenderness that left me speechless. My body jerked involuntarily, and a mental switch flipped from lust-induced haze to lucid reality. I'd never been held like this.

My body stiffened. I felt raw, exposed, and confused. *What the fuck am I doing?*

He stroked my hair. "Don't overthink this. Just feel," he coaxed.

I squeezed my eyes shut for a moment, trying to do the opposite of what he'd demanded. Feeling was exactly what had allowed me to get hurt by Kyle so many years ago. Feeling was what I'd sworn not to do because it hurt too damn much when my heart eventually got broken. And that was exactly what would happen with a man like Core.

No, it would be better to keep whatever we had strictly sexual. Sex, I understood. Relationships and emotions were not in my vocabulary.

My heartbeat raced, nearly exploding. "This is bullshit. I don't want to fucking feel." My voice broke. I cleared my throat. "I want to fuck you and be done with all of this." I wanted him to get angry. I needed his rejection to fuel my will to hightail it away from him and away from this intimacy.

I needed him to save me from myself.

He stepped back and grabbed my chin roughly. His eyes were clear and determined. "It will never be done between us, Sin. You're mine. All of you."

Momentarily, I was unable to speak. "No." My voice trembled. "Friends with benefits."

The muscles jumped near his jawline. "I'll have all of you or none of you," he clipped out. "That's the only way it will be." He removed his hand from my chin, pinning me with his hardened eyes.

I held back a scream of frustration. My aching desire for him threatened to drown me.

His mouth compressed into a thin line. "Sin, you can waste a whole lot of time pretending this isn't happening, but it is. The sooner you come to terms with your new reality, with me in it, the sooner I can get to shoving my cock into your sweet pussy and fucking you sideways." His nostrils flared, and every muscle in his body seemed to tense. "But that's not going to happen until you surrender to me, in every way a woman can surrender to a man."

He brushed a hand against my breast and teased the tight bud of my nipple between his fingers. Liquid heat poured through me, and my stomach quivered.

Jesus.

The mere thought of surrendering to Core on an emotional level made me dizzy with fear. My hands started shaking. I swallowed hard and bit my bottom lip to hide the emotion that had set it trembling. Clamping my fingers together, I tried to remember how to breathe.

Emotionally, I was falling down the rabbit hole. It was dark, cold, and disorientating.

"What is this?" I'd meant to sound abrupt and firm, but the words came out kind of breathy.

He arched down, and his teeth grazed over my ear before sucking the lobe into his mouth, eliciting a gasp from me. "Like I just told you, you're mine. All of you. And you will submit to me in every way I see fit."

"Like fuck buddies?" I squeaked, feeling like I was losing my ever-loving mind.

"No." His expression was serious. "I want more than an occasional fuck. I can get that shit anywhere."

I almost swallowed my tongue. "Are you talking about us dating?" *Oh God.* I didn't know shit about dating.

He ran his tongue along the seam of my lips, tempting me to open for him. "I don't date. I fuck. That means me fucking you whenever I want, wherever I want, and however I want. Exclusively." He wrapped a strand of my hair around his finger and tugged. "Because I damn sure don't share or play nice with others."

Uh, what? My mind screamed, *Run,* but my body froze, allowing him to fondle my hair affectionately. *What the hell is wrong with me?* I'd never reacted to a man like this, no matter how hot he was.

I pursed my lips. "No. That's you acting like some big, bad junkyard dog, using me as your fucktoy and then discarding me when you're done."

"No. It's us satisfying our urge to fuck each other senseless—" his chiseled lips curled "—with the added bonus of spending quality time with each other, seeing where this goes."

My heart instantly began to race with elation, but my stubborn mind refused to budge. "Sounds a lot like fucking with a hell of a lot of non-fucking activities thrown in. The sex part sounds hella good. But I don't do bullshit outings to the park, holding hands, or rolling around on picnic blankets, getting grass stains on my clothes." I pinched my lips together.

It was all true. There wasn't a girlie or romantic bone in my body.

He arched a brow. "Do I look like the type of man who likes to traipse through the damn park?"

He smiled, an honest-to-God, naughty-boy smile. Disarmed, I shivered.

"My idea of romance is me finger-fucking you under the table at my favorite restaurant and then denying you the pleasure of climaxing."

Okay...that sounds really good. My traitorous center quivered with lust. Ignoring the danger warning blaring in my head, I whispered, "Core, we have a deal."

He slid his hand between my legs, rubbing against my wet folds. "Do we?" He arched his beautiful brow. "I have very dark tastes when it comes to sex. And I'm planning on exploring every one of them, leaving nothing unfucked. Including your ass."

His words made my stomach flutter with excitement. It was a primal challenge no man had ever made me want to answer. There were no flowery, bullshit words, no complicated promises of forever, no judgment for the freaky things we both craved. He'd push my sexual boundaries, maybe even strip me emotionally bare, ruining me for any man after him.

But I wanted Core for however long this thing between us might last.

"Like I said, Core. Deal."

His hands slid under my arms, lifting me effortlessly.

"What are you doing?" I squeaked, my dress twisting around my waist. Instinctively, I wrapped my arms around his neck and my legs around his waist.

"I'm getting ready to spread your legs wide open and lick your sweet slit, darling."

Striding across the floor, he carried me over to his desk. With one hand, he swiped everything off of it before sliding me on top. In the blink of an eye, I was on my back with my legs hooked over his shoulders. He settled himself between the V of my thighs, pushing my panties aside before voraciously going after the damp petals of my womanhood. He lapped me from my clit to the end of my cleft. He swirled his tongue around my clit, repeatedly flicked it, and then sank it inside me. I panted, my hips arching. Holding me still, he fucked me unrelentingly with his wicked tongue. I hissed as he worked me into a frenzy, using long, sensual licks. His tongue constantly teased my opening.

"Who does this pussy belong to?" he gritted out as he pinned me.

Showing me no damn mercy, he flicked my swollen nub with his tongue until I screamed, "Oh my fucking God!"

I bucked as he continued to bathe me with his mouth.

"Whose is it, Sin?" He thrust two fingers into my trembling channel, curving them inside me while pressing his thumb on my clit so his hand was clamped around me.

I knew he had no intentions of letting me come until I verbalized his claim. Frustrated, I was squirming helplessly and arching. "Technically, it's mine," I responded breathlessly.

He growled, the vibrations pushing me to the edge of crazed lust.

"But since you're doing such a bang-up job down there, I concede to your talented, wicked tongue. So lick away, Core."

He shoved another finger inside me, making me cry out and buck. "Concede to *me*, not my fucking tongue."

My toes curled. I was so close. Just one more swipe of his tongue. "Okay. This pussy is on loan to you on a very temporary basis."

"Don't make me smack your twat."

"You wouldn't." My mouth dropped open at the sharp slap against my slick clit. My nipples tightened with desire. "You—"

"Enough." He flicked my womanhood with his tongue. "Say the damn words, or I'll walk away, leaving your stubborn ass hanging."

I jerked my head up to stare at him. "What? You wouldn't?" My voice held a tinge of hysteria. I was so wound up with the need to come, and shamefully, I wasn't above begging.

I needed Core. *Now.*

He raised his head, peering at me with sharpened eyes. My juices glistening on his lips like liquor filled me with perverse satisfaction and possessiveness.

"I would," he growled. "This won't work if I don't hear what I need." He stood up, and with his free hand, he pulled out his thickness, rubbing it tauntingly. "This cock is all yours."

I swallowed hard, watching as he stroked it sensually. His manhood was by far the thickest, largest, most perfectly shaped shaft I'd ever seen.

"And this pussy is mine." He plunged his fingers, hard, inside my aching wetness. "Yes?"

I nodded. All the while, it was killing me that I was conceding so quickly. But dammit, it was hard as hell to find a man in Manhattan with the Holy Grail—a huge dick and a very talented tongue.

I was greedy for more.

He narrowed his steel-gray eyes. "No nodding. I need to hear the fucking words, Sin."

Sealing my submission, I uttered, "It's yours. Take all of me."

With one seamless motion, he withdrew his fingers, gripped my ass, and stabbed his tongue inside me. My back arched, and my legs moved to the back of his head as I cried loudly for air to breathe. Consumed with lust, he continued to fuck me relentlessly with his tongue.

I reached my fingers down, biting into his silky hair while he pumped me, drawing out my climax. Pulling my ass cheeks apart, he plunged one wet finger into the normally forbidden zone—my ass. My eyes rolled to the back of my head. I panted, drawing ragged breaths. Mercifully, he relented, pulling away, his eyes blazing with a focused, animal wildness.

Holy hell.

I couldn't even form a coherent thought. Every muscle in my body tensed with expectation. I was so horny that all I wanted was to fuck.

"Fuck me," I demanded, all cavewoman-like.

He growled before hauling me off the desk, holding me securely as my legs wobbled.

Light-headed, I closed my eyes to get my bearings.

"Open your eyes." His voice was taut with lust.

I hesitated. My body was a shuddering mass of jelly.

"Now, Sin." His voice hardened.

Trembling, I opened my eyes. His eyes were now dark gray, like molten silver.

"Strip." He widened his stance.

On shaky legs, I slowly slid my dress off my body and then pushed my panties down my hips and legs before kicking them aside. I stood before Core, wearing nothing but my sexy stilettos. Gliding my hands up, I cupped my cleavage before squeezing my hardened peaks between my fingers.

"Is that what you want, Sin? Pain?" He drew his lower lip between his teeth.

My whole body ached with longing. "I want it all."

"Sinful." He stripped off his shirt, leaving on his unzipped pants.

I caught myself staring and cleared my throat. His body, from chest to sleeve, was a wonderland of beautifully composed Japanese tattoos and other beast-themed ink. Stepping closer, he lifted my chin with a flick of his finger and kissed me hard and deep. It was a kiss of utter possession.

He broke off the exchange and growled, "Turn around, facedown, and present your beautiful ass to me. Now."

There was something different about his voice. The gruffness I had gotten used to was gone. There was a new tenderness that I hadn't heard before.

Pivoting, I pressed my chest against the desk. "Like this?"

The cool air glided across the backs of my thighs. He ran a hand across the curve of my ass before parting my cheeks. A strange tingling sensation gripped my body like a vise. My eyes shut at the revelation that Core was viewing me in ways that no other man had.

"Damn, you're so damn sexy," he praised while kicking my legs apart like I was under arrest.

With sweet lust whipping through my dripping sex, I glanced over my shoulder, and I watched him reach into his pocket and pull out a condom. He tore the package open with his teeth and quickly removed the latex.

In seconds, he sheathed his cock and curled his hand in my hair, snapping my head back. "Your pussy. Your ass. All of you. Mine," he whispered into my ear.

Releasing my hair, he pressed me facedown onto the desk and buried himself so far inside me that my whole body quaked from the sheer force.

"Oh fuck!" I cried out as he stretched me ruthlessly.

His engorged flesh sank deeper between my sensitive folds, and his balls slapped against my womanhood, sending tiny shocks through my body. My hips bucked, and my pussy burned from the width of his big, thick manhood.

With fingers buried into the flesh at my hips, he held me still. "Slow, darling. I don't want to hurt you." He gave my wetness time to adjust to his girth.

My body tensed from the burning fullness in my cunt.

"Relax," he hissed.

I took a deep breath, forcing my rebellious muscles to loosen.

He pushed forward, slowly at first, and then he increased his speed from a sensuous slide to hard, forceful pumping. "Fuck!" he cursed.

I couldn't move as Core rocked me, hard and steady. The feeling of helplessness ran through me, heightening every sensation in my body. He was driving me crazy with lust, and each stroke brought me closer and closer to the edge.

"Core," I groaned as he continued to fuck me like a man possessed.

The pressure tightened inside me before I came brutally hard. I gasped and moaned as my interior muscles convulsed around him.

His fingers squeezed my hips. Again and again, he pulled out and plunged back inside me like a man on a mission. He tensed, and every muscle rippled before he uttered a guttural groan that sounded like, "Sinful," as his smooth pumping became jerky and harsh. He roared. His entire body shook as he came and came, his cock twitching inside me. He slumped over me, catching his weight on his hands. He nuzzled my neck and then pressed his sensuous mouth to the top of my shoulder before gently pulling out of me.

I sighed heavily, feeling utterly empty.

"Let me take care of the condom." He disappeared for a second to dispose of it.

When he came back, tremors ran through me as his lips trailed gently across the back of my neck, causing my stomach to do flip-flops. Twisting me around, he enveloped me with his body by wrapping his arms around me. Effortlessly, he picked me up, cradling me. Pressing my head into the hollow of his shoulder, he carried me over to the sitting area as if I weighed nothing. He sat down with me in his lap.

I felt safe and comforted. Boneless, I curled against his chest while he pushed the damp strands of hair away from my forehead. In that instant, I knew I had been stamped *Property of Core*. There would be no pretending this was just a one-time occurrence, and from the determined glint in his eyes, he wouldn't let me even if I wanted to. It was way too late in the game for that.

His chest was damp with sweat, slick under my cheek, salty on my tongue when I gave it a lick. Through the muscles covering his chest, I could hear his heart beating in a steady rhythm. He traced his fingers over the tattoo piece written horizontally from my abdomen to my back.

"Love all, trust a few, do wrong to none," he recited aloud. "Shakespeare," he ended.

I curved my mouth up into a smile. "Wow. I've never seen this side of you, Core."

His sensuous mouth twitched. "I have many sides, darling." His hand moved to my ass, lightly touching. "Good."

"Bad," I whispered.

"Hard." His voice rumbled through his chest as he stroked my hair.

"Gentle," I finished.

He arched a brow. "Gentle? I'm afraid not. Gentle is not in my vocabulary." He tweaked my nipple hard.

"I can deal with that." I traced my fingers along his jaw and across his lips.

He bit one finger before letting go. "I'll be right back," he muttered while gently scooting me off his lap before he stood up. Confidently, he swaggered over to the wet bar.

Lust curled in my cunt.

Damn, what a magnificent ass.

He stormed back with a tall glass of ice water. Without a word, he sat down, pulling me back onto his lap. Cradling me in his arms, he held the glass to my lips, and I drank thirstily. When I'd had enough, he drank some of the water.

"Do you want more?" he inquired, gesturing to the glass.

I shook my head. "No, I'm good."

Putting the glass down, he tucked a strand of my hair behind my ear, his fingers leaving a tingle in their wake. I tried to burrow closer, but I was already plastered against him like wallpaper. My chest was mashed against his, and my hips were cradled against his stomach.

Arching down, he crushed his lips against mine before pulling back. His gray eyes searched my face as if he were trying to figure out a puzzle, and I was that puzzle.

"For better or for worse, Sin, we're in this together."

CHAPTER 8
SINTHIA

"Wake up, darling. We're here." Core's voice was low and sensuous.

I popped my eyes open to find him staring at me. "Sorry. I fell asleep." I was curled against Core's side, totally satiated after our energetic sex romp.

With languid movements, I stretched. He traced a finger across my cheek.

"What?" I wiped my eyes. "Did I snore?"

"No." He took my hand and turned it over so he could kiss my palm, the sensation making a beeline for my sex. "You just look so cute when you're sleeping and not spewing four-letter words."

He gently placed another kiss on my palm before licking it. His touch stabbed through me, and moisture pooled between my legs.

I smiled impishly. "Fuck off, Core."

He laughed huskily. "And there she is, my foul-mouthed sex kitten." He threw open the limo door and stepped out, holding his hand for me to grab. "Time to get you inside."

I clutched his hand, hopping out.

Releasing my hand, he pressed his palm to my lower back, ushering me up the stairs. "So do I at least get to see where the fashion magic happens?"

I burst out in laughter. Turning around, I rolled my eyes heavenward. "Okay, is that your subtle way of asking to come inside and have your freaky, naughty way with me?"

He offered a bemused smile. "I didn't know I needed an invitation."

"With your talented cock, you can come over to service me anytime, Core." I leaned in, pecking him, before twirling around to resume my climb toward my front door. Pulling my key out of my mini clutch, I started to push the key into the lock when I noticed the door was already open with the lights on inside. A sense of dark foreboding weighed on me.

With shakiness in my limbs, I rushed forward, but Core yanked me back, pushing his muscular body in front of mine.

"Sin, let me go inside first." He nudged the door and stepped over the threshold. His body stiffened. "Holy shit!"

His wide, muscular back was blocking my view. "What?"

I shoved against him, but he refused to budge.

"Move the fuck out of my way, Core."

Slowly, he stepped aside, allowing me entry.

I froze, rooted to the spot.

It was like a tornado had ripped through my townhouse. Furniture had been slashed and thrown about. Kitchen drawers were pulled out. Broken glass and dishes littered the floor. Throw pillows had been cut, and down feathers were scattered everywhere. Nothing had been left untouched.

My lips trembled. "Who the fuck would do something as horrific as this?"

I was stunned into silence. My pulse raced as I continued my visual inventory. My flat-screen television and laptop were still there. I clasped my hands together to keep them from trembling, and my eyes widened when I saw the remnants of my collection ripped into pieces and thrown around like confetti.

"Oh God." My breathing sped up until I was gasping for air.

My legs gave way, and I felt myself crashing toward the floor when Core caught me.

His deep voice sounded from behind me. "Breathe, darling."

Unchecked tears streamed down my cheeks. "I don't understand what's happening right now." My voice broke as I shook uncontrollably.

He spun me around to face him, and his hands framed my jaws, anchoring me in place. "Sin, eyes on me. Calm down."

I forced myself to remain calm even though my insides screamed bloody murder.

He released me, righting a barstool that had been toppled onto the floor. "Sit down before you fall. I'll handle this." A muscle in his jaw twitched.

Shakily, I sank onto the chair, hooking my feet around the legs. Core stalked over to the refrigerator, pulling out a bottle of water. Wasting no time, he strode back, handing me the bottle.

I waved it away. "I'm not thirsty." My voice croaked as I set my palms down flat on the counter. My mind raced a mile a minute with questions. *What if I had been home? Would I be dead right now? Who the fuck would do something like this?*

He tucked a lock of my hair behind my ear. "Please drink it, darling."

I drew in a deep breath, taking the bottle with stiff fingers. Opening it, I sipped it absentmindedly.

"I need to call the police. Don't move." He kissed my forehead before pulling out his cell.

But I didn't care. All I could think about was how truly fucked my life was right now.

～

Hours later, uniformed and plain-clothes police officers stomped through my home.

Calming deep breaths, Sin, I chanted to keep myself from going completely insane.

After doing a walk-through with the police and Core, I could easily see the damage was worse than I'd originally thought. When pressed by the police to give an inventory of what had been stolen, I couldn't pinpoint what was missing. All my jewelry and other expensive items remained untouched. Not that I gave a shit. Material possessions could be replaced, but my collection could not. The intruder had ruthlessly destroyed it with a thoroughness that was mentally and emotionally disturbing.

Why would anyone do this?

I couldn't think of one competitor who hated me this much. My life was uncomplicated. There was no drama, no rivals. I frowned. But there was one man who had been following me from the past—after one night of sex, now he was my stalker.

Is Jaxon back to claim what he thinks is his—me?

My mind rejected the possibility, but the scary memory of the utter rage that had clouded Jaxon's eyes before he'd sliced my shoulder made me shudder. The all-too-familiar dread seeped into my bones. I gritted my teeth as I tried not to freak out.

Sin, stop it. He's gone.

But I knew he wasn't. The vase of white roses and the note with the letter *J* scribbled on it that had been left on my doorstep a couple weeks ago proved it.

My hand flew to the light scar on my shoulder. "Never forget," I whispered.

Fighting the cold fear running down my spine, I thought about the day Jaxon had grabbed me, pulling me into a dark alleyway, with a knife pressed against my throat.

He babbled words of love over and over as he brutally ripped off my clothes with sick lust in his eyes. Bitterness coated my tongue when I realized I was nothing but a piece of property to him, his possession that he had every intention of claiming over and over again until I broke. Tears streamed down my face as I braced for the impending savage violation. Shivering on the cold ground, I turned my head away, letting my mind go blank. Then a lone homeless man stumbled upon us, saving me, and I was thrown a lifeline. But I knew Jaxon wasn't finished with me, and that had just been a momentary reprieve.

My thoughts snapped back to the present. I shuddered. The break-in showed me just how vulnerable I really was. I'd never needed a security system in this affluent neighborhood, but getting one was the first thing on my agenda today.

Wandering back into the living room, I tried not to let my eyes linger on the pieces of my collection that lay in ruin across the floor.

"What the hell?" I muttered under my breath when I tripped over an object.

Glancing down, I toed the offending large chunk of old, splintered wood that had once covered the false bottom of Dad's beat-up trunk. The trunk was lying on its side with all the contents spilled out like seashells on a beach. Righting it, I scanned inside. The false bottom was missing, and so was the red leather ledger that had been hidden in the secret compartment.

Standing up, I scanned the entire area. *No ledger.* "This shit keeps getting stranger and stranger."

"Sin?" Core lifted an eyebrow, eyeing me from across the room. "Are you okay?"

"Yes, I'm good." I forced a smile.

Core glared at me with an intensity that made me uncomfortable before his gaze pivoted back and he continued talking to one of the officers.

I drew my lower lip between my teeth while staring at him.

A man I'd at one time thought of as my enemy was now my lover. Smoothly, Core had stepped in, taking charge of fielding the barrage of questions from the officers while I numbly rode a roller coaster of emotions—shock, fear, denial, and anger.

"Ms. Michaels?"

I snapped my head up at the sound of my name. A well-groomed, middle-aged man moved toward me.

"Yes?" I answered.

He adjusted the lapels of his jacket. "I'm Detective Talbot." His face flushed as he studied my attire with thinly veiled interest. "Seems like you were out when the break-in occurred." He furrowed his forehead. "You're very lucky."

"That's what everyone keeps telling me," I replied dryly.

Talbot inclined his head. "I do have some questions to ask you. First—"

I massaged the back of my neck. I'd had enough of the questions. I was exhausted, mentally and physically. I sighed with relief when Core sidled up, wrapping an arm around my waist.

"We've already been through the scene with your officers," Core interjected.

"And who are you?" Talbot's voice was clipped, as if he were irritated.

Core let out a harsh breath. "Core McKay," he snapped. "Now, no more questions. She's in shock. Can't this wait until later today?"

Talbot scrutinized me and then nodded slowly. "Sure." He turned to face Core. "Just make sure you bring her to the station today." He gestured toward the officers. "Come on, guys. Let's clear out." He pivoted and marched out the door, closing it behind him.

Core swiveled me around to face him. "Are you okay?"

"No." Feeling raw and vulnerable, I wrapped my arms around his waist. "I'm so totally screwed, Core." I gulped hard so I wouldn't lose my voice. "My collection is gone. I'll have to start all over again."

"Whatever you want and need, I'll move mountains to make sure you have it, darling." He kissed my forehead and whispered, "But right now, I need you to gather whatever is salvageable. You're staying with me until we get this whole thing sorted out."

I buried my face into his chest. In Core's arms, I felt safe.

CHAPTER 9
CORE

Disgust twisted my mouth into a sneer. I still couldn't believe Jeff had destroyed Sin's house. I gnashed my teeth as I climbed the stairs. I couldn't wait to get over to the warehouse and wrap my hands around his neck, watching the life slowly drain from his eyes. Reaching the top of the landing, I rolled my shoulders to relieve the tension. First things first, I wanted to make sure Sin was settled in before leaving.

I went poker-faced before entering my master bedroom.

Sin whirled away from my floor-to-ceiling window with awe transforming her face. "I'm jealous that you get to wake up to this beautiful view every morning, Core."

Sheer, boy-cut panties accentuated her voluptuous curves, and a body-hugging black tank top encased her tempting tits. She bit her lip as my eyes traveled from the top of her head down her curvy body.

"Unfortunately, I don't get to enjoy the view. I normally get in really late at night, and then I leave at the crack of dawn."

Damn. She was absolutely gorgeous with her hair cascading to her shoulders and her face freshly scrubbed. My length stirred, stiffening against my pants.

"Well, that's a fucking shame." She shifted from one foot to the other before swaying across the room. She climbed onto my king-size bed and slid under the sheets. "By the way, thank you for letting me stay here." She yawned. "And don't worry. I'm not moving in." She smiled impishly.

I shrugged. "I'm not worried about it." Walking over to the bed, I sat on the edge beside her.

Reclining back, she swallowed hard. "I feel stupid for saying this." She peered at me from under her long eyelashes. "But I was fucking scared shitless about being in my townhouse after—"

"Sin, stop torturing yourself. It's natural to feel that way." I handed her the glass in my hand. "Drink this. It's brandy."

Her long-fingered hands wrapped around the glass. Her gaze clouded, going distant. "I guess I wouldn't feel as creeped out about the intruder if something of value was actually stolen." Her face turned sullen. "Why would someone want an old ledger?" she muttered under her breath.

"What ledger?" I queried in a deliberately neutral voice.

She drew her brows together. "What?"

I stroked her hair. "You just mentioned something about a ledger."

She took a deep breath before letting it out slowly. "A couple weeks ago, I found a ledger stashed under a secret compartment in my father's ratty trunk. But nothing in the damn thing made a bit of sense. It was only random handwritten codes and numbers—essentially gibberish. The thing is—" she bit her bottom lip "—my father was an accountant, unglamorous and boring. So I can't figure out why he would even want to hide something like that."

Fuck. This shit was getting complicated. "Can't you ask your mother?"

Sin blinked her eyes rapidly. "Grace? Not a chance in hell. We don't talk."

She rubbed her brow as if to ward off a headache. Her pinched expression told me that matter was off-limits.

"Core, I'm sorry for snapping at you, but the topic of Grace isn't something I like to talk about." She sighed heavily. "Just put it this way, I cut her out of my life for a reason." One hand almost curled into a fist and then straightened. "Are you close to your mother?"

My muscles tensed slightly. "She died when I was young."

She gasped. "Oh God, I'm sorry."

There was a heaviness in the pit of my stomach. "It's not a subject I enjoy talking about."

She bowed her spine. "Believe me. I understand." She glanced away, then back.

Caressing her leg, I decided it would be better to change the subject quickly. "I'll have a couple of my investigators work on the break-in first thing today."

She inclined her head. "You don't have to do that. Talbot's got the case."

I pinned her in place with my steady gaze. "I would feel better if I conducted an independent investigation."

She took a large gulp of the brandy. "God, I feel absolutely nauseous about starting my collection all over again. All that work… gone." Her voice cracked.

I stroked her cheek. "You don't have to do it all by yourself. Whatever you need, I'll take care of it."

Placing her glass on the nightstand, Sin grabbed my face between her hands. "Thank you, Core." Her fingers shook. She jerked them away. She closed her eyes, her long, thick lashes fanning down on the glowing skin of her face.

"Sin," I demanded, lifting her face with my forefinger, "what's wrong?"

Within the expression on her gorgeous face, there was definitely something complicated.

She fluttered her eyelids half open, revealing the startling beauty of her eyes. "You don't know how much this means to me—you being here for me."

My heart jerked at the vulnerability and truth laid out in her words. I knew then that I would cut off my own arm before I'd ever let anyone harm her. "I always protect what I care for."

"Core, you're more of an enigma than I thought." She leaned in, tracing a finger along the light scar on my cheek and then farther up onto the jagged scar running across my eyebrow. "What are these from? A wicked bar fight?"

"Bad memories. Demons from my past that shaped the person I am today."

She curled her lips up into a slight smile. "Maybe someday you'll reveal the Core within."

"Maybe." My throat closed up. "But sometimes, the truth isn't so simple."

"We all have secrets we don't want to talk about because it hurts too much."

Drawing a breath, I released it before speaking, "Some more than others."

Her tongue darted out to touch her lips. "Someday, Core...we'll be able to let the demons go." Arching forward, she brushed her lips against mine before sliding under the sheets, closing her eyes.

I tucked them tightly around her soft, warm body. "Sleep tight, darling. I'll be back in a couple hours."

Her eyes snapped open. "Don't go." Her voice wavered.

Threading a hand through her hair, I murmured, "Okay, darling, I'll stay."

"Thank you."

I watched her nuzzle the pillow. Her eyelids drifted closed, and she promptly fell asleep. The bed dipped when I stood up. I headed to the bathroom, closing the door behind me. I groaned at the chaotic scene of Sin's personal items sprinkled around my master en-suite bath—bottles of body wash and lotion, her dress hanging next to her towel, her toothbrush next to mine. It reminded me of a happier time in my life with Maya. She had been my balance, my rock. I was willing to give up my criminal empire for her and my unborn child. One tragic moment and she'd been taken away, leaving me emotionally void. No woman could replace Maya in my heart. Until now.

A smirk rolled across my face. *Life is full of compromises*, I thought.

Then it dawned on me, the number of compromises I would be more than willing to make for this woman. Just the thought of her lying in my bed with those fucking barely there boy-cut panties displaying her luscious ass and her tight T-shirt outlining her voluptuous globes made my flesh go rock hard.

Turning on the shower, I adjusted the temperature to cold before stepping beneath the rain shower head, hoping the frigid water would get rid of my aching arousal. The jets beat against my body, but I was still at half-mast. As I soaped myself up, my hand lingered on my erection. I needed to stroke one out, or I'd end up turning her over and fucking the shit out of her.

Taking myself in my hand, I closed my eyes and tugged my cock. I thought about the taste of Sin's glistening sweet slit, my tongue licking her hard little nub, her hands tightly clutching my head against her weeping womanhood…

"Holy fuck," I hissed. I threw my head back, groaning as I ejaculated.

Quickly, I washed my body and hair, rinsing away the shampoo and soap. Snatching one of my luxurious towels, I dried myself off before putting on my lounge pants.

I left the bathroom to find Sin curled up in the middle of my king-size bed. She was snoring lightly. Turning out the light, I sat on the edge and the bed dipped. Then I lifted the covers and slid in beside her. As I edged my body closer, she mumbled something incoherent while inching her back until it fit snugly against my chest. I put my arm around her waist, and my legs pushed against the backs of her thighs, my nose nuzzling the back of her neck. I slowly dozed off. At that moment, I knew I had everything—Sin and Bigsby—and surprisingly, the anger was finally gone.

And one woman had unknowingly made it all happen—Sin.

CHAPTER 10
CORE

My phone vibrated on the nightstand, and I jerked straight up in bed. I grabbed it quickly, not wanting to wake Sin. The display told me it was Ram.

"Where the hell are you?"

Leave it to Ram not to beat around the damn bush.

"We've been waiting at the warehouse for hours."

Shit. I'd planned to call him, but I'd fallen asleep.

Now totally alert, I swung my legs over the bed and stood up. "Ram, give me a minute. I'm going down to my office."

Turning, I examined a fast-asleep Sin. I couldn't believe how peaceful and relaxed she appeared to be.

"Your office? Why can't you talk…?" Ram's voice trailed off. "Oh, fuck no. Don't tell me she's there, bro."

Silently padding out of my bedroom and closing the door behind me, I strode downstairs. I rubbed my forehead. "Of course she's here. I couldn't leave her in that fucked-up mess." Stepping into my sound-proofed office, I slammed the door behind me.

"What mess?" Ram asked.

I paced back and forth. "Jeff's mess," I growled. My hand tightened on the phone. "What the hell, Ram? Why didn't Max and Rocco stop him?"

There was a long pause.

"What are you talking about?" Ram asked calmly.

Jerking to a stop, I pounded my fist on the desk. "Sin's place, along with her collection, was trashed."

"What? Shit. Hold on. Let me get Max."

There was another long pause.

"I have Max here, and you're on speaker."

"What's the big emergency?" Max asked.

"What the fuck is wrong with you?" I barked. "I walked into her damn townhouse to find the whole place ripped to shreds. It was horrific. How could you let this happen?"

"We didn't let shit happen. In fact, we followed your instructions to a T," Max hissed. "You said hands off until we saw that damn ledger in Jeff's hand, and that was exactly what we did. Now you want to blame us because your brilliant plan turned into a clusterfuck? Come on, Core. This is bullshit."

My chest rose and fell with rapid breaths. "No, what's bullshit is I have to pick up the damn pieces because you and Rocco botched this job. Damn. I can't even trust you two to handle a fucking simple task." I knew my statement was irrational, but I didn't give a shit. Someone had to answer for this debacle.

"Core!" Ram snapped. "Are you even listening to yourself? What the fuck did you think Jeff was going to do when he broke in? Pussyfoot around and gently sift through her shit while searching for the ledger?"

"It was a damn break-in. That means shit gets broken." Max interrupted. "Did we think Jeff was going to fuck her place up? The answer is no. Obviously, you didn't either. Not that you gave a shit. All you cared about was getting that damn ledger. So, guess what, bro? You have the ledger and Jeff, too."

"Damn, you're right." I massaged the back of my neck. "We didn't know this shit was going to go down like that."

"And now that we have everything we need, what are your plans for Sin? Unless you're falling for her," Ram mused. "I hope not." He snorted.

I stiffened. "I'll be there in a few hours," I gritted out before throwing my cell onto the desk. I strode out of the office and back upstairs into the bedroom.

Closing the door behind me, I stood there for a good two minutes, wondering what the hell was wrong with me. She was supposed to be a means to an end. Nothing more. No attachments.

Shit, I never want to let her go.

All I wanted to do was go to her, wrap my arms around her, and protect her from the world.

Sin stirred. Her eyelids fluttered open, revealing the startling beauty of her almond-shaped hazel eyes. "What's wrong? You can't sleep?" she mumbled.

"I just called my team. I thought it'd be better for my guys to start on the trail while it's still fresh."

Sin smiled softly. "Come here, Core." She beckoned me with a little finger.

There were so many sides to Sin—sexy, rebellious, sassy, smart, vulnerable—and I wanted them all.

Marching over to the bed, I slipped between the sheets.

"You smell so good," she whispered before grabbing my hips.

Leaning in, she licked my lips and then plunged into my mouth with a persistent tongue. Her tongue slid around the tip of mine and then rubbed under it. I thought about her doing that to my cock, and I almost exploded.

Dammit!

I couldn't hold back any longer, not with her soft and pliant in my arms.

Groaning, I plundered, possessed, and nipped at her full lips before flipping her onto her back. I straddled her, one knee on each side of her waist. She gazed up at me, her eyes dilated. Her sensuous mouth curved into a smile.

I leaned down, biting her bottom lip. "I can't get enough of you."

She trailed her fingers across my chest. "I'm yours, Core. Fuck me."

I simply growled in response.

Wasting no time, I tugged off her tank and then her panties before sliding two fingers into her heat, stretching her open. She squeezed those fingers tightly, and I moaned just imagining how good she would feel around my cock.

"So beautiful," I murmured with approval as I slid down.

Molding her breasts with my hands, I sucked and bit her nipples until she was writhing beneath me, and then I journeyed down her body, pressing my mouth against her stomach, nibbling and kissing until all she seemed to want was to burst into flames.

Rising up on my elbows, I surveyed her hungrily before pushing her legs out a little. Now she was even more exposed and vulnerable before my gaze.

I cupped her wet sex. "Knees up to your stomach. Wide."

Giving me a salacious grin, she did what I commanded.

Damn. She follows instructions so well.

I pressed her knees outward, tipping her womanhood up in the air while gazing straight into her eyes. "This is how I always want you—open and ready for whatever I want and need from you." I slid my fingers between the wet folds of her heat. "This cunt is mine to do with as I please."

She arched up, wiggling closer, as my thumb circled and played with her clit.

"Whether it's with my cock or mouth, this pussy is all mine."

I stroked her smoldering wetness. She shivered as if she was on the verge of exploding. But I had no intention of letting her until she offered what I needed to hear—her soft request.

"Core," she whispered. "I...need—dammit. Please lick my pussy." Her breathing was ragged.

"My pleasure, Sinful."

My hands curled around her thighs, spreading her wider, and my tongue thrust into her heat. That one lick sent her spiraling over the edge.

She wailed, "Core," like a prayer.

I pulled my head back, watching how her skin glowed and her eyes dilated, as my fingers continued to stretch her. "Louder, Sinful."

Her fingers gripped the sheets. "Dammit, Core."

"Louder," I demanded.

She was panting as her hips bucked wildly. My fingers pushed harder. She moaned louder when my finger found her clit again, playing with it mercilessly. She cried out and came again.

Panting and wasted, she lay boneless while I kicked off my pants and put on a condom. Getting back onto the bed, I hovered right above her, my weight on my knees between her thighs. Directing my head into position, I slipped in smoothly.

I couldn't take my eyes off her.

Her hazel eyes smoldered with intensity as my girth stretched her tight cunt.

With her nails desperately digging into my back, I grunted, "This cunt belongs to me," while fully seating myself with my balls bumping against her ass.

Feeling possessed, I grazed her lips and jaw. After pulling out, I sank back in with ruthless precision, hitting her G-spot. I wanted to fuck her until she was begging for air to breathe.

Her legs wrapped around my waist as I continued to hit her G-spot, making her legs quiver. I groaned when her slit sucked me in farther as I pumped harder. Her hips tilted up, and I adjusted my movements so, with each stroke, I brushed against her clit. The deeper I pumped, the louder she screamed. Her head thrashed back as I slid in and out. She wriggled beneath me. She was trembling, humming low. She stilled her hips so she could feel every inch of my pulsing manhood.

"I can't get enough of your cunt. I'm going to fuck you all night until you can't stand, darling," I growled into her ear, my cock forcing its way inside her again and again.

"Yes, yes, yes," she chanted, digging her nails into me like a wild woman.

I continued pumping, hard and controlled, making her mine with each stroke.

The entire time, we never looked away from each other. I couldn't help but love the way our bodies connected—stroke for stroke, touch for touch.

Sin was my equal.

Her breathing was fast and shallow with periods of whimpers intermixed. "Oh God, Core. Yes. Harder." She grabbed my head, pulling me closer, biting my lower lip. "Your gifted cock is mine."

Her words unleashed the fire within me. I let myself go, moving faster, pushing her into another orgasm. Arching, she screamed as her moist center spasmed around me. She collapsed right after, worn out and sweaty.

Pulling out of her body and flipping her onto her belly, I guided her up onto her knees. She mewled when I bit her neck. I brushed my lips over the tattoo of a guardian angel inked on her left shoulder and then on the large dove in flight on her right. Continuing on, I rained kisses along her spine.

Nudging her forward onto her hands, I massaged her buttocks. "You have the most beautiful ass," I rumbled. My fingers slid down the crack between her cheeks, touching her folds so intimately she gasped. "Fuck. You're so wet for me."

I slid my fingers through her wetness over and over until her hips squirmed uncontrollably. The air was sultry around us as my hands gripped her waist and I thrust into her smoothly.

Sin cried out with pleasure as one of my hands gripped her hair, with the other wrapped around her waist. I rocked my body into her. Our slick bodies were in perfect synchrony, with a strange magnetic energy encircling us.

She looked so comfortable against my skin.

"Don't stop," she whispered, shivering, as she gripped the bedsheets.

Growling, my fingers clutched the sides of her lush hips. I reared back and pushed forward. Every inch of me was sheathed in her. Her body shuddered, her legs quivered, and her core pulsed.

"You and me, darling, for better or for worse," I stated roughly, thrusting faster.

"Yes. For better or for worse, Core," she hissed.

"Fuck!" I cursed when she moved again.

"I'm going to come," she wailed.

"Not until I allow you."

My body slapped against hers ruthlessly. She rocked back into me, taking everything I had to give.

"Core, please."

My body burned for sweet release. "Now!" A strangled shout escaped my lips before I felt the orgasm ripping up my spine, tearing through my limbs.

Sin came so hard that she shouted my name at the top of her lungs. Her inner muscles contracted, milking me as both of us crested.

I kissed her on the shoulder before pulling her farther up on the bed. I clutched her body against mine. I wouldn't release her. I wouldn't let her go.

"Shit. That was fucking hot," I whispered against her lips.

"Hell yes, it was." She smiled even as she gasped for air.

I kissed her neck, her chin, her cheek. But it wasn't until I devoured her mouth with sweeping strokes of my tongue, slow and deep, that I realized I wanted Sin more than any woman I'd been with—even Maya.

TWISTED LIES 4

"Some of us think holding on makes us strong, but sometimes, it is letting go."
—**Hermann Hesse**

CHAPTER 1
SINTHIA

I jolted awake, rolling onto the other side of the bed, flipping over onto my stomach, and pressing my face into the pillow. I inhaled Core's scent—amber and sandalwood.

When we'd woken up early this morning, he'd taken me in every part of his master suite and bathroom. And when I'd thought my pussy couldn't take another round of pounding, he'd taken me again while we showered together—me with my legs around his waist, water raining down on us, and him fucking the hell out of me.

Hell… he fucks like a damn stallion.

Granted, I was no stranger to freaking fantastic sex, but this thing with Core felt… different… in ways I didn't understand.

From the first day I'd met him, there had been an instant connection, a spark that tethered me to him. And for weeks, almost every night, I'd crawl into bed with his name on my lips and my trusty and reliable vibrator, Beast, between my thighs. And I'd find myself waking from dreams of Core with needs Beast couldn't fully satisfy. It was embarrassing and problematic because wanting a man who was within my reach that I couldn't have was fucking with my head—big time—until I finally gave myself to him at the McKay Club. Well, technically, I'd had sex with him in his Noire lounge—his private, members-only playground, where the rich and famous indulged in discreet sexual fantasies.

Rolling over onto my back, I kicked off the blanket that had been tangled around my body before swinging my legs off the side of the bed. Trying to clear my sleep-fogged brain, I leaned forward, putting my elbows on my knees and clutching my head. I was exhausted from the last round of sex with Core.

This was way too much. I needed to take a moment to focus on something else besides fucking Core.

Sighing, I sat up before scrubbing my hands over my face.

I stood, deciding to take a hot shower to loosen up my muscles. Walking over to the chair with his black T-shirt draped across it, I picked it up, tugging it over my head. Instantly, I was engulfed in his very virile and masculine scent.

The image of his sexy eyes flashed through my mind.

Yep… he's destroyed me. The cocky but well-hung fucker.

I padded into his impressive master bathroom and spotted all of Core's toiletries lined up and perfectly organized on his marble countertops, as opposed to my stuff that was scattered about, creating a hot, disorganized mess.

He was the poster child for a man who demanded control and dominance, which was everything I deplored in a man… or at least I'd thought I did. But the more time I spent with him, the more confused I became about what I really wanted from our relationship and from him.

Do I want just sex or more?

He was complicated and dangerous with a whole lot of crazy mixed in. Plus, there was something about him that I couldn't quite figure out.

He was like that box of chocolates from *Forrest Gump*. I never quite knew what I was going to get next.

Dominant Core.

Asshole Core.

Caring Core.

Sensual Core.

Or take-no-shit Core…

On the flip side, he was constantly shattering everything I'd expected him to be—cold, narcissistic, and uncaring.

My thoughts drifted to last night when he'd shocked the shit out of me by taking care of me and protecting me when I felt exhausted, mentally and physically, after my townhouse had been broken into. Smoothly, Core had stepped in, taking charge of everything, including calling the police and fielding the barrage of questions from the officers, while I numbly rode a roller coaster of emotions—shock, fear, denial, and anger.

Damn. This shit with Core is uncharted territory for me.

My mind went back to the incident between us this morning when he'd gotten out of bed, tucked the sheets tightly around my body, and then kissed my forehead.

Before he'd walked out of the room, I'd heard him mumble, "Damn. What am I doing? I could get used to this…"

And, silently, I'd agreed.

With feet slapping against the marble floor, I turned on the rain shower, adjusting the temperature to hot.

Am I really thinking about trying to have a… relationship with Core?

My gut started churning with fear.

Breathe, Sin.

Take control of yourself.

There will be no attachments and absolutely no relationship.

Nope. Hard pass on that shit.

I stripped off Core's T-shirt before stepping beneath the shower-head and scrubbing at my skin as the jets beat against my body.

My heart was permanently closed off, and I planned on keeping it that way. Many had tried, and all had failed. Besides, there were just too many sides to Core. Some I knew, and some I suspected he deliberately hid from me. But what I did know was he was smart, savvy, and calculating in everything he did. And when it came down to it, I was his business asset.

And if there was one thing I knew without a doubt, it was that business and sex did not mix. Yet here I was, allowing Core to disassemble me like a fucking toy and remake me into a woman I didn't know. Now I felt exposed in a way that scared the living shit out of me. I hadn't spent the night in a man's bed in forever... yet I had with Core.

Stupid, stupid, stupid. I'm doing everything I swore I'd never do... Get attached.

CHAPTER 2
SINTHIA

Internally, I was screaming while I quickly washed my body and hair, rinsing away the shampoo and soap. Snatching one of Core's luxurious towels, I dried myself off before leaving the bathroom. After getting dressed, I clasped the silver bracelet Dad had given me for my seventeenth birthday around my wrist before gathering all of my stuff.

When I bolted for the bedroom door, I felt like I was in a burning building and all I could see were the little lit-up red exit signs. "I'm so fucking out of here," I mumbled under my breath while walking out of Core's bedroom with my overnight bag in tow.

"All right. A cup of coffee. Okay, maybe two," I groused while padding down the stairs, "and then I'm getting the hell out of here." Unabashedly, I was never one to forgo coffee in the morning, even despite a potentially awkward situation with Core before I hit the road.

I marched through Core's palatial penthouse that was so huge that I could do cartwheels. His home was stunning, and it seemed like every detail had been considered at its conception—from the marble foyer with its discreet keyed private elevator that opened directly into his residence to the high ceilings, the marble-and-glass-enclosed fireplace in the living room, and the wide-plank, rift-sawed white oak flooring throughout.

From somewhere in the space, I heard Core's voice bark, "That's none of your fucking business, Ram!" There was a beat of silence before Core hissed, "Would you fucking stop whining like a damn girl?"

I rolled my eyes. He must be on his cell, and he sounded pissed. But that was nothing new. The fucker was always mad at something or someone. I was just happy it wasn't me... yet.

I followed the sound of his deep voice.

"Yes, Ram. I know you've had Jeff on ice for hours," he responded. "I've been busy." Silence again. "Oh, fuck off! I don't give a shit what you think." Core paused for another beat. "Yeah, real funny, fucker. Now let's get to business. Have you finished softening him up?" There was a long pause. "Good. When I get there, we'll start the real work..."

Ice for hours?

Softening him up?

What the hell?

Exactly what type of shit is Core into?

Is he a self-made billionaire, crime boss, or both?

I scowled. And what did it say about me that I was so far in with Core that I didn't give a damn either way?

I skidded to a stop when I found him standing in the kitchen, talking on his cell with his shirt off and annoyance written all over his face.

His head snapped in my direction. "Ram, I've got to go. Yes. I'll be right there," he roared before ending the call and sliding the cell across the countertop.

"Business deal gone south?" I inquired.

His face twitched. "Something like that." He flicked his eyes to the overnight bag I'd dropped by my feet. He rasped, "You going somewhere, Sin?"

There was no smile. When he crossed his muscular arms, my eyes traveled up his tall, well-built body that was pure, rippling muscle. Hardened abs trailed downward to the waist of his black designer-looking jeans.

Damn, no man should look this fucking good all the time.

And why the hell wasn't he wearing a damn shirt? His body, from chest to wrist, was a beautiful composition of Japanese tattoos and other beast-themed ink.

"Yep," I replied. "I've got shit to do."

He arched a brow. "Like?"

"Like it's none of your business," I replied while slowly plodding toward him, stepping into his massive kitchen.

We stood face to face as I leaned my hip against the granite kitchen counter.

He made a face. "That's where you're wrong. Everything about you is my business." He was studying me too closely, his expression brooding.

Keeping my gazed fixed on him, I replied, "The only thing that's officially your business is my company. Well, ninety-seven percent of it anyway." My statement was a deliberate jab. A reminder that he didn't own me and that I was still in control.

"You're the most infuriating woman I know." His calm response ignited my frustration.

I wanted to piss him off.

I needed his anger to fuel my will to hightail it away from him and away from this suffocating intimacy.

I needed him to save me from myself.

"I'll take that as a compliment, McKay."

"It wasn't." His lips curled into the faintest of ironic smiles.

"Why, sure it is. Besides, you love my sassiness and my sexy ass, which I'll be hustling on out of here once I have my coffee." I leaned in and tapped his cheek before allowing my hand to drop away. "Okay, enough of this morning chitchat. Coffee, McKay."

"What's the magic word?" He countered.

"Now," I chirped.

He growled.

"Please." I comically batted my eyes.

In answer, he reached out, grazing the side of my cheek, leaving a tingle in his wake before abruptly walking away from me and toward his espresso machine.

Holy shit! Core McKay is actually going to make me coffee.

I wasn't used to a man doing something remotely nice for me because I was so used to doing things alone.

I drew my lower lip between my teeth while staring at him.

He pressed the button on the gadget and placed a cup beneath the brew head to capture the wonderful stream of black liquid gold. When a sufficient amount of coffee had flowed into the cup, he filled another one and brought them over.

He pushed a cup into my hand. "So?" He started in his quiet, rough voice.

"So what?" I grumbled, lifting the cup to my lips and taking a small sip, savoring a much-needed awakening.

Glancing around, I took in his kitchen, which was a chef's dream—with top-of-the-line stainless steel appliances, including a wall oven and cooktop with a concealed range hood, a subzero refrigerator, and wine storage. Everything in the space gleamed—from the lacquer and glass cabinetry to the granite countertops and backsplash as well as a dishwasher with a built-in lacquer panel.

"What are your plans for today?" Core asked.

I choked on a mouthful of coffee.

Idle morning chitchat?

Is this what normal people do?

I shifted uncomfortably, feeling out of my depth as I tried to recall the number of times I'd engaged in casual banter the morning after having sex with a man. The number was zero.

With most of my previous sexual encounters, I'd actually had an exit strategy before having sex. My solution was to keep one high-heeled boot dangling just outside the door at all times. I would time it perfectly. After we both climaxed, I would simply follow the evacuation instructions I had practiced over and over in my head, and—*poof*—crisis averted. I was out of my hookup's bed before he could even pull out of me.

Ignoring Core's question, I took another sip, eyeing the cup sitting on the counter. "Why aren't you drinking your coffee?"

"It's for you."

I frowned. His sweet gesture instantly raised my guard. I waited for the other shoe to drop. *Is he fucking serious?*

This shit is too good to be true.

What is he after?

"So that's your evil plan? Ply me with coffee, hoping to get my agenda?"

"Yep. Is it working?" He winked at me.

"No," I mumbled before draining the cup and placing it on the counter. "But I know you're like a dog with a bone, and you won't let this shit go until I tell you." I pursed my lips. "I'm going home to assess the damage that bastard did to my townhouse." Something I really wasn't looking forward to.

My mind spun just remembering the chaos waiting for me in my home. The image from last night's mayhem was burned in my mind.

An intruder had violated my personal space, my home and sanctuary, and then destroyed all my shit. It was like a tornado had ripped through my home. Furniture had been slashed and thrown about. Kitchen drawers were pulled out. Broken glass and dishes littered the floor. Throw pillows had been cut, and down feathers were scattered everywhere. Nothing had been left untouched. And all I could think about was...

What if I had been home?

Would I be dead right now?

And who the fuck would have done some vile shit like that?

"Sin," Core started, "there's no need for you to run home. In fact, I'd rather you didn't until I can sort out who broke into your house."

"Hell no!" I snapped. "I'm not going to cower in your penthouse, waiting for your ass to figure this out." I clenched and unclenched my hands at my sides.

I refused to let terror control my life. By facing my fears head on, I not only was confronting what was making me so afraid—seeing months of hard work on my collection ruined and coming to terms with the daunting task of starting over—but I was also taking back control and choosing not to let the break-in dictate what I could and could not do. No one had the right to stop me from achieving my dreams.

"Core, I'm not running away from this. I'm going home."

Rage coursed through my veins when I thought about the worst part of the destruction—the remnants of my couture collection ripped into pieces and thrown around like confetti.

"And you will. But not now." He kept his voice low and soft but left no room for doubt that he'd issued a command.

"What?" I spluttered. I was the damn girl boss here. "Don't tell me what to do, Core. I'm a grown-ass woman."

His taking sexual control in the bedroom, bathroom, and any other available surface we'd fucked on was one thing, but telling me what I could and could not do outside of those circumstances was another damn thing.

"Yes, you are. All I'm saying is at least let me lessen the stress of you starting over."

My temper eased a bit when I realized he wasn't trying to control me. He was trying to help. I just wasn't used to accepting assistance. I was a go-it-alone and fix-it-myself type of chick.

"Core, I appreciate everything you're doing for me. I really do. But I'm really angry right now… well, angry and creeped the hell out." I studied him. "Someone broke into my townhouse and destroyed my collection. And if that isn't fucked up enough, the only thing they stole was my dad's ledger. Don't you think that shit is strange?" I took a deep breath before slowly letting it out.

Frustration was clouding my mind over the whole break-in situation, but the fact that the old ledger was now gone had been nagging at me with an incessant sense that I was missing something important. I just couldn't figure out what it was.

A couple weeks ago, when I'd found the ledger stashed under a secret compartment of Dad's ratty trunk, it had been puzzling to say the least.

Why did Dad take the time to hide the damn thing in the first place?

When I'd opened the book to check it out, nothing in the damn thing had made a bit of sense. It was only names, random handwritten codes, and numbers—essentially gibberish. There were too many pieces to the puzzle, and none of them fit together perfectly. But now I couldn't shake the feeling that I was overlooking a key connection between Dad, the break-in, and the ledger.

"Sin, yes, I do think it's bizarre the ledger was stolen. I already have my team working on getting to the bottom of the break-in. I've also arranged for a housecleaning service to stop by and clean up your place."

"That was fast."

The man was efficient.

How did he manage to get them to come out at the last minute and on a Saturday?

"And as far as your collection," he declared, "just tell me what you need to make you whole, and I'll take care of that, too."

Holy hell. He did all that shit for me? Without me even asking?

Core's demonstrated ability to be selfless and take care of me without my asking was a refreshing change of pace. His actions brought me peace of mind. I relaxed, deciding not to push him so hard. Besides, it was Saturday, and I didn't have any client dress fittings until tomorrow. Maybe it was best to spend a stress-free day—away from the scene of the crime—going through images of my designs stored on my Mac and coming up with a logical game plan for tackling the re-creation of my collection.

"You've thought of everything, huh?" I countered.

"No." He scowled. "Not everything. I didn't think someone would destroy all of your hard work. That shit was totally fucked up and damn unexpected. But whoever did it… I'll make them pay for that." His jaw tightened. "Does anyone have an ax to grind with you?"

I widened my eyes. "With me? Fuck no. I keep my life drama-free. I don't have any enemies." I frowned. I couldn't think of one competitor who hated me this much. My life was uncomplicated. There was no drama, no rivals. "Except…"

My heart thumped hard in my chest.

Is Jaxon back to claim what he thinks is his—me?

My mind rejected the possibility, but the scary memory of the utter rage that had clouded Jaxon's eyes before he sliced my shoulder made me shudder. It was Core who brought me back to the here and now.

He caught my chin, and his gaze bored into mine. "Except what?"

My pulse accelerated at his question. "Nothing." I shook my head. I couldn't tell him the truth because it was ugly. I felt like a fool for lowering my guard and allowing an unstable asshole like Jaxon into my life.

He stroked my cheek. "Tell me." His eyes never left mine as he waited for my response.

It felt like being dissected, and no matter how hard I tried, I just couldn't hold up under the scrutiny.

"Years ago, there was this guy named Jaxon who started stalking me," I said softly, my throat tightening. "He became obsessed with me after just one night of sex."

"And?" His fingers stilled.

I shrugged. "And nothing. He's gone. I haven't seen him in years. Thank God."

"So you're telling me he just up and disappeared?"

I nodded.

He dropped his hand away from me and narrowed his eyes. "Sin, that's bullshit. Stalkers don't just walk away from their prey. They get what they want—their ultimate prizes and their victims. They're obsessive, sick fuckers who get off on harassing, terrorizing, and in some fucked-up cases, killing their victims or anyone else they think is in the way of their desired goal."

The truth of Core's words terrified me. The idea that Jaxon was indeed skulking around in the shadows, waiting to attack me, was way too much for me to stomach.

I shivered with disgust, remembering how the utter madness years ago had spiraled out of control after Jaxon broke into Jade's apartment and left the rose and my underwear on my bed.

"White roses," I blurted out. "I fucking hate the smell and the sight of them." I'd lived through agonizing months of huge, elaborate vases filled with white roses being delivered to me every day with one creepy message scribbled on each card.

Love you.

—J.

"Then one day, the roses mysteriously stopped showing up. I thought the madness and his obsession with me were over." I laughed cynically. "But, of course, I was fucking wrong. My Jaxon nightmare was just beginning. The bastard started showing up at every party I attended, and he chased away any guy who attempted to talk to me. When I confronted him, telling him to leave me the hell alone, that only seemed to enrage him."

Just thinking about the months of torture and fear he'd put me through, my heart raced. "Paranoid that he was lurking in the shadows, waiting to hurt me, I locked myself away in my house, only venturing out for work. After weeks and months passed without incident, I thought my world was safe again—until it all came crashing down."

His stoic expression turned grim. "What did that fucker do to you?"

The vehemence of his response surprised me. Core sounded like he would destroy anything and everything that dared to hurt me.

"He grabbed me, dragged me into a dark alleyway, and pressed a knife to my throat." I shuddered, fighting the familiar dread that seeped into my bones when I thought about that day. The memories lingered. The fear remained.

Tone as flat as ever, Core replied, "That fucker did what?"

Nothing could erase that day from my mind. The insane words of love Jaxon had babbled over and over as he brutally ripped off my clothes with sick lust in his eyes. The moment of total hopelessness I'd felt. I could still remember the bitterness that had coated my tongue when I realized I was nothing but a piece of property to him, his possession that he had every intention of claiming over and over again until I broke.

The tears had streamed down my face as I braced for the impending savage violation. Then my resignation to my fate as I lay shivering on the cold ground and letting my mind go blank. Like a petulant child, Jaxon had tried to steal what I refused to give him— illicit permission to be his. Unlike Core, who only took what I'd freely given him… me.

I recalled Core's words to me last night.

"I'll have all of you or none of you," he had clipped out. "That's the only way it will be."

And I had agreed with, "Core, we have a deal."

Core softened his voice, bringing me back to the present. "Sin?"

"A homeless man stumbled upon us, saving me. But before Jaxon walked away, he sliced me across my shoulder." I rubbed the scar that was covered by my T-shirt. "Never forget…" I whispered, fighting the cold fear running down my spine. "His words were, 'Never forget you'll always belong to me.'"

Core paced back and forth before me. "Last name?" he snapped.

I arched a brow. "What?"

He stalked over to me. "Tell me his last name," he demanded.

"Why?" I raised my chin in a gesture of defiance and met his gaze. "He's gone, Core."

"Is he?" Catching my upturned chin, he bored his eyes into mine. "What are you not telling me?"

My breath hitched as a flush of adrenaline tingled through my body. It was frightening how he knew me so well. "A vase of white roses with a note with the letter *J* scribbled on it was left on my doorstep a couple weeks ago."

"Like I asked, last fucking name?" He lifted an eyebrow. And waited.

My resolve faltered beneath the steady, authoritative regard.

"Jaxon Webb," I offered tentatively. "What are you going to do, Core?"

Not that I was averse to the idea of Core finding and beating the shit out of Jaxon… but killing him? No. That line I wouldn't cross. I didn't want that type of shit on my conscience. But more importantly, I couldn't allow Core to get into trouble with the authorities for any illegal actions he'd taken to keep me safe.

"His name has just been added to my Assholes to Destroy list."

"Core." My voice croaked as I spoke. "You can't just go around New York like some vengeful Viking, destroying everyone in your path."

"I can, and I do. I seek and destroy motherfuckers every damn day. And I don't lose a fucking wink of sleep about that shit."

Core had a certain intensity about him that always made him seem intimidating, but this was different. He was fierce, dark, and unyielding. Every word rang with power and authority. Frankly, it had me feeling a little turned on, if I was being honest.

I inclined my head. "And what will you do when you find him?"

He arched a brow. "Do you really want the answer?"

"Yes."

"He won't live." His dark words rang with deadly promise.

I swallowed. Hard. The silken threat of violence in his civilized tone reminded me that, although Core was a billionaire, wore expensively tailored suits, and negotiated million-dollar deals, he was still a ruthless predator and not a man to be fucked with.

"Well... shit," I whispered. "That's badass and unnervingly savage."

"Sin, there're things I don't tolerate." He spoke with quiet menace. "And one of them is men who abuse women." He reached out and grazed the side of my cheek with the back of his hand.

"I can protect myself, Core. Shit, I've been doing a damn good job for twenty-six years."

Despite the fact that he thought he could protect me, no one could but me, and I refused to cower behind Core's back, letting him fight my battles. I was strong and in control, and I would not let Jaxon win. And if Jaxon was back to claim what he thought was his—me—then I was ready to fight as if my life depended on it—because it did.

Core kept his answer short. "I'm all yours. If you're all mine."

My breath caught in my throat as I blinked hard. His words gave me goose bumps, stirring a longing in me I hadn't known existed until now. For a moment, I wondered what it would be like to be loved, adored, and worshipped by a man like Core, but I quickly dismissed the dumb thought.

Without thinking, I blurted out, "Until?"

He eased back, eyeing me. "That's up to you, Sin."

He was right. How far this shit went between us was completely up to me. I was in control... and I planned on keeping it. That was why I had to get out of there.

"I always trust my gut." I bit my bottom lip.

My fingers itched to trail across the all-seeing eye tattoo etched into the skin of his neck, but then I caught myself. Tenderness was not something I embraced. I fucked men and then disconnected. But that was B.C.—Before Core. Now here I was breaking all the rules with the one man I shouldn't.

No. I will not give in to him.

He reached forward, threading his fingers through my hair. "And what is your gut telling you about me?"

"Run because you're nothing but trouble." It was the damn truth.

Yes, I was very attracted to him. Yes, I wanted him like no other man I'd ever met. And yes, he scared the living shit out of me because of all of the above. Core was an itch I couldn't stop scratching. No matter how much I wanted to run away from him, I just couldn't muster up the strength to do that.

His fingers dropped away, and he stepped back slightly, making no attempt to conceal the erection tenting his jeans. "And just when I thought we had an understanding..." His gravelly voice sent vibrations of lust throughout me.

Sin... eyes off his cock. Focus.

"It's complicated, Core." My voice broke. I cleared my throat.

He stepped forward, caging me, making sure my body was flush against his. I sucked in a breath when his huge, hard bulge pressed against my stomach. Warmth flooded my pussy and then coursed through my veins like fire. My nipples strained against my bra.

"This seems pretty simple to me. I made the terms of our relationship very clear last night. It's you and me, satisfying our urge to fuck each other senseless." His chiseled lips curled. "With the added bonus of spending quality time with each other, exclusively, and seeing where this goes." He tilted his head and studied me. "And you agreed to the arrangement... happily. The deal has been made, and I'm not allowing you to back out of it. You're mine," he growled.

"Yours, like an object? We went over this last night." Pursing my lips, I pushed at his chest, and he moved back a little, his gaze burning me. "See, when you say caveman shit like that, I want to Superman-punch you in the damn face. I'm not something to be owned like one of your fucking expensive sports cars, McKay."

"No, not like an object. You're so much more than an object to me, Sin. But I won't make excuses for the man I am. I'm greedy, ruthless, stubborn, and yes, an asshole… at times. But I protect and cherish what's mine. And you, Sinful, are most definitely mine." He reached up and pinched one of my nipples through my shirt and bra, and I whimpered with a combination of pleasure and pain. "And I'm not letting you go until we both are duly satisfied. Like I've already told you, I have very dark tastes when it comes to sex, and I'm planning on exploring every one of them, leaving nothing unfucked. Including your beautiful ass."

My heart thumped wildly in my chest. I'd thought after our all night and morning fuckfest, my lustful urges had disappeared, but there was nothing settled between us.

"I agreed to sex…" I placed a hand against his cheek, enjoying the prickle of his stubble against my palm. "Not… this…" I croaked, dropping my hand.

"This? You mean us?" he replied before he angled down, grabbing my face between his callused hands.

Our mouths were a breath away, the desire and tension almost more than I could take.

"Yes, us." I confirmed.

Shit… is there anything he doesn't know about me now? Just the thought made me uncomfortable and jittery. My feelings for him were so powerful that fear flowed through me.

"Yes… that's right… us," he whispered before swooping in for a tantalizing kiss.

My body betrayed all my mental defenses, and I lifted my soft lips to his hard ones. As he slipped his tongue along the seam, a low moan escaped me, and then he was inside, exploring and teasing. He gave my lower lip a nip, followed by a soothing rub from his tongue.

Shit. Core is sexy and lethal.

And when I expected him to press his advantage, he gave me one last swipe of his tongue, bit my lower lip again, and retreated.

"Are you hungry?" he asked.

Utterly mystified by the change of topic, I stared at him. "What?" I rasped, blinking in confusion.

Yes, I'm hungry… for your cock. Is this a damn trick question?

He brushed a hand against my breast, and my nipples stiffened immediately. Liquid heat poured through me, and my stomach clenched.

"Of course you are," he purred simply. A smile twitched across his lips.

"McKay"—I suspiciously eyed him—"are you fucking with me right now? Because being a cunt tease is beneath you."

"I'm not fucking with you. I need to feed you." He smiled. The man was beyond handsome when he smiled.

My heart skipped a beat because he was taking care of me in a way no man had before. Core was being unbelievably caring and kind, and that terrified me because it was easy to walk away from someone who wasn't.

"Let me see what I can scrounge up to eat." He lifted me, setting me on the countertop.

Turning, he walked over to the subzero refrigerator and pulled out items—a plate of assorted sliced cheeses and curls of thinly shaved prosciutto and a bowl of figs and strawberries.

I arched a brow. This feast felt a little highbrow for Core. "You prepared all of this?"

"Hell no." He shook his head. "Zuri did. She calls it community service by fixing my 'sad bachelor fridge.'"

Wasting no time, he placed the items on the table next to the granite counter. Then he plucked a piece of cheese from the plate and held it out before my lips. I nibbled on it while glaring at him. I waited for his next move, but Core watched me with those devastating gray eyes, his expression giving nothing away. Before long, we were eating in comfortable silence as I examined the aftermath of my passion-fueled antics on his skin.

"Jesus. You've got lots of bite and scratch marks on you."

I wouldn't admit it out loud, but there was something so damn satisfying about marking him for the world to see.

"What can I say?" He grinned. "You're a wicked sex kitten when my tongue is stroking your pussy just… right," he purred.

"Quiet, McKay. Don't be a cocky asshole." I smacked his shoulder. "Besides, I'm no quiet lady when it comes to sex."

"I can attest to that shit." He swooped down and nipped my neck.

"Jesus. The filthy, naughty words and sounds that came out of that pretty mouth of yours would even make a porn star blush." He laughed huskily. "And I loved it."

"Ooh!" I dug my fingers into his hair, yanking him away. "It's not polite to fuck and tell, McKay."

"Who gives a shit about being polite?" He winked. "What happens in the bed… bathroom… and anywhere else that I decide to fuck your luscious, beautiful body is all up for discussion between us, darling."

We looked at each other and then burst out laughing.

Damn, the vibe we had was so fucking easy and natural. I hadn't realized until now that I actually liked Core—as a person.

"You know this thing between us is crazy, right?" I asked. "I don't know anything about you, except for the shit I've read about you in the gossip section of the newspaper." I gave him a quizzical glance.

Core didn't respond right away.

"Believe me," he replied. "What they write about me is bullshit. All speculation and made-up garbage just to sell more newspapers."

Before I'd met him, I'd heard all the rumors—none of them good—circulating about the ruthless but utterly handsome Core McKay, the wealthy New York City recluse, business mogul, and eccentric owner of McKay Corporation and the McKay Club—his invite-only playground for the elite, rich, and kinky, a place to indulge in discreet liaisons, allowing all your freaky fantasies to come true.

I quirked a brow. "So you're telling me the Manhattan gossip hags have it all wrong?"

"Wrong about what?" he asked in a low tone.

"That you built your billion-dollar empire using money from drug trafficking, money laundering, and prostitution."

"Prostitution?" The look on his face was something close to disgust. "I've never messed with that shit. It's not my thing. I don't believe in sexually exploiting women."

His nostrils flared. "Hard damn work. That's how I built my empire. Nothing was handed to Ram and me. We had to fight for everything we've got, and that shit wasn't easy. But I'm not going to lie. Some of the shit we did… Well, it wasn't pretty." He scoffed. "The world of organized crime is a dog-eat-dog world. We made a fucking lot of money, and life was good… for a while." He flexed his arm muscles. "Until everyone around us got nabbed by the police, ending up serving hard time in jail, or got killed by business rivals over territory, money, or just for the fuck of it. So Ram and I decided to get the fuck out while the getting was good. We had to look out for own interests, and we went legit."

"Okay… so that would be a big check in the criminal activities box."

"Does that change how you feel about me?" He compressed his mouth into a thin line.

Mystified, I stared at him. "What? Hell no. At least, not now." I shrugged.

Before I had gotten to know him, the rumors about Core had definitely affected how I felt about him. But now? I didn't care what the tabloids proclaimed.

"I'm not perfect. You're not perfect. Shit. Perfection just doesn't exist. Besides, everyone's journey in life is different. As far as I'm concerned, it's the destination that matters."

He nodded in agreement.

"Okay, so… how did you get these?" I leaned in, tracing a finger along the light scar on his cheek and then farther up onto the jagged scar running across his eyebrow. "A gang fight over territory in Brooklyn?" I finished saucily.

He frowned while a long, uncomfortable silence dragged on. I fidgeted awkwardly when I realized Core was still on the fence about just how honest he wanted to be with me. It was as if he still didn't trust me. I pushed down the emotional hurt and replaced it with my old standby… anger.

"Okay. I'm done." I threw my arms up in the air. "This is definitely not going to work between us if you refuse to open up even a little bit."

With jerky, furious movements, I attempted to hop off the counter, but he quickly stopped me.

With an aggrieved sigh, he responded, "Sin, calm the fuck down."

"Oh, fuck off, McKay! I've shared stuff with you that I haven't said aloud in years, and the minute I ask you a question, you either deflect or I get nothing but crickets. You're the most infuriating man I know."

The tension between us was almost unbearable.

His mouth flattened. "I'm an open book, Sin." He folded his arms over his chest. "It's just that you might not like the answers you get." He bit out the words. "My past is very dark and sordid. I'm just not sure you're ready to hear about that part of me… yet."

I refused to let him intimidate me. With my chin tilted at a stubborn angle, I held my ground. "I'm not afraid of knowing the truth, Core. I'm more terrified of the unknown shit."

Running his hands through his hair, he grunted, "Fuck it." He scowled. "I got the scar on my cheek from a car bomb."

My breath caught in my throat as I blinked.

He carried on, eyebrows squeezing together. "It happened years ago." His voice went flat. "One minute, I was walking away from my girlfriend, Maya, who was pregnant with my child and sitting in my parked SUV, waiting for me to get something she'd left inside our apartment. The next instant, I heard an explosion." His hands almost curled into fists, and then he straightened them. "The force of the blast threw me back, slamming me into the sidewalk." He pointed to the scar on his cheek. "That's how I got this." There was tightness in his expression. "It's a reminder of what I lost in that burning SUV—Maya and my baby." He finished with a grave expression, the loss and pain evident in his eyes.

I felt like shit for making him relive something so fucking painful. I thought the story about the scar was going to be some epic tale about how totally badass he was. But this? My mind was still reeling from his story. Core would have been a father if Maya and his baby had survived.

Core, a father?

I blinked rapidly. That was a side of him I hadn't even known existed.

Abruptly, he turned on his heel, storming over to the refrigerator and pulling out a beer. He eyed me. "You want one?"

It took several moments before I could compose myself enough to reply. Even though it was early, I nodded. "Yes."

He twisted off the caps on both bottles before walking back and handing me an icy-cold one and taking a long swig from his.

"I'm sorry for your loss, Core."

He drained his bottle before saying, "It's been fucking years, but I'd be lying if I didn't admit that thinking about Maya still hurt like a motherfucker." He spoke with quiet menace, "The irony of all this shit is that the major reason I'd decided to turn my back on my criminal empire was for fear of losing her and my unborn child. But I lost her anyway, and my world shattered. Just one tragic moment, and she was taken away, leaving me empty. When she died, I lashed out at everyone around me, including my friends." He shrugged one massive shoulder. "Without her, my life was cold, and I wasn't alive."

"And now?" I asked tentatively.

"No woman could replace Maya. That's what I believed… until now…" His voice trailed off as he brushed my cheek.

His touch and words sent a shiver through me.

Oh. My. Fucking. God.

He continued. "But I'm at a crossroad. There's so much that you still don't know about me—and me about you."

I nodded. "You're right. There is still a lot we don't really know about each other. But I'd be lying if I said that what I know about you so far doesn't make me want to run the other way." Especially not since he'd just laid his heart bare by spilling his past and about the loss of his girlfriend and unborn child.

Maybe Jade's advice was right; I needed to heal and let go of the hurt from what Grace and Kyle had done to me.

Now it was my turn to reveal a piece of me. "I've had a pretty fucked-up past with relationships. So getting close to someone again? Trusting someone? Not gonna happen overnight." I sighed heavily. "The problem got worse when my dad died."

He kissed my forehead and whispered, "I'm sorry for your loss, Sin."

I nodded in acknowledgment. "It was such a shock. A reckless driver slammed into him, sending him off a bridge." How abruptly I had lost him hurt. It had changed me, leaving me vulnerable and scared to let any new people into my life for fear of losing them.

"Shit. That must have devastated you and your mother," he said.

"I was devastated. My mother… Grace, well…" I snorted. "She didn't even shed a tear. But she did happily burn through the money from my dad's insurance settlement on a massive shopping spree."

Just thinking about how Grace had spent the settlement on extravagant purchases, including a new condo with a homeowner's association fee that was more than what most people paid for their monthly mortgage alone, my lips pursed.

Core lifted an eyebrow. "Damn. She sounds like some piece of work."

I snorted. "Yes… she's fucking special, but not in a good damn way. That's one of the many reasons I cut the heartless hag out of my life when I was eighteen."

"Doesn't sound like a great mother-daughter relationship."

I drew my lower lip between my teeth while staring at him, hesitant to unearth the bones of my past that I had buried deep. "No, it wasn't, and it's not a subject I enjoy talking about."

Core glared at me with an intensity that made me uncomfortable. "Sin, we're talking, so let's be open."

I let out a calming breath. "Grace was never… well, a mother. As long as I can remember, there was always this wall between us. Do you know I can't recall a time when she actually hugged me?"

Painful feelings—of being unworthy and unlovable—and memories I'd repressed came rushing back at the remembrance of how Grace didn't love me. For years, I'd felt defective because she never taught me the things most mothers taught their daughters—allowing them to express their emotions, their pain, and their vulnerability without repercussions.

I continued. "I remember one day I came home from school and hugged her. You know, just to see what would happen. She shook me off like I was some pervert molesting her. I knew then that there was nothing in the world I could do to make her love me." But like an abused puppy, I still tried for way too long.

I cringed inside, thinking about back then, how fucking hard I'd worked to be everything she expected me to be—flawless. I'd even dyed my long naturally auburn hair blond like hers, which looked utterly ridiculous with my olive-colored skin and exotic, dark features. What was worse had been the sheer disdain in her eyes when she saw my failed attempts to be perfect. In comparison to her ethereal, porcelain features, I wasn't pretty enough or thin enough or smart enough. I just wasn't enough. And frankly, that truth had hurt like a motherfucker.

Unwanted memories—a bitter past I'd thought I'd buried deep—surfaced, one of the many arguments between Dad and Grace...

I was happy... for once—at least for now—because I was with Dad, and he was alive. I had just finished watching him slave over Thanksgiving dinner while I served as his little helper by setting the table that we now sat down at, still, tense, watching the clock, and letting the food get cold while we waited for Grace to come home. With every breath I took, my heart sank deeper. She should have been back by now.

6:34 p.m.

8:27 p.m.

10:05 p.m.

Then around 11:30 p.m., Grace stumbled into the house, laughing to herself as she staggered over to the table.

Dad snapped, "You've been drinking again."

"No..." Her breath reeked of alcohol. "I swear." Then she broke out in a fit of giggles.

I hated that she laughed when she lied.

Dad looked at Grace with disappointment. "Grace, it's Thanksgiving. I promised Sin we'd spend the day together for once and have a nice family dinner."

I held my breath, waiting for Grace to say something, and she did.

"You promised her? Well, you didn't ask me shit. You always do this," she slurred. "I can never have a good time. Now you've ruined my night." By now she was screaming. "You and that little brat of yours always do!" She leveled me with a disdainful glare. I squirmed under its intensity. "Besides, look at her. She could stand to miss a couple meals." She cackled.

Tears rushed to my eyes.

"Grace! Enough!" Dad shouted.

Grace wobbled. "You're always taking up for her. Well, I don't need this crap," she yelled before she opened the door to leave again.

"Grace." Dad jumped up from the table, and I followed him as he went outside where Grace stood, trying to get into her car.

"Grace, get inside," Dad demanded. "I'm not letting you drive drunk." He tried to stop her from getting into the vehicle.

She kept pushing him away like he was some sort of pest she wanted to get rid of. "Don't try to act like you give a shit if I live or die. All you care about is Sin. What about me? Don't you love me? Or am I just here to pretend that we have a happy family life?"

"Grace, how many times do I have to tell you that I love you?" He sighed. "Now get inside. You're making a scene."

The neighbors were peeking out of their windows, watching the spectacle.

"No," she hissed. "Ian, come with me. Remember how we were before her?" She pointed at me. "It was about us… about me. Now my life is a living hell with us moving around because of her."

"Shut up, Grace," Dad hissed. "She can hear you."

"I don't care because I've never wanted her. She's not mine. She's Aub—"

"Don't," Dad yelled.

I sobbed because it hurt that she'd rejected me and thought I was a burden to her. But it had always been that way, my entire life. Dad would get into trouble for being nice to me.

"Go or stay. I don't care anymore," Dad replied.

"You're such an idiot," she chided before jumping into her car and driving away.

Dad brought me back inside the house, closing the door.

"Dad, what's Aub?"

He touched my hair. "Nothing. You know how she gets when she drinks."

"But why does she hate me so much?" I asked.

"It's not about you, Sin. She's hurting inside." He sighed heavily. "Her dad was awful to her throughout her childhood. She had no attention whatsoever. And I think every time she sees what a good relationship we have, she relives her childhood all over again."

• • •

Core's voice drew me back to the present. "Shit. That's rough, but that's her fucking loss."

"Loss?"

"Missing out on the experience of loving and caring for a beautiful, smart woman like you."

My mouth parted and then closed at such an unexpected but touching compliment. Damn... he was redefining my initial perception of him in every way. He had a fucking heart under his ice-cold demeanor.

Emotions welled up within me, and I cleared my throat, deciding to change the topic before I said or did something I'd regret like throwing caution to the wind and lowering my emotional barriers, letting him in. "What about your mother? How was your relationship with her?" Last night, he had briefly mentioned his mother had died, but he had seemed hesitant to talk about the topic any further.

"The exact opposite of your mother." He paused. "And if she were alive today, the moment she met you, she would have welcomed you into her home with no reservations because that was the kind of nurturing woman she was."

Wait... met me? Core McKay would have brought me to meet his mother?

I swallowed hard. He couldn't have meant that. I was reading way too much into his words.

Get a grip, girl!

Without missing a beat, he carried on. "To the world, she was a hard, street smart, take-no-shit kind of woman. But with me, she was so much different." He smiled wryly. "She couldn't stop hugging me, even at the most inappropriate times, like when I was trying to look cool and tough in front of my friends. And even when I was being a badass, stubborn prick, she loved me unconditionally, so I felt safe enough to be myself. Most significantly, I learned the importance of honoring my word and commitments from her. Her word was her bond. And so is mine."

"Sounds like a good woman, Core." I loved seeing that happy glint in his eyes. "It must have been nice to have that kind of foundation in your life." I envied him at that moment because it reminded me of my nonexistent relationship with Grace.

Core let out a harsh breath. "It was." A brief flash of sadness glinted in his eyes before they hardened. "Before she was murdered by a cold-blooded killer."

Oh shit. I wasn't expecting this response at all.

"Murdered?" My eyes widened.

"Yes. She was killed right in front of me."

"I'm so sorry, Core." I touched his arm. "I hope the animal is in jail at least?"

"He's not. He got away with fucking murder, and my world changed forever the day she died. I've spent my entire life waiting for the day I'll finally find him and avenge my mother's death."

I heard the agony in his voice when he mentioned his mother. The rare display of his emotion made me want to know more about the man, to dig deeper under his hard facade. My wanting such intimate emotional access surprised the hell out of me, given the fact that I stubbornly refused to give Core the same access to what lay beneath my emotional mask.

"I don't blame you for feeling that way." I swallowed hard. "If you don't mind me asking… what happened?"

I grabbed his hand, weaving my fingers through his. His fingers stiffened before they relaxed.

His eyes glazed over like he was reliving the bitter memories. "I was doing my homework when I heard my mother's bloodcurdling scream. I'd never heard something like that before. The shit was terrifying. I ran into the kitchen, and this man had her pinned against the wall."

"Did you know him?" I whispered.

"No." He shook his head. "He was beating my mother's face to a bloody pulp. I didn't give a shit who he was. I jumped onto his back while trying to claw his fucking eyes out of his head. All I cared about was saving my mother."

I squeezed his fingers, imagining the horror of witnessing that shit. It'd had to be emotionally scarring.

He continued. "It's been twenty-six years, and I can still hear the thud my mother's body made when he slammed her to the floor before grabbing me off his back and throwing me clear across the kitchen.

And I just fucking lay there, helpless and weak, before he shot her and then me."

"Don't you dare blame yourself for this shit. You were young, and there wasn't anything you could do."

It was painful, watching the emotions—sadness, guilt, pain, and then back to anger—flick through his eyes. Everything he was feeling resonated with me. It was exactly how I'd felt the minute I found out Dad had died because he was out driving around, looking for me when I broke curfew.

"Fuck that. It was my fault. She needed me, and I didn't do shit to help her or save her. She's dead because of me. Just like Maya and our baby." He hunched his shoulders. His eyes sparked with rage as they locked on to mine.

"Because of you? Core, no. That's not true. None of this shit is your fault."

I was so enraged. I wanted to wrap my hands around the neck of the person who had killed Maya and the man who had murdered his mother and choke them both to fucking death. The emotional damage those people had caused him was a stain he would never be able to remove.

He released my hand. His fists clenched and unclenched at his sides. "I could have done something… anything… when that bastard placed the gun to her head. But I didn't," he gritted out.

"Stop!" I couldn't stand to hear him tear himself up like that. "You're fucking ripping yourself apart for something that's not your damn fault. Blame the fucker who killed her. Be angry with him, not yourself."

"That's easier said than done. Especially when her killer is alive, and she's dead." His eyes blazed with ire. "He stole her from me. Took away the one person who meant anything to me. And I won't rest until that asshole is taking a dirt nap." He ran a hand over his head. "I was near death, and Ram saved my life. We made a pact that day that the man who had killed my mother would pay with his life."

The rage balled up in my stomach at the senseless deaths of both his mother and Maya. And fury because the person who had run Dad off the road was never punished. Lives lost and the broken children—Core and me—left behind to deal with the emotional baggage.

"I'm so sorry." I wrapped my arms around his waist, pressing my cheek against his chest.

Core mimicked my motion, tightly holding me, as if trying to anchor himself in the here and now. "There's nothing to be sorry for. I've moved on. I've survived. I always do."

Easing out of his arms, I stared up at him. I knew he hadn't moved on. There were threads of pain and fury intertwined in his voice when he retold the story. Core's hurt, guilt, and bitterness ran deeper than a river. There was no way in hell he'd find peace until he got retribution for his mother's death. And frankly, I didn't blame him. I understood the hole in the soul death left that could never be repaired. No matter how hard you tried to mend it, the loss from death lingered forever. But the truth of the matter was that revenge wouldn't bring his mother back.

"Shit happens." His nostrils flared. "The way I see it, you can't go through life untouched by suffering. But the smart ones understand that the only way to survive is to find the meaning behind the suffering." His eyes transformed; they were now cold, hard, and flinty.

The man behind the mask was starting to make more sense to me now. He'd lived a rough life and made it out alive when most of the kids he had grown up with probably didn't.

"Core, I know how much losing someone you love can hurt." I swallowed hard. I felt Core's pain and knew it intimately. "When my dad died, I was lost for so long. He had been my lifeline. I fucking miss him every damn day."

"Death is a cruel motherfucker," he grunted.

"That it is," I whispered, comforted in the knowledge that Core and I had a connection that ran deeper than sex.

We'd both lost someone we loved, and the loss had devastated and molded us into the people we were today… for better or worse.

But is this enough to force me to tear down the emotional walls that protect me, letting Core close to me, revealing my true self? And if I do… could he accept me… the broken woman inside?

"Core…"

"Yes."

Without thinking, I blurted out, "I have a shitload of trust issues."

"Sin, you—"

I was a tangled knot of anxiety, waging an endless battle between my head and my heart.

"Don't." I placed a finger over his lips to silence him. "If I don't say this now, I won't ever." I swallowed hard. "Grace cheated on my dad when I was a kid, and to add insult to injury, she verbally treated him like shit. It wasn't a happy household, to say the least, so I inherited a lot of relationship issues from that. It's hard for me to trust anyone."

Reaching up, I grabbed his head, yanking it down so that we were now face to face. "I'm not looking for you to define what's happening between us. In fact, I'd rather you didn't." Because if he did, it would be like a spray of insect repellent, making me want to fly as far away as possible. "But what I am demanding is that you never lie to me... because if you do, this thing between us is over. I can't be with a fucking liar. I need you always to keep it one hundred percent real with me. Are we clear, McKay?"

He narrowed his eyes. "Clear as water." He grunted before swooping down, claiming my mouth while squeezing my ass with one hand, the other possessively wrapped around my waist.

I almost came undone when he sucked my tongue into his mouth, twining his around it. He plundered, possessed, nipped, storming through my defenses, demanding my surrender. And I did. I couldn't do anything else.

His tongue slid over mine, around, seeking every inch of me. A fist in my hair angled my head back, granting him deeper access. He growled, a sound that rumbled down in his chest as he effortlessly hoisted me up, kneading my ass with two hands. Instinctively, I wrapped my legs around his waist, completely gone... lost in the sensation of Core.

CHAPTER 3
SINTHIA

Core strode through the house and up to his bedroom. With his hand on my back, he lowered me onto the bed and gently pushed me back while his legs forced my knees apart. He yanked off my boots, jeans, and panties, tossing them aside. One hand grabbed a firm hold of my wrists, and the other slid into my pussy, two fingers pushing inside and stretching me open. I moaned as I clenched around those fingers.

He growled again. "So fucking beautiful," he murmured with approval, pressing his mouth against my stomach, nibbling and kissing until all I wanted to do was burst into flames.

My nerve endings stirred and tingled. His touch and our physical connection felt intense, like a slow, smoldering fire. It was so much different. So much more because of the way we had both just opened up, baring our souls to each other during our conversation. It was as if we both wanted to slow down, savor the moment, linger in the essence of the momentous corner we'd turned together in our relationship.

Rising on his elbows, he hungrily looked at me before pushing my legs out a little. Now I was even more exposed and vulnerable before his gaze, just as I'd opened myself up to him, telling him about my dad and my relationship issues. He pushed my knees to my stomach before pressing them outward, tipping my pussy up in the air. As he slid his fingers between the wet folds of my heat, I arched up, wiggling closer when he slipped his fingers inside. His thumb circled and played with my clit.

I was dying for more even though I was on the cusp of my first orgasm. As I stared at him, my mind went numb. I needed more, but I was helpless. He stroked my pussy. I shivered, on the verge of exploding.

"Give it to me, Sinful," he demanded huskily.

I knew exactly what *it* was from our numerous hot-and-heavy fuck sessions.

Core dominated.

I submitted.

It was Core's sensual power play, forcing me to leave all my inhibitions at the door. In exchange, he'd push my sexual boundaries.

There were no flowery bullshit words.

No complicated promises of forever.

And no judgment for the freaky things we both desired. It was beautifully uncomplicated and liberating. Finally, I'd found a highly skilled lover with whom I didn't have to orchestrate every touch and stroke. Shit, the man fucked like a tireless machine.

And the way his eyes bored into me while fucking… It was as if I were his goddess and he were worshipping me at my altar. It was humbling, sensual, exciting, and intense.

He ensured that my sexual pleasure came before his. It didn't hurt that the man was very skilled at fucking.

In the bedroom, bathroom, and anywhere else he chose to take me, I was his be-all and end-all.

"Please," I whispered. "Lick me," I finished because I knew he had no intention of pushing me over the edge until I offered what he needed to hear.

"With pleasure."

His huge hands curled around my thighs, spreading my legs wider. His tongue thrust into my heat. That one abrasive lick sent my mind and body spiraling over the edge, and I screamed his name like a prayer.

He pulled his head back, watching as his fingers continued to stretch my greedy slit. "Scream louder, darling."

I was writhing and panting as my hips bucked wildly. His fingers thrust harder. I moaned louder when his thumb found my clit again and mercilessly played with it. I screamed and came again, feeling light-headed from the passion.

He nipped my inner thigh. "I love the taste of your cunt."

His lustful words made my toes curl. I wanted Core more than my next breath.

He eased back, standing before me for a moment, and then he stripped naked.

I shivered deliciously. He was gorgeous, fit, and muscular with a thick cock jutting out in front of him.

"Fuck me," I demanded.

His face darkened. "Who's in charge, Sin?"

"Me," I answered.

My willful streak pushed to the forefront. Core had taken me several times that morning, and each and every time, I'd submitted to his demands… willingly. But the sadistic streak in me wanted to push the envelope. I wanted to know how far Core could take our sensual play.

"Tsk, tsk," he shot back before opening a condom packet and sheathing himself. "You know better, darling." He moved in front of me, stroking his length.

I inhaled sharply, loving the sensual way he touched his staff.

"I'm in charge," he insisted softly, his voice still full of authority.

Truth be told… behind closed doors, in his bed, I wanted him to be in charge. Core knew what I wanted without me even having to ask, which was scary and exciting.

Our gazes locked when he stated, "I'm going to stick my dick up your ass."

I swallowed hard. I'd never had anal sex in my entire life.

His laugh made me shiver. "Everything in you is probably saying no, that you wouldn't like it. But the spark of excitement in your eyes… it says differently."

Core was right. My body was on fire, the need unlike anything I'd ever felt.

"On your fucking knees," he demanded.

My eyes widened. Butterflies fluttered in my stomach.

Oh shit. This is really happening… ass action.

I froze with indecision.

Do I trust him enough to be that vulnerable to him?

When it came to sex, Core had not hurt me and had given me things I hadn't known I wanted—freedom to unleash my freaky dark desire with no judgment about my sensual wants and needs—until him.

"Now," he barked.

I rolled over, getting on my hands and knees. My shoulders were pressed against the soft sheets. My ass high in the air, I glanced over my shoulder at him.

"Damn. Beautiful," he whispered. "Spread your knees wider." He used his muscular thighs to spread my legs even more.

My breath caught in my throat when he reached for the lube, squirting it onto his fingers.

The realization sank in. I was excited. The need to have him take me surpassed any desire I'd ever felt. My throbbing folds felt like he'd already fucked me. The silky feel of the bedding against my nipples sent ripples of need to my center.

"Fuck me," I hissed.

He was on top of me in seconds, his body pressing against me.

"Beg me," he whispered into my ear, "and make it good, Sin."

A soft moan escaped my lips. "Fuck me, please. Put your cock inside me. Make me yours."

"I've already done that, Sin."

I shivered as the truth of his words registered.

He taunted. "Say, *Pretty please, Core, fuck me.*" He ran a hand over my ass cheek and then to the crease. His lips trailed down my back, sending a combination of heat and shivers through me.

I became consumed by the helplessness of my position as a lube-coated finger slid into my ass with no warning. My cheeks squeezed against his invasion. Automatically, I tried to move away. He applied a little more pressure at my puckered opening. The cold and unrelenting push into my anus held me captive while he pushed his lubed finger deeper and then slowly thrust in and out.

My forbidden hole relaxed around his finger and opened up. The most amazing pleasure shot through me. Arching my back, I lifted my bottom, opening myself fully to him. He added a second finger. Again, he was very slow and cautious before he thrust in and out with his two fingers. Then he tried three fingers.

I repeated, "Pretty please, Core, fuck me."

"My pleasure," he drawled, withdrawing his fingers. "Once I've fucked your ass, you'll know just who you belong to." With strong hands on my thighs, he lifted my ass high, using his muscular thighs to keep my legs spread wide.

My hips rocked, needing him to fill me, but I was not at all certain that I wanted him fucking my ass.

Will it hurt? Will I even like it?

"Core. Um… I don't know if—"

The tip of his cock touched my opening. I tugged at the covers in an attempt to move away from him while at the same time raising my butt higher.

Shit. There was something about the sting of the head of his cock pushing against my puckered hole that was simply alluring.

"Core," I whispered.

With long strokes up and down my back, he kept me bent over, my ass in the air.

"Your ass looks so beautiful in this position." He nudged his cock a little more firmly against my bottom hole.

I groaned, burying my face in the bedding as the head of his cock pressed insistently into me. "Core… Oh! It burns." I struggled to adjust to his thick heat opening me wide.

The unrelenting pressure as he forged his way deep inside me persisted, making it impossible for me to catch my breath. The raw dominance of it staggered me. Core's hands squeezed my hips, his deep growl filling the room as his cock pressed another inch deeper.

"You're fucking tight. Just a little more, darling," he whispered.

I gulped in air, fisting my hands in the sheets. "It's so fucking deep. Core..."

His balls were against my ass as he slid the rest of the way into me.

I couldn't breathe.

I couldn't think.

I felt so taken... so consumed.

He was possessing me as no man ever had, the sharp primitiveness of the act freezing me into immobility.

This act, more than any I'd ever experienced, filled me with a sense of vulnerability I'd never before imagined. I was aware of each shift of his staff, each breath he took. He stretched me wide, moving inside me as he bent over my back, pressing his lips to my neck.

"You belong to me," he hissed. "Say it."

I felt fragile.

He completely owned and controlled me with every move of his cock, each movement drawing a trembling gasp from me.

"I can't," I breathed out.

When his hand came around my waist, settling on my mound with a rough finger pressing against my clit, the sensation was so intense I drew a sharp, shaky breath. He began to stroke, slowly moving in and out of me, the friction over my inner walls robbing me of reason.

"Sin, let go. Give me everything."

Tilting my bottom upward, I cried out as the thick head of his cock pressed impossibly deeper.

"You're mine to take. Mine to fuck deep. Mine to enjoy. Mine to protect. Mine to care for. Mine to make happy."

Nothing in my life had ever felt so intimate. So all-consuming. The connection between us made tears prickle behind my eyelids.

My nipples craved his attention. My clit burned for his touch. My arousal was so intense that I couldn't think of anything else except coming. I teetered on the edge, the erotic pleasure too good to be real... but I resisted in giving him what he wanted—all of me, both emotionally and physically.

I countered. "You have no right to ask for this."

"I have every right." Wrapping his arm around me again, he leaned over my back, his fingers parting my folds. "You are mine... and every time you look at me, you're going to remember this. You're going to remember how I can make you feel… because you belong to me and I to you."

He belongs… to me?

I stiffened as his fingers started stroking my clit, inadvertently clamping down on his cock and making my anus burn.

The flash of fire hit me so hard and fast that I froze, unable to move at all as I came so hard that I saw stars. I couldn't draw a breath deep enough to cry out. The cock inside me felt even larger as I tautened on it, stretching me so intimately and making me feel even more defenseless and exposed.

I couldn't escape it any more than I could escape the insistent strokes on my throbbing clit, his hold keeping me still, forcing me to accept all he had to give me, making me give him even more than I had known I had to give.

Fuck. He's reaching in, snatching part of my damn soul.

Core lifted me, keeping me on my knees in front of him as he buried himself deep in my ass at the same time he buried his face in my hair.

"Fuck, Sin," he growled harshly, holding me, pulling me back against him, and he came deep inside my ass. "Mine."

With a shudder, he released my hands before sitting on his heels, pulling me down to sit over his thighs. His cock pulsed inside me, drawing a moan from me as my head fell back against his shoulder.

His arms wrapped around me, the muscles beneath my thighs rock hard. "I've never wanted a woman more." He cupped my breasts. "You okay, darling? Did I hurt you?"

No, I'm not okay. I was emotionally shaken and struggled to shore up defenses that had been eradicated by the intensity of his lovemaking.

Core had made me feel beautiful and desired. I loved the feel of his muscular arms around me and the way his thighs trembled beneath mine. The level of trust it had taken to allow him to do what he'd just done to me scared me.

My body stiffened when the most frightening and, frankly, disturbing thought flashed through my head. Core could easily make me break all my rules about not getting emotionally involved with a man.

And if that happens… will sex continue to be enough for me?

My heart raced as panic started to set in.

Oh God. What if I actually fall in love with him?

Heaviness settled in the pit of my stomach.

Shit. That would be a fucking disaster.

But I knew the possibility of sex morphing into something else was real and damn unnerving.

Jesus, I'm so fucked right now.

CHAPTER 4
CORE

Weaving in and out of Manhattan traffic in my Porsche, I reveled in the sounds of the heavy metal music I used for meditation. I needed something to distract me from the powerful arousal that coursed through my body like fire when I remembered how, mere hours ago, Sin had screamed my name over and over again as I devoured her cunt, licking from bottom to top, teasing her clit and lapping up her cream like warm honey.

Damn. And her tight ass is incredible.

The vision of Sin's eyes dilating with lust flashed in my mind. Basic, raw hunger surged through me, beating at my self-control. My cock swelled, and the wild thought of turning my car around and going back to the penthouse flittered through my mind.

Shit... the things I could do once I got there... like order her to get on her knees and suck me hard and fast. Damn. Just the thought of how her warm, pink tongue would feel against my skin while she teased my cock before taking me to the back of her throat...

I shook my head to clear my lustful, wicked thoughts.

Sin is an addictive distraction.

Even with a string of women and business successes over the years, it had been so long since I was with anyone who looked remotely like a real woman with soft curves, pretty girl-next-door looks, and a sassy, take-no-shit personality like Sin, and it was a bonus that she more than satisfied my distinct and dark tastes in sex.

Shit, my obsession with Sin was crazy and fucking reckless, but the more time I spent with her, the more I wanted her… in and out of my bed.

It wasn't just her body that captivated me, but her wit, mind, and compassion also drew me in like a moth to a flame. My thoughts drifted back to our conversation and how Sin had instantly recognized and understood the anguish and guilt I'd felt over Mom's, Maya's, and my unborn baby's deaths.

"I'm so sorry," she had whispered before wrapping her arms around me, pressing her cheek against my chest.

Her impulsive yet simple act of affection and comfort had been unnerving at first. Frankly, it had been so long since I allowed a woman to get close—the last one Maya—that I didn't even know how to react to her consoling touch. I was always fairly detached with women, and while I kept some of them around for a few months, it was only to hook up with them. I had no emotional investment what-soever. But with Sin, it was like the emotional walls I'd worked so hard to erect were crumbling down.

Without a doubt, Sin was the full package. She was everything I wanted in a woman—strong, feisty, intelligent, and beautiful. And I wanted her more than any woman I'd been with—even Maya.

This was a real fucked-up predicament.

I had no damn business thinking about Sin that way.

She was supposed to be a woman I was using as bait.

Just a casualty in my war against Bigsby.

I pressed on the bridge of my nose and took a deep breath. "Shit."

I really didn't need this Sin complication. My life was difficult enough, and I didn't need any distractions, especially now that I'd found my mother's killer. Besides, I wasn't relationship material, and I never would be. I fucked women and then showed them the door. Well… that had been my mode of operation before Sin.

Now my plans for Sin had changed, and I'd decided once I destroyed Bigsby, I'd tell Sin the truth about everything. Not that I'd ever lied to her in the first place. I'd just omitted and dodged telling her some pertinent information so I could keep my Bigsby mission on track and her under my control. I'd already told her the truth—that I'd spent my entire life waiting for the day I'd finally find him, my mother's killer, and avenge her death.

And Sin had replied, "I don't blame you for feeling that way, Core."

So I knew she would understand my motives when I told her the truth about Bigsby.

How could she not?

We'd both lost people in our lives that we loved.

The loss had devastated and changed us forever.

Yes, there was no doubt in my mind that Sin would forgive me, especially when I revealed that the same bastard who had killed my mother also murdered her father.

My cell rang, echoing throughout the confines of my car and rousing me out of my thoughts. Glancing at the caller ID that flashed on the dashboard, I turned down the loud music before pressing the button on my steering wheel.

"What's up, Kevin?" I answered.

"My connection came through and sent me the info you asked for on Webb."

"Damn, that was fast."

As soon as I'd gotten in my car, I'd texted Kevin, instructing him to dig up everything he could find on Jaxon Webb, Sin's stalker.

"Getting this info was a piece of cake compared to the other crap you asked me to do today."

"Come on, bro. Just hit me up with the damn info already."

I was fortunate to have Kevin on my team. He was not only one of my closest friends, the equivalent of a brother, but he was also one of the smartest men I knew. He was a valuable member of my team, handling the financing and accounting for all my businesses as well as all my private intelligence-gathering efforts. If I needed answers, Kevin would reach out to his deep well of intel connections and get that shit, pronto.

My fingers tapped on the steering wheel.

"Jaxon Webb. Caucasian. Thirty-one years old. He's the only son of a filthy-rich family from Connecticut."

My lips compressed as I waited for him to get to the point.

"Mother, Claire Webb. Father, Daniel Webb." Kevin paused for a beat. "Jaxon's parents are both attorneys…"

Is he kidding me?

I frowned. "Who gives a rat's ass that they're attorneys?" I complained under my breath.

Kevin droned on. "At their prominent Manhattan family law firm—"

I cut him off. "Fuck, Kevin!" I banged the steering wheel. "I don't give a shit about his parents. Just tell me about that asshole Jaxon!"

"Shit. Calm the fuck down, Core," he replied calmly. "There's nothing about Jaxon that's any different than most trust fund babies running around Manhattan. Shit. I've lost brain cells just reading his intel report. Why are you investigating him anyway?"

"He's stalking Sin," I gritted out.

My heart jerked as I remembered the vulnerability in her eyes and the truth laid out in her words as she'd told me what that demented asshole had done to her. I had known then that I would cut off my own arm before I'd ever let anyone harm her.

I always protected what I cared for.

"Stalking her?" Kevin responded. "Shit. Well, that's not good."

"Why?" I countered.

"Because according to the police report, he has a bad track record with women, and that raises a red flag."

"Go on." I prodded, overcome by an edgy, twitchy feeling.

"He's been accused of sexually assaulting several women. But get this; he's never been arrested or charged in connection with any of these alleged incidents."

I snorted. "Let me guess; his parents intervened." It wasn't a question, but a statement.

My business dealings with blue-blooded fuckers had given me a glimpse into their world of bribes and other shady undertakings. I'd quickly learned from watching their maneuvers that if you had money and the right connections and pedigree, you could get away with anything, including murder, without any repercussions.

"Exactly." Kevin confirmed. "His parents quietly dealt with the women while Jaxon left the country."

"Where did he go?"

"He hopped around Europe for years. But it didn't take long for his same pattern with women to start. He was accused of sexually assaulting five women in Europe. But this time, two of them ended up missing and are now presumed dead."

"Shit!" I stiffened. Disgust twisted my mouth into a sneer. There was no way in hell that I was going to allow that sick fucker to hurt Sin.

She's mine to protect… to care for.

And no one…

Absolutely no one…

Messes with what's mine…

Sin.

My pulse elevated.

"Yeah, well, that's not all," Kevin replied. "Jaxon recently came back to the US, so that can't be a good thing for Sin. Once a stalker, always a damn stalker."

This confirmed Sin's theory about Jaxon leaving roses on her doorstep. I tightened my fingers around the wheel. If there was one thing I despised, it was men who got their rocks off on harassing and intimidating women. And all the signs pointed to the fact that Jaxon had picked Sin as his next victim. Not on my damn watch. That shit was not going down.

Adrenaline rushed through my body.

"Kevin, you've got twenty-four hours to get me his address." I couldn't wait to find that coward, wrap my hands around his neck, and watch the life slowly drain from his eyes. "I need to pay that fucker a little visit and permanently shut his ass down."

"Smart move. I'll get back to you ASAP."

"Next topic," I grunted. "Did you decode Bigsby's ledger?"

Once Max and Rocco had nabbed Jeff leaving Sin's house with the ledger in hand, they had taken him to our warehouse for interrogation.

Kevin's role was to take the ledger and start piecing together exactly why it was so important to Bigsby that he'd ordered Jeff to break into Sin's house to steal it.

"Shit. That was easy," Kevin bragged. "Each entry in the ledger documents the client's name, their credit card number, how much they paid, the date they hired the escort, and the name of the escort they fucked."

"Escort? How the hell did you jump to that conclusion?"

"Jemma Kane," he disclosed dryly. "She's a Manhattan madam who got busted about twenty-seven years ago because of a sting that had targeted her massage parlor. Her establishment was really a cover for her high-end escort service, and all her clients were the who's who of New York. I'm talking about politicians, judges, and Wall Street executives."

"So what's her connection to Bigsby?"

Kevin replied, "It was a painstaking process, but for each ledger entry, I ran a check on the credit card number associated with it. And every single credit card number came back to black cards issued by various financial firms and services. The charges were expensed on corporate accounts, disguised as computer repair, trading research, or consulting for market compliance. And every client credit card charge listed in that damn ledger links right back to Jemma's escort service, which funneled money to several offshore accounts listed in the ledger. Now here's the smoking gun. Every single one of those offshore accounts is closed, except one. And that active account connects to a shell company called Pomtonic International, which I confirmed is owned by Bigsby."

"Holy shit," I answered. "Is she still serving time? Because if we can get to her and offer her some cash, I'm sure she'd be willing to implicate Bigsby as part of her escort business, and then—"

"Great idea, Core. I like where you're heading, but that shit is not going to happen."

"Money talks—"

Kevin cut me off. "Jemma never served time."

"Did she make a deal with the prosecution?" I inquired.

"Don't know. She went missing without a trace while she was out on bail."

"So when you say Jemma's missing, you really mean she's presumed dead," I returned.

"Officially, according to the police, she's missing. Unofficially, she's presumed dead. It's speculated that she either jumped bail and fled to Mexico or she was killed by one of her rich clients when she threatened to reveal the names in her black book, which I think is the fucking ledger we now have in our possession."

"This shit is getting deep," I mumbled as my mind raced with questions and theories. "But why would she have kept a ledger with all this information?"

"I'd guess it was her security, her plan B, if shit went south and she got nabbed by the police."

"Exactly," I interjected. "That's what I'm thinking. So maybe when she got busted and had her back to the wall, she threatened to out her clients as a part of her plea deal with the authorities." I frowned. "This is all speculation, but it makes sense. She probably revealed the names and then went into witness protection."

"Maybe," Kevin shot back. "This whole Jemma story is just fucking odd. I can't put my finger on it, but something is off. I couldn't find any information about her background. No birth certificate, no driver's license, no photos, not even a blip of personal information about her anywhere. That shit doesn't happen unless someone wiped her background clean."

"It doesn't matter. She's gone, and so much time has passed since she went missing that even if we wanted to find some of the escorts who had worked for her, that would be a big fucking waste of time."

I thought about my conversation with Sin this morning when we'd talked about the person who'd broken into her townhouse and destroyed her collection, but the only thing they'd stolen was her dad's ledger. A ledger that Bigsby had sent his errand boy to break into her house and steal. *But how had Bigsby even known where to search for it?*

"Did Sin tell you how she ended up with the ledger in the first place?" Kevin asked.

"Her father. And before you ask, she has no clue what the information in the ledger even means."

Kevin scoffed. "And you believe her?"

"Hell yes, I believe her."

From what I'd experienced so far, Sin didn't have a deceitful bone in her body. She pulled no punches in everything she did and said—a trait I admired and respected.

"Then how did her father end up possessing Jemma's ledger—aka little black book?" Kevin inquired.

"Bro," I barked, "if I knew the answer, we wouldn't even be having this conversation. All this shit... and the connection between Jemma, Bigsby, and Sin's father is a big damn mystery. I suspect all three have something in common." I just couldn't figure out what.

"You mean all four," Kevin stated.

"Four?"

"You forgot Sin," he informed me.

"Sin is just the unwitting owner. Well, she was the owner of the ledger. We need to focus on our target—Bigsby. It's taken us over twenty years and a fortune paid to dead-end tips to get this far."

Bigsby was unfinished business, business I'd been waiting to resolve for far too many years. I had thought of nothing but revenge. It'd consumed me. Just thinking about the night when the unknown assailant wearing a gold ruby-and-diamond-encrusted horseshoe ring had shot my mother and left me choking on my own blood fueled my hate fire. My mother had died, but I survived. I'd finally found the owner of the ring—Bigsby. I had been searching for that ring for years, and it was right under my nose.

"Yeah, but what about Jemma?" Kevin started. "And her missing background is a loose end I don't like. Until I figure this out, it's going to be like a piece of corn stuck in my teeth. Fucking annoying."

I sighed heavily. Sometimes Kevin was way too smart for his own good. He had this need to solve everything, and his need for perfection was borderline obsessive.

"Kevin, one mission at a time. Let's finish the Bigsby mission first. Then if you want to chase down the unsolved Jemma disappearance, knock yourself out. Shit, I'll even fund it. Hell, I love a good thriller and suspense story just like everyone else, so it would be nice to get to the bottom of what actually happened to Jemma. But right now, I've got the team waiting for me at the warehouse, so can we move this crap along?"

"Yes. Anyway, moving on, back to Jemma." He paused. "Here's the part I think you're going to really love. Jemma had two business partners. The first was Bigsby Calhoune. The second was Sin's father."

"Which one?" I asked.

Kevin's previous investigation into Sin's family background had unearthed that she had two birth certificates, each one showing a different set of parents. The first birth certificate had her father listed as Ian Michaels and her mother as Grace Michaels. The second certificate had her father listed as Greer Lorne Cruickshank and her mother as Aubrey Cruickshank.

"Greer," Kevin replied.

I frowned. "It still doesn't answer how Bigsby knew Sin had the ledger."

"Or if he suspects that Greer might be Sin's real father," Kevin chimed in.

I scratched my chin. "I don't think it's a coincidence that the only two people who can tie Bigsby to his former life as a pimp are either missing or dead."

"Exactly," Kevin intoned. "A narcissistic man like Bigsby would terminate anything linking back to his seedy history."

New York City's mayoral hopeful, Bigsby Calhoune, was a dirty criminal underneath his slick, cleaned-up politician veneer. He might have a new identity and life, but he was still the power-hungry thug who had killed my mother and left me to die.

My stomach felt like a rock had taken up residence when I realized Sin could be in danger.

What if Bigsby thinks Sin is one of the loose ends from his past and decides to put her on his hit list?

Knowing what I knew so far about Bigsby, I was sure he had come too far to let his new life disintegrate, which meant Sin's safety was in serious jeopardy.

My chest tightened.

I was an all-in-or-all-out type of man, and that meant doing whatever I needed to do—no matter how dark and bloody—to reach my goal.

But how far am I willing to go now that Sin's life might be on the line?

Will I offer her up as a sacrificial lamb?

The old Core would have without hesitation, but that was before I'd really gotten to know Sin. But without me even realizing it until now, the line between what I needed—vengeance—and wanted—Sin—was thin.

When push comes to shove, will I sacrifice Sin's life to avenge my mom's death?

A couple weeks ago, the answer would have been a resounding, *Yes!*

Today? I was second-guessing every damn move and decision I made. And that shit was not how I operated… ever.

When I made a strategic decision, I stuck to that shit and didn't deviate, letting the chips fall where they may. Outside of my team, people were pawns to maneuver any way I wanted. For years, I'd built alliances while doing things like blackmail, coercion, and extortion, and that had made me one of the wealthiest and most feared men in New York City. I was the puppet master, pulling the strings and making CEOs, politicians, and the very affluent dance for my amusement. Billionaires would quake in their custom-made shoes for fear of being exposed by the cache of intelligence I had about their shady business dealings and sordid sexual tastes. Information that would ruin them if I chose to reveal it.

I'm Core McKay, a billionaire, and I'm always in control.

The vision of Sin's eyes dilated with lust flashed in my mind. Indecent hunger surged through me, beating at my self-control. Sin was everything I wanted in a woman—strong and feisty. The idea of having her in my bed every night, submitting to me, for the rest of my life had my cock throbbing and my balls aching.

Shit. How the hell did I let it go so far?

I snapped out of my reverie. "Kevin, I'm pulling up to the warehouse now. I'll give you a call later."

Finally, the time had come to get answers and put all this shit with Bigsby behind me. Of course, after I destroyed his ass.

CHAPTER 5
CORE

I parked beside Ram, who was leaning against his own car with his cell in hand, texting. As soon as I stepped out of my vehicle, closing the door behind me, the nauseating smells of stale food, garbage, and exhaust fumes slammed into me.

Damn. I hate Newark.

Ram pushed away from his SUV and stormed up to me. "About fucking time," he hissed. "I've been waiting hours for you to haul your ass down here."

"I was busy," I barked.

"Busy being cock deep in pussy doesn't fucking count." Ram countered.

Leave it to Ram not to beat around the damn bush.

"Fuck off, Ram," I grunted, walking away, but he easily kept pace.

"Look, bro, I'm just calling it like I see it." Ram defended. "We've had Jeff on ice for hours, and you went MIA on our ass. It's not in your fucking DNA to neglect business, especially when we're so close to bringing down the man who killed your mother."

"Sin needed me."

The man I had been before I slept with her and got to know her better would have wondered what the hell was wrong with me. She was supposed to be a means to an end. Nothing more. No attachments.

The man I was now… I was her mercenary gladiator, ready to fight and kill anyone who dared to harm her.

I want to protect Sin from the world.

"Did she now? And since when did you start caring about her needs?"

I retorted, "It's fucking complicated."

"Did you actually just say, 'It's fucking complicated?'" He burst out laughing. "It's confirmed; you're losing your mind."

He was right.

How did casual fucking with no strings, no emotional attachments, and no expectations turn into this—me getting greedy and wanting more?

Now I never want to let her go.

"We all think this shit between you and Sin is messing with your head and making you lose focus on the business at hand."

"All?" I countered.

I knew that *all* meant the entire team—Zuri, Kevin, Rocco, Max, and him. That was one of the many downsides of working on a close-knit team. It was like a fucking high school.

"Yep." Ram nodded.

"Not that it's anyone's damn business, but in the interest of shutting down the little girl's gossip clique you're obviously the president of"—I looked at him with hard eyes—"my head is fully intact, and I'm completely focused on our mission."

"Are you sure about that? Because the Core I know wouldn't have ghosted us like you did last night. For that matter, the fucking Core I know wouldn't have brought Sin to his damn place to play house with, especially since she's a woman he's using as a pawn." He paused. "And if I didn't know better, I would think that you've claimed her ass and marked her *Property of Core McKay.*"

"I have," I confided bluntly.

Ram skidded to a stop. "What?"

I stopped, turning to face off with him. "You heard me. I've decided to keep her and see where this relationship between us goes."

Ram's mouth dropped open, and then he closed it. "Keep her?" He laughed. "She's not some damn puppy you can play around with and then give away when she stops being cute and cuddly."

The reminder that I was breaking my number one rule of never mixing business with pleasure was fucking with my mind. My obsession with Sin was crazy and fucking reckless, but I found myself shaken by how my need to possess her had quickly changed to my need to keep her as mine... forever.

"Who said anything about giving her up?" I crossed my arms.

"Hold the fuck up." Ram held up his hand. "Are you actually talking about dating her?"

"Come on, bro. You know me..."

Ram arched a brow. "Do I?"

"You do. And you know I don't date. I fuck. That means me fucking her whenever I want, wherever I want, and however I want. Exclusively."

"That means you're dating her."

I shrugged. "Whatever. I'm not trying to label what Sin and I have."

"Whatever?" He looked at me like I had two heads. "Core! Use your damn head and not your cock."

"Relax," I answered.

"I will not fucking relax. Sin makes you vulnerable."

"Ram, everything is under control. I've got this." I wrinkled my forehead.

Ram snorted. "You've got this? No, you don't. I'm not the smartest person when it comes to figuring out women, but I have enough common fucking sense to know when Sin finds out she's been used and manipulated just so you could get to Bigsby, this is not going to end well—for you." He eyed me. "Believe me. Hell hath no fury like a woman fucked over by a man. Men have been castrated for less."

"Like I explained, I've got this shit." But the tightness in my chest bore witness to the effect Ram's words had on me.

Ram is right.

I rubbed the back of my neck.

When, not if, Sin found out the truth—that I'd manipulated her just to get to Bigsby—she was going to go ballistic on my ass.

Frankly, her anger I could deal with.

But her walking away from me? From us? Now that possibility is fucking with my head big time.

I pressed my lips together in a slight grimace.

Ram just stared at me. "Bro, just tell her the fucking truth, and if she walks… good riddance. Not that you'd care…" Ram's voice broke off with a small frown. "Wait… what the fuck? I know that look on your face. You do care."

My irritation rose. "What look?"

He shrewdly assessed me. "The look you get when we're about to take over a company—predatory, focused, and possessive."

Ram knew me well. He was right—again. I wanted Sin despite the fact that there were a million reasons I shouldn't.

Ram went on. "After all these years and so many other women, what's so special about Sin?"

Everything—from her take-no-shit attitude to her point of view about sex and me.

Sin pulled no punches and was a welcome change from the women who threw themselves at me because of my money and those I slept with to sate my sexual cravings. None of what I'd had with previous lovers was real, and all of it had been exhausting.

Sin was my kind of perfect. A woman I'd never dreamed of encountering after Maya—the first woman who had loved me for me, stood by me when I was poor, and grounded me. Maya had been my balance, my rock. The major reason I'd decided to turn my back on my criminal empire was for fear of losing her and my unborn child. But I'd lost them anyway, and my world had shattered into a million pieces. For too many years to count, without her, my life had been cold, and I hadn't been alive. Until Sin. Now I could let go of the memories of my life with Maya and move on.

"None of your damn business," I snapped.

"Seriously?"

In that moment, I realized I needed Sin because she filled an emotional gap I'd thought was buried deep and lost forever. Her taste, smell, and body were imprinted on my mind. Ingrained in my mind from the first time I'd fucked her. I couldn't remember the last time I'd wanted someone with the intensity I felt for Sin.

I sighed heavily. "Because Sin's the only woman who truly understands me. Fuck! She's the only woman I ever told about Maya or my mom. That's what she does to me. And even after I told her all that shit, she still accepts me for who I am. She doesn't want to try to change me. And that's the kind of woman I won't ever walk away from."

"If she means that much to you, then tell her the truth," Ram insisted.

"When the time is right, I'll tell her what I did and why. Sin's smart. She'll understand, and we'll move on… together."

Ram laughed. "And everyone thinks I'm the fucking crazy one." He shook his head. "She won't understand that you've used her. No woman would. And there will be no moving on *together*. Look, bro, I get it. You're the master of everything you survey. You're Core motherfucking McKay. Billionaire. Ballbuster. In control of everything you touch. But Sin is different. This whole fucked-up situation is different. She'll walk away from you once she knows the truth."

"If it happens, I'll deal with it." My stomach tightened with the knowledge that there was a big possibility of losing Sin… and frankly, I didn't know if I could deal with that shit.

Now that I'd had a taste of life with Sin in it, going back to my cold, sterile world of caring about nothing but money and my team felt empty. My muscles tensed as I just imagined a world without Sin by my side. Strangely, the thought made me feel like a man deserted on an island… alone.

Ram laughed. "Seriously, this shit is hilarious. You were the mastermind behind this whole plot to get close to her and then use her as a fucking pawn to get revenge on Bigsby, and then you lied to her—"

I cut him off. "I've never lied to her. I've omitted information and evaded talking about need-to-know information that might jeopardize our mission. But I've never fucking lied to her. Ever!"

Ram shook his head. "If that's the excuse you're going to give her, then, bro, you're in a shitload of trouble. Because if there is one thing I know, there isn't a sane woman walking this earth who's going to blindly accept the load of shit you just told me."

"When I explain everything to her, she'll understand my motives."

"Uh-huh." Ram looked at me with wide eyes. "And how do you think she'll feel when she finds out you were the puppet master behind all her deals with the retailers screeching to a halt?"

I winced when I remembered the fact that Ram and I had contacted every retailer we owned a major stake in and told them the deal to carry Sin's line was dead until we personally approved it. More importantly, how Sin had flinched as if I'd physically slapped her when I told her that my sources had informed me that her retailers were getting cold feet about the viability of her collection and were pulling out of her deals. What she didn't know was that, with just one phone call to my shadowy connections—who were wealthy, deadly, and ruthless—I had killed all her retail agreements.

"I fixed that situation," I retorted. "I called them all and approved her deal to go forward."

Ram cocked his head, looking at me like some horrible experiment gone wrong. "Um… let me get this straight. You're taking credit for fixing a situation you created? Man… this is classic Core McKay bullshit."

"Like I said, she'll understand."

"Okay, Core. If you say so…" He clapped me on the back and walked away, laughing.

I'd be damned if I'd admit it aloud, but he was on point about this, too. This situation between Sin and me was a messy, fucked-up predicament that, for the first time in my life, I had no clue how to fix without losing her in the end.

CHAPTER 6
CORE

When I opened the warehouse door, slipping inside the dark building, I quickly snapped my mind into business mode and to the matter at hand—interrogating Jeff. I'd planned on the process of breaking him down to take hours. So I'd told Sin I wouldn't be back home from taking care of business until tomorrow morning.

The first thing on my agenda was finding out where Jeff was holding Lexis, Ram's sister, and then getting her back... hopefully alive. The second was getting confirmation from Jeff about why the ledger was so important to his boss, Bigsby.

I glanced at Ram, who was pacing back and forth while talking on his cell.

"Kevin, are you sure?" He paused a beat. "Don't be a dick. I just want to be sure." There was another moment of silence. "Yeah. Okay. I'll tell Core. Talk to you later." He ended the call before striding up to me.

"Tell me what?" I asked.

"Kevin just got word from his sources that the Feds are mounting an investigation into the Super PAC backing Bigsby."

"Why should I give a shit if they shut UF-Star down?"

It was no secret that UF-Star was a Super PAC—an independent political action committee that had been spending a ton of money to promote Bigsby for New York City's new mayor. No one but us knew that for a huge fee, Bigsby had arranged to help a group of traffickers clean their money through his shell company, Pomtonic International. In addition, in exchange for the traffickers contributing to UF-Star, Bigsby had made a deal with them that once he got elected, he'd turn a blind eye to all their illegal activities for a percentage of their profits.

"But it's not just UF-Star," Ram interjected. "It's the sex trafficking ring Bigsby's involved in. Kevin's intel says it won't be long before the Feds arrest Bigsby."

"Shit. That's not good."

"What's the problem?" Ram asked. "That's what you wanted, right? To destroy Bigsby? Now you don't have to get your hands dirty. The Feds and prosecutors will end him."

The truth of the matter was that I wanted to get my hands dirty.

I wanted to personally destroy him. It was the only way to ensure that everything went according to plan.

I was close to finally destroying Bigsby Calhoune by stripping away everything he held dear—his wealth, freedom, political career, and trophy fiancée, Cate.

Now I had everything—Bigsby and the one woman who had unknowingly made it all happen, Sin.

But why is the taste of revenge so bittersweet on my tongue?

"I've waited too many goddamn years to destroy that fucker. I'm not going to sit back and let him slip through my fingers. He has to pay for killing my mother. Besides, I'll be damned if I trust the incompetent Feds. They could mess it up, allowing him to get off on some technicality. No. I've got to personally make sure he ends up in jail for the rest of his life or six feet under. Either way, my job will be done, and I can mark this mission complete."

"Well, we'd better wrap up this shit fast because once the Feds nab him, he'll be out of your reach."

We moved off through the space, our boots sounding like trumpets as they slapped against the hard concrete floor in the cavernous, dark space. Rats almost the size of kittens ran across the floor to hide. The air was stale and cloying.

"What's the status of Project Jeff?" I asked.

"Like we planned, Max and Rocco have been softening him up for us and keeping him awake all night with rounds of throwing ice-cold water on his ass. Max reported that it wouldn't take us long to break him."

Sometimes, it took us days to break our captive and other times, hours.

"Good," I answered. "We'll start with questions about Lexis's location, and then we'll grill him about the ledger. I need him to corroborate what Kevin found out."

We made our way down the metal stairs and through the corridor.

"You don't know how bad I wanted to storm into that room last night and wrap my hands around Jeff's neck," Ram replied.

I knew that, deep down, Ram felt guilty for Lexis's disappearance. Well, more like guilty for not pressing her for more information about Jeff Barolo—a man who had become her boyfriend after dating her for only two weeks.

Ram had grown suspicious when Lexis refused to introduce Jeff to him, so Ram had driven to her college—Massachusetts Institute of Technology—only to find out from her friends that Lexis had dropped out and vanished with Jeff.

After a background check, we'd found out Jeff was some budding yuppie pimp who had a track record for ensnaring pretty young college freshmen women into a life of sex trafficking.

It had been hell trying to find any information on the location of Lexis because the human trafficking world was dirty and secretive. One tip after another had led to dead ends, which had frustrated us and pissed us off.

Every time we'd gotten close to finding Lexis, Jeff would transport her across state lines, leaving no trace. The last hot lead we'd gotten was that she'd been traded to a trafficker in San Diego.

After months of attempting to infiltrate the seedy traffickers' world, playing games of subterfuge while trying to find Lexis, we'd finally gotten a solid clue from Sarah, one of the girls Lexis had worked with who had escaped Jeff's clutches. She had given us one name—Ben Vargos—that ultimately led to Jeff and Bigsby.

After we'd kidnapped and interrogated Ben—who was also among the human traffickers cleaning his money through Pomtonic International and pumping a hell of a lot of money into UF-Star—he had given up information on his connection to Bigsby and who Bigsby was working with to get women… Jeff Barolo.

Ram ran his hand over his hair. "I swear, if Jeff killed my sister, I'll—"

"Don't even fucking think it," I barked.

We both knew the odds of Lexis being alive were slim, but I was still optimistic. We had done some more digging into her disappearance and unearthed info that corroborated our current belief. Lexis had not dropped out of college or run away. From all the dots we'd connected, she'd probably thought she was going on a weekend getaway with her "perfect" boyfriend, Jeff, and then got trapped in the world of sex trafficking.

"She's been missing for almost a year," Ram grumbled with bleak eyes.

It was hard as hell to watch my levelheaded friend slowly become emotionally unhinged with each passing day Lexis remained trapped in that horrid world.

"Even if she's still alive, she won't be the same Lexis she was before she got abducted by that piece of shit."

It was grim but true. We both knew that the old Lexis—who was always happy and cheery with an *I believe there are more good people than bad* perspective—would no longer exist. There was no way that she'd come back from whatever hell she was currently experiencing without some emotional and mental scars.

We'd heard all the dark things that happened to the women Jeff had lured from their normal lives and made into sex slaves. Many of the victims weren't just runaways or kids who'd been abandoned. Lots of them had come from what would be considered good families and had been coerced and trapped by clever predators like Jeff.

My eyes narrowed as I just remembered Sarah's horrific tale of her life with Jeff…

. . .

Sarah was nineteen when she had been approached by an older man—Jeff— who promised he would change her life forever. It'd started as a whirlwind romance. The pair had bumped into each other time and again around Brooklyn. She'd proclaimed that it'd felt like a series of coincidences. He'd called it fate. It was neither of the two. It was part of the game. Then things between them had progressed quickly. He'd met her family, and the two had made plans to go on a trip to California. It hadn't been until they were there that Jeff's intentions became clear.

"I met Jeff the same way all of us did, including Lexis—at a party. I didn't realize I had been marked. We all had," Sarah revealed to us. "He even met my mother."

She confided that the change had happened quickly and dramatically. "One morning after we arrived in California, Jeff shoved a pair of heels and a tiny black dress into my hands and told me to 'get to work.' I thought he was joking, but I was wrong. He took my clothes, my shoes, my keys, my phone," Sarah recounted. "He explained that he was actually a pimp, and this was how escorts were made."

His plans for her were detailed and disturbing. He took her directly to a wealthy client's house and forced her to have sex. It would not be her last client.

"Jeff kept all of us off the streets. We only had sex with people he knew. It was like all these rich, perverted men knew each other... like it was some dirty sex club."

During that time, Sarah explained she hadn't tried to escape because Jeff had threatened her and terrified her. "He swore his clients were rich and powerful and would think nothing of going after my family. I believed him because the client homes he'd brought us to were so huge and fancy. It was like shit you only saw on a reality television show."

Ram and I realized then that the fact that Sarah and all of Jeff's girls, including Lexis, were kept off the streets was what made it almost impossible for us to track Lexis down.

Sarah reported that she'd spent eight months being moved from state to state—essentially, she was on tour—servicing clients at their homes or parties to have sex. It was at one of those client parties that she'd met Lexis.

"Lexis was lucky," Sarah whispered. "She didn't have to work the parties like the rest of Jeff's girls. It was as if Jeff was showing her off to his customers

like some trophy. I'd heard several clients making offers to Jeff to fuck her, but he'd just tell them that she was his. But I knew better. Jeff was trying to get the best offer he could for Lexis."

"Did you talk to her?" Ram asked.

"Yes"—Sarah fidgeted nervously—"but she was high."

Ram hissed, "Lexis doesn't do drugs."

"But Jeff does," Sarah replied. "And he would force us to take drugs all the time. He suggested it made us less uptight and more fun around the clients." For Sarah, sleeping with those men was like a death sentence, and she finally worked up the nerve to escape. "I waited until the client was almost asleep and told him I was going to go outside and smoke a cigarette. And then I ran for my life."

I snapped back to the present.

"We're getting closer to finding Lexis—alive," I told Ram. "The sooner we find her, the better, bro."

"Stop bullshitting me, Core," he hissed. "I know what animals like Jeff and Bigsby are capable of doing to women they view as prey."

"Yes, but we've still got to hope for something good to come out of this clusterfuck."

Ram huffed out a breath of air. "Lexis and I had a big argument before she disappeared. I ordered her to come back to New York, and she told me that it was her life and for me to fuck off. I'm not going to lie; her defiant attitude pissed me off. So I shouted some shit to her that I'm not too proud of… but dammit, it was time for tough love."

"So now you're blaming yourself because she trusted that fucker Jeff?"

The only one responsible for this mess was Jeff. He'd manipulated Lexis into putting her trust in a man who didn't deserve it or her.

An image of Sin's smiling face flashed into my mind, and the irony and similarity of the Lexis and Jeff situation chilled me to the bone.

Didn't I do a very similar thing to Sin by making her believe she could trust me? When my intention from the very start was to use her just to get to Bigsby?

There was a heaviness in my body.

I didn't deserve Sin's trust, and I damn sure didn't deserve her. But I was a greedy man who wanted more than I was entitled to.

Ram's voice broke into my thoughts. "Yes, I spoiled her too much and sheltered her from the realities of life because I wanted to make up for the rough way we had grown up. If I'd just told her straight up that she didn't know shit about love or men, then maybe she wouldn't have hooked up with a predator. It's my fault she chose Jeff over me. I fucking pushed her too hard, and maybe she's dead because of me." His eyes took on a steely glint.

"Ram, you know I have your back, no matter what, bro."

Ram roughly blew out a breath before nodding.

I continued. "So let's not jump to any conclusions when the answers are right behind this damn door."

Adrenaline pumped through my veins as we stood before the door.

What we were about to do would be brutal, but we had to get Lexis back, and there was nothing I wasn't willing to do to accomplish that.

My mind slipped into the dark and lethal place, and the ugly monster that I kept caged came out to play. He didn't give a shit about anyone or anything but his prey—Jeff.

Grinding my teeth, I grabbed the doorknob, yanking open the door before stepping into the damp-smelling cell.

My eyes quickly adjusted to the darkness as we strode in. Ram closed the door with a decisive click.

I nodded curtly to Max and Rocco, my enforcers, before my eyes locked on the man in his early thirties—according to our intel—who was lashed to the metal chair sitting between Max and Rocco and was surrounded by buckets, a stack of towels, a bottle of pink solution, and a watering can resting on the floor.

Jeff's body was wet, stark naked, and shivering.

His eyes widened at the sight of Ram and me. "What the hell is going on now?" he squawked and then warily eyed me.

My nostrils flared slightly before I responded, "Hello, Jeff."

"Who are you?" he furtively glanced around.

"I'm your worst fucking nightmare." I fixed him with a cold stare.

"Do you know who I am?" Jeff stuttered while trying unsuccessfully to move his legs that were spread eagle and bound to the chair

"Dead," I replied, "if you say another damn word without my say-so. I'll kill you right here."

Jeff glanced around, and I could see the sheer fear in his eyes.

The room was silent, except for the low whir of the air conditioner. Ram moved toward the table smack dab in the middle of the room.

"Meet Ram." I jabbed a finger in Ram's direction. "Lexis's brother."

Jeff's face turned ashen.

"And I'm going to break you in half," Ram hissed while snatching up a pair of black latex gloves and impatiently snapping them on. "If I don't get my baby sister back… alive."

Jeff bucked against the rope binding him to the chair. "Untie me!" he shrilled.

Max growled, slapping him on the back of his head. "I will snap your damn neck. Shut the fuck up."

Ram sneered but remained eerily silent as he moved to sit on the edge of the table.

Jeff's face contorted with pain. "What the fuck is this shit about?" he squeaked while watching me move unhurriedly toward the narrow table.

I ignored him while taking off my leather jacket, folding it, and then laying it over the table ever so carefully. I cracked my knuckles before slipping on a pair of black latex gloves.

"All I was doing was visiting a friend when these two men"—his eyes darted toward Max and Rocco—"kidnapped me, brought me here, stripped me naked, and started torturing the shit out of me."

My eyes were cold, my voice flat. "And they're the nice ones. Me?" I shrugged. "Not so much."

"Come on, man. This is totally fucked up," Jeff screamed. "And illegal." He struggled uselessly against the rope.

Rocco snorted. "Ain't this some crazy shit? You're a sex trafficker complaining about us doing something illegal. Men like you should be buried alive."

"So Sinthia Michaels is your friend?" I asked with a sharp tone.

"Yes." Beads of sweat dripped down his forehead.

I arched a brow. "Do you really want to lie to me?"

"She's a friend of a friend," Jeff stuttered. "And I was picking up something from her house."

I cracked my knuckles. "Now we can do this the hard way or—"

"The easy way?" Jeff croaked.

"No." I shook my head. "I was going to say the harder way. And if you interrupt me again, I'm going to knock out your damn teeth."

Jeff gulped.

I smiled coldly as I rolled up my sleeves, displaying my tattooed forearms. "I'm not going to lie to you. There's no way you're going to get through my interrogation without a lot of blood spilled—yours—because I happen to hate lowlife motherfuckers who deal in human trafficking."

"This is bullshit!" Jeff's panic was distinct. "I don't do that shit. I swear."

"You lying fuck." Ram stormed up to Jeff and punched him in the face. He grunted in pain. "You pimped out my sister."

Jeff spit out blood along with a couple of teeth before screaming, "I didn't. Not Lexis. She's mine. Bigsby wanted me to, but I didn't. I swear."

"She's yours?" Ram roared. "My sister is not your damn property. She fucking trusted your ass, and you treated her like a whore."

Jeff's lips and chin wobbled before he mumbled, "I'm sorry."

I eyed Jeff. "This is how it's going down. I'm going to ask you some questions, and I want straight answers." My voice was harsh. "Where's Lexis?"

"If I tell you, Bigsby will kill me." Jeff's body trembled.

"And if you don't tell me, I'll kill you. So it sounds like you're in a real fucked-up predicament. But the difference between Bigsby and me is I'll make sure you stay alive for five long, agonizing days until you beg me to end your life." I smiled coldly. "Your choice."

"Fuck you," he spit.

My voice dropped to a lethal, low whisper. "No. Fuck you."

I nodded to Rocco and Max. They yanked the chair Jeff was sitting on all the way back so it dangled precariously on its back legs. Picking up the damp towels from the floor, I slapped them onto Jeff's inclined head before pouring water over his scalp. The damp cloth was not essential but was a bonus multiplier of the torture. I continued pouring water over his face, and Jeff struggled and inhaled. In turn, the inhalation brought the damp towels tight against his nostrils as if a huge, wet paw had clamped over his face. His legs, chest, and arms twitched involuntarily. The inhaled water was an instant, life-threatening situation; even the smallest amount of liquid in the larynx and trachea was an immediate, hardwired hotline directly to the panic portion of the brain that death was imminent.

He struggled, but not as much as before. I nodded to Max and Rocco, and they righted Jeff's chair. I yanked off the soaking, stifling layers. His head lolled back, and he was barely coherent.

"I know your lungs are burning." I stepped back, drying my hand on a clean black towel. "I can see the panic in your eyes. You want this to end, and I promise I will end it. Just tell me what I want to know. Where's Lexis?"

He coughed. "She's in Connecticut with the other girls. And if you keep me alive, I'll take you to her." He looked around with uneasy eyes.

Ram snapped, "Either tell us where she's at or we'll do to you like they castrate the bulls." He held up the metal forceps. "We'll put a rubber band around your balls, cutting off the blood circulation until they fall off like rotten grapes. Your choice, Jeff."

Ram squeezed the castrater as if testing out the device. Jeff looked on with disbelief.

"Okay, okay." He stammered out a Greenwich, Connecticut, street address.

Ram quickly entered the information into his cell and then glanced over at me. "I just sent Kevin the info to check it out." He then stared at Jeff. "And if it isn't correct, this shit is going to get real nasty."

It didn't take long for Ram's cell to beep with an incoming text. He tapped the screen and reported, "He's heading over to the address right now. He'll brief us once he gets there."

I twirled a chair around, and I sat in front of Jeff. "See how easy this shit can be? Now let's move on, shall we?" I leaned forward. "Let's talk about Sinthia Michaels. Why did Bigsby send you to break into her house to steal the ledger?"

"I don't know what you're talking about," Jeff stuttered.

"You don't?" My voice dropped to a threatening whisper.

I nodded. Rocco yanked the chair back. Max slapped the damp towels over Jeff's face and then started pouring water over him. Jeff struggled, but Max didn't relent. Jeff thrashed more frantically until Rocco righted the chair. Max whipped off the towels, and Jeff gasped for air.

"Why does Bigsby want the ledger?" I yelled.

"I don't know anything!" Jeff screamed.

Ram walked over to him and punched him in the face. Jeff whimpered as blood trickled down his cheek.

"Jeff," I started, "come on, man. I thought we had an understanding that you were going to tell the truth."

Jeff silently looked at me.

I continued. "How about this? I'll tell you what we know, and we'll start all over again."

Jeff nodded while nervously licking his lips.

"Good," I grunted and fixed him with a cold stare. "How we hear it, the reason we had such a hard time finding you is because you're being protected by Bigsby. We know you're now his errand boy. You recruit the women for him, and he pimps them out to his rich friends. We hear there's a huge demand from his rolling-in-it friends to fuck fresh, untrained women any way and anywhere they want."

Jeff nodded. "Yes… to everything."

"See how easy that was?" I replied. "Moving on… Bigsby sent you to Sin's house to break in and get the ledger, which you did. But you also did a little more than that, didn't you? You trashed her house."

"What?" Jeff squeaked. "No." He shook his head in denial. "Don't know what you're talking about, man. Yes, I broke in and stole the ledger, but I left the house exactly how I found it. Trashed." His Adam's apple bobbed.

Max's body tensed. "You lying piece of shit!"

He stalked toward Jeff before hitting him hard across the head. I watched with disinterest.

"I'm telling the truth," Jeff replied. "I took the ledger for Bigsby, but I didn't trash the fucking house. I swear." He paused. "I'm not dying for Bigsby. He ordered me to do a job, and I did it. If you just let me—"

"Max," I hissed, "go find out who trashed Sin's place."

"You actually believe that piece of shit?" Max asked.

I glanced over at Jeff, who stammered, "I swear. It's the truth."

He looked like a desperate man with nothing to lose who was fighting for his life, which he was.

"Yes, I do," I gritted out to Max. "Get on this now!"

Max nodded before walking out of the room with his cell in hand.

I eyed Jeff. "What were you told about the ledger?"

"I'm not saying anything more until you release me," Jeff demanded.

"You will talk," I replied and then eyed Ram. "Let's try the castrater, shall we?"

"My pleasure," he answered with a wicked gleam in his eyes.

"It might take him a couple tries to lock on to your shriveled-up balls," I informed Jeff. "But practice makes perfect."

"I'm not talking, you sadistic bastard!" Jeff yelled.

"Well, that's the spirit. How about we kick this party up a notch?" I countered before nodding at Rocco, who brought me the small machine with two metal pads attached to it. He placed the device on the floor by my feet.

"Let's play." I flipped on the machine. I picked up the two metal paddles attached to the device and asked him, "Have you ever watched the show *Naked and Afraid*?" I slowly touched the paddles together, causing sparks to fly into the air.

The color drained from Jeff's face.

"Rocco, let's proceed," I ordered.

Rocco pushed the button on the machine, causing the electricity to pulsate harder through the paddles.

"Time for the fireworks to begin." I pressed both pads to Jeff's scrotum.

His face contorted as he howled with pain.

CHAPTER 7
SINTHIA

The doorman grandly opened the door for me before I stepped out of Core's building after he left for his urgent business meeting. Hurriedly, I zipped up my leather motorcycle jacket as the cool, crisp air engulfed me.

I loved October; it was the best time of the year to walk around New York City because all the touristy summer crowds had disappeared. It was a beautiful Sunday, but I had to forgo my leisurely walk through Manhattan.

Yesterday, I'd worked until late night on my designs and then eaten a quick meal before falling into a deep sleep. When I'd woken up this morning, I'd felt pleasantly refreshed but missed Core's warm body. He'd given me the heads-up yesterday that his business deal would take a while to negotiate, so he wouldn't be back until today. But before leaving, he had insisted that someone from his team drive me around today. At first, I'd resisted, not liking the idea of being followed around the city like I needed a babysitter, and we'd passionately argued back and forth about the topic. But eventually, his logic and concern for my safety due to the break-in at my townhouse had finally won.

Truth be told, the idea that the person who had caused such

destruction of my property, including my collection, had not yet been caught caused me unease. Now that I'd left the cocoon and safety of Core's penthouse, a sense of dread and paranoia seeped into my bones, and I was glad Core had been so insistent.

I inhaled deeply, taking in a lungful of the fresh air, and mentally shook myself. I had to stay on my game.

Buck up, Sin. Put on your big-girl panties.

I straightened my back and slung my leather handbag over my shoulder before walking toward Zuri. She was Core's well-paid minion—her words, not mine—whom I'd met for the first time on Friday when she dropped off Core's invitation to the McKay Club along with an expensive, beautiful dress he'd purchased for me to wear that night. Frankly, when Zuri had strode into my townhouse, I hadn't known what to make of her due to the fact that things were a little tense between Core and me, and anyone linked to him had been on my shit list just from their mere association. But after Zuri and our mutual on-the-spot should-I-like-you analysis of each other, we'd concluded that we liked each other so far.

I waved at Zuri, who was leaning against her expensive black SUV. She looked like she'd just stepped off the fashion runway. Her dark autumn skin tone along with her sleek flaming-red tresses, pulled up into a high ponytail, gave her an exotic look. Her eyes, as usual, were shielded by aviators.

She pushed away from her car, stepping forward and then hugging me. I returned the embrace before pulling back.

"Well, don't you look absolutely hot in that outfit?" Zuri complimented me. "Damn. You're giving me a lady boner."

I laughed. "I aim to please."

Today I was rocking a cool graphic tee and cuffed skinny jeans that I'd amped up with statement accessories. A pair of gold hoop earrings, a logo handbag, and red-bottomed shoes.

"So you drew the short straw today and got assigned to be my driver, huh?" I gave her a mock frown, but frankly, I wasn't put out by Core assigning Zuri to be my babysitter. I liked her, and that was saying a lot for a person like me who didn't easily click with people and therefore kept her circle of friends really small.

"Assigned?" Zuri whipped off her sunglasses. "Hell no. I volunteered." She smiled impishly. "I wanted to hang out with you today. Believe me. The alternative of having the other guys on the team drive you around would make you pull your hair out. I love them and all, but they can be a bit abrasive. Just way too much grunting and knocking stones together like cavemen if you ask me."

"So basically what you're saying is they're assholes, just like their boss?" I grinned sassily.

"Exactly." Her eyes lit with a twinkle of mischief.

I opened the passenger door and slid in, watching as she sauntered around to the driver's side. Zuri got into the car, fastening her seat belt.

"So where are we heading today?" She turned on her vehicle and revved the engine.

"To my friend Cisco's boutique." I rattled off the address while fastening my seat belt. "Today is the last dress fitting for my two best clients." I sighed heavily. "Luckily, I sent their gowns to the boutique days ago for alterations. It would have been a mega clusterfuck if the dresses had gotten destroyed last night along with the rest of my collection."

I'd already designed the gowns for Ariana Bellisario—the mother of my bestie, Jade—and Erika Watson—Ariana's best friend and Jade's television executive boss—to wear at an upcoming fundraising gala. And I needed to make sure their gowns were perfect. So I'd sent their gowns to Cisco's—the boutique where all of my clients' fittings were done—so my friend Summer, who was a top-notch seamstress and the only one I trusted to work on my designs, could put the last-minute touches on the gowns.

My mind drifted to Jade. I missed her. There were so many times yesterday and today when I had been so tempted to call her, telling her everything that had happened since she left for New Zealand to start production on her first directorial feature. But I didn't want Jade to worry about me or feel compelled to hightail her ass back to New York, ruining her movie shoot. Just because my dreams were on hiatus didn't mean Jade's had to be destroyed over my drama.

Zuri pulled out of the parking space. "Core told me about your break-in." She ripped her gaze away from the road long enough to give me a sympathetic look before turning back to concentrate on weaving through Manhattan traffic.

"I'm kind of numb about it, frankly." I stared out the window, looking at everything but processing nothing. "The funny thing is I couldn't give a shit about all of my personal possessions that were destroyed. Those things I can buy back, but it's all the damn work I put into finishing my collection. That's the part that hurts like a fucker."

I bit my bottom lip, staring at the bumper-to-bumper gridlock.

I'd had only five more over-the-top pieces to complete before I sat down with the buying and marketing teams to decide which designs would make the final cut, essentially eliminating designs to be made and sold via the retailers. And I'd excitedly anticipated the final stage —when my collection would go on sale.

Damn! My collection was almost complete. Now I have to start all over again.

The thought was frustrating and daunting.

Horns honked loudly, mercifully jolting my thoughts back from an impending descent into depression.

"Sin, I'm really sorry about your collection," Zuri replied while zipping in and out of the snarl of taxicabs and buses. "The pieces that I saw when I was at your house were so beautiful. It's going to take a lot of work, but you can rebuild the collection. And whatever you need, you can count on me to help you."

"Thank you, Zuri." I smiled at her while fiddling with my seat belt.

"And I just heard from the cleaning company. There was more work than they had originally estimated, but they'll have your townhouse finished today." Zuri cursed and hit her horn. She mumbled under her breath about terrible New York drivers while tapping the steering wheel as we sat in heavy Manhattan traffic.

"I appreciate it, but no amount of cleaning is going to make me feel comfortable in my house again," I returned. "Whoever broke in violated my space… my home. Honestly, I'll feel better once the police find out who did it."

The gridlock eased, allowing Zuri to smoothly drive ahead. "Unfortunately, the police probably moved on to another case. But I wouldn't worry about it. Core will find the person who did it and make them pay."

I clenched my fingers around my leather handbag. "You have a hell of a lot of faith in him."

"Don't you?" Zuri shot back.

I contemplated my response before uttering a word. Zuri was employed by Core. More importantly, she was his friend, so I knew where her loyalty lay. However, I wouldn't be me if I didn't keep it real with her.

"I have faith in myself." I shrugged. "I've learned the hard way that people tend to have their own agendas. It's just second nature for me to question people's intentions."

My past experience with toxic relationships, with Grace and men, made me so conscious of people—what they said and why they wanted to be with me.

"Sin, no one is perfect, especially not Core. It's just..." She shook her head. "Never mind."

"Zuri, spit it out."

"I just assumed that after spending time with Core, you saw that little bit of potential of sticking it out with him."

"Look, Zuri, I like Core... a lot. Probably more than I should, especially given the fact that our business relationship didn't start out on the best foot." Not with him swooping in out of nowhere and taking control of ninety-seven percent of my business. "Yes, our relationship has changed for the better, but how I feel about Core is complicated."

My mind was telling me one thing—not to get too attached—but I felt like I already was.

"Hmm... complicated. That's code for: *He scares the shit out of me—emotionally.*"

I blinked, startled that she'd read me so fast. "Hell yes, he does," I answered. There was no need to lie about it. "I've moved from wanting to shank him to wanting..."

"More than just sex," Zuri finished.

"Yes," I replied. My throat instantly went dry as I just felt the emotions stirring inside me while I tried to wrap my mind around the concept of Core and me together... like in a real relationship.

"Trust me on this," Zuri confided. "This is new territory for Core, too." She paused. "Zero. That's the number of women he's brought to his penthouse."

My mouth dropped open with shock before I shut it. "I don't understand…"

"You don't know much about the man, do you?" Zuri asked.

"Apparently not." I nibbled on my bottom lip.

Abruptly, Zuri pulled over to the farthest lane and out of traffic. She double parked and then put on her hazard lights. "Do you want to?" she asked before unsnapping her seat belt and turning to squarely look me in the face.

"Want to what?" I asked.

"Know about him?" She pursed her lips.

I ran my fingers through my hair. "You work for him, and you're his friend. So why would you tell me anything about him?" I unfastened my seat belt to get more comfortable.

"Core is not just my friend. He's the big brother I never had. He has my back, and I have his. And I would never tell you anything that would betray the trust and bond Core and I share." She blew a strand of hair that had fallen across her eye. "All I'm saying is I don't give a shit about the who, what, and why he came into your life. That's the past. This is the now."

She jabbed her finger in the air. "He has everything a man could ever want—money, friends who love him, freedom, and power—but he doesn't have that one person. I want that so much for him because he fucking deserves a chance at something real. You are that real. A chance for happiness." She scowled. "But you two are the most stubborn people I know. You're scared of being hurt. Core wants to stick his head in the sand and pretend he won't be fucked up emotionally if you walk out of his life for good. This shit is not rocket science. Will you both just lay your damn cards on the table with each other and see what happens?"

"I wish it were that simple, Zuri. I've been through some things in my life that I haven't quite healed from."

"Sin, so has Core. Growing up, he went through some crazy shit that would have broken a lesser man."

"Don't you think I know that? Shit. I thought my life was fucked up, losing my dad the way I did, but damn... with Core's mother being killed so brutally and in front of him..." I swallowed hard. "I'm not going to lie; I think that would have broken me."

Zuri's mouth parted and then snapped shut.

"What?" I asked.

"Wow." She shook her head. "I can't believe he told you about his mother. Talking about her is pretty much taboo for him, even with us—me, Ram, Kevin, Max, and Rocco—and we're family."

I silently digested what she'd revealed. Core had shared this deeply personal experience... with me.

Any traces of doubt that he cared about me disappeared along with the little nagging voice in my head that berated me for trusting him, for agreeing to give our relationship a chance to grow.

I guess I should listen to my heart... right?

CHAPTER 8
SINTHIA

"Zuri," I said while stepping off the elevator with her by my side, "you know you don't have to hang around for this."

"Wait." She skidded to a stop, giving me a mock glare. "Are you trying to get rid of me already?" She pouted playfully. "And just when I thought we had this bestie vibe happening. Don't you like me?" She dramatically fluttered her eyelashes.

I rolled my eyes. "No."

Zuri cocked her head to the side.

"Maybe," I replied before my lips curled up into a smile.

Zuri fist-pumped. "Yes! I knew it."

"Okay, okay. Now move your needy ass on," I demanded before swaying away from her. It didn't take her long to catch up with me. "Are you sure you won't be bored? Watching client fittings is not exactly exciting, and they tend to be long." But for me, it was the exact opposite. I loved everything about my design process—from creation to seeing my clothing on my clients—but I was a fashionista and loved all things clothes.

"Bored? Are you crazy?" Zuri countered. "Jesus. My heart is pounding like a high school virgin about to get her cherry popped."

She winked at me. "I mean look at this place. It's a paradise for a clotheshorse like me." She gestured widely to Cisco's boutique.

The space was sleek, modern, and very glam. The walls were painted black, which allowed the rich colors of my designs on display to pop against the beautiful darkness. It contrasted against the plush velvet furniture and natural light in the space that had been designed with a contemporary look in mind.

I smiled at her. "I knew there was a reason I liked you so much."

I scanned the studio. I loved the ambiance at my friend Francisco "Cisco" Rodriguez's upscale boutique and that it was blissfully quiet. Unlike other boutiques in this neighborhood, Cisco's place was by appointment only, which his rich and discerning patrons loved.

"Those are your designs, right?" Zuri gestured to my pieces that were displayed like eye candy in the middle of the space.

"Yes." I confirmed proudly. "They're some of my pretties."

"Damn. Your designs are badass."

"Okay. So now you're just bucking for a discount," I groused good-naturedly. "But that shit isn't happening. I have damn bills to pay."

Zuri laughed. "Jesus. You're funny and straightforward, and you live your life unapologetically. I really like that about you. Core's lucky I'm not into chicks, because I'd shank him for you."

"Girl, you're cray-cray. I love it," I replied with a wink. "Follow me," I ordered, dropping my leather handbag onto a plush ottoman. "Let me give you the tour," I instructed, looping an arm through hers, ushering her across the space. "Okay, these are all my designs." With one hand, I gestured to the wall-to-wall racks.

Zuri fanned herself while gawking at the clothes. "Oh Lord. There's movement in my vajayjay, an honest-to-goodness tingly fucking sensation. I want one of everything."

I gave her an impish smile. "Aren't you even going to look at the price tags?"

"Nope." Zuri lovingly stroked a dress. "It's all going on my McKay black charge card. These outfits are my bonus for having to put up with a bunch of cavemen assholes."

"Shit. Why didn't you say that from the get-go? I'm more than happy to help you spend Core's money on my clothing." I stepped forward, pulling out a bright, sparkling orange halter top and a full, ruffled black silk organza skirt. "This is new and would look fab on you."

Zuri squealed like a schoolgirl. "Love it."

"Pick whatever you want and put it on the empty rack. Cisco will bring everything upstairs and set up a fitting room for you."

I dug into my pocket, pulling out my cell and aiming it at her. "Zuri, smile and hold up the dress. I'm sending Core a photo of what his money is buying."

Zuri struck a vixen pose. "Cha-ching!" she chirped as I took the photo and then hit send.

"I can't wait to see Core's face when he gets his charge card statement," I crowed before shoving my cell back into my pocket.

Zuri started putting clothes on the empty rack. "Nothing fazes him. Believe me," she answered while looking through the other outfits on display.

"Fill the rack up, sweetie." I urged. "You deserve it." I winked at her.

"Sin!" Cisco exclaimed, rushing over to me.

Dressed in black jeans, a crisp blue shirt, and his signature old Rolex, he barely paused before closing the space between us and then yanking me into his arms. I hugged him back without any hesitation.

"Sin, don't be angry," Cisco muttered into my ear before pulling away and clasping my hands. "This is not my fault," he finished as his eyes swept over me from head to toe. At thirty-six, he still looked boyish, but he had intense dark eyebrows that conveyed his seriousness. He released my hands, dramatically fanning himself with his hand. "*Ay, Dios mío!* I really don't need all this drama today."

I knew from experience that when Cisco started spouting Spanish, shit in his world had hit the damn fan.

I arched a brow. "What the hell are you talking about?"

"Sin!" a woman's voice exclaimed. "Jesus. I'm so happy to see you. Listen, I need—"

"Tabitha?" I cut her off.

What. The. Fuck?

Just a couple weeks ago, we had been at the McKay Club, laughing and drinking. Gone was the polished veneer of Tabitha Thorp, celebrity designer. Now she looked haggard. Her face was gaunt. The head-to-toe black ensemble she wore looked at least two sizes too big and accented her now-unattractive, rail-thin body. Her hair appeared frizzy and unwashed. Essentially, she was a hot mess.

I watched in disbelief as she swayed toward me with a huge grin on her face like we were besties, when all I wanted to do was cunt-punt her ass across the damn room. I was so glad Cisco's was an appointment-only boutique, which was now empty except for the four of us, because I was about to go Brooklyn on Tabitha's scheming, conniving ass.

Tabitha grinned. "Yes, it's me, darling. In the flesh."

Cisco had told me about the Manhattan gossip mill running rampant with news that Tabitha, my former mentor and longtime friend, was back in town and frantically calling around, begging friends for money. The last place I'd expected to see her was here. Well, not after she'd abruptly shut down her boutique, disconnected her cell, and left New York without a trace.

"So the rumors are true. You're back in town and begging for money?" I directed at Tabitha.

"Begging?" Tabitha scoffed. "Hardly. I'm asking for generous donations just to tide me over." Tabitha sniffed disdainfully. "You see, I've run into a bit of trouble. And I'm reaching out to good friends like you and Cisco in my time of need."

With every haughty syllable she'd uttered, rage raced through my veins at her gall to act like everything between us was the same. It wasn't and never would be again.

All I saw was red.

"Trouble?" I hissed at Tabitha while steadying myself, using Zuri's frame as I hopped from one foot to the other, pulling off my red-bottomed shoes and tossing them aside. "You don't know what trouble is, you backstabbing bitch!" I lurched for Tabitha as I demanded, "Cisco. Move."

"*Ay, Dios mío!*" he whispered. "No!"

Zuri quickly wrapped her arms around me, restraining me.

"Zuri! Let me go," I commanded.

"No," Zuri answered while turning me around to face her. "Lord knows I like a good catfight, but this bitch is not worth your time."

"Bitch?" Tabitha screeched.

"You heard me." Zuri taunted Tabitha, still eyeing me. "Sin, don't do this. Take a deep breath. Walk away from this shit."

She was right. Tabitha wasn't worth the effort or the scene I would be making by beating her ass. But there was no way I was leaving that room without a fucking explanation from Tabitha.

Nope. I want—no, need—damn answers.

Zuri stared at me. "I need to make a call. So are you calm and collected now?"

I nodded.

Cisco's face was flustered when he asked, "You okay?"

I nodded.

He slowly stepped aside, giving Tabitha the evil eye. Zuri pulled out her cell and started texting rapidly but still kept an eye on Tabitha and me.

I squared off with Tabitha. "Okay, Tabitha, let's get this ugliness over with. Why didn't you tell me that my investor was McKay?"

When Tabitha had called me out of the blue, all excited about one of her business connections being willing to provide financing in exchange for a small percentage of my future profits, I had been skeptical but desperate for funding to expand my business and start my new clothing line. So I'd just blissfully signed the contract. The ink hadn't even dried on the document when two million dollars was deposited into my business account with the promise of another million in six months. Little had I known that the investor was Core McKay or that I had stupidly given away ninety-seven percent of my business.

"What difference did it make who he was?"

"You know why. And you know me. I would never have gone into business with a man like Core."

"Hey!" Zuri protested. "What the hell is that supposed to mean?" she asked with narrowed eyes.

"Oh, don't get all snippy," I responded. "You and I know that I've changed my original viewpoint about him. But I'm keeping it real."

Given what I'd heard about Core through the grapevine before I met him—that he'd built his billion-dollar empire from illegal activities—I never would've been desperate or stupid enough to pick him as my investor.

I eyed Tabitha. "Now, back to our conversation. Why did you hide the truth that my secret investor was Core McKay?"

"It's complicated," Tabitha replied sharply.

Heat flushed through my body. "Complicated?" A bitter tang coated my mouth. "It seems pretty straightforward to me. You steered me into a deal you knew I wouldn't have taken if I had known it involved Core. And given our former long-standing friendship, in my eyes, that was a really fucked-up thing to do."

For fuck's sake, she had been my trusted mentor, and I'd thought she was my friend. That type of betrayal was not something I could just sweep under the rug and walk away from without finding out why.

"I didn't make you do anything, Sin." Tabitha snarled. "I made a business introduction; that's all. You signed the deal."

I blew out a noisy breath. "Let's be clear. I'm not blaming you for my stupidity in signing the damn contract without looking at the fine print." I pointed to myself. "That fucked-up move is all me. But damn, I trusted you as my friend. You could have been straight with me and told me Core McKay was the secret investor. You owed me that much."

"I don't owe you shit." Tabitha jutted out her chin.

I tilted my head. "Don't make me hurt you, Tabitha." I countered. "Answer the fucking question. Why didn't you tell me the truth about McKay?"

I was like a dog with a bone, and there was no way in hell I was going to stop until I had the answers I'd waited so long to hear from her.

Tabitha's eyes darted around. "I can't talk about this," she whispered. "You don't know him like I do. He'll…" She swallowed hard.

I arched a brow. "He'll what?"

Is she actually scared of Core? No. That's bullshit. She was stalling. Playing games with my head by trying to avoid telling me the truth.

Tabitha's mouth formed a thin line. I knew she wasn't going to budge on her stance. So I decided to come at her from another angle.

"What's your relationship with Core? Are you friends?" I demanded.

I suspected the answer was no because they just didn't seem like the type of people to run in the same social circles. Plus, there was something about how Tabitha had reacted when she mentioned that she couldn't talk about Core; she looked terrified.

"Sin!" Zuri interjected.

I threw up a not-now hand. "Mind your damn business, Zuri," I retorted.

"No," Tabitha drawled. "Core and I are not friends."

Warning bells started ringing in my head.

I pushed on with my inquisition. "Let me get this straight. Everything you told me about your business connection, Core, was a lie?"

"Not exactly," Tabitha said.

What the fuck is going on?

"Not exactly? What the hell does that mean?" I was pissed at the fucking trust and friendship violation. "Did you even know Core?"

"I knew him, but we're not friends." She paused. "We grew up in the same neighborhood."

Okay. That I believe.

From what Core had told me about his difficult childhood and what I knew about Tabitha—that she had grown up in the rough streets of Brooklyn, doing things she wasn't really proud of—her words, not mine—it made sense that they knew each other from years ago. But what didn't make sense was how or why they'd reconnected over my business.

"And?" I prompted.

"And what, Sin?"

I huffed with exasperation. "You would have me believe that you just happened to reconnect with Core—a man you weren't even friends with? And he just happened to be interested in going into business with me?"

She threw her hands up in the air. "I don't have time for this fucking interrogation. I have shit to do, so let's get to the damn point.

Core approached me about meeting you. He had money. You needed money. Problem fucking solved."

My body stiffened. "Wait. Core approached you? Why?"

"Ask him. Now, are we fucking done?"

"Tabitha, you're such a bitch to everyone!" Cisco snapped.

"Oh, shut up, Cisco," Tabitha replied.

I glanced over at Zuri. She was still tapping furiously on her cell.

Who the hell is she texting while this reality show is in midswing?

"Look, Sin," Tabitha retorted, pressing her hand into my arm.

"Don't touch me," I roughly shot back.

Her fingers dropped away from me.

Tabitha stepped closer, whispering in my ear, "I'm not who you need answers from. You need them from Core."

I frowned at her words even though I knew she was right. There was no way he was going to squirm away from my questions tonight.

Tabitha carried on. "All I'm asking for is some money to tide me over until I can get myself together."

"You're really a piece of work, Tabitha." I looked her up and down. "After what you did to me, you actually think I'm going to give you money?" I snorted.

"Why not?" Tabitha whined with a sullen look on her face.

"Because you probably sold me out to the first bidder—Core." I jammed my hands on my hips. "You already got your penny out of this pound of flesh. Now get the hell out of my damn face."

Tabitha twisted her expression into an ugly mask of hate. "I mentored you. You were my protégé. I showed you the fucking ropes."

"That makes what you did to me even more tragic," I pointed out.

"I was the one who took you under my wing and helped you make all the right connections!" Tabitha screamed.

"Like Core?" I sneered.

"I made you."

I felt nauseous from the way Tabitha was looking at me. It was *The Silence of the Lambs* creepy. Like she wanted to rip off my skin and wear it like a fucking fur coat. Tabitha was a selfish, self-serving cunt who only cared about herself and money.

Fuck! Jade was right all along. Tabitha is jealous of my success.

"You made me?" I arched a brow. "What the fuck are you smoking?" My nostrils flared with anger. "I worked hard to get to where I am today. It was my blood, sweat, and tears."

"You fucking owe me, Sin!"

"I don't owe you shit. And anything you've done for me, I've paid back threefold by allowing your lazy, washed-up designing ass to sell my clothing at your bargain basement boutique."

"You little…" Tabitha sputtered.

I backed her into a clothing rack. "I dare you to say it."

She swallowed hard.

"Give me a reason to go Brooklyn on your ass," I hissed, shoving her head back. "And just so we're perfectly clear, you are officially on my *To Be Shanked with a Dull, Rusty Knife* list. So stay clear of me from this point forward."

Someone cleared their throat loudly. "Are we interrupting something?"

My head snapped around to see my clients and friends, Ariana and Erika, looking on with wide eyes.

"Nope," I answered. "Nothing to see here."

I snidely looked at Tabitha before stomping over to my handbag and then shoes, picking them up before walking away toward the stairs, which led to the dressing lounge.

Tabitha had destroyed years of friendship, and I was pissed and damn hurt. But I was also grateful that the truth about her loyalty to me had finally been revealed. Now my blinders had been yanked off. Now my eyes were wide open. And even though she had answered some questions, there were still so many left unanswered. But there was one thing that was apparent; Core had actively sought me out via Tabitha. But why? It didn't make any sense.

Why would a billionaire want to buy my fledgling fashion business?

It was as if he'd used Tabitha just to get to me.

No. That couldn't be right. My conclusion made no sense.

Before meeting Core, I had been in debt and hadn't even had a mainstream clothing line. Yes, I'd had a strong cult following, but in order to take my business to the next level—fashion mainstream status —I'd needed money and an investor to get my clothing line into all major retailers. Frankly, from a financial perspective, I'd needed Core more than he could ever need me.

I bit my bottom lip. Still… there was something that needled me about the fact that Core had asked Tabitha to vouch for him.

I pulled out my cell and tapped his name on my contacts list, instantly calling him. My eyes narrowed when it went to voicemail.

Why is his phone off?

"Core, call me now," I instructed before ending the call and marching up the stairs.

I didn't like secrets… especially potentially dirty ones.

No. I have to address this shit straight on.

My chest tightened.

But am I making a big deal out of nothing? Maybe Core's rationale will be simple and straightforward…

But, if it is… then why was Tabitha petrified to talk about the subject?

CHAPTER 9
CORE

It was Sunday morning, and I was still in the cell with my team, Ram and Rocco, and our prisoner, Jeff.

I had all the information I needed from Jeff Barolo, who was tied to the chair, his body slumped against the bindings that tethered him to the seat. His muscles were still twitching from the electrical current I'd tortured him with. And I felt no guilt about Jeff's predicament.

Jeff was a bottom-feeder and Bigsby's errand boy, and they both dealt in human trafficking. The brutal realities of human trafficking were deplorable and destroyed the lives of tens of thousands of women like Lexis every day.

Pulling off my black latex gloves, I tossed them into a black garbage bag. Now that Lexis and the women had been saved today when Kevin arrived at the Greenwich address Jeff had given us, we could move on with our Bigsby mission.

Damn. I still can't believe it. After all these years, I might finally have the ammunition to take down Bigsby. Shit.

The ledger combined with an actual recording of Bigsby bragging about his kills would be ironclad evidence.

Impatiently, I was waiting for Kevin to get back to us, confirming the existence of Jeff's evidence—a secret recording of Bigsby bragging about killing several people—that he'd stored in the cloud.

My cell rang; I put it on speaker so Ram and Rocco could hear, too. "Did you get it?"

"Yes. Just like Jeff insisted, there was a password-protected audio file. After unlocking it, I cleaned it up a bit."

"But it's legit?" I asked. "Nobody's tampered with it?"

"Yes," Kevin replied. "I checked. It's authentic. I had my computer program compare Jeff's file against a recording of Bigsby's mayoral debate. No anomalies between the two were found. You ready to hear the shit or what?"

"Go," I snapped, sitting down on a chair.

The recording that Jeff had made started…

"I'm not fucking around with you, Jeff," Bigsby shouted.

The recording was peppered with the sounds of scuffling and grunts of Jeff being roughed up by him.

Bigsby demanded, "Where the hell is Ben Vargos?"

I snorted. *Dead… by my orders.* There was no way in hell I could let a piece of shit like Ben back on the street after we'd interrogated him for intel that pointed us right back to Bigsby and Jeff.

Jeff's high-pitched voice screamed in the recording, "I told you I don't know. I swear."

Bigsby barked, "If I find out you're lying to me…"

"I swear. I'm not." Jeff huffed and puffed as if Bigsby was choking him. "Just like you asked, I tried to find him, but he's disappeared. No one knows where he is."

I nodded. *Truth… Max and Rocco buried him somewhere he won't be found.*

Bigsby bellowed, "You think he's the one talking to the Feds about me?"

"Probably," Jeff stammered. "How else would they know you're laundering money through Pomtonic? Someone is talking."

"Yeah! Someone's snitching all right," Bigsby snarled. "It could be Vargos or… you, asshole!"

I arched a brow. Bigsby was right. Someone was dropping a dime on him. But it wasn't Ben; he was dead. And it couldn't be Jeff; that fucker was terrified of Bigsby.

So who's talking to the Feds?

I made a mental note to have Kevin find out.

"Bigsby, I swear," Jeff blubbered on the recording. "It's not me. I would never betray you."

Bigsby growled, "It'd better not be you because that shit will earn you a damn dirt nap."

There was utter silence and then the sound of something creaking open.

"What's in the safe?" Jeff asked with a nervous voice. "Bigsby? What the fuck?" There were sounds of objects dropping. "Come on, Bigsby," he yelled. "Why are you pointing that gun at me?"

"You scared?" Bigsby taunted.

"Yes!" Jeff squeaked.

"You should be."

"Be careful with that gun, Bigsby." Jeff's voice trembled.

"What did I tell you that I do to people who betray me?" Bigsby asked in a menacing tone.

"You. Kill. Them!" Jeff yelled.

"Exactly," Bigsby growled. "See this gun? It reminds me of what I'm willing to do to get what I want. More money. More power. More pussy. And I'll crush anyone who even thinks about getting in my fucking way."

Jeff blubbered, "Listen to yourself, Bigsby. Why would I want to stop you? I want what you want. I stopped recruiting women for Ben and came to work for you. I didn't have to. I could have let Ben be the middleman between us, but I didn't because I knew you were the man with the master plan. You and me… we're partners."

"We're not damn partners," Bigsby snapped. "You work for me, asshole."

"I thought…" Jeff's voice trailed off.

"Leave the thinking to me, idiot." Bigsby laughed coldly. "I'm the brains. You're the help who gets the girls. That's where our business arrangement starts and ends."

"But I thought if I bagged more bitches, you'd think about—"

"Making you partner?" Bigsby asked. "Hell no." He chortled. "The last business partner I had was Greer Cruickshank, and he was a hell of a lot smarter than your dumb ass."

My shoulders bunched, but I kept my face expressionless. Cruickshank was the person Bigsby had bragged about to Mom before killing her.

Bigsby carried on. "In fact, Greer was too damn smart for his own good. That's why I had to burn his ass alive." He chuckled. "The idiot wanted out of our business arrangement because he had fallen in love with that Jemma Kane bitch. She'd pussy-whipped the chump." He snorted. "No one leaves me... ever. Not unless it's in a damn body bag." He paused. "My only regret is that I put too much trust in our friendship by letting him bring Jemma into the business—especially when I didn't know that bitch at all. Shit. By the time I realized they were fucking each other and she was pushing him to get out of the business, it was too late. She'd already sunk her greedy little claws into his ass." There was a beat of silence. "But I got even with that conniving wench by snitching her out to the Feds. I just never knew she and Greer had a baby together—that Sin Michaels chick—until years later. Shit. If I'd known about their child, I would have cut that baby right out of that backstabbing whore's belly."

What. The. Fuck?

I stood up and started pacing across the cement floor.

Sin's parents are Greer Cruickshank and Jemma Kane?

"Holy hell!" Ram hissed, running a hand through his hair. "This shit has officially crossed into high-drama, reality show territory," he yelled.

Startled awake by the sound of Ram's voice, Jeff bucked against the rope binding him to the chair. "Untie me!" he screamed in a high-pitched tone.

Rocco growled, "Shut the fuck up!" before punching him so hard in the head that the chair rocked onto its back legs from the weight of Jeff's naked body tethered by the rope. Rocco's hand snapped out, righting it.

Jeff blacked out again.

I stopped midstride. "Not another word from anyone," I ordered.

The room went silent, except for the low whir of the air conditioner and the sounds from the recording.

"What's happening?" Kevin's voice inquired through my cell's speakerphone.

"Press pause," I instructed Kevin.

"Done." Kevin confirmed.

I needed a minute to process the information from the recording plus everything that I knew. Kevin's investigation into Sin's family background had unearthed that she had two birth certificates, each one showing a different set of parents—the first, Ian Michaels and Grace Michaels, and the second, Greer Lorne Cruickshank and Aubrey Cruickshank.

My mind raced to connect the dots.

Is Jemma an alias for Aubrey?

I made another mental note to have Kevin find out if my assumption was correct.

"Kevin, go back a couple seconds in the recording," I demanded. "And then resume playing."

Kevin did just that, and the recording started playing again.

Jeff asked over the recording, "Damn. You would have killed their baby?"

"Shit, I've done worse," Bigsby confided in a chilling voice. "Like that stripper Stella who tried to blackmail me after she overheard me talking about killing Greer. She had the nerve to threaten me by saying she'd keep her mouth shut for a price."

My fists tightened. Stella was my mother. The woman he'd killed without a damn thought.

My mind snapped back to the present when I heard Jeff's voice on the recording. "Did you give it to her?"

"Yeah, she got it all right." Bigsby laughed. "Right in the fucking head with this .357 Magnum."

Fucker.

I clenched and unclenched my fingers.

Then there was the sound of a phone ringing on the recording.

"Shit," Bigsby exclaimed. "It's that nagging bitch Cate calling me again."

I tilted my head to the side at the mention of Cate Bellisario—Bigsby's socialite fiancée.

Bigsby continued. "If I have to hear her ass whining again about some fucking detective her sister hired to dig into my background, I'm going to wrap my hands around her scrawny neck and choke her to death." He mocked Cate's voice. "Bigsby, Irvin is an excellent detective. Are you sure there's nothing he'll find?" He paused again. "Fuck Cate and her uptight bitch of a sister, Ariana. Shit. Once I become mayor, I won't need her or the Bellisario family name anymore."

Jeff inquired, "Will Irvin find anything on you?"

"Fuck no," Bigsby spit. "I paid a lot of money to make sure my past was buried. There's nothing linking me to that time in my life, except that fucking ledger."

"What ledger?"

There was a long pause before I heard a heavy sigh.

"When I was running girls with Greer and Jemma, we kept records of our business. It was like our little black book. I thought the ledger burned up along with Greer… until Grace contacted me."

"Grace?" Jeff asked.

"She's the wife of Ian Michaels—Greer's brother. Her greedy little ass wanted money in exchange for giving me back the incriminating ledger. Little did she know that book was both a curse and a blessing. Yeah, it links me back to my past, but it's also the only leverage I still have on rich and powerful fuckers in this city."

"But how the hell did she know about you and the ledger?" Jeff jabbered.

Bigsby replied, "She told me when Ian heard I was sanitizing my past and starting to go legit, he got nervous and told her if anything happened to him, he needed her to protect Sin because he had incriminating evidence against me that could get them all killed. Apparently, Grace saw dollar signs and went behind his back, trying to extort money from me."

"So why didn't you kill her?"

"She gives good head." There was loud laughter. "I was going to kill her after she gave me back the ledger… Well, I was going to kill them all."

"All?"

"Grace, Ian, and Sin. But Ian found out his wife was trying to make a deal with me, and he threatened to expose me with the ledger if I didn't leave him and his family alone."

"Stupid bastard." Jeff snorted.

"Yeah… no one threatens me. So I hired someone to run him off the road, killing him. And that's when shit went left. Grace couldn't find the ledger in any of Ian's stuff. She was drunk most of the time, and it was years before she remembered some old trunk that used to belong to Ian that she'd allowed Sin to take. Grace swore up and down that was the only place the ledger could be—in that trunk."

The playback of the recording stopped, and Kevin relayed, "Core, that's all there is."

"Shit. That's more than enough." Rocco grunted.

"That's for sure," Ram remarked while looking over at me. "Now we have everything we need to destroy Bigsby. The ledger and this secret recording. We can call this mission a success once we leak this information to the media, and Bigsby's life as he knows it will be over."

My jaw tightened. "The plan has changed."

The original plan to strip away everything Bigsby held dear—his wealth, freedom, political career, and trophy fiancée, Cate—had been scrapped the minute Jeff exposed just how ugly a monster Bigsby was—a psychopath that had gotten away with a shitload of murders.

Rocco sighed heavily. "That's what I thought you'd say. I knew there was no way you'd let that fucker live now that we've gotten solid confirmation about all the people he's killed."

I narrowed my eyes. "Once I'm done with Bigsby, no one will ever know he existed," I answered. "And I can finally move on with my life."

"So what's the new game plan?" Ram asked.

I cracked my knuckles. "We need to draw Bigsby out and then kill him, putting an end to this crap once and for all."

"Agreed," Ram and Rocco roared in unison.

"Damn." Rocco shook his head. "I can't believe that fucker put a hit on Ian Michaels."

"Or the fact that Ian is Sin's uncle and not her father, like she thinks." Ram chimed in. "Shit. Her whole world is going to be blown apart when she finds out the truth."

I bit back the expletive hovering on my tongue. Sin had told me that her father—or rather, the man she thought was her father, Ian Michaels—was killed in a freak car accident.

How is she going to handle the truth? That it was a damn hit by Bigsby?

"Well, this confirms Kevin's intel," Ram declared. "The apartment fire that killed Greer was arson. And now we know why Bigsby did it; he was pissed that Greer wanted out of their business partnership." He frowned. "The fucked-up part is that Bigsby thought the ledger was burned in the fire"—he shook his head—"and if Ian had just kept his mouth shut, he would still be alive today."

"Probably," I muttered. "Damn! This Bigsby shit is one big cluster-fuck." Adrenaline rushed through me as I just thought about all the lives Bigsby had destroyed. "But at least after all these years of wondering why that sick fuck killed my mother, now I know why." It didn't make losing her any easier, but I had answers now.

"And we got Lexis, and she's safe," Ram disclosed.

I nodded. We were all grateful that Lexis and the women were now under the protection of the authorities. But with Lexis, we had a whole other bag of issues. Even though she was happy to be rescued from her nightmare with Jeff, she was emotionally traumatized and embarrassed by the whole incident, and she refused to come back to Manhattan with Kevin. She tearfully offered that she wasn't ready to face Ram or my team or her old life. It wasn't the happy reunion Ram and the team had been anticipating, but we knew she needed time to heal. So Kevin had called one of his trusted contacts who could spirit her away to a highly secured facility that specialized in rehabilitating victims of domestic sex trafficking.

"But doesn't anyone think it's a bit strange that Bigsby didn't mention anything about killing Jemma or Aubrey?" Rocco asked.

"Exactly," Ram answered. "Plus, I bet you right now Jemma and Aubrey are the same person."

"I wouldn't take that bet because I was thinking the same thing," I gritted out. "Kevin, I need you to check out a couple things. One, who's talking to the Feds about Bigsby? And two, is Jemma an alias for Aubrey?"

"Okay," Kevin responded. "I'm out. I'll see you all back at the compound." He ended the call.

"So we know that Bigsby's a psychopath," Rocco hissed. "Do you think Sin's safe?"

"Hell no," I replied. "Bigsby's a loose cannon, and he wants the ledger back. So who knows what he'll do to get it?" And I wasn't about to find out. I would protect Sin with my last breath.

"Time to wrap this shit up," Ram suggested, looking at the unconscious Jeff.

"Shit!" Rocco barked. "I missed a 9-1-1 text from Zuri."

My eyes narrowed. "What's going on?"

Rocco read the text aloud. *"Tabitha's here. Asking Sin for money."*

Tabitha Thorp was a disposable piece of trash who had served her purpose when I recruited her to help me get close to Sin.

Rocco continued to read. *"Catfight going down. Get your ass over here now!"*

I hurried over to my cell. "Zuri," I voice-dialed with the phone on speaker.

"About damn time!" Zuri whispered urgently.

"Can you talk in private?" I asked.

"Hold on." There was a pause. "Okay, I can talk now."

"Where's Sin?" I questioned.

"She stormed upstairs… pissed. Look, I can't talk long. I need to make sure Tabitha doesn't dash after Sin and cause more trouble."

"What did Tabitha tell her?" I demanded.

"Enough."

"Shit." I flattened my lips.

Weeks ago, when I'd gotten the call from Kevin about Bigsby's interest in Sinthia, my first question had been, *Who the fuck is Sinthia Michaels?*

It hadn't taken Kevin long to do a thorough investigation, but he hadn't found anything linking Bigsby to her. I had known though that if Bigsby was interested in Sin, there had to be a sinister motive, which was why I had to acquire Sinthia Michaels's business fast. I'd had

Kevin search through her background again, looking for anything that could be used as leverage. Surprisingly, Sin was squeaky clean and free of scandal. Frustrated and running out of time and options, I'd found a chink in her armor—money.

She'd needed money, and I had lots of it. But to my frustration, I couldn't find a way into Sin's small inner circle without raising suspicion or scaring her off.

That was when Kevin had found the game changer—Tabitha Thorp. I had known Tabitha from the old neighborhood. When we were young, we had hung out in the same criminal circles. The only difference was back then, the now-famous Tabitha had run drugs for her boyfriend, Ben Vargos. I'd even fucked her several times behind Ben's back. She was a money-hungry whore who could be easily manipulated.

So when I'd found out the currently successful Tabitha Thorp owed a shitload of money to her unsavory criminal ex-boyfriend, Ben, I'd swooped in. One call later, I'd recruited Tabitha to help me get close to Sin. Tabitha had convinced Sin of the value of getting an investor—specifically, me—to help her expand her business. In exchange, I'd agreed to take care of Tabitha's debt to Ben and send her on a very long vacation.

"But Tabitha didn't tell her everything." Zuri countered.

"And she wants money," I groused. It wasn't a question but a statement.

"Yes," Zuri replied. "Apparently, she's broke."

Tabitha could go fuck herself. Our business had been done the moment she took my money.

"She implied money was exchanged between you two," Zuri reported.

Fuck.

I hadn't twisted her arm into taking the money. And the recording of Tabitha and our business arrangement would surely enlighten Sin.

"Where are you?" I asked.

She rattled off an address.

"Max should be in the vicinity," I replied. "Hold tight. He'll be there to get Tabitha." I ended the call.

It was time to turn the screws on Tabitha and permanently shut her down. I had so much dirt on her shady dealings with Vargos that by the time I was done snitching her out to the authorities, she'd end up in jail, designing uniforms for the entire prison.

"Max," I voice-dialed.

"Hey, bro," Max answered. "What's up?"

"We just got a text from Zuri. Tabitha has finally surfaced." I gave him the address. "I need you to get over there and shut her up. But don't kill her. I just want to make a statement that I can find her anytime, anyplace. Call me when it's done." I ended the call.

"I don't like this shit, Core. Too many fucking loose ends," Rocco grumbled.

I didn't need his ass telling me something I already knew.

Ram stared at me. "I guess the *talk* between you and Sin is going to happen sooner than you expected, huh?"

I ignored his gibe. "Let's get this Bigsby shit over with."

Ram nodded over to Rocco.

Rocco dumped the tub of water over Jeff's head.

Jeff's limbs jerked into action. His eyes snapped open. "What…" he garbled.

"Good. You're awake," I responded. "I wouldn't want you to miss this." I quickly swiped my finger over my cell, tapping the number and putting it on speaker. "Bigsby."

"McKay?" Bigsby answered. "What can I—"

"Bigs!" Jeff yelled, his voice so hoarse it sounded broken with panic ringing in it. "Help…"

"Jeff? What's going on?" Bigsby asked sharply.

I paced back and forth. "I have your ledger," I responded, "and a recording."

"What fucking recording?"

My nostrils flared. "Apparently, Jeff didn't trust your dumb ass and needed some insurance. Frankly, I don't blame him, given the fact that you've killed so many people—Greer, Ian, Stella, and her son." I wasn't going to reveal—yet—that I was Stella's son, the little boy he thought he'd killed so many years ago. No. That little eye-opener would be unveiled right before I killed the fucker. "Poor Jeff was afraid he'd end up on your shit list, too. So he recorded you confessing to a lot of crimes."

"That dumb fucker!" Bigsby exclaimed. "I'll—"

Losing patience, I stopped him. "Let's cut to the chase, Bigsby. I can make this all go away for twenty million dollars and control of your empire. And, of course, I'll expect you to disappear." It was all a bluff. I wanted to know exactly what Bigsby would do now that his back was against the wall.

Bigsby sputtered before saying, "Fuck you, McKay. I've built this. I want the fucking recording and my ledger back."

"What about your boy Jeff? Don't you want him back, too?"

"I don't give a shit what you do with his ass. He wasn't worth shit to me anyway," Bigsby hissed.

Jeff started screaming because he knew he was going to die.

"I want my ledger and the recording. And if you don't give them to me, Sin's dead."

What the fuck?

I stopped midstride. The muscles in my shoulders bunched.

I didn't respond well to threats, especially against someone I cared about.

"What makes you think I give a shit if she dies?" I did… and I wanted to break every bone in Bigsby's body for threatening Sin's life.

Bigsby laughed. "I've been keeping tabs on you and Sin. And it seems like you've got something going on with Michaels. I can't really blame you. She's simply delectable."

He was trying to push my buttons, but this was not my first rodeo, dealing with assholes who thought they could best me. Every day, I ate motherfuckers like Bigsby for breakfast and enjoyed it.

I deliberately infused nonchalance into my tone. "Shit. I like a woman who gives good head. What man doesn't?" I laughed coldly. "But I ain't planning on marrying her."

Bigsby sneered. "There's no honor among thieves, McKay. So let me make things very clear. I either get my fucking ledger back, along with any copies you've made of it and the recording, or your sweet little cunt, Sin Michaels, is dead." He rattled off an address. "I'll meet you there in seventy-two hours. Ticktock, McKay."

Our call ended.

"Fuck!" I banged my fist against the table.

Despite the fact that I'd just gotten what I wanted—a meeting with Bigsby—I didn't want to tell Sin the truth... today. Or that she already knew part of it—due to Tabitha's big mouth—and wasn't happy about it.

The only upside of this clusterfuck was that Bigsby's world was about to collapse. And that he was a desperate man on the verge of losing his power and wealth—equivalent to death for a social climber like Bigsby. I'd heard the desperation in his voice, and I knew he'd do anything to avoid losing it all, even if he had to lie, steal, cheat, and in this case, kill... both Sin and me.

Killing Sin or me? That shit is not happening. Not on my damn watch.

It was time to go to fucking work... meticulously planning Bigsby's death.

I looked over at Rocco. "Bury Jeff somewhere he won't be found, and then clean this place and get rid of all the evidence."

Rocco nodded.

"Please! Don't... I can help you." Jeff bucked against the rope binding him to the chair. "Give me a—"

"Time's up," Rocco revealed flatly.

Jeff struggled uselessly against the rope.

I looked over at Ram while grabbing my jacket. "Let's go. We've only got seventy-two hours to put things in motion." And for me to figure out how to finally tell Sin the truth and lay out the plan to protect her.

As I walked out of the warehouse with Ram at my side, my mind buzzed with all the things I needed to do to keep Sin safe from Bigsby. My team was already stretched thin. Rocco was getting rid of Jeff before cleaning up the warehouse. Max was hemming up Tabitha. Zuri was protecting Sin; it was a good thing Zuri was carrying a gun and knew how to use it. Kevin had intel work to get done. Ram and I had to start working on the logistics of my meeting with Bigsby.

And the clock was ticking.

Damn. Seventy-two hours. That's all we have to get our shit together.

My gut instinct urged me to go to Sin, but logic ruled. I had to work on a plan to take Bigsby down. There would only be one shot to get it right. Any mistakes would get us killed.

I ran my fingers across my hair. Logically, the smart thing would be to move Sin into my penthouse until this shit got resolved. But Sin agreeing to move in would be difficult… especially after I told her the truth tonight.

Ram loudly cleared his throat. "Bro, look… What I said about Sin earlier. Everything cool between us, right?"

"Yeah." I sighed heavily. "And you're right. This shit with Sin is a real fucked-up predicament. I had no business getting involved with her." I eyed him. "But I did, and there ain't no going back with her. Only forward. No matter the consequences, Sin's worth the fight to keep her by my side."

Truth be told, from the moment she'd allowed me into her body, I had known that our fates were sealed and she was mine to protect and care for.

Sin is my present and future… and I'll fight tooth and nail to keep her in my life.

"Shit," Ram said, "that's deep." He shook his head. "I guess I never thought any woman could replace Maya."

"Me either. Until Sin."

Maya had been my balance, my rock. But in one tragic moment, she'd been taken away, leaving me emotionally void—until Sin had unwittingly turned my world around.

Now the thought of Sin walking away from me, from us, was totally unacceptable.

Despite losing every woman I'd ever loved—Maya and Mom—to death and the fact that I still felt haunted by their passing, Sin made me want to try again for another chance at a relationship, companion-ship, and hopefully… someday… even love. With her.

"Damn, I never thought I'd see the day Core McKay officially took his ass off the *Single and Available* list."

A smirk rolled across my face. "Life is full of compromises, and I'm more than willing to make them to be with Sin." There were so many sides to Sin—sexy, rebellious, sassy, smart, and vulnerable—and I wanted them all.

He clapped me on the back. "Okay. Well then, we'd better hurry up and sort this shit out with Bigsby because we're going to need to start working on *Operation Save Core's Ass*, pronto. How I see it, there's no doubt in my mind that when you tell her the truth… Sin's going to go Amazon warrior princess on your ass."

"Fuck, I'm screwed." I grunted.

"Yep. So gird your loins, motherfucker."

CHAPTER 10
SINTHIA

Pacing across Cisco's lounge, I dropped my bag before checking the fitting rooms, making sure each had the correct client gown.

"Still no call," I muttered after checking my cell clutched in my death grip.

Maybe he was busy.

Walking over to the soft, comfy gray couch and sitting down, I ignored the open complimentary champagne bottle and waiting glasses. No alcohol. I needed to keep a clear head.

I inhaled. Exhaled. Tried to chill the fuck out… then *bam*! My mind went right back to what-the-fuck mode.

What in the world is going on between Core and Tabitha?

It seemed like no one was who I'd thought they were. I recalled the conversation Tabitha and I had weeks ago when I asked her about my secret investor.

"Why can't I know his damn name?" I demanded.

Tabitha's eyes hardened. "Darling, the less you know, the better. Believe me. Sin, I swear to you he's legit. I wouldn't get you involved if he wasn't.

You can't have it both ways. You asked me to find an investor, and I did. You've got the money. Isn't that all that matters now?"

Is it?

Frankly, I didn't know, but what I did know was that I wouldn't have been able to complete my collection without Core's money.

But the nagging feeling that something was off wouldn't go away.

Why did Tabitha hook me up with Core? And what did she get out of the deal for doing it?

A second thought crept into my mind, and it was hard to dismiss. *What is Core really after? My business? Me? Or both? And why?*

Ariana finally breezed into the room, cell pressed against her ear, with her new bestie, Erika Watson, walking beside her. Both women—in their fifties, slim, and tall—wore their beauty and class well.

Ariana—the older, classically refined version of my bestie, Jade—had porcelain skin, a square face, blue eyes, an upturned nose, and wore her long black hair loose. She was stylish, and as usual, she was looking radiant, wearing a black mid-length sheath dress with peplum detailing around the waist. She'd paired the dress with a cozy gray cape, tan top-handled purse, and matching pointed-toe stilettos. A bold red lip and matching manicure completed her look.

Erika was stunning. The dark richness of her skin contrasted beautifully against her long, white belted coat, black Christian Louboutin pumps, and classic diamond jewelry. She'd styled the look with oversize shades and a slicked-back ponytail.

"Cate, enough!" Ariana screamed into the phone.

"Hello, Erika," I greeted.

Erika dramatically whipped off her shades and kissed me on the cheek before sitting down and saying, "The full moon must be coming tonight because everyone is losing their damn mind. Between Ariana and Cate going at it all day and you and that woman downstairs, everyone is either battle ready or battle weary. Which one are you?"

I replied, "Definitely battle ready." I poured her a glass of champagne.

Erika laughed. "A woman after my own heart. That must be why I like your ass so much." She winked at me. "Just let me know if you need backup, because I'm not afraid to kick off my red-bottoms and get to kicking ass."

I grinned at the television producer voted most likely to bitch-slap an actor. "And that's why you're my favorite client." I gave her a high-five.

I wasn't kidding. I adored Erika's vibe. She was remarkably laid-back for a woman who'd achieved so much, so fast. She was an award-winning writer and producer who created hit TV shows. She was also the first black woman to create and executive produce a top ten network series—a series starring Jade, my best friend.

"Love the bracelet," Erika commented. "I meant to compliment you on your excellent taste in jewelry when you wore it to Bigsby's gala." She paused. "It's Victorian Scottish, right?"

"Yes. It's special… an heirloom that belonged to my Scottish great-grandmother. My dad gave it to me before he died." I swallowed hard over the emotions welling up inside me. "It's the only piece of my heritage and my family that I have left."

"Oh, sweetie." She comfortingly touched my shoulder. "I'm sorry for your loss."

"It's been years, but you know… the shit still hurts." It did, and the pain would never go away.

"I know. Losing people we love is never easy." Her eyes clouded over with emotion. "It leaves you hollow."

I nodded in agreement.

"Do you mind?" Her fingers hovered over my wrist with the bracelet clasped around it.

I shrugged. "Nope."

She examined the jewelry. "It suits you." Her lips curled up at the edges. "And I'm happy it finally found a home." Then she abruptly slapped my leg. "Enough of this sad stuff. *Viva la vida.*"

We both held our glasses in the air before taking a sip.

"Wait… *viva la vida*… Isn't that a Coldplay song?" My lips curled up.

"Yep," Erika retorted. "It means *live life.* And you and I are going to rock the hell out of this life while we still have it." She winked. "So are you ready for me to get all sexy?"

"You're set up in the second room," I responded.

I completely forgot about the phone war Ariana was waging until she growled into her cell, "I'll be damned if I let you marry that sleazy bastard."

She didn't mention his name, but I knew exactly who the "sleazy bastard" was—Bigsby.

"Bigsby at it again?" I asked Erika.

"Of course." Erika rolled her eyes. "But what's new about that shit?" She pursed her full lips. "The man is an utter douche bag. After what Ariana just found out about him, at least I can finally convince my husband to drop his support of Bigsby for mayor of New York. Now my world is complete."

"I can't blame you." I shuddered. "Every time I'm around Bigsby, I want to douse my body with holy water to rid myself of his evil vibes."

"He creeps everyone out. It's his greasy used car salesman person-ality." She stuck her tongue out in disgust.

"Are we done?" Ariana yelled.

"And, as usual, Ariana and Cate are like two pit bulls in skirts." Erika grimaced, eyeing Ariana. "If I wanted to hear that shit, I could have stayed at work and listened to the overpaid divas bitch about who had more lines." Getting up, she swayed toward the fitting room, slamming the door behind her.

"Blah, blah, blah. I don't give a shit what he thinks. God, I hate that fucker Bigsby," Ariana hissed. "I made no damn secret about the fact that I'd hired Irvin to investigate his ass."

I recalled what Jade had told me—that Ariana, Cate, and Jade were the last members of the Bellisario dynasty and each worth millions. And if anyone wanted to date a Bellisario, they got investigated thor-oughly. According to Jade, most guys just ungracefully bowed out because they couldn't deal with Irvin, the investigative proctologist.

"I'm done with this conversation, Cate. And no, I'm not going to tell Irvin to back off until you publicly call off your engagement. Good-bye. Yes, I'm hanging up, Cate," Ariana barked before tossing her cell into her handbag. "Family. Can't live with them. Can't fucking kill them."

She flopped down next to me and kissed my cheek. I loved Ariana because she was beautiful inside and out. When Dad had died and Grace had disowned me, Ariana had taken me into her family, treating me like I was her daughter.

"How are you, darling?"

"You saw that shit downstairs. I'm pissed, but I gather from your conversation, you're not too chipper yourself." I arched a brow. "So what's going on?"

Ariana Bellisario—a philanthropist, heiress, and successful businesswoman—was Jade's mother and also a member of the illustrious group of New York socialites. Her sister, Cate Bellisario, was older than Ariana by a couple years. To some, that made Cate the most powerful member of the Bellisario family. She was using that status among the New York elite to get her fiancé, Bigsby Calhoune, a wealthy shipping mogul, elected as New York City mayor.

"Irvin, my private investigator, finally found the skeletons in Bigsby's closet."

Erika peeked out of the dressing room, making eye contact with me in a *See, we were right about Bigsby* moment before disappearing back into the room.

My mouth fell open before closing with a snap. "What did Irvin find out?" I had no qualms asking because Ariana and Jade were family. All three of us had been by each other's sides in the best and worst of times. And I would never reveal anything they'd told me because I loved and trusted them as much as they did me.

"The Feds are secretly investigating Bigsby over some shady business going on with Pomtonic International." Ariana scowled. "Irvin says his source told him it's a shell company that's cleaning sex traffickers' money."

I blinked in shock. "Sex traffickers?"

"Oh, it gets worse." Ariana took a huge swallow of champagne. "According to Irvin, those same traffickers are laundering money through UF-Star. That is why the Feds were digging into UF-Star in the first place."

My brows came together in a puzzled frown. "He's into sex trafficking and money laundering, and he has the Feds on his ass? That news bomb can't be good for Cate or the Bellisario name."

"Exactly. There's no fucking way we want our family name being linked to this shit. That's why I told Cate she has to break off her engagement to Bigsby and publicly denounce any association with him."

I replied, "Well, there goes his political ambitions and his bid for New York City mayor."

"Exactly. It's a wrap, and the only one who doesn't get it is Cate." She ran her fingers through her hair.

I pressed my lips together in a slight grimace. "Knowing Cate, her reaction must have been a hissy fit worthy of a reality show cast member."

Cate was a ruthless, conniving, manipulative woman who would think nothing about taking down the most powerful people in New York unless they played nice with her and kowtowed to her every whim.

"When I told her what I found out, it was a clusterfuck. Cate accused me of being jealous because she's finally found the love of her life and I'm still alone." Ariana's upper lip curled in disdain. "I'm not alone. I'm in a relationship with a lawyer Erika hooked me up with—not that I'd ever tell Cate that because she'd just use that shit against me and try to break us up because she can't stand to see me happy." She paused. "With Cate, it's always some damn competition that I've never been interested in participating in. She can't get past the fact that our parents always favored me when they were alive."

I snorted. "That woman only loves herself."

"Exactly. Anyhoo, things got ugly, and Cate left my house in a huff. She's been calling me all day, trying to get me to back off, but I won't. Push comes to shove, I'd even go as far as leaking the Bigsby information to the media."

"That's not a good idea, Ariana. The bad press might backfire, hurting you and Jade in the end." I countered.

"Yes, but we're damned if we do and damned if we don't. I need to get ahead of the Manhattan gossip rags by putting my own spin on the information and releasing it first. But more importantly, despite the fact that Cate and I have never been on the best of terms, she's family, and blood is thicker than water."

I frowned. "Hopefully, Cate will dump him."

Ariana sighed heavily. "I know my sister. She's not going to turn her back on Bigsby. She's invested way too much of her time, money, and connections into molding him into her perfect Ken doll. No. She'll turn her back on our family first. In her eyes, I've just declared war against her and Bigsby."

"Does Jade know what's going on?" I asked.

"Yes. And she's angry with Cate, and she wants to come back to the US. You know, to have my back when shit gets ugly between Cate and me… and believe me; it will."

"You and Jade are not on your own. You both are my family." I grabbed her hand. "You're like my mother, and if I can help, I'll do it with no questions asked. Let me be there for you while Jade's away."

She squeezed my hand back. "Sin, you already have enough going on in your life. Plus, I don't want you getting hit with shit when Cate starts slinging it. You know how cruel she can be."

"I'm not scared of her, Ariana. You and Jade are the only family I have, and I'll fight tooth and nail to protect you two."

She smiled at me. "What a damn tiger. I raised two beautiful women." She nudged me in the side. "So are you going to tell me what the hell happened downstairs between you and that woman?"

"That was Tabitha," I answered.

"Really?" Her eyes widened.

I nodded.

Ariana pursed her lips. "She looks different. Time out of the fashion spotlight has dimmed her remarkably."

"I know. She looked like a hot mess. Not that I feel bad about her predicament at all."

"Okay. Get me up to speed," Ariana said.

I leaned my head on her shoulder. "Where should I start?"

"From the top and leave nothing out."

She stroked my hair in her familiar, comforting way, and it didn't take long for the drama playing out with my townhouse break-in and the Tabitha reality show to come tumbling from my mouth.

$$\sim$$

Several hours later, Ariana had already left. And Zuri had sent me a text saying she was in the vicinity, taking care of business and for me not to leave without her. And still... there was no return call from McKay.

Fucker!

We—Erika and I—stood before the floor-to-ceiling mirror while I made the final adjustments to her gown. I was proud of my creation; Erika was stunning in the gown that accented her perfect, tight, curvy body. The dark richness of her skin contrasted beautifully against the formfitting chartreuse drape-back dress. Next to Jade and Ariana, she was the best walking commercial for my clothing line.

"Damn!" Erika exclaimed. "My ass looks spectacular in this dress. It's like I've had a butt lift." She did a sexy butt shake.

I laughed. "Well, look at you. Twerk it."

"Age ain't nothing but a number." She shimmied. "I've still got it."

"Yeah, you do." I impishly tapped her ass. "But I'm gonna need you to stop watching Cardi B music videos." I smiled saucily before stepping back, examining her.

"Never!" Erika dissolved in laughter before walking over to her bag, reaching in, and pulling out a piece of paper. "This is for you," she explained, extending her hand.

Walking over, I took the check, blinking at the five-figure number written on it. "Erika, you're overpaying me again." I handed it back. "I can't take it."

"Nonsense." She waved away my objection. "Just the pleasure of my husband drooling over me in your design... that's worth the price of this gown and more, darling." She grinned at me. "When Mitch sees me in this, he won't be able to keep his hands off me. And let me tell you, the man's foreplay game is on point."

Ugh... no. Why do my clients insist on oversharing?

Her statement was the equivalent of realizing that your parents were still having sex. Hard pass on that kinky image.

"Well, if my designs get women laid, then my community service is done. You're welcome." I bowed playfully.

She cracked up before walking over to the mirror again. "What do you think? Up or down?" She gestured to her hair.

"Up." Coming up behind her, I twisted the hair hanging freely from her ponytail, wrapping it around into a tight, high knot. I stilled when I noticed the small infinity tattoo at the base of her neck. "Well, look at you. A tattoo?"

Erika didn't seem like an ink chick. I squinted at the letter G etched at one end of the infinity symbol and the letter A at the other.

She lifted her head, meeting my eyes in the mirror. "It's to remember someone I loved and lost years ago," she confessed, and her famous sassy smile was nowhere to be seen. There was an unmistakable sadness in her eyes.

I pressed one hand against her shoulder. "I'm sorry for your loss."

"Thank you," she whispered. My hand fell away when she turned around to face me. "He died too young, but when he was alive, he did give me the best gift a woman could hope for, his love." She cleared her throat. "Sin, I overheard your conversation with Ariana about your break-in and that horrid Tabitha woman." Her eyes locked with mine. "And I hope you don't get offended, but I'm worried about you. Is everything okay money-wise? I know how close you were to finishing your clothing line. I'd just hate for you to give up on your dreams because of everything that's happened."

My thoughts flashed to Core…

Would he do anything for me?

Or is he just running a game? Using me to get what he wants?

"I'm okay." I warmly smiled at her. "Believe me; I'm not remotely close to giving up designing for a job at a fast-food restaurant."

Erika drawled, "I know that." She reached out, grabbing my hand. "But if I can help in any way, I will. My show has millions of viewers, and I'd love to have your pieces on set. I want the world to know about your clothing."

Heat radiated through my chest at her generous offer. "I'll never say no to business or publicity. I'm game." Just the press coverage would be enough to keep the fashion hags talking for days.

"Good. I'll have my people contact you." Her hand tightened around mine before quickly pulling away as if she'd just realized she was still clutching mine. She smiled at me before walking away toward the dressing room, and then she stopped abruptly, turning around to stare at me.

"Sin, I—" She fidgeted and twisted her large, sparkling diamond engagement ring coupled with the diamond-encrusted wedding band. A look of uncertainty flickered in her eyes. "Uh… nothing."

Without another word, she dipped into the dressing room.

"Well… that was strange," I mumbled under my breath.

CHAPTER 11
SINTHIA

After leaving Cisco's boutique, I stood in Core's kitchen, fuming silently. "Fucker!" I mumbled under my breath while glancing down at my cell again. "Who does he think he is, not returning my call?" But I'd be damned if I blew up his cell. I refused to chase his ass for answers about Tabitha.

"Sin—" Zuri started.

"Nope." I cut her off. "No excuses."

And then there was another problem. The tenseness between Zuri and me that permeated the confines of the kitchen was uncomfortable.

There were so many unanswered questions.

What was going on between Tabitha and Core? Why had he sought me out through Tabitha? And why would a billionaire like him want to go into business with a fashion designer? And lastly, what does Zuri know about this debacle?

Even if she knew the answers to my questions, which she probably did, I suspected she wouldn't tell me. She was loyal to Core.

Besides, it would be unfair to interrogate her, given her close relationship with him.

My cell chirped. Glancing down, I saw it was a text from Core.

Dinner tonight. We need to talk. Max will pick you up at 8 p.m. sharp. C.M.

I promptly texted back. *Fuck off! S.M.*

"Take that, asshole," I muttered.

Zuri exhaled loudly. "That was Core, wasn't it?"

"Yes. Your lord and master has finally decided to acknowledge my existence, ordering me to be ready to go out to dinner with him tonight." I snorted. "That shit is not happening."

"Why not?"

"Because I don't jump to attention and salute when he snaps his fingers."

Zuri shook her head. "You two are the most stubborn, most bull-headed people I've ever met. All I know is that both of you need to talk this out, clear the air. Don't you think?"

"I called him hours ago… and nothing. Not an, *I'm busy right now, and we'll talk later.* Just crickets. This is not normal. He's not fucking normal." I huffed, plopping down onto the barstool nestled under the granite kitchen counter.

"I'm sorry… Were you under some perception that he was normal?" She arched a brow. "Because you and I know he's not. For that matter, you wouldn't want his ass if he were. Admit it."

I rolled my eyes. "Maybe not. But I do expect some level of communication."

Zuri sat down with a heavy sigh. "Then go out with him and let him communicate. Let him explain what the hell is going on. Don't you want to know?"

"Of course I want to know, Zuri. Hence my call to him hours ago." I eyed her. "Something is going on. I feel it in my bones, and my instinct is never fucking wrong. Never."

"Sin, I—"

I held up my hand. "Zuri, stop. I don't need you to explain anything. It's not your place to clean up his shit."

"Sin, you know me better by now. I'm not going to touch this whole Tabitha drama. That's between you and him." She leaned forward. "But I will say this—he's my family. I love him. I really do, but he's stubborn sometimes." Zuri sighed heavily. "When Core wants something, he goes after it with a single-minded, calculating focus, and he won't stop until he gets it. But he's a bull in a china shop. He doesn't give a crap about finesse. So all I'm saying is to be patient with his ass because he's going to make all sorts of mistakes when it comes to you. Just"—she cleared her throat—"try to forgive him when he does because he's really a good guy and worth it."

"Why are you telling me all this?"

"Because I want you to understand the man behind the mask. I want you to take the blinders off and really see him. And when the time comes when he pulls off the disguise he wears to protect himself emotionally, I want you to be open to forgive some of the things he does or says. Because sometimes Core forgets the human aspect of being human. You know what I mean?" She pursed her lips.

"No, I don't," I replied, feeling like she was passing on some secret message that I didn't quite have the code for.

"You will. Just give it time," Zuri finished, lightly touching my arm.

I could feel the beginning of a migraine when my cell rang. I smiled when I saw the name on the caller ID. "I've got to take this," I explained to Zuri.

"Sure. No issues," Zuri replied, getting up. "I'll be in Core's office," she finished, striding out of the kitchen, giving me privacy.

"Hey, Jade!" I answered.

Jade was scheduled to be away on her shoot for months, and even though she hadn't been gone long, I already missed her something fierce. We'd been friends since high school. We pushed each other further. Our friendship had tightened over the years, creating a perfect synergy unmatched by any other relationship to date. We were an unstoppable team who stuck by each other, no matter how rough the circumstances.

"Don't *hey* me." Jade countered. "My mom just told me about what happened at your place. Are you okay?"

"Yes."

"Thank God." I could hear the relief in her voice. "Shit. Where were you when it happened?"

"With Core." I leaned forward, putting my elbows on the counter.

"Wait! What?" There was a beat of silence. "Core? As in Core McKay?"

"Who else?" I answered, nibbling on my bottom lip.

"Oh, please tell me you fucked my favorite bad boy."

"Sure did… several times."

Jade squealed. "About time!" She followed that with a rambunctious rendition of the "Bad Boys" song, and then she abruptly asked, "Wait. You did come, right?"

I burst out laughing. "Yes… and it was magical."

"Ah, shit… I knew he had potential. Damn. My favorite alphalicious billionaire rained pixie and fairy dust on your vajayjay. Leg on his shoulder. Boom! Fairy dust. Doggy style. Bam! Fairy dust."

"Jade." I interrupted. "You want to hear my story or not?"

"Hell yeah! And since it's been such a pathetically long time since I've had sex, I'm going to need details. Lots of sweaty, hot, and hopefully very filthy details." She paused. "Hold on a second. Let me take a sip of coffee and get all comfy." I heard shuffling sounds, and then Jade shouted, "And… go!"

Putting my phone on speaker, I gossiped. "So Friday, he invited me to his McKay Club's private playground—Noire." Thirsty, I went over to the refrigerator.

"I've heard about that place. The gossip hags say Noire is the anything-goes section."

"More like anything your kinky little heart desires," I replied, grabbing a bottle of Pellegrino, cracking it open, and taking a long sip. "Believe me; the gossip is nowhere near the reality of Noire. It's total sexual energy and chaos."

I opened the cabinet, looking for a snack. "Oh, jackpot! Macarons." Pulling out the box, I ripped into the package, biting into the cookie's crisp outer shell that gave way to a soft, chewy center with an intense burst of flavor. "Lordy… it's yummy."

"Wait. His cock was yummy?" Jade asked.

"I was talking about my macaron. But his cock was quite tasty, too," I sassed cheekily.

"Sin!" Jade screeched in an impatient tone. "Focus. Details."

I chewed. "Put it this way." I swallowed. "If I threw his cock up in the air, it would rain sunshine. That's how good he is."

"Oh, I want one of those." Jade gasped comically.

"You know… he does have a friend named Ram."

"Ram?" she sputtered. "What kind of name is that?" She paused. "Never mind. I don't even want to get into that topic."

I laughed. "Yes. Let's not go there."

"Anyhoo," she replied, "I'll hard pass on the *Ram*."

I nearly choked on my mouthful of cookie at her dramatic emphasis on the word *Ram*. "Girl, you're a hot mess."

"I'm just saying…"

"Anyway," I quipped, "after the club, when he dropped me home, my front door was wide open. And when I walked in, my place was destroyed." I swallowed hard. "Everything, including my collection."

"Jesus," Jade hissed. "This story just turned left." She paused. "Not that I don't care about your work, but I'm happy you weren't home when they broke into your place. You can re-create your collection. Your life and safety are more important," she remarked. "Was anything stolen?"

"Nothing I could pinpoint but that ledger of my dad's."

Jade had been with me when I was looking in Dad's ratty trunk and found the well-worn leather ledger that had been deliberately concealed in the false bottom.

"You sure you didn't just misplace it?" Jade asked.

"I'm sure. I put it right back where I'd found it. I had every intention of looking through it again when I had time, but I never did."

I also remembered that while the police were at my house after the break-in, I'd found the large chunk of old, splintered wood that had once covered the false bottom of Dad's old trunk on the floor, and the trunk had been lying on its side with all the contents spilled out. When I'd righted it and scanned inside, I could see the false bottom was missing and so was the red leather ledger that had been hidden in the secret compartment.

"That's odd," Jade uttered. "Why would someone want to steal that?"

I shrugged. "How would I know? There was nothing in the ledger that made any sense to me." I guzzled my water.

I recollected lifting the cover and flicking through the thin paper. The first several pages were a collection of names, which were not in my father's handwriting. Then there were the initials G.L.C. scrawled in red ink at the bottom of every page, along with random numbers and phone numbers. All the pages had codes running along the margins.

"Anyway…" I carried on. "It's gone, but all my jewelry and other expensive stuff remained untouched. Not that I give a shit. Material possessions can be replaced, but my collection can't."

"Sin, it's going to take hard work, but you can reboot your collection," Jade responded. "I'm just relieved that my bestie didn't get hurt."

I heaved a sigh, twirling the bottle between my fingers. "You're right, but what's messing with my head is that the intruder just destroyed everything, down to the smallest details. It was spiteful, as if they were trying to break me emotionally."

"You see, that… I just don't get," Jade said. "Unlike me, you don't have any enemies or rivals. It's just fucking freaky that someone would do that shit to you. Sin, I don't feel comfortable with you staying alone at your townhouse. Why don't you stay at my place while I'm away?" She urged. "I have twenty-four-seven security. You'll be safe there."

I seriously contemplated her offer. Staying at Jade's place seemed like the smart thing to do. I had no guarantees that the intruder wouldn't come back, but next time, I could be home. Staying by myself wasn't ideal, particularly since the intruder was still out there, but what were my alternatives? Definitely not camping out at Core's place… especially not after he'd ignored my phone call. But the townhouse was my home, and no one was going to chase me away from it.

"I can protect myself, Jade. Shit, I've been doing a damn good job for twenty-six years."

"Don't get all huffy with me, Sin Michaels. I'm worried about you; that's all."

I sighed heavily because I was being irrationally bratty. "I know. I'll be okay. I promise."

Jade confided. "I don't feel right about being so far away from Mom and you right now. That's it. I'm coming back home. Fuck shooting this movie. You two are my family. We have to stick together."

I banged my fist against the counter. "Don't you dare, Jade." This was exactly what I didn't want to happen. Her dropping everything just to come back to New York. "You worked too damn hard to make your project a reality. I'm going to be fine. I swear."

"Dammit," she swore. "I hate being so far away. Especially when everyone I love is going through some major, real-life crisis shit. My mom is feuding with Cate over that fucker Bigsby. And now you and your break-in. I can't just sit here with my thumb up my ass. I feel useless."

I hated hearing the despair in her voice.

"Jade, we'll both be okay. Stay where you are. Your movie is important to you… to all of us."

"Not as important as you two." Jade countered.

My jaw hardened. There was no way I could live with myself if she gave up her dream just to come back here and babysit me. That was exactly why I hadn't called her when everything in my life went to shit… starting with the break-in. I didn't want her to worry, and I damn sure didn't want her to give up her dream because of me.

"You are not coming back to New York until you finish what you started. At least one of us has to have their dreams come true. This movie is yours."

"But—"

"Enough, Jade. If shit gets unmanageable, I'll call you. And only then will you hop on a plane and come home. Okay?" I insisted.

"Okay." She confirmed in a tired voice. "Well then, tell me something… anything to distract me from the clusterfuck of my life."

"Well…" I bit into another macaron, chewing thoughtfully. "I can officially cross *have an all-night sexathon* off my to-do list."

"All night?" Jade interrupted.

"And morning," I shot back.

"Holy shit! You stayed until morning?"

"Yes." My lips pressed together in a slight grimace.

"Interesting…" Jade murmured.

I furrowed my brows. "What do you mean by that?"

"Oh, nothing. So you know the drill. What's his performance score?"

"Eleven." I grinned. "No, scratch that. He's a twelve. I forgot to add points for this genius and wildly creative thing that he does with his tongue that makes me so delirious every time he does it. Like this morning when he was mid-swirl, I swore I saw a unicorn frolicking through a meadow."

Jade screamed, "Oh. My. God. You've never rated a lover a twelve."

I shrugged. "Because he's that good."

"Okay, bonus round. What's his conversation score?"

I thought about all the conversations Core and I had. But there was one moment last night that stuck out—when I'd decided to lay my feelings out like a rug before Core…

"You don't know how much this means to me—you being here for me," I whispered to him.

His eyes were passionate, and his words were fierce in response. "I always protect what I care for."

My heart had jerked at the truth laid out in his words. They confirmed what I'd secretly suspected—that Core would destroy anyone and everyone who dared try to harm me.

Frankly, I liked that kind of devotion because it was something most men didn't have anymore.

"Same score," I answered. "Twelve. He's intelligent, funny, and very intense, but he keeps me interested."

I bit my lip, contemplating the enigma that was Core. He was the complete opposite of everything that I'd thought he was, and little by little, Core McKay was unveiling who the man truly was.

A man who cared about me.

A man with a damn heart.

"But he's complicated," I started, "and dangerous with a whole lot of crazy mixed in." I stared into space. "Plus, Tabitha's back."

Jade scoffed. "Back from where? The asylum?"

"She sure as hell looked like it… but it was more than that. It's the unnerving shit she mentioned today."

"Like what?"

"That Core had sought me out. He came to her to broker an introduction to me—like he used Tabitha just to get to me. Worse, they're not even friends. What do you make of that?"

Jade snapped, "Anything that comes out of Tabitha's mouth is utter bullshit. I warned you about her years ago. I never liked or trusted her. She's a pretentious bitch who's fixated on outshining you—her protégé."

"And you were right."

Jade and Tabitha never got along. Jade hated Tabitha's biting, acidic personality, and Tabitha resented Jade's privileged lifestyle.

"But today, what Tabitha disclosed about Core rang true. Though, for the life of me, I can't figure out why he wanted to meet me."

"Did you ask him?"

"I called him and left a message for him to call me back."

"Nope," Jade simply stated.

"Nope what?" I asked.

"Not the way to go about this shit. In person. Have the discussion with him face to face. You'll be able to tell whether he's lying then."

I sighed heavily. "You might have a point."

"I always do," she quipped and then yawned. "I'm exhausted already. I haven't been sleeping well lately."

"Try that sleep app with white noise that I nagged you to buy before you left." I urged. "You should be asleep in no time."

"Okay, but call me… no matter what time, and tell me how it goes with him."

"I will."

Jade sighed. "And, Sin… please be careful, all right?"

"I will. Love you, girlie."

"Love you more, Sin."

CHAPTER 12
SINTHIA

Striding out of Core's building, I felt sexy but warrior-tough in my little black dress, paired with thigh-high boots and a leather jacket. Now I was ready to do battle against Core at dinner tonight.

Zuri was talking to a sandy-haired man who was leaning against a sleek black SUV.

The man pushed away from the vehicle, tilting his head toward me. "Well, hello, sweet cheeks. Remember me?" He grinned.

I eyed the man who was built like a tank. "How could I forget? You and your sidekick—"

"My brother, Rocco." He interrupted. "I'm Max."

I arched a brow. "Well, Max"—I widened my stance—"you and Rocco refusing to let me onto the rooftop was a prick move."

"Oh, come on, sweet cheeks. Don't hold that against us," he replied. "At the time, the roof was reserved for Core. But I do recall we did let you onto it to spend some private time with Core." He suggestively waggled his eyebrows at me.

Zuri rolled her eyes before jabbing him in the side. "Don't be crude, Max."

"Ouch!" he grumbled. "Woman, don't poke me with that bony elbow of yours." He glared at Zuri. "I was just pointing out a fact."

She eyed me. "He's like a little boy sometimes. You'll get used to him… eventually." She pursed her lips. "I'm going home. Max will be driving you over to the restaurant to meet Core." She touched my elbow. "Sin, you have my number. Call me if you need to talk, okay?"

I smiled at her. She looked exhausted.

"Yes. We'll chat." I hugged her before stepping back.

She winked at me. "Have a good time tonight." She got into her vehicle and drove away.

Max opened the back door to his SUV.

"Thank you," I replied, maneuvering inside.

Shutting the door, he strode around to the driver's side before sliding in and driving off into the Manhattan traffic.

After a few minutes of zipping in and out of the snarl of taxicabs and buses, it didn't take long for Max to pull up in front of a restaurant that I recognized from a foodie magazine—Redemption.

Anxiously, I smoothed out the nonexistent wrinkles in my dress, waiting for Max to open my door.

"Have a good time," Max remarked as I stepped out.

"Thank you," I replied before striding toward the inconspicuous doorman, who opened the door, allowing me to step into the dim, upscale restaurant. I was trying to hide my excitement and morbid curiosity. This was my first time at the well-known private restaurant owned by a former model named Vivica.

I observed the celebs inconspicuously sauntering around before a willowy redhead with ample cleavage on display approached me with a huge smile, which I returned, immediately recognizing that she was wearing one of my designs.

"Love the dress," I complimented, trying not to act like a total fangirl. But inside I was jumping up and down. One of the most recognized and famous models in the world—Vivica—was wearing something I'd created.

"Well, I love your designs, Sinthia Michaels," she answered.

I was flattered that she'd recognized me. "Thank you. Believe me; it looks fab on you."

"Thank you, darling." She winked. "And welcome to my sinful establishment"—she gestured dramatically—"Redemption."

"I'm meeting Core McKay," I replied.

"I know. He's waiting for you," she replied. "Right this way."

We sliced through the space, and I admired the exquisitely designed restaurant draped with rich fabric across the ceiling. The Moroccan flair made the space feel both exotic and elegant. Bypassing the seated patrons, we eventually arrived at a long hallway that led to a flight of stairs. At the top of the staircase, she pushed open the door.

"And here we are," Vivica announced. "Have fun, darling," she drawled before sauntering away.

My gaze swept across the lit rooftop with its medieval architecture and vines hugging the bricks. Candles were strategically placed, giving the space a sultry, romantic vibe. A table nestled in the center of the rooftop was set with candles and an elaborate table setting.

Core stepped out of the shadows, studying me with no smile. In fact, his eyes were the most serious I'd ever seen.

I tilted my head, and my eyes traveled up his tall, well-built body. Muscles bunched beneath his crisp, tailored white shirt, and his rolled-up sleeves displayed the tattoos on his forearms. His collar was unbuttoned, and all I could focus on was the all-seeing eye tattoo on his neck. He looked delicious and dangerous.

My stomach popped and gurgled like a freshly opened bottle of Pellegrino.

Damn. This doesn't bode well for me.

I felt my hands grow moist.

His searing steel-gray eyes made me visualize seriously wicked, naughty things.

Shit. Shit. Shit. Sin, focus.

Keep your eyes on the prize. He has some damn explaining to do about his relationship with Tabitha.

He regarded me for a long time before smoothing a hand across his blunt-cut midnight-black hair.

"You look absolutely beautiful," he drawled in that ridiculously gruff tone.

My cunt clenched like it recognized its master's voice. As the cool air whirled around us, I sashayed toward him. Stopping before him, I tilted my head, and my eyes traveled up his body. Core under the bright moonlight was like a work of art.

"And you're late," he informed me with a velvet voice.

I considered him from head to toe and looked back again to his hard lips. "Well, hello to you, too," I replied before leveling him with an irritated stare.

He arched a brow.

I coolly glared at him before gliding around him to take in the beautiful views of downtown and uptown Manhattan, as well as the Hudson River.

There was a loud clearing of a throat from the entrance to the rooftop. Laden with dishes, the waiter and another server stood looking at us as if asking for permission to enter.

"Sin, let's have a seat." Core urged.

I nodded, allowing him to escort me to the table where he pulled out my chair, and I sat down while watching him take the opposite seat.

Both waiter and server approached the table.

"Bone marrow with veal cheek marmalade, foie gras fried rice with shredded duck and coriander, crispy duck wings with yuzu kosho, grilled clams flecked with Calabrian chilies, pasta spiked with pink peppercorns, and squash-stuffed ravioli with hazelnuts," the waiter announced as the server grandly set the small sharing plates down in the center of the table, carefully avoiding a stack of papers held down by a glass. "Enjoy," he finished with a bow of his head.

"Are you feeding an army?"

Core smiled, a slow lifting of perfect lips to reveal straight white teeth. "I didn't know what you'd like, so I took the liberty of ordering some of their popular dishes for you to try."

"I see," I croaked before clearing my throat. I kind of liked that he had taken the initiative to make sure I was properly fed with a well-selected sampling of a foodie's wet dream.

The server poured water into our glasses while the waiter beamed at me. "What would you like to drink?"

"I'll have a Moscow mule," I answered.

"And I'll have a Jack on the rocks," Core replied.

The waiter and server roamed away.

We eyed each other for a full minute before I couldn't stand the silence anymore. "Busy day?" I asked.

"It was very… enlightening." He narrowed his eyes as he continued to assess me with a combination of curiosity and intense interest.

"For me, too." I knew he was toying with me, but I was in no mood for games.

Core put a small plate in front of me, scooping a teeny portion of foie gras fried rice and putting several crispy duck wings with yuzu kosho onto it.

With butterflies fluttering in my stomach, I was not in the mood to eat right now, despite the delicious offering. "So are we going to talk about Tabitha or not?" I brought the glass of water to my lips, sipping slowly.

"We'll talk about Tabitha, but first, I need to get this out of the way. There's something on the table for you." He gestured to the stack of papers under the glass before filling his plate with food.

What is Core up to now?

I picked up the papers. "What's this?" I asked.

"A contract giving you back full control of your company." Core leveled his gaze on me.

My breath hitched. "Why?" A flush of adrenaline tingled through my body.

He ate a forkful of rice while staring at me. He swallowed before asking, "Isn't that what you wanted?"

"No!" I snapped my mouth shut, gathering my thoughts. "I mean, yes. It's just… sudden. Only weeks ago, you seemed pretty adamant that our business relationship was going to remain intact, and now… this?"

Yes. I am happy but also perplexed.

"Sin, sign it."

I scanned all the papers, and the contract was exactly what he'd explained. He was giving me back full control of my company. Happiness zinged through me, and then I froze.

But what does this really mean?

Is Core withdrawing all financial support for my business?

And if he did, I would be screwed. The only reason I wanted a financial investor from the get-go was because I needed money, lots of it. And now that my collection was ruined and I was starting from scratch, I needed Core—I mean, his money… more than ever.

My heart raced when another horrible thought filled my head.

Is he breaking up with me?

I wasn't egotistical, but a woman had to have her pride. It was all good when I was considering walking away from him, but for Core to beat me to the punch? That shit was frankly ego-bruising.

Heat flushed through my body. My emotions went from calm to rage in seconds.

Oh, hell no! Who the fuck does he think he is?

Then the numbness set in, and my emotional walls went up.

Fuck him. I'll survive.

I zeroed in on where it was flagged for me to sign. My fingers shook a little before I steadied myself.

He quickly signed, too. "It's done." He confirmed, pushing the documents back under the glass.

The server arrived with our drinks on a silver tray. Swiftly, he placed them in front of us before scurrying away.

My throat was parched for liquid courage. Picking up my Moscow mule, which was in a cool copper mug, I drank thirstily, feeling the smooth burn of alcohol before placing the cup down. "All right, Core. Now tell me what the hell is going on." I looked in his direction, my eyes suspicious.

He studied me for a moment, long and hard. Then he frowned, deep creases forming around his brow and lips. He rubbed his fingers over his lips, and more time passed before he spoke. "What if you had to tell a person the most important thing that they needed to know, and you knew they wouldn't believe you?"

Uh-oh… this is bad.

I'd never seen Core this somber.

"I'd tell them," I whispered.

"Bigsby is the man who killed my mother."

I blinked and then blinked again.

Wait. What?

"Bigsby Calhoune?" My question came out with a tinge of hysteria because right now, I felt like I was losing my fucking mind. "How did you come to that conclusion?"

"The man who placed the gun to my mother's head still wears the custom-made gold ruby-and-diamond-encrusted horseshoe ring on his middle finger."

A ring?

I let the words roll around in my head before I sputtered, "You're basing such a serious accusation on a damn ring?" I frowned. "Do you know how many men could have that same piece of jewelry?"

"One," Core answered, holding up a finger. "Bigsby told me he's had his ring for over forty years and that it's custom-made."

Okay… none of this shit makes any sense.

"Cut to the fucking chase, Core. What the hell does this shit have to do with me?" My heart was racing like a rabbit because I suspected I wouldn't like his answer.

"The man who shot me and my mother wore a gold ruby-and-diamond-encrusted horseshoe ring. I've been looking for years for that man. When I finally found the owner of the ring—Bigsby—I had Kevin dig up everything he could on him."

My eyes narrowed. "And?"

"Kevin found out that Bigsby was looking into your business. And I knew if he was interested in your business, there had to be a pretty damn good reason."

That was the truth bomb I'd been waiting for.

My mind screeched to a stop, and slowly, I began to reverse-engineer all the information I knew. And the pieces to the puzzle that had been plaguing me for hours all started to fit together.

Why Core had sought me out through Tabitha—because she was my friend and his only way to get close to me. That was the answer to the riddle about why a billionaire like Core had wanted to go into business with me, a fashion designer.

Core couldn't give a rat's ass about me. He'd needed my business as the bait to lure Bigsby in. That simple truth cut my heart like a dagger.

I was nothing to him.

Nothing but a pawn he'd used to get him closer to his end game… Bigsby.

My blood started to boil. Rage slithered through my veins like poison.

Breathe, Sin. Breathe.

Picking up my glass of water, I drank quickly. There would be no more alcohol for a bit; I needed to keep my mind focused for this conversation.

I was mad as hell right now, but I needed to think logically, not emotionally. And when I did exactly that, more pieces clicked into place. "You purchased my company so he had to deal directly with you." It was a statement, not a question.

"Yes," Core replied. "Kevin did a thorough investigation, but he couldn't find anything linking Bigsby to you. But I was sure if Bigsby was interested in you, there had to be a sinister motive, which was why I had to acquire your business fast. I had Kevin search through your background again, looking for anything that could be used as leverage."

My heart clenched and then dropped to the pit of my stomach. His words confirmed what I'd suspected—that all I was to him was a resource to be used to suit his needs.

"Leverage?" I asked in a low voice and through clenched teeth.

He furrowed his brows as he continued to stare at me. He slightly tilted his head, and then his frown deepened.

I inhaled a deep breath and held it for a beat before speaking. "You dirty fucker."

He spoke in a low, soothing tone. "Sin…" He leaned forward to touch my hand.

I snatched it out of reach. "Don't. Touch. Me. McKay," I gritted out.

His angular, rough-hewn face clenched.

"Continue…" I ordered before I steepled my fingers, cool eyes on him. "I want to hear exactly how I've been used for leverage."

Core inhaled a long, ragged breath before dragging his hands over his face. His cool, controlled demeanor dropped for just a moment before it reasserted itself. "I found out that you needed money, and I had lots of it." He sat back and cocked his head. "But I couldn't find a way to get into your small inner circle without raising suspicion or scaring you off. That was when Kevin found out you were friends with Tabitha."

The more Core had unveiled, the more pissed I got at myself for trusting Tabitha Thorp.

So this was all part of his big game plan... to maneuver me like a chess piece.

Everything that had occurred right before and during our relationship sank in. It was no happenstance when Tabitha had called me out of the blue, all excited about one of her business connections willing to provide financing in exchange for a small percentage of my future profits.

Core had put her up to making the business arrangement and the call. And that truth stung like a motherfucker.

My brain started working overtime. *What else don't I know about Core and Tabitha's relationship?* I knew for sure that they weren't friends; Tabitha had told me that much. *So if they weren't friends and didn't run in the same social or business circles... then how did they know each other?*

Then a horrible thought occurred to me. In the past, Tabitha had recounted her many excursions to the McKay Club to hook up with prime hotties—her words, not mine. Tabitha unapologetically slept around.

Is Core one of her many lovers?

"Did you fuck her?" My lips mashed together.

"I did." Core confirmed grimly.

I sucked in a sharp breath as the anger sparked inside me. "You had sex with Tabitha?" I jumped to my feet, toppling the chair behind me. "I knew it! Something about you two just didn't feel right." I clenched and unclenched my fists.

He stood, towering over me. "Sin!" he barked. "I slept with her years ago. Back when Tabitha and I were young. Way before I met you, we hung out in the same criminal circles. The only difference was, back then, the now-famous Tabitha worked as a mule for her seedy drug kingpin boyfriend, Ben Vargos."

Keep it together, Sin. There's more. I can feel it.

I held a breath before releasing it. "I'm listening," I replied in a sharp tone.

His jaw clenched so tight; if it were glass, it would have shattered. It seemed like he had to unhinge it just to speak. "When I found out she had a shitload of debt, I recruited her to help me convince you of the value of getting an investor—specifically, me—to help you expand your business. In exchange, I agreed to pay off Tabitha's debt to Ben and send her on a very long vacation."

"That's why she cleaned out her house and abruptly pulled up roots as if she never existed. You made her leave."

"Yes." He intensely watched me for a few moments. "It was part of our deal."

"Deal? That's all I am to you, isn't it?" A bitter tang coated my mouth. "An object. An acquisition to add to your collection." My hands were shaking with anger. Deep down, I knew that was all I meant to him, but it still hurt like hell to hear him say it.

I briefly closed my eyes, still processing what he was telling me… the truth. Despite my best efforts to calm the hell down, the warmth from my rising anger became an inferno.

I launched at him. "You lying, manipulative fucker!" I punched my fists against his chest. All of the anger and pain from being lied to and manipulated like a pawn on a chessboard erupted inside me like a volcano.

I can't believe I actually thought Core could be the one…

This man had inspired me to do and want things sexually that no other lover could.

This man who I'd thought did sweet, genuine things for me without me even asking…

This man I had been falling for…

Was this all part of his grand plan?

To trick me into trusting him? Falling for him? Wanting him? Maybe even… loving him?

My stomach twisted with pain because he was just like every man I'd encountered over the years, selfish… a liar… a manipulator.

A man who would use people—me—for whatever he needed without giving a shit.

Who the hell is the real Core McKay? Because everything I thought I knew about him—and liked about him—was all an illusion. Smoke and mirrors.

My voice was harsh when I whispered, "I let you into my body… my life… and you used me like a whore." I wanted to wrap my hands around his thick neck and squeeze the living shit out of him. I pummeled his body with all my might.

"Sin!" He easily grabbed my hands. "Stop!" he pleaded in a gentle but warning voice that didn't have the desired effect. Instead of calming me down, it just added fuel to my fire.

"Let. Me. Go. Now!" I yelled.

"I will if you just calm the fuck down." His voice was softer, calmer, and in direct contrast to mine.

I took some deep, cleansing breaths. "Let go," I ordered.

He released me, slightly stepping back. The uncomfortable tension between us didn't vanish.

I moved back to maintain the distance between us. All the trust that I'd had in him was gone… and there was no coming back from this shit. I knew that, and from the look of remorse in his eyes, he did, too.

"Core, you used me as fucking bait, like my life and business meant nothing." I cocked an eyebrow, putting a hand on my hip. "Really?"

"Sin, I needed closure." His voice was hard and decisive.

I threw my hands in the air. "Oh, to hell with you and your fucking closure." I stormed away from him, nearer to the railing. Being close him was making me claustrophobic. "You fucked me… literally and figuratively."

"I am who I am, Sin." His usually vibrant gray eyes seemed dulled by regret and intense thought. "I can't change that." He sighed. "Could I have done things differently?" he asked in a coarse voice, and deep brackets formed around his mouth as he frowned. "Fuck yes, but I did what I did because Bigsby needed to be destroyed."

"At my expense," I whispered.

I shook my head. For the first time, I really saw the man behind the veil. He was a broken man who'd waited his whole life to get revenge on his mother's killer. Core didn't give a shit who he had to use to get it.

Then another horrible thought occurred to me. "You were the one who caused all of my retailers to pull out of their deals."

He studied me for a long moment, and when he spoke, his tone was quieter, apologetic. "Yes."

I flinched as if he'd physically slapped me.

No. No. No. This shit can't be happening. I'm such a damn idiot. I allowed myself to do what I'd promised myself I'd never do again... trust a man.

"And was Lily Sanchez a part of your plan, too?" I inquired, looking for more traitors in his web of deceit.

Lily Sanchez was a buyer who'd pushed her bosses to carry my Sin Michaels collection in their Fifth Avenue luxury goods department stores. But when the stores had mysteriously backed away from my deal, Lily had seemed just as puzzled as I was.

"No," he replied sharply. "Lily was insignificant in the food chain of New York City power. I went above her head and called in some favors. She didn't know why her bosses had decided to pull out of your deal because I'd ensured that everyone involved in killing your deal kept their mouths shut... or else..."

All the information was painful to hear, but I had to know.

"Or else?" I asked.

He didn't blink. "I'd destroy them."

I studied Core, a scowl etched over his features, his nostrils flaring.

He is a monster.

And if by chance I'd forgotten Core was a powerful predator, it was abundantly clear at that exact moment.

Clearly, Core was a ruthless man of action.

What would he have done to me if I'd refused his proposal as my business investor?

Would he have destroyed my reputation? My business? My life? All three?

Now knowing everything about him... the answer was a resounding, *All of the above.*

After moments of uncomfortable silence, I asked, "And how exactly did you kill my deals?"

"Sin, that's not important. I just did." His voice turned commanding.

Wrong answer.

I didn't give a shit if he was the baddest motherfucker in New York. Because in this moment, I felt like the baddest bitch around, and I wasn't backing down from him. Not one damn inch.

"You don't get to decide anymore what's important for me to know. I do, McKay." I moved closer to him. "Now how did you destroy my retail deals?"

His face tightened. "I called all my connections at the retailers and had them end the agreements."

Exactly how powerful is Core that he could so easily destroy deals I'd worked months to get?

I straightened my spine and glared at him. "I want to know, Core. I want to know all the dirty details. What types of connections would do such a despicable thing?"

"Let's not play games, Sin. You know I'm not some fucking Boy Scout." He walked over to me, tracing a finger across my cheek.

His touch incensed me. I stepped back.

His hand fell away.

Irritation glinted in his eyes as he continued in a low voice. "My connections are shadowy, wealthy, deadly, and ruthless. I've built alliances while doing things like blackmail, coercion, and extortion, and that made me one of the wealthiest and most feared men in New York City."

After a long moment, I said, "So in essence, you're their puppet master, pulling the strings and making everyone, including me, dance for your sheer amusement."

His face hardened.

Oh… did I hit a nerve, McKay? Good.

I wanted him to fucking hurt just as much as—no, more than—I was hurting right now.

I'm a vengeful bitch.

"Sin—"

I cut him off. "Did Bigsby tell you why he wanted my business so badly?" My lips flattened.

"Yes," he snapped. "When he found out I was a stakeholder in Sin Michaels Corporation, he requested a meeting with me. During which he told me he knew you were set to manufacture in Thailand, and your first run to the United States would be in weeks."

"And?" I inclined my head for him to continue.

Core cleared his throat. "He wanted a small area within your cargo shipment to put his merchandise—women. If I agreed, he'd ensure there were no issues at Port Authority when your shipment arrived in New York."

My heart clenched before speeding up.

What. The. Fuck?

My business and sex trafficking?

"And let me get this straight," I croaked. "You agreed to get my company entangled in sex trafficking?" The thought of it made me angry all over again.

He studied me in silence. His nostrils flared. "Yes, and—"

"You fucker!" I screamed before swallowing several times and then sucking in a slow breath that didn't help. I began to pace, aware that he was watching me.

Now Bigsby's interest in my business made more sense. No one would ever suspect a naive designer was part of a sex trafficking ring. Frankly, Bigsby's plan was brilliant.

My heart started to pound in my chest at the thought of women, men, and children being robbed of both their lives and freedom by sexually depraved predators.

It's disgusting.

I glared at Core, and I didn't like the man I saw.

Who is this man? And why the fuck did I let him into my life?

Did he ever care about me?

Or was it acting?

Dammit! How did I let this shit between Core and me even happen?

"Let me finish," he requested in a rigid voice. "I had no intention of trafficking women. That's not my shit. You should know that. You know me."

I shook my head. "No, I don't… but please, continue."

"Sin, I just wanted to know exactly what he had planned for your business."

I shouted back, "Oh, go fuck yourself, Core!"

I started to storm away, and he grabbed me from behind, pressing me against his body. I stiffened and then tried to pull myself away, but the heavily muscled arms that encircled me refused to budge.

"Let me go."

"Only if you calm down," he said, his mouth brushing against my ear.

My skin prickled. I struggled hard to get free.

His arms tightened. "Sin, just let me finish what I have to say to you." His voice was soft, lighter than I would have expected from him, but firm.

"Okay. Whatever… just get off me," I croaked.

His touch repulsed me. I had given him everything, and he still made a mess of things.

His hold loosened.

I scrambled away from him before swinging around to face him. "I hate that you did this to me." I pointed at him. "You used me like I meant nothing."

My face felt like it was on fire.

Core was a horrible mistake.

And I had done everything with him that I'd sworn I would never do with another man. I had opened up and shared a piece of me, all because he'd weakened my defenses, made me believe that he cared about me and that I could trust and be trusted.

All of it was a damn lie.

"Sin, what was I supposed to do when I found out Bigsby had killed my mother? Let him walk away?" he replied in a cool, level voice. I could tell he was trying to get a handle on his anger.

"I never said that," I protested.

There was no doubt in my mind that Bigsby deserved to pay for his crime. But using me to do it? That shit was inexcusable.

"Good," he barked. "Because that wasn't fucking happening. My mother deserved better than to remain some unsolved crime sent away to the cold case unit that the police officers didn't give a shit about anymore."

I saw the raw pain and fury in his eyes and understood the emotions. It was what I'd felt when Dad died. I blamed the police for not searching day and night for the person who had run him off the road, killing him. I remembered calling the cops for months, pleading with them not to close his case and for them to keep looking for his killer. But they didn't.

"And what do I deserve, Core?" I pointed at him. "To be treated like some stepping-stone? An expendable object to be used just to get what you want… justice?"

I recognized this topic was a slippery slope for both of us. He'd lost a mother, and I'd lost a father. Each death and loss had torn us apart.

But how many lives had to be destroyed in the process of him getting his mother's killer? My life? Core's life? Just how far was he willing to go? From everything he'd done… very far.

The moments of silence drifted to minutes, and his eyes narrowed. "There are always sacrifices in war." His voice dropped to a growl.

His words were like a dagger to my heart.

"So I'm the damn sacrificial lamb?" My words were clipped.

The silence stretched.

I waited for something…

Anything…

That could erase this vile *I want to firebomb his damn car and then go to his penthouse and destroy all his shit* feeling that took up residence in my soul. I despised that he was the cause of these foreign, dark, heavy, sordid emotions.

This isn't me. I never look for drama, but dammit, why does drama always come looking for me?

"Sin." He blew out a hard breath before sliding his hands over his face. "You and I shouldn't have gone this far. I didn't want this." He chewed on his lip for a moment in consideration and seemed to be carefully choosing his words. "But I've come to understand there's a big difference between what I want and what I need."

I ignored everything he'd just disclosed, except for one word. *This?*

Irritation colored my words. "What part of this"—I gestured between us—"didn't the great Core McKay want?" I jammed my hands on my hips. "Because it seems to me like you've gotten everything you wanted. Your mother's killer. My business. To fuck me… literally."

What an arrogant asshole!

Every time he opened his mouth, I had to resist the urge to shank him… repeatedly.

"Sin, I won't say that I'm sorry. I do what I have to do. That fucker took my damn mother away from me. Do you understand me?" he asked in a coarse voice. "Bigsby shot me and my mother…" His eyes looked haunted while his fists clenched and unclenched. "And he walked away like we didn't mean a goddamn thing. What would you have done if he did that shit to you and to someone you loved? Walk away? Or make him answer for his crime?"

I swallowed hard. He had me there. Memories marred my mind. Dad's senseless death had destroyed me emotionally and burned me to the core. It'd changed me in ways I didn't even really understand until recently. Even years later, with his murder unsolved, it burned me that someone had gotten away with murder.

I turned my back on Core when I felt a tear—from anger—roll down my cheek.

Looking out on the cityscape, I rubbed my damp cheek on my shoulder. "You think I don't want retribution for my dad's death? But at what cost?" I shook my head. "Using you to get what I want? Manipulating you? Fucking you? I'm not that type of woman. I've never done shit in my life that made me question my morals—whether you believe it or not." My lower lip trembled. "I have a code of honor, and I tell the straight-up truth. I'm simple. Transparent. Real."

"And where the fuck has that gotten you?" he lectured in a low, even voice.

I shot a glare at him over my shoulder. There was a quick flicker of emotions—anger, then regret, to confusion, and then back to neutrality —in his eyes.

Is Core so blinded by his need for revenge that he didn't give a shit about anything or anyone? Including me?

Jerking my eyes away, I stared at the bustling city below. With a voice deliberately devoid of any emotions, just matter-of-fact, I replied, "At least I can look at myself in the damn mirror and know that I haven't backstabbed my way to the top. And if that shit makes me naive in your eyes, well, fuck you and the horse you rode in on."

"Well, in my world, it doesn't work that way," he retorted, his voice cold, hard. "Watching my mother getting killed changed me."

I felt rather than heard him come up behind me. A tsunami of energy swirled along my hypersensitive nerves.

Core pressed his body to my back.

"Core. Don't." I stiffened, clutching the railing for dear life, trying hard to ignore how comforting the heat emanating from his body felt pressed against mine.

Damn. Damn. Damn.

I swallowed hard.

Focus on the matter at hand. I scolded myself, but I had a hard time redirecting. I was so pissed off with myself that he still affected me this way. *Don't fold, Sin.*

"Sin." He pressed his hands over mine. They were so much bigger and darker than my slender, feminine ones that trembled underneath. "I will not apologize for what I am."

"I never asked you to," I mumbled.

"No. What you're doing is even worse. You're condemning me for being broken and, yes, fucked up in the head," he replied hoarsely. "But I am the product of my environment. Seeing what I saw and living through what I lived through… those things aren't easily forgotten." He paused. "Waking up in the middle of the night to sounds of people being gunned down. Coming home from school and witnessing single mothers giving blow jobs in alleyways so they could pay rent and put food on the table…"

I calmed a bit as I listened to him. The horrible sense of rage faded slightly.

"Sin, the things I've seen either break you or make you. I chose the latter."

"Core, you don't understand."

"Please… make me understand then." He lowered his head on top of mine.

After a few moments of uncomfortable silence that were riddled with distrust and tension, I asked, "How can I trust you anymore?"

"Sin, you never did." His breath puffed the delicate hairs at my temple.

I pulled one hand out from under his.

I bit my bottom lip and remained silent. He was right. I never did trust him—and with good reason. He had done everything that I'd feared a man would do if I ever lowered my defenses and let him in—hurt and betray me.

"What? Did you think that I didn't know? That I couldn't feel you were ready to bolt from us, from me, like some nervous rabbit? You had one damn foot in and one foot out of my bed."

I frowned. "I'm not good at trusting men. And everything you've done just proves why I never let my guard down. You manipulated me to get what you wanted, with no damn consideration for my feelings or how it would affect me."

"We both didn't trust each other," Core answered in a deep, velvety voice. "And without trust, there's only fear." He turned me around to face him.

I studied him as he studied me.

He carried on. "I trust you now, Sin. Despite the things I've done, given time, don't you think you can come to trust me?"

I rolled my eyes skyward. "Are you kidding me right now? Of course I can't trust your ass! Not after all the lies you told me."

"Not once did I lie to you."

I arched a brow. "Oh, really? Then what would you call it?"

"I omitted information, but I didn't lie."

I sputtered, "Don't play word games with me, Core. The way you manipulated me—your lies of omission—was infinitely worse. I can't forgive you for that shit."

Core angled his head and watched me. "Putting all my cards on the table, it did start out as me using you and your company to get to Bigsby. But it all changed when I got to know the real woman that you are. You became more than business; you became someone I needed in my life. And you can call bullshit on this if you want, but in my world, the less you know, the safer you are."

I stiffened. "Safe from what?"

He intensely watched me for a few moments. "You're going to need to sit down for this, Sin."

"No. I'm good. Just tell me," I declared with quiet resolve.

He furrowed his brows as he continued to stare at me. He slightly tilted his head, and then his frown deepened. "Kevin's investigation into your family background unearthed that you have two birth certificates, each one showing a different set of parents."

I sucked in a sharp breath and held it for a moment before releasing it. "What are you talking about?" I croaked.

"The first birth certificate had your father listed as Ian Michaels and mother as Grace Michaels. The second certificate had your father listed as Greer Lorne Cruickshank and mother as Aubrey Cruickshank."

"What?" My knees buckled.

Core caught me and escorted me back to the chair. I plopped down, feeling light-headed.

"I don't understand. Ian Michaels is my dad."

"Sin, no… he's not."

With those four words, my world shattered, along with everything I'd ever thought I knew.

CHAPTER 13
SINTHIA

My appetite had vanished after hearing Core's earth-shattering revelation, so the waiter and server cleared the table of food and plates. Core had also instructed them that we no longer needed their services for the rest of the night.

I sat stiffly in the chair on the rooftop as the Manhattan air chilled me, staring at Core in disbelief. "Let me get this straight. My supposed parents, Greer and Aubrey, started having an affair behind Bigsby's back and then cut business ties with Bigsby?"

"Yes," Core replied.

"And Bigsby got so pissed," I started after moments of uncomfortable silence, "that he killed Greer in an apartment fire. But Greer gave his brother, Ian, the ledger just in case something went wrong?"

"Exactly."

Tilting my head in quiet consideration, I studied him. "And Jemma, whom you suspect is my real mother, disappeared while on bail after Bigsby snitched her out to the Feds?"

"I know this shit sounds crazy, but it's true." He spoke in a soothing tone.

I bit my bottom lip, examining him for a beat. "And during all this drama, Bigsby had no clue that Jemma was pregnant with me—until now?"

"Also true," Core answered.

I eyed him like he'd lost his fucking mind. "So Ian is not my father. He's my uncle and Greer's brother?"

Core nodded.

"Oh God," I whispered. I felt like I was about to hurl. My emotions were churning from anger to confusion to dread and back to anger. "My whole life is one big lie."

Dad is not my biological father?

He's really my uncle who loved and raised me as his own?

Part of me wanted to reject everything Core had just told me, and the other part… wholeheartedly believed him because this was the answer to the question I'd been asking myself for years.

Why didn't I look anything like Dad or Grace?

Because I was not their biological child.

I stared into space while images of my dad flashed through my mind. He had been the doting dad who took me to zoos, aquariums, and planetariums, and I always marveled at how fortunate I was to have a parent who loved me unconditionally.

But now those memories were complicated by this extraordinary drama that was unfolding.

Once again, Core spoke in a simple, even tone. "Sin, I have information to verify everything I just told you."

Jerking my eyes away, I stood and began to pace the terrace, aware he was watching me.

I stopped and stared at him. "But if Bigsby killed all of them—Greer, your mother, and Ian—isn't it plausible that he killed Jemma, too?"

He pushed up to his feet, striding over, and stood just inches from me. "Bigsby is a psycho, so if he killed her, I'm sure he would have bragged about that, too, on Jeff's recording. But as far as I know, he's still looking for her."

Sex trafficking.

A Manhattan madam who is also my mother.

Greer is my real father.

What. The. Fuck?

But the crazy thing was Core's story did make part of my life make a hell of a lot more sense—like how much Grace disliked me, especially after Dad's death. Grace was probably pissed that she was stuck with me… still having to pretend to be my mother. Given how self-centered and selfish she was, having me around as a constant reminder that I wasn't her biological child probably sucked big time—especially in light of the fact that she didn't have a damn maternal bone in her body.

I stiffened when I recalled an argument between Dad and Grace years ago that I'd buried. It was one of their vicious spats that took place on Thanksgiving. My mind traced back to the memories of that fateful day.

Grace was in the midst of one of her infamous tirades, and Dad hissed, "Shut up, Grace. She can hear you."

And Grace shouted back, "I don't care because I've never wanted her. She's not mine."

Yes, her words had cut like a knife, and I had cried hysterically because of them, but I'd thought Grace had said them to hurt me and Dad—not because what she'd stated was actually the truth. Now I knew that all of her actions and barbed words were because she resented the fuck out of me since I wasn't her child.

"Bullshit! This doesn't make any sense. There's no way someone with Bigsby's past can run for mayor of New York, much less attract a socialite like Cate."

He studied me for a few minutes. "What past?" he requested in a low, rigid voice. "Do you know how hard it was for me just to get this much information on him?"

Three deaths—possibly four, including Jemma. All orchestrated by one man—Bigsby. I wasn't sure which feeling was more overwhelming—anger, frustration, or rage.

I paced back and forth, still trying to make sense of it all. "I believe everything you revealed about Bigsby being involved in an escort service. Ariana—Cate's sister—hired a private detective, who dug up information about some trafficking ring Bigsby's involved in. According to Ariana, the Feds are close to nabbing him for money laundering." I skidded to a stop, glaring at Core. "But what I don't understand is why Bigsby would pay someone to kill my dad."

"Which one?"

The headache from stress had been just a minor ache earlier; now it was raging. "Ian. Despite what you've told me, I'll always consider him to be my dad."

Maybe he wasn't my biological father, but he'd raised and loved me. That shit counted for something… my loyalty and devotion to his memory and all that he had given me unconditionally.

Core replied, "Ian had incriminating evidence about Bigsby's sordid past. A ledger—essentially the escort service's little black book."

"That's why Dad hid it in the trunk." I swallowed several times and then sucked in a slow breath that didn't help.

"How did you even find it?" he asked.

"The night of Bigsby's fundraising gala, I was looking for an heirloom piece of jewelry that I'd stowed inside my dad's old trunk. When I was digging inside, I saw red leather peeking out of the broken bottom, so I tried to yank it out. But when I hit the bottom, a secret compartment shifted, completely revealing the leather ledger."

"Didn't you think it was strange that Ian had put it there?" Core's lips pulled into a straight line.

After a long moment of consideration, I confided, "Yes. But when I looked through the ledger, nothing in it made any sense to me. There were several pages of names, and I knew it wasn't my dad's handwriting. And there were the initials G.L.C. scrawled in red ink at the bottom of every page."

Core interjected, "G.L.C. Greer Lorne Cruickshank. Your biological father."

"I knew there had to be a good reason my dad had hidden it because he was the most transparent person I knew." I paused. "But it's obvious now that he had a whole lot of damn secrets." And the unveiling had turned my reality upside down, forcing me to question every core thing I'd ever believed to be true. Now I was struggling to come to terms with all these shades of gray. I needed to make sense of them and hopefully achieve some sort of peace with them.

"So what did you do after you found the ledger?" Core asked.

I shrugged. "I pushed the journal back into the false bottom, banged the base back into place, and then dumped everything I'd pulled out back on top of it, promising myself to further investigate the ledger over the weekend. I just never had a chance to—"

"Sin, that ledger documented all of the clients who frequented your parents' and Bigsby's escort service. Those clients are rich, powerful people whose lives would be destroyed if that information got out. It's leverage Bigsby can use to blackmail people to do anything he wants. Greer knew that, and it's probably why he gave it to Ian for safekeeping. The ironic part about all of this is that Bigsby thought the ledger had burned along with Greer. Ian probably knew if Bigsby found out that he had the ledger, Bigsby would kill him to get it back."

"That's why my dad kept us moving from state to state like we did." I gasped. "We never settled anywhere for too long until… right before his death. I remember being so happy that we were staying in New York permanently, and then out of the blue, my dad decided he wanted to move again." I bit my bottom lip. "Core, shit, that ledger was stolen during the break-in." I froze with my eyes wide. "Wait. Did that fucker Bigsby steal it?"

My body shook with rage at the violation of my space… and my home and, worse, at the destruction of my clothing line that I'd spent months creating—all because of a ledger. And if Bigsby had wrecked my house just to get his hands on it, was my life now in danger since I'd had the ledger?

Fear weighed heavy on me as I considered the possibility of Bigsby coming back to my townhouse when I was home alone to tie up loose ends—me. Adrenaline and fear didn't mix well, and the combination was coursing through me, making me anxious and jumpy.

"Core"—the tension and fear were there, tightly bound around me like a cocoon—"did Bigsby break into my house just to steal the ledger?" I worked hard to control my breathing, steady my heart rate, and temper my fear.

He scowled, and his voice dropped to a rumble. "He ordered Jeff, his little minion, to break in and steal the ledger."

Fury chased the fear away. "But why did Jeff have to destroy my clothing line?" I asked through clenched teeth. "Was he trying to send me, or maybe you, a message?" Bitterness burned in my belly. It all felt like a blanket that wrapped around me too tightly.

"Sin, I don't know who destroyed your house. But what I'm sure of is Jeff didn't do that damage. He told me that he stole the ledger, but he didn't do all that shit to your house."

"And you actually believe a word that fucker said?" I arched a brow.

I was still trying to make sense of it all when a horrible thought raced through my head. *If Jeff didn't destroy my house, who did?*

"Yes, I do," he growled. "Believe me. With the shit we put him through last night and today, it wasn't in his best interest to lie to us. Trust me. No one can withstand—" Core stopped, jaw clenched, and shook his head as if clearing away whatever he'd been about to say.

"Torture?" I squeaked.

My thoughts flashed back to Core's telephone conversation yesterday morning and his statements about "ice for hours" and "softening him up."

"Exactly what type of criminal shit are you into, Core?"

When he finally spoke, he carefully chose his words. "Not something you need to know about. We got the answers we needed about Bigsby via the recording that Jeff had secretly made."

"What happened to suddenly put Da—Ian on Bigsby's radar?"

"Ian's greedy-ass wife."

"Grace?" I asked.

He nodded. "Ian told Grace about the ledger, and apparently, she figured out the value of the book. She snuck behind his back and went to Bigsby, asking him for money in exchange for giving him back the ledger."

"That bitch!" I hissed.

"Well, she was the one who put a bull's-eye on Ian's back," Core replied. "Bigsby thought the ledger had burned up in the fire, along with Greer. And when Ian found out what Grace had done, he met with Bigsby and threatened to expose him with the evidence contained in the ledger if he didn't leave him and his family alone. And you know how well Bigsby took that threat. He decided to put a hit on Ian."

"But why did Bigsby wait so long after that to come after the ledger?" I asked.

"My best guess is he figured that once he acquired your company and got you wrapped up in his illegal business, you would just turn it over with no questions asked."

"Oh God." My tears welled up, more so out of anger than anything else. "For years, I blamed myself for my dad's death"—tears rolled down my cheeks before I dashed them away—"because the morning of his death, I argued with him and then deliberately disobeyed him by not coming home straight after school. He died because he was out looking for me when that driver slammed into him. But now… Bigsby hired someone to kill him?" I stared at Core, blinking back the tears. "His death wasn't because of me."

The memory of that morning and the shouting match I'd had with Dad still made my heart heavy with emotion. Now I couldn't hold back the tears that fell. I was still racked with so much guilt and self-loathing about that day. Instead of telling him, "I hate you," I wished all I had said was, "I love you, Dad."

"Sin? Sin, come on. Please don't cry."

He wrapped an arm around me. I struggled, but he pulled me into his broad chest anyway. I nestled there, enjoying his warmth.

"When I arrived home," I mumbled, "a cop car was pulling away. I raced up the front stairs and slammed into the house to find Grace sitting on the stairs with a drink in her hand, reeking of alcohol." My mouth felt like sawdust had made a home inside. "She told me that Dad was… dead. That he'd gone out searching for me and a car crashed into his, sending him off the bridge."

"It wasn't your fault, Sin. It was Grace who had gotten him killed."

"I know that now! But why did she let me believe all these years that it was my fault that Dad—Ian—had died?"

It was still so hard for me to believe that he wasn't my real father. But despite the fact that he wasn't my biological father, I loved him as such. He had been my lifeline, the man who'd wiped my tears and loved me so much.

"She doesn't hate you, Sin. She hates herself."

"No. I'm pretty sure Grace hates me. I'm not her child. I'm just some other woman's baby that she has been forced to parent. It is a recipe for disaster because Grace doesn't have a nurturing bone in her body. She is a selfish, hateful bitch who has never loved me, but how could she betray her own husband?" That I couldn't understand.

I'd always suspected by her actions and words toward Dad that she didn't love him, but if she'd resented him so much, why hadn't she divorced him? I shook my head. There was no way to figure out why people did the crazy things they did, but as far as Grace was concerned, her ass could rot in hell.

"And all those lives destroyed because of one man… Bigsby."

I hated Bigsby for taking so much away from me. Maybe if my real parents were alive, I wouldn't have had such a fucked-up life, being at the mercy of Grace's emotional abuse. Dad had done his best to shield me from her, but frankly, he hadn't done enough.

"Your mother," I started, "my dad, my biological parents are all gone because that fucker Bigsby thinks people are disposable, like razors." I pushed away from Core, staring at him with narrowed eyes. "Their lives were nothing but damn footnotes. He has to pay the price for taking away their lives."

I was teeming with a level of rage that was new for me, and I didn't know how to subdue it. Vengeance rode me hard.

"I agree. He has to be stopped before he tries to hurt you." His tone was hard and sharp. His lips twisted into a snarl.

"Hurt? What the hell are you talking about now?"

"Bigsby gave me an ultimatum. If I don't give him back the ledger and any copies I've made, plus the recording that Jeff made, within seventy-two hours, he's threatened to kill you."

"Great!" I threw my hands up in the air. "This shit just keeps getting better and better. He's going to kill me." Bile crept up, and I pushed it down.

With a dismissive wave of his hand, he intoned, "That shit will never happen. I'm going to end him before he can even try to kill you or me."

I sighed heavily. "And the ledger and recordings are the only leverage you have to bring him down?"

"No." He scowled. "There's a gun stowed away in Bigsby's safe. Kevin's working on finding out how we can get that, too."

"What's with the gun?" I asked.

"It's the gun he used to kill my mother," he stated in a low, ominous voice.

I narrowed my eyes. "He kept it?"

Core just nodded.

"Damn. Bigsby is a real piece of shit."

There was a special place in hell for a man like Bigsby, who had taken at least three lives without any remorse and then kept a trophy from his kill. Anger rolled over my skin, raising the hair on my arms.

"We can't let him go unchecked," I breathed out. "You've got more than enough evidence to bring him down, Core. So what's the fucking problem?"

Silence stretched for long moments. Core's eyes shone with a clear understanding. Behind them, I saw the same ire and exasperation I had felt.

"Bigsby disappeared," he snapped. "But my intel says he hasn't left New York City… yet."

More silence. The muscles in Core's forearms bulged from clenching his hands into fists.

"Oh shit! Bigsby went underground? That's not good."

Now Bigsby was lurking in the shadows, just waiting to kill me if he didn't get the ledger.

"No. The situation is not good."

I sucked in a sharp breath as the fury sparked inside me. I was not going to let Bigsby get away with taking and destroying so many lives. My dad's life had stood for something. Core's mother's life wasn't just some afterthought, never to be revisited. And rage burned deep inside me that Bigsby had taken away the life I could have had with my biological parents. I'd be damned if I was going to cower in some corner, waiting for Bigsby to come after me, too. I would fight for my life tooth and nail. And if I lost the battle against Bigsby—which I damn well hoped I didn't—I was going to make sure he paid the price for his misdeeds one way or another.

"Well, you're not giving him that fucking ledger or recording back," I snapped. "I don't give a shit what happens to me. Bigsby took my family away from me. He has to pay. How do we make that happen?"

"We're meeting him in seventy-two hours. That's Thursday. He's expecting me to hand over the ledger and recording then. We'll use that meeting to kill him."

Bigsby has to be dealt with strategically and with brute force. And if that means his death... so be it. No one will mourn a world with one less psychopath in it.

"So we just sit around waiting for seventy-two hours?" I ranted. "Are you out of your mind?" I shouted. "He could be plotting anything by now."

Fear and apprehension coursed through my veins. Fear was something I hated to experience because it made me impulsive, which was the worst way to handle things and people like Bigsby.

"We're trying to track his money because he's going to need cash to leave the country. The minute we have some good intel, we'll try to take him down before the meeting. But you won't be safe, Sin, until we get him."

Core is right. I'm not safe. Shit. This situation has turned into the cluster-fuck of all damn clusterfucks.

Bigsby was a psychopath, willing and capable of taking a life—mine. Fear shook me to the bone. But when the image of my dad's face flashed through my head, resolve steeled my nerves. There were only two ways to handle Bigsby—flight or fight. I decided to take the latter route. I couldn't control Bigsby's actions, but I could control how I felt about them, and I wasn't going to go down without a fight.

"Safe? Honestly, Core, I don't give a damn."

But that was the furthest thing from the truth. I gave a lot of damns. Because at the end of the day, there could only be two outcomes from our battle against Bigsby—me ending up dead or remaining alive—

and I had too much shit to live for, so I chose to duke this shit out gladiator-style until the bitter end.

Core grabbed my face between his hands. "I care for you, Sin… and you're mine," he proclaimed while one hand slid down. His thumb stroked my lips.

I barely held back the urge to run my tongue over the callused pad of his finger. "I'm not your property, McKay."

"You can deny it." He traced along my cheek, down my jaw, across the curve of my neck, and over my collarbone. Gentle, languid movements. "Argue about it. Try to run away from it. But you're still mine. I will not hurt you, and I will always protect you. And when you realize that you and I are forever… you'll begin to trust me." He paused. "I'm a patient man, Sin."

My heart thundered. I liked that he wanted to fight for me… for us.

Is it too late to salvage our relationship?

"You're insane, McKay. You manipulated me for your own ends. I can't trust you anymore."

And while knowing I had to trust Core in order to survive a Bigsby attack, actually doing it was a completely different thing.

"Sin"—his voice was still low, a sultry, deep rumble—"in the beginning, it was business, but that changed for me a long time ago. You mean so much more to me now. Just give me time to prove it to you."

"Crazy—that's what you are," I whispered.

"That makes two of us." He curled his mouth into a smile. He slowly lowered his head, watching me. When I tensed, he whispered, "I haven't tasted you in hours. One kiss, and then you can go back to being mad at me." His hands pressed into my lower back as he pulled me closer.

He waited inches above my lips for consent.

Shit. This is wrong on so many levels.

He'd manipulated me into his business spiderweb, claiming ninety-seven percent of my business, all while using me as a pawn to get revenge on the most repulsive man I knew—Bigsby.

Frankly, everything Core had done earned him a top spot on my shit list because he could have come clean with me a lot sooner.

I sighed heavily, pushing aside the dark, ugly thoughts, and considered the positive things that came out of having a mutual enemy—Bigsby. Everything Core had done was in my best interest, too, since we were tied together because of Bigsby's nasty deeds.

If Core hadn't come into my life right when he did, my life would have turned out a lot differently. If Bigsby had gotten what he wanted from me—to become a major stakeholder in my business—I would have been unwittingly shoved knee deep into his sex trafficking business. And given how devious Bigsby was, he would have figured out how to easily get the ledger from me. And when Bigsby was done getting everything he wanted from me—business and ledger—he probably would have killed me because I knew too much.

I took a deep breath. For better or for worse, Core's and my destiny, future, and very life were tied together. For how long… I didn't know. But there was no doubt in my mind that Core and I would be stronger working together than apart.

I glanced from Core's smoldering eyes to his ridiculously sexy mouth. The tension melted from my traitorous body.

He felt my resistance disappear. His mouth covered mine.

My eyes fluttered closed. His lips, warm and firm, moved with a featherlight touch against mine, as if he were discovering their shape and texture all over again.

His kiss was slow, confident, unhurried, and sensuous. I tried to hold on to the anger, distrust, and hurt from everything he'd done to me when pleasure zinged through my body and grew liquid. Lost in the sensation, I touched his jaw. He licked and nibbled at my lips, his breathing deepening.

My fingers traveled up from his jaw and threaded through his hair. He opened his mouth and drove into me with his tongue. The pleasure spiked higher, sharper. He growled deep in his throat before reaching down to hike up my dress and pick me up. My legs wrapped around his waist as he carried me over to the corner of the rooftop where there was a long bar, and he plopped me on top.

He angled my head, so he had better access and could plunge deeper into my mouth, his body hardening. He drove his thigh between my legs, pushing up against the area that had grown wet in response to him.

I made another muffled noise as I kissed him back with escalating excitement. He growled and pushed harder with his thigh, deeper with his tongue. He hit just the right spot.

I gasped and arched my pelvis. Both of my arms were now wrapped around his neck. He cupped my ass and pulled me up more tightly against him. He wound his other arm behind my neck, holding me pressed along the length of his body.

He found a wicked rhythm with mouth and thigh that stole all thoughts from me until I was so torched that I was wantonly eating at him.

He devoured me with starved greed. My hands ran over his muscular shoulders while his thick, hard erection pressed against me.

If we were undressed, Core would have slid inside me.

The feel of his cock burning against me made me wiggle closer, trying to settle my throbbing heat against him to get that fraction of an inch closer. I felt his breathing slow.

I want his clothes off.

I want him inside me… holding me down as he pounds into me hard and fast, making me temporarily forget the ugliness of the Bigsby mess and Core's violation of my trust.

But there was still so much residual stuff between us due to all the manipulative crap he'd done.

There was a part of me that was furious with Core. I wanted to shout at him, tell him how much he'd hurt me by not telling me the truth about Bigsby sooner, that I didn't know if I could ever trust him again, that he was the first man in a while I'd let get so close to me emotionally, but that he'd gone and fucked up everything.

And without trust, aren't we building a relationship on a foundation of sand?

The fact that he hadn't been forthcoming with the truth about Bigsby from the get-go contaminated every area of our relationship.

How can I believe anything he says anymore without the urge for me to play detective to confirm it's true?

Trust was a pretty big fucking deal in any relationship, and I wasn't sure if I could wholeheartedly trust him again.

I had to pull way the hell back now.

I yanked my mouth away. "Stop," I pleaded. "It's too much."

He reared back his head and hissed. He crushed me to him and didn't move, his body strung tight.

I turned and buried my face against his hard, bunched biceps. I whispered, "I'm going home. I need some space to think… alone." I looked up at him, determined to make it clear that he wasn't forgiven for his transgressions.

And even though I was terrified of the possibility of Bigsby attacking me, I needed breathing room from Core. As soon as I got inside my home, I planned on having my cell in hand at all times with 9-1-1 on speed dial and ready to call at the slightest sound of trouble.

He was looking down at me, the planes and angles of his dark face cut sharp. "It's dangerous with Bigsby underground and plotting against you and me. It's better if you stay with me until we catch him."

"What didn't you understand? I can't be around you right now." I became decidedly defiant, a scowl pulling my face tight.

With a piercing gaze, he studied me for a long time. "You'll stay at my penthouse, and that shit is not negotiable." He snarled.

I glared at him even though, internally, I conceded to the fact that I was acting on emotions and he was the voice of reason. I knew Bigsby wanted to kill me. I wasn't an idiot, and I damn sure didn't have a death wish. "Separate rooms."

"If that's what you want." The tension in his body eased.

"Yes, that's what I fucking want," I replied. "But I need to go to my place to pick up some essentials for a longer stay at your house."

He lifted me off the bar, giving me a long, lingering once-over, his eyes roving over me inch by inch as I fixed my dress, smoothing it into place.

His eyes blazed with raw sensuality as they raked over me. "Let's go. I'll drive you home." He placed a hand on the small of my back, escorting me off the rooftop.

The deeper I went into Core's world, the more I understood him.

Core was dangerous, deadly, and focused—all traits that, instead of repelling me from him, drew me closer like a magnet.

CHAPTER 14
SINTHIA

Once we were in the car after leaving Redemption, we had a brief conversation about Jaxon, and then time ticked by as we drove in silence. The hush made the rest of the drive to my townhouse seem longer. Much longer.

Moments stretched, and Core spent more time glancing at me than looking at the road.

I felt as though I'd been through a tornado. Resting my head against the soft leather headrest with my eyes closed, now that my brain had started working again, I grappled with the fact that my entire view of the world had been proven false.

Ian is not my dad. He's my uncle.

Grace is not my mother... which, frankly, is a blessing in damn disguise.

Greer and Aubrey—Jemma—are my real parents but are both dead.

I frowned. Scratch that. Greer was conclusively dead, but Jemma... that was still an open question. But she had to be dead. *If she were alive, wouldn't she have contacted me?* My stomach hardened. Not if I was some sort of pregnancy mistake and she didn't want anything to do with me. Given my lifelong experience with a non-maternal woman—Grace—that was likely the situation.

Then there was Bigsby, who was planning to kill me unless he got the ledger back—his little black book.

Fuck. My. Life.

I felt like someone had hit me in the head with an ax. Really. All I wanted to do was lie down. Everything I'd believed to be true was now called into question.

Since Dad—Ian—had died, I'd never had so much go wrong with my life in such a short span of time. And all of my bad luck, misadventures, and misfortunes centered around one man… Bigsby.

I peeked at Core. The muscles of his neck bulged as he clenched his jaw. I wasn't sure if he was silent out of respect, giving me time to gather my thoughts about everything he'd just told me, or because he was plotting how many different ways he'd torture and kill Bigsby once he found him.

Turning my head, I stared out the window at the passing Manhattan landscape. I wasn't quite sure what I wanted to do about Core or his deception.

On the one hand, I really did understand his burning desire to find his mother's killer—Bigsby—and seek retribution for her death. On the other hand, he'd mercilessly used me as a pawn to get what he wanted —revenge.

Then there were the other things I now knew about Core. He was a very dangerous man who'd outright told me that he'd torture, kill, bribe, and manipulate to get what he wanted.

Can I really open up my heart to a man like him? Not to mention trust him again?

Is he even the one I can open my heart up to?

Shit. Is it even worth my while to spend more time with him to see where our relationship can go?

Damn. There were so many questions that I didn't have the answers to right now. Not with my mind churning with all of the information about my biological parents and Bigsby's ultimatum fogging my brain. But what I did know was if I did decide to go down the relationship rabbit hole with Core, there would be no going back. Any life with Core would be all-consuming and utterly dangerous.

I slid my eyelids closed to soothe the headache now emerging.

The sound of Core's phone ringing echoed throughout his vehicle.

"What's up, Max?" Core answered. "I'm with Sin and on my way to her place. She needs to pick up some stuff before we head over to the penthouse."

My eyes snapped open. I studied him in silence.

"Got it. But…" Max started.

"Go ahead, Max. Sin and I talked, and she knows everything." He glanced over at me. "So speak freely."

Core pressed a hand to my thigh and squeezed. I pushed his hand off. His face tightened.

"We can't find Jaxon," Max's voice boomed out. "We had a solid lead from his credit card purchases. There was a pattern of Uber rides to the same location in the span of a month."

"And?" Core requested in a tense voice.

"I broke into the apartment he was renting, but it's empty now. I suspect he was doing a stakeout in the joint; essentially, it was stalker central. And here's the kicker… It's only a few blocks away from Sin's townhouse."

"Oh God," I mumbled. "This is bad." My heart clenched and dropped into the pit of my stomach.

Core's hands tightened around his steering wheel. His nostrils flared. "Did you try his parents' house? Their law firm?" He frowned, his anger showing as he accelerated, passing the cars that had the audacity to go the speed limit.

My head got a little lighter from holding my breath. I kept thinking about what Max had reported.

"We can't find Jaxon."

Damn. Damn. Damn. I swallowed hard.

"Come on, bro," Max replied. "Of course I did. I staked out both locations—their office and home. At the latter, there was no sign of activity. So I talked to the security guards and administrative assistants at their law firm. His parents aren't even in town. They're in Europe on vacation." He paused. "But everyone I talked to said they hadn't seen Jaxon. They said he was still in Europe."

Core pressed his lips into a thin line. Several moments passed before he spoke again. "How do you know they didn't lie to—"

"Core." Max cut him off. "None of the people I interviewed today lied to me. For fuck's sake, I'm a former Green Beret who's faced all kinds of liars. Nothing slips by me… ever. You know that shit."

"I want that stalker caught so I can show him exactly what I do to anyone who fucks with mine." His hands clenched the wheel.

"Come on, man. Relax," Max urged. "I know how bad you want to get Jaxon. We all do."

"Tell Kevin to stay on the trail. I don't care how much money it costs for more intel. And I need you to meet me outside Sin's townhouse. I'll be there in a few." He pressed a button on his steering wheel and ended the call. "You okay?" he asked, glancing over at me.

My lungs relaxed into an exhale. *This is what breathing feels like.*

The restricted feeling had gone away.

"With Jaxon loose? Hell no," I sputtered, glaring at him.

He scowled, and his voice dropped to a rumble. "Sin, you're safe."

"I'll never be safe," I pointed out. "Not with Jaxon stalking me."

"We'll catch him and then get rid of him—permanently." His voice was matter-of-fact.

"You're going to kill him?" I finally replied after moments of uncomfortable silence.

His features clenched as he drove down the street. "After everything I've told you about him, do you really care if he lives or dies?" He was silent for a while, allowing me to contemplate and consider his words.

It didn't take a genius to figure out that Jaxon was a big problem for me.

"No, I don't."

Not after everything Jaxon had done to me and now that he was back to stalking me. He had to be stopped—by any means possible.

I stared out at the passing city scene of looming glass towers, along with spectacular architectural sights like Grand Central Terminal, the Chrysler Building, and the Seagram Building.

Before long, we pulled up in front of my house with Core parking behind the SUV Max was leaning against. He stood up, striding over to us, and waited for us to get out.

Turning off his car, Core unbuckled his seat belt and then reached over to the glove compartment, unlocking it. My eyes widened when he pulled out a gun.

"Are you expecting trouble?" I asked.

"I'm always expecting trouble, darling." He threw open his door, hopping out while simultaneously holstering the gun, hiding it underneath his jacket. It didn't take long before he was at the passenger door, opening it for me.

Max grinned at me. "Hey, sweet cheeks!"

"Hi, Max," I replied, taking off my seat belt. I stepped out, ignoring the hand Core held out for me to grab.

"Eventually, you'll forgive me, Sin," he answered in a deep, velvety voice.

"Overly confident, aren't you?" I replied as he pressed his palm to my lower back, ushering me up the stairs with Max pulling up the rear.

I became hypersensitive to the way Core's firm hand pressed into my back. His thumb lightly stroked me, and I liked it—too much.

"No, just realistic." When he spoke, his warm breath brushed lightly against my ear.

For a brief moment, I thought about all of the wicked, sensual things his talented lips and tongue had done to my cunt just yesterday morning.

Sin, focus.

Ruthlessly, I pushed all the sinful thoughts out of my mind.

Turning around, I poked him hard in the chest. "Well, I think you're aiming too high, McKay. I'm not so forgiving. In fact, I'm a card-carrying vengeful woman, and you are now on my *To Be Shanked* list. So if I were you, I'd sleep with one eye open," I stated coolly before whirling around to resume my climb toward my front door.

"Damn," Max grumbled. "I like her." He laughed huskily.

"What's not to like?" Core countered. "She's a pit bull in a skirt with an amazing ass."

"Keep your eyes off my ass, McKay." Pulling my key out of my mini clutch, I pushed the key into the lock and then opened the door. I felt both Max and Core present behind me. "Okay, I've got it from here." I turned around to eye them. "You two wait outside. I don't need your help."

I felt secure that if Jaxon were to do a stalker drive-by, he wouldn't even think about stopping after the mere sight of a muscular, scowling Core and hulking Max standing outside my door like warrior sentinels.

Core frowned. "That shit is not happening." He gently tugged me back, pushing his bulky body in front of mine. "Sin, let me go inside first."

He nudged the door, and both he and Max stepped over the threshold.

With them both tall and built like a wall of muscles, I barely squeezed around them to turn on my lights.

With eagle eyes, they scanned the area.

I remembered the last time Core had been at my place—when we found out the break-in had occurred—and the door had been open when we arrived. So I felt pretty sure everything would be fine while I gathered my things.

"Will you both leave? You're hovering, and I need some space." I eyed Core. "Especially from you."

Max replied, "Damn. Zuri was right. She's the perfect match for you, Core. I'm loving her take-no-shit attitude." He clapped him on the back. "It's going to be interesting seeing her keep you in check." He stared at me. "Core's one lucky man. Do they make more like you?"

"You wouldn't be able to handle another of me. But my bestie, Jade, is a ballbuster like me and will give you a run for your money."

"Many have tried," Max revealed, "but I've yet to meet a woman who can handle a man like me." With a gleam in his eyes, he added, "But I'm willing to give Jade a shot."

I scrutinized his tough military demeanor.

Shit. He looks like he could bench-press a car—easily.

I was intrigued about a possible hook-up between Jade and Max.

Would it be fireworks? Or oil and water?

Knowing Jade, probably the latter. She liked her men pliable and ready to succumb to her every whim and demand in and out of the bedroom. But something told me that shit would never work with Max.

Max's cell rang. He scanned the caller ID and relayed, "It's Kevin." He turned to Core. "I'm out. Core, I'll meet you outside." Then he left.

Core strode over to me. He wasn't smiling, but he didn't look angry, more contemplative than anything. "Now back to us."

I rolled my eyes. "I'm sorry if you haven't gotten the memo." I gestured between us. "But the whole *us* situation has been put on hard pause… by me." Jamming my hands on my hips and looking him up and down, I continued. "Like I said, I need my space. So I'm going to need you to exit left." I wasn't budging on my position. I needed alone time to decompress before I was shuttled over to his place for God knows how long.

He lowered his head to mine, eyes open, almost daring me to look away from him. It was predatory, determined… and primal. He was letting me know that he was top dog and what he said goes.

In the bedroom, I'd allow him to dominate me.

But outside? Hell no.

And it would be my pleasure to set his ass straight.

"Does your mean-mug expression actually work on other people?" I asked. "Because all it's doing is annoying the hell out of me," I sassed.

"You can have your space while I wait right here," he explained. "And pack enough clothes for a couple of weeks. It might be a while until we wrap up this Bigsby and Jaxon situation."

I scoffed. "Weeks?"

"I'm hoping sooner," he replied grimly. "Do you need help with moving your packing along?"

Okay, that's it. His "Me, Tarzan; you, Jane" attitude is pissing me off.

"Out, McKay." Marching over to the door, I yanked it open. "I don't need your ass micromanaging me while I pack up my shit." I desperately needed the time alone to come to grips with my feelings.

His eyebrows lifted in amusement, and then he shook his head. "Damn, your dirty mouth is making me so hard right now."

He's not making adulting easy at all.

I pointed at him. "Is that your attempt at sweet nothings?"

Core tilted his head as he considered me. "Yes. Is it working?" He gave me an honest-to-goodness, panty-melting bad-boy grin.

I sighed, running a hand through my hair. "No, it's not. And as far as you and I are concerned… you're on a pussy diet." I pointed to the door again.

He stared at me with his mouth open.

Look at that. I got him quiet.

He swallowed the distance between us, and when he spoke, his warm breath brushed against my lips. "No pussy for me. And no cock for you." His voice was low and sensuous. "It's going to be a rough couple of days for both of us, huh?" He leaned in and kissed me. He didn't move when he finished. He kept his lips gently pressed against mine.

A few moments passed before he kissed me again, more commanding, hungry, urging a response that I freely gave before my brain caught up with what my body craved. Quickly, I put a hard stop to Core's seductive play by breaking our kiss.

"Don't worry about me, McKay." I softened my voice to saccharine sweet. "My vibrator, Beast, and I will be A-okay."

He licked his lips, as if still savoring my taste. "Normally, I don't share when it comes to you, but I can definitely get with a threesome—you, me, and Beast. Can't wait for our date. Say… in three days? In my bed, when you're not so pissed off at me?" He winked at me.

"Don't hold your breath, McKay." I countered, even while my cunt tingled and my nipples puckered as I envisioned a gloriously naked Core lying between my legs, pressing Beast against my slit while he finger-fucked me.

Oh, sweet Jesus… I've found the trifecta—a man with a big cock and a wicked tongue and who loves playing with sex toys. Damn. Damn. Damn. It's like Christmas and my birthday wrapped into one. Surprise!

As if he could read my sexy, dirty thoughts, he grinned. "I'll be right outside, waiting." He leaned into me, his voice dropping to a low purr. "And don't forget to pack your toy, darling."

Dammit. Focus. Eyes on the prize. Give him hell for betraying my trust. He's an asshole—a sexy one, but an asswipe nonetheless.

My racing thoughts revved up my anger all over again.

He strode out the door before I could launch my final shot.

"Whatever," I clipped out before closing the door but leaving it unlocked. I knew no one had a chance in hell of getting past him and Max—two mixed-martial-arts-looking fuckers.

I padded over to the kitchen and grabbed a bottle of sparkling water from the refrigerator. The cleaning company did an excellent job. I leaned a hip against the kitchen counter and stared at the rows of empty racks that were in part of my townhouse. Racks that had once held around twenty outfits, ranging from shredded organza dresses with flowers at the hem, cobweb gowns that fluttered from neck to floor, crystal tank tops over short sequined skirts, to peacock-print silk dresses tumbling off one shoulder.

I'd have to make the outfits again. Trying to calm the anxious ball of energy bouncing around in my stomach, I took a deep, cleansing breath. It didn't help.

I wasn't a quitter, and despite the daunting task of starting over, I'd do it because being a fashion designer was my life and getting my designs into major retailers was a dream I'd never let go of.

"Okay, Sin," I muttered, "no wallowing in sadness. Get your shit together." Pushing away from the counter, I made my way upstairs, mentally cataloging what I needed to pack for my stay over at Core's place.

Finally in my bedroom, I kicked off my stilettos before walking over to my dresser. I started pulling out my neatly folded lingerie when I heard something drop in the hallway right outside my bedroom door.

I rolled my eyes. "McKay," I yelled over my shoulder, not bothering to stop what I was doing, "what part of 'I need my space' didn't you understand?"

There was no response. I sighed heavily. My back was facing the door, but knowing Core, he was probably standing there with his usual *I'm the king of the world* glare.

I huffed. "I'm not going to move any faster with you cracking the whip. So go on. Get." Gathering my stacked pile of bras and panties with one hand, clutching it against my chest, I swiveled around to face him, my resting bitch face firmly in place.

I screamed. The muscles in my arms went slack, everything in my hand dropping to the floor, as I watched with disbelief and then horror as Jaxon, dressed in all black, strode toward me with a knife held in one hand.

Panic quickly took over the darkest parts of my mind, and the fear blossomed into terror. I had to escape.

He was blocking the path to the door—the only exit. I spun on my heels, running to the left, where my bathroom was located. If I could just make it inside, lock the door… I'd be safe.

He grabbed me. There was a sharp yank on my hair and then the burn of strands being ripped out of my head as he jerked me backward.

Damn. He caught me.

I still fought the backward momentum by pressing forward, ignoring the sting of my hair being pulled out at the roots, courtesy of his brutal tug. My head throbbed, but I didn't give a shit about the pain because I knew Jaxon had much worse planned for me.

Slamming me against his hard body, he pinned my back against his chest with one muscled arm. My fight response amped up, and I was immersed in survival mode.

"Let me go." I snarled, wildly swinging my arms, scratching and punching and kicking. I felt like a rabid animal foaming at the mouth until I felt the cold, sharp prick of his knife against my throat.

"Cut it out, or I'll fucking slice that pretty little neck of yours." His words came out in a growl, his anger was blistering, and the muscles of his arms were taut.

I froze. *Oh my God, he's going to kill me.*

How the hell am I going to get out of this mess?

And where's Core?

The headache from stress was raging.

Why the hell did he have to listen to me when I told him to get out?

Fuck. Fuck. Fuck.

This is it. This is how I'm going to die.

Panic threatened to consume me, but I fought for mental control. I took a calming breath as my brain raced with multiple scenarios of how this night would end. None of them were good.

Sin, it's time to reason with the psycho.

"Jaxon, what is it that you want?" I worked hard to control my breathing, steady my heart rate, and temper my fear.

When Jaxon spoke, I felt like he was taunting me. *Asshole.* "You. I've always wanted only you." His sour breath made me gag, but when he pressed the knife harder against my skin, my body tightened. "We belong together. Do you see?"

"Jaxon, there is no *us*," my voice shrilled.

"I've been waiting for you," he muttered. "I wanted to talk. I wanted to apologize for destroying your clothes and your house."

Everything in my mind froze. "That was you? You were the one who destroyed my collection?"

"Yes. When I saw you all dressed up and then getting into that car, I knew you were going on a date with lover boy. You're cheating on me." His hand trembled. He was becoming more enraged. I felt the knife piercing my skin as a little bit of blood trickled down my neck. "How could you do that? To me? To us? I needed to teach you a lesson."

He's a damn lunatic.

This fucker had broken into my house, destroyed my shit, and now he was violating me because he had some delusional notion that I was his girlfriend because I'd fucked him years ago?

But I knew his crazy went deeper. He was pissed and obsessed with me because I'd said hard pass to anything more than a one-night stand.

Rage coursed through my veins.

I wanted to claw his eyes out. Kill him. Bathe in his blood. That was what I had been reduced to. Primal urges—attack, maim, kill, using whatever was available to succeed, including kicking Jaxon in the groin, which became a priority.

I remained silent, emotionless, knowing that would bother him more than me talking. He wanted my attention, my adoration, my begging. Well, that shit was not happening.

He leaned in, and his tone dropped to a low growl as he spoke. "And now you show up again with lover boy? Are you fucking him, Sin?"

I kept a sharp eye on the entrance to my bedroom. *Come on, Core. Get a clue.*

It had been ages since I kicked him out.

"I'm talking to you, bitch!" Jaxon shouted.

I'd seriously had enough of his shit. "Bitch? Is that the best you could come up with? I've been called worse by a better class of people than your ass," I pointed out.

Core's voice bellowed from downstairs. "Sin? What's taking you so long?"

"Good. Your boyfriend's here," Jaxon whispered.

I croaked, "Core—" But I was quickly silenced by a sharp dig of Jaxon's blade. At first, it felt like someone was pinching my skin with a metal claw—like a nipping feeling but a lot worse—and then I got pins and needles before it went numb.

"Time for some fun," Jaxon jabbered before dragging me over to my open closet with the blade firmly pressed against my throat. Then he flung me inside.

His gaze rested on me, and then his eyes traveled along my face, down the curve of my neck, and to my breasts. Then they lifted lazily to my mouth again. "It's been so long," he chattered. "I can't wait to kiss you."

"I'd like that, too," I replied in a saccharine tone, "so you'll be close enough for me to rip your cock off."

He grinned. "I find our banter amusing."

I frowned. "Banter?" I spit. "That's a fucking threat."

"Sin?" Core's voice called out again, and this time, he seemed closer.

"Co—" I shouted.

"Shut it," Jaxon warned while simultaneously lunging at me with his knife.

Dodging his blade swipe, I clumsily fell back onto my ass—hard. "Goddammit." That was going to leave a mark. "Asshole," I groused, scrambling onto all fours and scooting farther away.

Jaxon narrowed his gaze on me. "Keep your damn mouth shut," he warned, "or you'll both die." He slammed the closet door shut.

My heart raced with fear as I stumbled to my feet in the dark space.

My mind raced with all of the horrible possibilities and scenarios psycho Jaxon had planned and would inflict on Core and me, given the opportunity.

The only bright spot to this clusterfuck was that Core was one tough motherfucker and could handle Jaxon. And so could I.

My counterattack strategy quickly came together. As soon as the closet door opened, I would be ready to brawl. Scrambling over to my shoe shelf, I snatched one of my highest stilettos and tightly gripped it with the thin, long heel pointing outward like a deadly weapon.

"I'm no one's bitch," I mumbled while making practice swipes with the shoe, slicing it through the air.

I never realized how deadly my stilettos were. One stab with full force would easily cause serious injury, and with laser focus on a soft part of the body—like the throat or eye—it could give me enough time to escape from Jaxon… or piss him off. Either way, it was him or me, and I chose me.

I blew out a breath. "Okay, Sin," I mumbled, "no fear."

Bouncing on my bare feet, I readied myself to go full-on survival-of-the-fittest beast mode. If Jaxon somehow made it past Core—highly unlikely—then it would be a shoe to Jaxon's face.

"It's go time, motherfucker. Stiletto fucking city."

There was an audible bang that pierced the air. I knew it was gunfire.

I heard Max's voice bark, "Clear."

The closet door was thrown open with Core standing at the threshold. Dropping the shoe, I rushed into his arms, relieved as hell that he was alive and so was I.

"Thank God," I whispered, clutching him for dear life. I wanted to cry, laugh, and yell—all at the same time.

"I've got you, Sin," he declared huskily before kissing me.

Warm, soft lips covered mine. The kiss became more fervent, and when it ended, I leaned into him, lingering in his arms that protectively engulfed me as if he never wanted to let me go.

He released me, clutching my face in his palms with eyes sweeping me for injuries. "Are you okay?"

"Some cuts to my throat, but I'll be fine," I answered. "How did you know he was here?"

"Because Max smelled cologne when we were downstairs. He didn't think anything of it, but when you were taking so long, he put two and two together, and we knew something was wrong."

Glancing over, I saw Max standing there with a gun in his hand and a fierce look on his face. "Core, go. I'll take care of it. I already sent a text to both the cleaner and Rocco. They're all on the way. We'll make sure to clean up the body."

I blinked and then blinked again.

Cleaner?

Clean up the body?

Both Core's and Max's expressions were *There's nothing to see here, folks… just a dead man lying on the bedroom floor* neutral. It was as if we were standing in a grocery store, waiting for a cleanup on aisle ten.

What type of world does Core live in that makes this situation remotely normal?

And is this a world I can learn to get used to?

My heart started to pound in my chest at the thought of it.

My gaze landed on Jaxon, who was lying faceup.

"Sin, don't look." Core's voice became low and commanding.

But I couldn't help myself. My eyes zoomed in on Jaxon's body crumpled on the floor with blood running out of his head, eyes wide with shock, and lips parted slightly in death's awe.

I felt nothing about his death. Jaxon was going to kill me. So it was either him or me. Yet there was a part of me that was a little concerned that my conscience was silent, on a hiatus, unmoved at the loss of life. But I also knew that the body on the floor could very well have been me, and just the thought of that near-miss tragedy settled my lack of emotions toward his demise.

I croaked, "Who's the cleaner?" I split my attention between Max and Core.

Max's lips flattened into a straight line.

Core narrowed his eyes. When he finally spoke, his tone was slow and restrained as he carefully chose his words. "It's our connection that takes care of messy situations like this for us."

My eyes widened.

What the fuck?

Exactly how many situations like this has he been involved in?

My lips parted to ask more questions.

"Sin, the less you know, the better." He grazed his finger along my cheek. "You got me?" Fastened on me were determined and unwavering eyes.

I nodded because, strangely, I did.

They'd killed Jaxon with a weapon they probably shouldn't have. Plus, I'd watched enough police procedural shows to know that calling the police would only land the three of us in jail while the cops sorted out the who, what, why, and how of this major clusterfuck.

And I damn sure didn't relish the probability of spending time behind bars, fending off sexual passes from Big Bertha, who was eager to make me her new prison yard bitch.

"Good. Let's go," he demanded, grabbing my hand. Escorting me toward the door, he led me out of the bedroom. "Don't bother with your stuff. I'll buy you whatever you need. Right now, we have to clear out of here. I'm not sure if your neighbors heard the commotion that took place just now."

Still in shock from everything that had gone down, I didn't look back. I didn't need to.

Jaxon was gone, and I had one less person out to hurt and kill me. Then my new reality sank in. I'd never be able to be in my bedroom… in my home… without the memory of what Jaxon had done and his eventual death tarnishing the peace and sanctuary that I'd built.

My home was where I'd felt the freest of worries. Where I'd felt comfortable and safe. Now not only Jaxon, but also Core and even Bigsby had broken that barrier in my home as well as in my life.

I felt vulnerable and scared.

I didn't know how to process the fact that my world had shattered around me.

What do I do now?

And how do I move on from this?

And will it be with or without Core?

CHAPTER 15
SINTHIA

Unable to sleep, I sat in the serene environment of Core's private terrace overlooking Manhattan. It was late, a little after midnight, and the sky was dark. The crisp fall air whipped around me as I tucked my legs under me.

"Now this is living," I murmured under my breath, enjoying the panoramic view of the Manhattan skyline, East River, and Central Park.

Cradling a cup of coffee in one hand, I sighed heavily. It was Thursday, only four days after my world had imploded due to Core's truth bomb about my real parents and Jaxon getting killed at my house. The situation had gotten worse when Grace was found dead inside her business. The police had speculated that it was a robbery, but we—me, Core, and his team—all suspected it was Bigsby's doing. He was systematically going down the list, killing everyone who knew about his connection to the ledger. It didn't take a genius to figure out I was next, so Core and his team went on high alert, putting me on lockdown at Core's penthouse until his meeting with Bigsby today.

Adding to the tension permeating the house, I'd moved myself into Core's guest bedroom, deciding I needed time to get my shit together emotionally. I'd asked for space, and he was giving it to me.

"Be careful what you wish for…" I muttered.

I hated to admit it, but I missed him.

Compounding my feeling of isolation, I hadn't spoken to Jade since Sunday, even when there were so many times I had wanted desperately to call her. Jade had her own little family drama brewing after the press had gotten wind of the authorities linking Bigsby to a sex trafficking ring. The media circus had kicked into high gear when Bigsby went into hiding. The tabloids had become dogged in their twenty-four-seven news coverage of the Bellisario family—following them around and camping outside of both Cate's and Ariana's homes. I was relieved as hell that Jade was still in New Zealand, avoiding the public drama this Bigsby fiasco had become.

Taking a sip from my cup, I voice-dialed the only person I wanted to talk to right now.

"Jade?"

"Sin? Why aren't you sleeping? It's past midnight in New York. Is everything all right?"

I grumbled, "Nothing a couple of shots of Patrón can't resolve."

"What's going on? Issues with Core?"

I sucked in a ragged breath and held it for a long time before exhaling. "Yes," I replied.

"And?"

The silence stretched.

"And my life is so fucked up right now." Dammit, I needed to keep it together. I pressed my fingers along my temple, trying to ease the pressure from the stress. It didn't work.

"What does that mean?" Jade countered.

"My life is a reality show, and the results are in. Ian is not my father, and Grace is not my mother," I responded flatly, curling up into the plush cushions. "My real parents are essentially a pimp and a madam."

Jade was silent.

"Did you hear me?" I asked in a strained voice.

"I did, but what's the damn punch line?"

I swallowed hard before launching into the full details.

Moments later, Jade cleared her throat. "Oh my God! This explains a lot," she hissed.

I frowned. "Like what?" I finished my drink and carefully set the mug down on the table.

"Why you look nothing like Ian or Grace."

I sighed. She was right about that fact. I had olive-toned skin and dark, exotic features. Grace had ethereal, porcelain features, and Ian had been just as fair.

I inhaled a ragged breath. "Is that all you got out of the fucked-up lowdown I just went into?" I nibbled on my bottom lip.

"Sin," Jade replied in an even voice, "what you told me about Bigsby frankly isn't surprising. My mom and I have never liked or trusted him. So Core taking that fucker down is just community service in my eyes."

I jumped up, wincing when I hit my toe on the coffee table. "And the fact that Bigsby is planning on killing me?" My heart started to pound in my chest at the thought of it.

I started slowly pacing the terrace and twirling my tresses around my finger, holding my cell in one hand.

Once again, she spoke in a simple, even tone. "Core sounds like a badass, so that shit is not going to happen." She paused. "I mean, come on. He took care of stalker boy. You can give him my thanks for that shit."

In Jade's typical MO, she was trying to calm me the hell down, but it wasn't working. I was too wired… too frustrated… too conflicted… too damn everything.

"Great!" I threw a hand up in the air. "So now you're a member of the Core McKay fan club?"

"Hell yeah! I don't have to worry about your ass while I'm away. He has your back."

"He manipulated me, Jade!" I snapped.

"And did you slap his ass for being a naughty boy, telling him not to do that shit again?"

I couldn't help the laugh that slipped out. Only Jade could lighten my dark mood.

"Jade, come on. This is serious. He manipulated me to get what he wanted."

"I got that, and knowing you, you laid into his ass about it."

"Yes. I told him if he lies to me again, then that's his ass."

"So what's the problem?"

"I can't trust him," I replied.

She exhaled an exasperated breath. "You mean that you won't."

"Can't. Won't. It's the same thing."

Jade snorted. "Come on, Sin. You and I know what this is really about. You're terrified of being hurt by a man again. Look, I get that what he did was fucked up, but the why is valid. Bigsby had killed Core's mother and left him for dead. That shit would stick in anyone's teeth like corn. Life is too short to stand on the sidelines because you're scared to trust and love. Zone in on the bad boy and make him yours."

"It's not going to work. I can't trust any man to do the right thing." I sighed. I hated feeling this way, but a whole lot of shitty life lessons had taught me nothing good came out of trusting men.

"Bullshit. You're just scared. Just let the past go, Sin. Scars remind us where we've been, not where we're going."

My heart raced. Trying to hide from the truth wouldn't alter the reality of this clusterfuck. "He scares the shit out of me. He's the one man who changes everything I thought I knew about myself." He was the one man who had stripped away my mask and laid me out, bare and vulnerable. "I've spent my whole life building a fortress and defending myself from being hurt again."

"Listen to me, Sin," Jade whispered. "Every relationship is different, and you can't carry your past issues into the future. Keep the ex baggage where it's meant to be—in the damn past."

I remained silent.

"If you don't open yourself up and trust him, your relationship will go nowhere. And without trust, you're putting a dead end on a future partnership. Now pull on your big-girl panties and be brave and open. Let him in."

I dashed away the tears rolling down my cheeks. That was exactly what I was afraid of doing. "I hate that I'm so fucked up in the head."

"You're not fucked up. We're both emotionally challenged, but I think it's time for a change."

"Jade, I've only known one good man in my entire life, and that was my dad. He was way more man than Grace deserved."

My upper lip curled in disdain. Even though Grace was now dead, she'd caused a hell of a lot of emotional damage while she was alive. I hoped her soul could find the peace she needed.

I walked over to the railing, staring down at the bustling city below. "I don't think I'm built for the level of commitment that a relationship takes."

Jade sighed. "I think that's what we've been telling ourselves for so long that we actually believe it. This much I know. Someday, I want kids and stability. Don't you?"

My mouth went dry. For the first time in my life, I was thinking about a future with children... with Core. "Maybe. I'm just so afraid that I'll be a cruel monster like Grace. I would never want to do that to a child. So I decided a long time ago that I didn't want children."

My life growing up had been an emotional roller coaster, all due to Grace. Dad had done the best he could to shield me from her verbal and emotional abuse, but still, it just hadn't been enough.

"Grace was a bitch. You're nothing like her."

"I hope not." My pulse sped up. "She never loved me or my dad, and it changed us for the worse. We both morphed into people who lived just to please her—hoping if we changed, if we could be every-thing she wanted, she would love us. It took me years to learn that loving myself was good enough."

"Loving yourself is important, but having the right man to love you for who you are is important, too. And a partnership of equals? That's icing on the fucking cake." Jade paused. "Just think about it, okay?"

"I will." I bit my lower lip, changing subjects. "I spoke to your mom today. She's holding up well. But how about you?"

"Stressed about being here while she's being chased by the media every day. But she's right; staying in New Zealand is best until all this shit dies down. That said, it helps that Cate is getting the brunt of the bad press and not Mom. Did you watch that freak show she orches-trated on Monday?"

Cate had called a press conference, tearfully announcing she'd called off her engagement to Bigsby because, according to her, "Like the good citizens of New York, I, too, was duped by the former mayoral candidate."

I snickered. "Hell yes, I watched it. In typical Cate, over-the-top, diva fashion, she gave a television performance worthy of an Emmy."

Jade laughed. "I guess I'm not the only actress in the family. Well, enough of my family drama. It's late… and you need to wrangle yourself a bad boy."

"Damn right I do. I'll call you later."

"Hopefully with good news that you and Core fucked it out, and there's a happily ever after," Jade replied. "Call me and let me know either way."

I ended the call, letting out a sigh of despair.

Jade was right. I wanted—no, I *needed* more with Core than sex. Deep down, I was a woman who wanted to be cherished and cared for. And given a chance, Core wanted to do both. Even though I knew he wanted more from me, from us, together we were facing a whole new set of challenges.

Can I trust him after he's manipulated me? The answer was unclear, and the only way I could find out if he was a man of his word was to break down the walls I'd built around my heart, allowing him to get close.

But I was afraid of letting Core into my life.

I was afraid of letting him see me weak and vulnerable.

I was afraid of getting attached and then losing him.

I was just so afraid of getting hurt. I knew it was going to happen—with Core or with someone else—but I was still terrified.

He'd wanted a chance to redeem himself in my eyes—a do-over.

Would it be so bad if I just gave it to him? Especially when he had the courage to ask for forgiveness?

I was far from perfect, and I damn sure couldn't promise him that I wouldn't make mistakes. All I knew was that any man I let into my life would have to have the strength to forgive me when I said I was sorry.

Not only that, but he would also have to have the ability to move forward without holding a grudge, leaving the past in the past.

In the same vein, the man I was with would have to be courageous enough to ask for forgiveness. Given that I knew how hard that shit was to do, I would respect him even more when he was able to admit his blunders—like Core had.

My pulse raced at the thought of belonging to him, and deep down, I wanted him. I walked into the penthouse.

Shit. Am I really doing this?

What would my reaction be if he changed his mind and he wasn't interested in a relationship with me anymore? Relief? Hurt? Anger? All three? The fucked-up part is I have no damn clue which of the three I'd feel.

I'd either have the pain of opening up and maybe getting hurt or have the pain of shutting down and being alone. There was no pain-free choice.

No one was in the living room, so I walked farther into the apartment, moving toward two male voices. One was distinctly Core's, and the other sounded like Ram. I hesitated outside Core's office, shamelessly eavesdropping on their conversation inside.

"Ram, the clock is ticking," Core stated. "And we have to get our shit together for our meeting with Bigsby today. Did you scan the perimeter of our meeting location with the drone?"

Ram shot back, "Of course we did, Core. This is not my first mission. I know what the hell I'm doing."

"I just want to be sure we're ready for anything during our meeting. I don't want any surprises," Core grumbled.

A shiver ran down my spine. *What if things go wrong at their meeting with Bigsby?*

"We'll be ready. Our game plan is airtight. Once you hand over the ledger and recording to Bigsby, our sniper will pick him off, and then our cleaning crew will take care of the body. Kevin will be handling the surveillance remotely. Rocco and Max will be sniper A and B. And I'll have your back on the ground during the exchange." Ram paused. "That means we won't have anyone to guard Sin during our meeting. What are you going to do about her security?"

I frowned at the mention of my name.

"This penthouse is an impenetrable fortress, but I've asked Zuri to stay with Sin just in case shit goes south at the exchange."

"Bro? You actually think Sin will just sit here twiddling her thumbs and wait for you to get back?" Ram argued.

I snickered under my breath. Ram was damn right. There was no way I was sitting out this faceoff.

"If I have to handcuff her ass to the bed, then that's exactly what she'll do. I can't risk putting her in even more danger." Core's voice got louder.

"Core, calm the fuck down."

"Ram, I can't risk losing her. My mother and Maya are gone because I couldn't protect them. I'll be damned if I lose another woman I care about."

Butterflies fluttered in my stomach. Core really cared about me. Then it dawned on me just how much I cared about him… so much that I'd risk my heart just to have him in my world.

"Core, bro, you're not going to lose her. Besides, from what Max told me about how she handled herself with Jaxon, she's one tough chick."

I smiled at Ram's words. He was right; I was tough, but I knew I wasn't invincible. Jaxon had taught me that shit… more than once.

"She got lucky. That fucker could have hurt her."

"No. Not lucky. She's brave, Core. And now she knows enough about you and our world to understand exactly what she's getting involved with."

Between how efficiently he'd handled the cleanup of the Jaxon incident and what I suspected he'd done to Bigsby's lackey, I knew exactly the type of man Core was. He took care of his own, no matter what it required. And that was the kind of loyalty and protectiveness I knew firsthand, given my feelings toward everyone in my inner circle. My friends had my back, and I had theirs, no matter what.

"Yeah. But what's fucking with my head is that she didn't know the truth when she got involved with me," Core snapped. "Maybe if she did, she would have walked away from me." He paused. "Shit. All I can think about right now is that maybe she should have hightailed her ass away from me a long time ago. If she had, then her life wouldn't be in fucking jeopardy right now."

My heart thudded with joy. Core was truly bothered by the fact that he hadn't been upfront with me from the beginning. The man had a conscience when it came to me and the damage he'd done.

But Core was right. Maybe if I had common sense, I would have walked away from him, but I wouldn't because I was just as fucked up in the head as he was. I wanted Core, and I wasn't walking away from him, not anymore. I'd made up my mind to see this thing with him through before I walked toward his office. But now, after I'd overheard his conversation with Ram, I was here to stay by his side for as long as our relationship lasted.

I stormed into Core's office. Ram stared at me while Core's eyes narrowed at my presence.

"Core…" I started and then stopped when something on the television flashed, catching my eye. "Do you see that?" I pointed to the television. "The news ticker on the TV says there's breaking news on Bigsby Calhoune. Can you turn up the sound on the television?"

The three of us stood before the flat-screen with our eyes fixed on the news anchor.

"We have breaking news," the anchor said. "New York mayoral candidate Bigsby Calhoune has been charged in one of the nation's largest sex trafficking rings." The hypnotic, repetitious evenness of her voice continued. "Federal authorities just announced charges against Calhoune and forty-three others in a conspiracy that allegedly trafficked hundreds of women throughout the United States. Now let's go to Anne, who's on location outside of Calhoune's campaign office. Anne, any sign of Mr. Calhoune?"

Anne smiled with excited eyes. "No. But we've just gotten word that Bigsby Calhoune is a fugitive and on the run. The former mayoral candidate is now on the Most Wanted list. Back to you, Jessica."

Core turned off the television and stared at Ram. "Well, we already knew the Feds were going to make this announcement, but now we have the news sniffing around for a scoop on Bigsby. So this is bound to turn into a media free-for-all. We know that Bigsby is dead set on getting back the ledger and recordings, so he'll show up for our meeting today. We just have to be ready to take him down. No errors."

Ram nodded. "Got it. I need to catch a couple hours of sleep. I'm going to bed. I'll see you both in a few hours." He strode out of the room.

Core eyed me. "What are you doing up?" He leaned against his desk, crossing his beefy arms.

I locked eyes with him. "I couldn't sleep. But that doesn't matter now. I heard your conversation with Ram about Bigsby."

"Eavesdropping, huh?" Amusement danced in his eyes.

I threw my arms up in the air. "Of course. I'm not going to lie about it. There's no shame in my game. I'm nosy." I invaded his space, giving him a peevish look. "So what?"

"So now that you know what's going on"—he gently grabbed my face—"take your sexy ass to bed and let me handle this shit," he stated flatly before his hands fell away.

I cupped his cheek. "Baby, I don't take orders. You should know this by now." I tapped his face hard before letting my hand drop. "But since I like you so much, I'm going to be clear so we don't have these communication issues again. I don't like *you woman, me man* caveman shit. Now I'm not asking you to get all poetic while communicating with me, but I—"

Core's eyebrows drew together. "Good, because that shit isn't happening."

I blew out a breath. *Patience, Sin.*

My gorgeous lover was going to take more work than I'd envisioned, but I was up to the job.

"Like I was saying before I was rudely interrupted…" I pursed my lips. "I don't expect you to be poetic. Shit, you're incapable of not grunting every other word."

He grunted.

I shook my head in dismay. "But I do expect you not to bark orders at me. I'm your equal, and I expect to be treated as such. Now, I'm capable of being reasonable, contrary to your belief."

He snorted.

I scowled. "So if you think I'm in fucking danger, communicate with me in a way that won't make me want to smother you in your sleep."

The vein along his jaw pulsed. "Do you even get that I'm worried about Bigsby trying to hurt you? Sin, you mean the world to me." He fiercely looked at me, his words barely above a whisper. "I wouldn't survive losing you." His own admission appeared to surprise him.

The tender affection in his words and in his eyes washed over me, making me feel cherished and desired. I hadn't realized until now that I'd needed to hear him say how much he wanted me.

He glanced at me with pained eyes. "So if you're expecting me to apologize for wanting to protect you, that's not going to happen."

I sighed, grabbing his hand, kissing his fingers one by one. "I get it, but you don't have to be so fucking abrasive about it. That's all I'm saying, Core."

"I'll work on my delivery," he answered. "But you're not going to the meeting."

"I'm going, Core. We're partners, remember? In business and…" I paused. There was a flutter in my belly. I was nervous about uttering my next words, but I had to push myself not to play it safe… to believe that everything would be all right… that he wouldn't make me regret giving him all of me—heart and soul. "Now in life. Fifty-fifty. And I'm not going anywhere, McKay." I stared at him. "I'm yours, mind, body, and soul."

He fisted his hand into my hair at the nape of my neck—a sign of his possession. "Sin, you don't know what you're saying."

"The hell I don't." My heart raced, bracing for the impact of telling him the truth. I bit my bottom lip. "I'm a hard woman, Core. What man will take the risk of loving me?"

"Me. I know who you are, Sin. You hide yourself with men who have no chance in hell of getting your heart or loving you. Give us a chance. Let me in."

I licked my dry lips. "I've spent my life hiding from relationships so I could feel safe. But I don't want to feel safe anymore. I want more with you. But I'll walk the fuck away from you, from us, if you ever lie to me again."

He released my hair. "I never lied to you, Sin—"

I held up a hand. "If you ever lie to me or are deceptive in any way, I'm gone. The only way this can work is if you go all in with me, because I fucking love myself too much to accept anything else. And even though you're a pain in the ass and way too cocky, I think every bit of the work our relationship is going to take is worthwhile."

"I belong to you, mind, body, and soul. And now that you're mine,

I'm never letting go." He kissed my jaw, down the column of my throat, and to my collarbone. There was more tenderness, passion, and meaning in those precious, gentle kisses, and they claimed me like no words ever could.

"Good, because I've decided to keep your crazy ass." I kissed him hard.

"Really? Decided? You had no choice, woman. Now let's get the formalities out of the way. You belong to me and no other... and I belong to you."

I frowned. "You'd better. I'm selfish, and I don't share."

"There's no other woman for me. I'm a mean SOB sometimes, but you'll deal like I can deal with your crazier-than-hell attitude."

I grinned. "Oh, fuck off, McKay. I don't have an attitude. I'm Brooklyn sassy."

He arched a brow.

"Well, I am." I ran my tongue over his firm lips.

I had let go of the terror. He was the man for me, the man who destroyed the fear.

"And for the record, I accept everything you're offering, McKay." I flattened my hand on his stomach. "There's no other man like you. I know this. And I'm crazy turned on right now." I ran my palm along his muscular thigh.

He regarded me with half-open eyes. "Like how turned on?" he demanded with a rasping voice.

I desperately wanted him. I stared at him, wondering how the hell this shit happened.

"Like on-my-knees hot," I blurted out without blinking. There was no shame in my game. I asked for what I wanted always. And I wanted him... now. I ran a hand over his crotch and winked. "Let the fucking commence. And I plan on keeping you busy until it's time to meet Bigsby."

He took my mouth with a kiss that sent me barreling into another world. His kiss left me with no doubt of his dominance as he explored my mouth with a thoroughness that rendered me breathless. His tongue tangled with mine, leading me in an erotic, sexy dance that made my senses reel.

I followed where he led with every stroke of his tongue on mine. I felt the power of his possessive seduction in every cell of my body.

Core broke off our kiss before standing, and in one sinuous motion, he lifted me and placed me on the edge of his desk.

I licked my bottom lip with anticipation as he shoved up the hem of my dress, grabbed my thighs, and pushed them wide open. I shivered deliciously as cold air brushed against my womanhood before he slid a hand between my legs, pinching my clit.

My lips parted. "Yes. Harder," I whispered.

He squeezed my thigh hard and then soothingly rubbed it.

"Ready to fuck, McKay?" I licked his lips and unzipped his pants, grabbing his cock. "Impressive." I bit his lower lip. "I want you —now."

The sultriness of the air skimmed across my skin. All the fun and games were over. This was the truth. There was no compromising.

"I'm never letting you go," he growled.

I reached up, digging my fingers into his hair, scratching my nails across his scalp.

He carried on. "This will never work until you trust me, giving me your submission, surrendering your heart, body, and soul, as I am willing to do for you. Trust is the only thing that can keep us together. Trust that you accept the man I am. And trust my acceptance of the woman you keep hidden."

I calmed my breathing. He'd stripped away my mask, leaving me bare, vulnerable, and raw. For the first time in my life, I would have a protective, caring man who would cherish me for as long as I allowed it. And I was pretty sure I wanted forever.

"And what if the woman you think I am isn't there?" I paused. "I'm more than what you see."

"That's what I'm counting on. Nothing is perfect. I'm far from it, but I'm half the man without you." He grabbed my face between his callused hands. "On your knees, darling. Now." He tilted his head. "Submit to me." His voice was hard and unyielding.

"Submission," I whispered as if rolling the word over my tongue like a fine wine. "And do you think you've earned my submission?"

"Make no mistake about it." He narrowed his eyes. "I'm wild and ruthless, and I don't give a shit about anything but what belongs to me. You."

After spending a lifetime of overthinking everything in my life, it was freeing to put my trust in his hands.

He gripped my hair, tilting my head back. I knew what he wanted now. It wasn't about sex… not anymore. It was about sharing a piece of me I had long hidden away, a part of me that needed nurturing, love, and acceptance. I knew he wouldn't push or force. He would wait for me to submit—not because it was what he wanted, but because it was what I wanted to give. That piece of me reserved and owned only by him.

I angled my head in submission. His body tensed. I wrapped my hands around his penis and squeezed hard.

He slightly stepped back, intently watching me. There was no need for words. He knew I was meeting him halfway. I slid off the desk and then started to get on my knees before him. He stopped me by grabbing the back of my neck, pulling hard on my hair, ushering me to stand.

"I want you." I trailed my fingers over his chest.

With our eyes locked, he asked gruffly, "Are you mine to enjoy… to taste… to explore?"

I couldn't look away from the stark need in his eyes. "Yes. Always."

Core's smile stole my breath.

"Good." Effortlessly, he nudged my back down onto the desk, pushing my knee-length slip dress up around my waist.

"Well… I thought we'd finish this in the bedroom. But I'm down for—" I swallowed the rest of my words.

Quickly, he removed my panties, tossing them aside.

He lightly ran a finger down my body, making every place he touched quiver.

"I want your sweet pussy," he demanded.

I watched, transfixed, as Core settled himself between my thighs. The first swipe of his tongue on my slit had me panting, my hips arching, before he held me down with one hand on my stomach. He dipped his tongue into my pussy, lapping at me, his slow, torturous caresses driving me insane.

"Please, Core. Faster." I needed more.

He knew just where and how to touch me.

He took his time and thoroughly explored my slit, his tongue caressing my folds before slipping into me again. He circled my clit with an unhurried precision that made me scream from frustration. Using my arms, I tried to rock, but Core slid his arms under my thighs, one hand pressing down on my abdomen, keeping me from moving, while his other hand cupped a breast, teasing my nipple.

With my thighs over his shoulders and his face buried between them, I couldn't move while he showed me no damn mercy as his tongue flicked my swollen nub until I screamed, "Oh my fucking God."

His warm breath blew over the throbbing bundle of nerves and set off another wave of sizzling heat. His long strokes had me writhing, my fingers clawing the desk. He thrust two fingers into my trembling channel, pumping me, drawing out my climax. My eyes rolled to the back of my head, and I swore I saw dancing spots. I panted, drawing ragged breaths—the experience more intense because I'd given myself to him fully. Mercifully, he relented, pulling away, his eyes blazing with wildness.

I was greedy for more. *Holy hell, I can't even form a coherent thought.*

"Fuck me," I demanded.

He growled, his expression savage. "I'll give you five minutes to get into my bedroom." He ran a callused thumb over my bottom lip. "And then you'll show me all the things your sexy mouth and sinful body promise."

He lifted me off the desk, securely holding me as my legs wobbled, my body a shuddering mass of jelly.

He softly kissed me on the lips. "You okay, darling? You look a little... dazed."

"Not dazed. Fucking amazed. Believe me; that's not easy to do." I smirked while cupping his hard cock. "McKay, we are going to do great things together." I wanted him right now.

He slapped my ass. "Off you go, vixen."

"Whatever you want, McKay." I squeezed his girth, smiling with satisfaction when he hissed. "I'll be waiting, McKay," I taunted before turning on my heel and walking away. I basked in the heat of his gaze as he stared at me all the way out of the office.

I padded through the penthouse and then up the stairs that led to his bedroom. Once inside, my heart thumped as I perched on the edge of his king-size bed.

Core stormed into the room. "Strip," he ordered as he walked over to the chair positioned next to the bed. He sat on that chair, facing me. He looked hard, sexy, and in control.

I flipped my hair. "Why, Core, you've read my mind. I'd love to strip." *Hell, I am adventurous.* It didn't hurt that I'd taken a few pole dancing classes with Jade for fun.

I swayed over to him.

"Strip. I want to see you take off your dress while I watch, thinking about all the dirty things I'm going to do to that sexy body of yours."

The thought of stripping before him ramped up my adrenaline, making me giddy with lust. I circled his chair, giving him my best smoldering gaze while trailing my fingers along his neck.

As I passed behind him, I leaned over, brushing my breasts against his back, whispering, "When I first met you, I wanted you to fuck me. Now I'm greedy. I want more. Now I want you to love me." I ran my tongue along his ear, trailing it across his neck.

He reached up, grabbing the back of my hair, and said in the sexiest voice I'd ever heard, "Loving a woman like you, who's so beautiful inside and out, won't be difficult."

I blinked back the tears of joy. "Damn. You're a romantic. Who would have thought?"

He shrugged. "Not romantic. Realistic. If I wanted sex, I could get it anywhere, and that gets real empty. But finding that… connection we have, well, that's priceless."

I twirled around him, stopping in front of him and bending over so he could peek down my dress. I spun around, placing one foot on the bed, bending over from the waist, practically putting my ass in his face. "Do you want to touch it, baby?" My breath hitched as I felt his fingers run along my ass seam.

"You have the sexiest ass I've ever seen. I can't wait to take you from behind."

I tauntingly wiggled my ass. "You sure you know what to do with all this ass?"

"Tease."

He slapped my ass cheek so hard that I knew I would have a handprint. I moaned when the delicious zing went straight to my cunt. He rubbed his hand over the cheek, soothing the pain of the sting.

I spun around, walking over to him. "Did I displease you, McKay?" I asked with a flirtatious smile.

"There's nothing your sexy body could do to displease me... besides disobey." He sternly looked at me. "Continue to strip."

"What if I don't? Will you punish me?"

Please say yes! Punish me, McKay.

"Take the dress off," Core demanded in a hard voice.

I inched the straps off. There was something so intimate and hot as I stared into his eyes while removing my dress, letting it drop at my feet. "Like this?"

He grinned, his teeth flashing white. "Just like that, darling."

Tweaking my nipples to make them erect, I asked him, "Do you like it when my nipples are hard?" I walked toward him, swinging my foot up onto his shoulder, stroking my womanhood.

"Shit," he groaned. "I didn't realize you were that limber."

I leaned in, licking the shell of his ear. "If only you knew how limber," I whispered.

"If you kiss my neck, it's done. We're fucking," he hissed.

Pushing back, I straddled one of his legs, lowering myself onto it, and then briefly rubbed my crotch against his thigh, making sure to press on his hard cock, giving him a lap dance. "If you like, you can touch it, baby."

"To hell with taking it slow. I need my cock lodged so deep into your pussy you can taste it in the back of your throat," he barked in a voice that was deep and smooth as he sprang up from the chair.

"Do your worst, baby." Instinctively, I wrapped my legs around his lean waist, digging my heels into his ass as he effortlessly carried me over to the bed and lowered me onto it.

His firm lips curved a little into a smile. He stroked my hair. "Ready to be tied, darling?"

"Yes," I whispered.

His eyes never left mine as he picked up my hands and lifted them toward the head of the bed, wrapping a soft strap around them.

Excitement bubbled up as he moved to lie beside me. He cupped my face in one huge hand, forcing me to meet his sensual gaze. "Do you trust me to take care of you?"

I nodded. "Yes. Always."

He brushed a tender kiss across my lips and nuzzled my temple.

I lay there, hands tied over my head, staring up at him. I remained as still as possible as the sexual tension heightened to a level that made it nearly impossible to breathe.

He stripped naked. His skin was a golden tan, tight over the bulging muscles beneath. He was without a doubt the sexiest man I'd ever seen… and damn, he was all mine.

I dropped my eyes lower. His huge erection was thick, hard, and jutting toward me. He joined me on the bed. He caressed my cheek before his tongue took full possession, darting in and out of my mouth.

"So beautiful," he murmured with approval.

I could hear his heart beating in a steady rhythm as he slid down. His fingers traced over my tattoo—*Love all. Trust few. Do wrong to none*—written horizontally from my abdomen to my back. He pressed his mouth against my stomach, nibbling and kissing until all I wanted to do was burst into flames.

He knelt between my legs, hungrily looking at me. He pushed my leg out a little. He cupped my pussy. "You know how I want you. Now assume the position, Sinful."

I brought my knees up to my stomach.

"Spread your legs, darling."

I did it without hesitation, eagerly following him into the world of decadent pleasure he'd created for me.

He gazed straight into my eyes while sliding his fingers between the wet folds of my heat. "Do you know what it does to me to see you this way?" Cupping a breast, he stroked the underside before tapping my nipple.

I wanted him more than I'd ever wanted anything, wanted his cock deep inside me.

I wanted his eyes on mine as he took me.

I arched up, wiggling closer as he slipped his fingers inside. His thumb circled and played with my clit.

"This pussy is all mine."

I was dying for more even though I was on the edge of my first orgasm. As I stared at him, my mind went numb. I needed more, but I was helpless.

He stroked my heat. I shivered, on the verge of exploding. I knew he had no intention of pushing me over the edge until I said what he needed to hear.

"Please," I whispered. "I just… Please… lick me."

"Was that so hard, darling?"

His huge hands curled around my thighs, spreading me wider, and his tongue thrust into my heat. That one lick sent me spiraling over the edge, and I screamed his name like a prayer.

He pulled his head back and watched me as his fingers continued to stretch me. "Scream louder, darling."

I was writhing and panting as his fingers thrust harder. I moaned louder when his finger found my clit again and mercilessly played with it.

I screamed and came again, feeling light-headed from the passion.

I am his.

I belong to him… and him to me.

"Core." I breathed his name and whimpered, all the fight going out of me.

As if it were the sign he'd been waiting for, he lifted his head, his smile gentle. "Nothing is sweeter than my strong woman's surrender."

I caught my breath. Core was right above me, his weight on his knees between my thighs. He directed his condom-sheathed cock into position, smoothly slipping in, looking at me with burning possession all over his face.

"So tight," he whispered.

I struggled to breathe as his cock stretched me.

He gave me a slow smile. "I've never wanted anyone more than I want you right now," he grunted, fully seated with his balls bumping against my ass.

The tender affection in his words and in his eyes washed over me, making me feel cherished and desired.

He kissed my lips, my jaw, and my eyes. I basked in his tenderness and love. He pulled out and sank back in, hitting my G-spot with precision.

My legs wrapped around his waist as he continued to stroke me just right, making my legs quiver. My pussy sucked him in farther as he pumped deeper. I tilted my hips forward, and he adjusted his movements so with each stroke, he brushed deliciously against my clit.

The deeper he pumped, the more I wanted him.

My head snapped back as he slid in and out. I writhed beneath him, meeting him thrust for thrust. I was trembling, moaning low and deep. He stilled my hips so I felt every inch of his pulsing cock.

He swooped down, taking a nipple into his mouth. He lifted his head, his eyes boring into mine. "Take me, Sin. All of me."

Instinctively, I knew that he meant more than just taking his cock, that he was asking me to take him the way he was—flawed and dominant.

Tears pricked my eyelids, and I wished my hands weren't tied so I could caress him.

I sucked in a breath as he withdrew and plunged deep again.

"I accept everything that you are," I declared.

"From you… I'll accept nothing less." Core's dark eyes raked over me. "It's going to last all morning, darling. No rushing," he growled in my ear as he released my arms from the bonds.

Dropping my head on his shoulder, I felt so connected to him.

Wrapping my arms around his wide shoulders, nails digging into him like a wild woman, I buried my face in his neck and breathed deeply, the scent of him somehow reassuring me. He continued pumping, hard and controlled. I was going insane from the heat building.

My breathing was fast and shallow with periods of whimpers intermixed. "Please… harder." I grabbed his head, pulling him closer, biting his lower lip. "Please?"

He let himself go, moving faster, pushing me into another orgasm. Arching, I screamed as my pussy clenched around him, my body collapsing right after, worn out and sweaty.

His face was harsh and controlled as he pulled himself from my pussy, flipping me over onto my belly. He pulled me up onto my knees. I moaned when he kissed my neck and shoulders and then rained kisses along my spine.

Nudging me forward onto my hands, he gripped my waist with his strong hands as his cock smoothly thrust into me. I cried out with pleasure when his one hand gripped my hair and the other wrapped around my waist.

His body rocked into me. The slickness of our bodies was in perfect synchrony. I gripped the sheets as he reared back and pushed forward with every inch of him sheathed inside me.

My body shook and my legs quivered as my core pulsed, racing toward blissful release as he thrust faster.

"Sin, you're mine to cherish, love, and protect." His thrusts grew stronger as his body slapped against mine.

I clenched the sheets as I rocked back into his body. My body burned for sweet release. A strangled shout escaped his lips before I came so hard that I screamed his name at the top of my lungs. My inner muscles contracted, milking him. He roared as both of us crested.

He kissed me on my shoulder before pulling me up farther onto the bed. Clutching me against his body, he kissed me, and with eyes closed, I kissed him back.

I couldn't stop trembling. I wanted to laugh. I wanted to cry. I wanted to be held in his arms this way forever.

There is no going back… not that I want to.

I knew with every fiber in my body that this man would love me hard and cherish me until his last breath.

I sighed, content, as we held on to each other, lips melding over and over as the tremors passed.

"So I guess you're stuck with me, McKay," I sassed, letting out a little laugh.

He nuzzled my neck. "I wouldn't have it any other way," he quipped, nibbling on my ear.

CHAPTER 16
CORE

I stepped off the elevator with Sin by my side, and we stormed down the hallway leading to my war room.

I'd tried everything in my power to make Sin change her mind about going to my meeting with Bigsby, but she was determined to come with me tonight.

I flattened my lips. Heat flushed through my body.

Why the hell does she have to be so fucking stubborn?

When it came to Sin, my protective instincts were on high alert, and all I wanted to do was lock her ass up in my penthouse, keeping her safe until I could take care of Bigsby.

And even when I'd pointed out to her—several times—that Grace's recent death was a perfect example that Bigsby had no qualms about killing anyone he deemed disposable, she'd calmly rebutted, "Core, I have a stake in this shit. Bigsby ruined my damn life. Just like you. I need closure. I'm coming with you. End of story."

She was right about needing closure, but I would get it for both of us. She didn't need to be there to get it. But when I had seen the damn determination in her eyes, I had known she wouldn't just sit around at my place, waiting for the end of the Bigsby saga. Like me, she needed to witness the job being done. And if I'd left her behind, denying her that right, she'd only resent me for it... and a pissed-off Sin was not what I wanted to deal with when I got home tonight. So my reluctant concession was agreeing to her request. I wanted no doubt in her mind that she was my partner in every way.

But what if Sin gets hurt... or killed, despite my best efforts to protect her?

I could lose her just like I lost Mom, Maya, and my child. Shit. If anything happened to Sin, it would literally break me.

I couldn't remember the last time I'd wanted someone—not even Maya—with the intensity I felt for Sin. Now the thought of living a life without her, in solitude, filled me with dread.

I would kill for her, live for her, do anything I needed to protect her.

I clenched and unclenched my hands by my sides as I took a deep breath. Somehow, I'd have to control my primal instinct to wrap her ass up in bubble wrap, protecting her from the hard-core shit that was about to go down in a couple of hours. And knowing Bigsby's sordid history of violence, there was no doubt in my mind that I was walking into a trap, which we'd planned for with our own counterattack strategy. But all of the damn planning in the world couldn't account for every possible scenario, which also meant there was a real possibility of Sin getting hurt. Again, I'd explained that to her several times but to no avail. She still wanted in.

Fuck my life.

I sighed heavily.

She grabbed my hand. "Core, stop worrying. It will be all right." She finished with a squeeze of my fingers before releasing them.

I growled menacingly, incensed that she was putting herself in unnecessary danger. "This is utter bullshit!" The words were out of my mouth before I could stop myself. "I can't focus on this mission and you at the same time." I was mad as hell, and it was making me act out emotionally instead of logically.

She stopped in her tracks, turning to stand in front of me. "Then don't." She countered. "I can take care of myself. Focus on taking down Bigsby."

"That shit is easier said than done."

"Core"—she reached up, touching a hand to my chest—"we're

going to be all right. Everything I need is standing in front of me. Through the ups and downs, baby, I'm going to stick around." Leaning up, she pressed her lips against mine.

Damn, I never want to let this woman go.

I leaned into her body, sucking her tongue into my mouth. The nagging fear of losing her like Maya threatened to drown me. Her tongue slid around the tip of mine and then rubbed under it. I gave her one last swipe of my tongue before I retreated, bit her lower lip, and then pulled my mouth away from her, keeping my hands on her face. I inhaled deeply, smelling her sweet scent lingering all over me.

"I promise we will be all right," she insisted. "Now let's go."

I released her, reluctantly stepping back.

She grabbed my hand, and we continued toward my war room.

I shook my head to clear my mind. I needed to focus. The sooner we could launch our attack on Bigsby, the sooner I could get Sin back to my penthouse, safe and sound.

We stepped into the war room, and I glanced around, taking stock of my team. Ram, Max, Rocco, and Kevin were gathered around a mini mockup of the warehouse and the surrounding area. Zuri was walking around the room with her cell pressed against her ear.

Sin assessed the team. "Wow. You guys are not fucking around. Y'all are ready for war."

And we were, including Zuri. They were geared up for battle in our standard uniform—black tactical clothing with a sidearm attached to their legs and black combat boots.

The guys' bodies tensed with their eyes locked on Sin.

And here we go…

I ran a hand through my hair, hoping I didn't look as stressed out as I was feeling.

Before I'd left the penthouse, I'd told my team that Sin was coming with us. They weren't happy about the idea—just like me—but we'd quickly adjusted our strategy to factor in her presence, protecting her at all costs.

Zuri ended her call, striding over to Sin and pulling her aside. Their conversation was animated but in low tones.

Shifting my attention, I stared at the myriad of monitors that hummed with energy. Pacing back and forth, I narrowed my eyes on the streaming aerial images of the warehouse area where we were scheduled to meet Bigsby tonight.

In my peripheral vision, I saw Sin sway to the center of the room with Zuri trailing behind her.

"Let's clear the air, shall we?" Sin started.

Everyone around her—except Zuri and me—stiffened, and an uncomfortable hush fell over the room.

"From the look on everyone's faces"—she glared pointedly at Kevin, Ram, Rocco, and Max—"I can tell no one is happy I'm going with you tonight."

"I am." Zuri raised her hand like she was in school.

Sin smirked. "Besides you, Zuri."

Zuri air-high-fived her. "I've got your back, girl."

"Now," Sin replied.

"What?" Zuri pouted. "But you just said that you and I were cool… and we're starting with a clean slate as of tonight."

Sin pursed her lips. "We are, but I want everyone in this damn room to be absolutely clear that there will be no more lies or omitting info, and there will be no putting Baby"—she pointed to herself—"in the damn corner. I'm all in with Core and everything that shit entails."

She didn't even flinch under their scrutiny; she boldly met their hard stares. And it occurred to me that it was very possible I'd found someone who could outstare all of us. Sin was a force to be reckoned with, and she was obviously not going to take any shit from my team.

"Preach, sista," Zuri chirped, throwing her hands up like she was in church.

Kevin, Ram, Rocco, and Max frowned at Zuri.

Ram snorted, crossing his arms over his chest. "Just what we need… another member of the I Heart Sin Club."

Zuri rolled her eyes at him before retorting, "Whatever."

Sin turned to Zuri. "I'm loving your support, but you're stealing the thunder from my epic vagina monologue. So hit the mute button." She ended with a smile, eyes glimmering.

Zuri gave her a wide grin with a thumbs-up.

Sin eyed my men. "Anyway, like I was just saying… You might not be thrilled that I'm coming along." She jammed a hand on her curvy hip. "But I am, so just suck it up."

I smiled, feeling some of the tension leave me. *Damn, I loved her feistiness.*

Max finally did something other than scowl; a faint smile brushed his lips. "Well, look at that… Sweet cheeks ain't afraid of the big, bad alphas."

Ram quipped, "She has balls of steel for sure." He waggled his eyebrows. "I like that."

Kevin tilted his head as he considered her. His expression clearly relayed his conclusion about Sin. She was a science experiment gone wrong.

A muscle twitched beneath Rocco's left eye. He was annoyed, but he remained silent.

Sin continued. "Look, I'm not planning on getting in the way or doing something stupid like pretend I'm Lara Croft or some shit." She glanced around. "But I have a right to be at that meeting, given what Bigsby has done to my family and me. I have to be there to see him get his due justice. So just tell me what you need me to do, and I'll do it, no questions asked. But I'm going with my man." She nodded at me.

The corners of my lips lifted into a smile.

Damn, how fucking lucky am I to have Sin, who is everything I need and a force to be reckoned with?

Now all I could think about was fucking her so hard she would taste my cock in the back of her throat.

I was proud of her for not cowering in a room full of alpha personalities. I loved it. She was the special woman in my life and here to stay, so it was important for her to assert her place, by my side as alpha female, among the team. Especially since she'd be seeing them a lot because, despite the fact that each team member had their own luxury apartment, it never failed that command central was always at my penthouse. I didn't know how, but over the years, our living quarters had turned into a quasi fraternity house with the one elevator giving us unlimited access to each other's space. Our living situation worked because none of us had a significant other in our lives—until me.

Kevin replied, "We've already got your security covered, Sin. You'll be with Zuri and me in the surveillance van." His lips kinked into a smile.

"Got it," Sin replied. "And nice to finally put a face to the voice, Kevin." Her lips twisted into a smirk.

Kevin and Sin had interacted in the past when he contacted her—at my request—about taking care of all her business financial matters, including providing the money to continue her line.

"So I've met the rest of you." Sin confirmed. She turned to stare at Ram. "And we've met twice. The first time at Core's office. The second when you were Core's sidekick at the gala."

Ram retorted, "You forgot to add *sexy* before sidekick." He gave her a salacious smile.

"Cocky much?" Sin countered with an arched brow.

"Just saying… the ladies love me," Ram answered. A smile spread over his face, brightening his eyes and his voice.

Zuri rolled her eyes heavenward. "So says the king of dirty hook-ups." She pointed at Ram. "He's our resident man-whore."

"I'm just spreading love." Ram countered with a suggestive pelvic thrust.

Kevin mumbled, "I hope that's all you're spreading."

Ram punched him in the shoulder. "Shut the fuck up."

Sin snorted. "Anyhoo, moving on… So Max and Rocco." Tilting her head in quiet consideration, she studied them. "We first met at Bigsby's fundraiser gala."

Max answered, "Where you threatened to kick our ass… which was the single most thrilling moment of that whole damn boring night."

"What can I say? I'm a very bad girl." Sin batted her eyelashes, almost comically. "But that will teach you not to fuck with a woman not afraid to street fight in a couture dress and stilettos." Sin countered, ending with a grin at Rocco.

Rocco scowled before his muscular forearms crossed in front of him while he stared pointedly at Sin.

Sin quirked a brow in his direction. "Well… ain't you the chatty one?"

Rocco grunted before running a hand over his blond five-o'clock shadow.

"Lovely… another one who loves to grunt like a caveman." She shot me a look.

I felt my mouth twitch into a smile. "Yep. And for fun, my team and I like to knock stones together to make fire."

Sighing in exasperation, Sin perked her lips into a half smile. "Smartass."

"I don't have time for this shit," Rocco muttered before making his way over to the monitors.

Zuri jabbed a finger at Rocco. "See? He talks."

"Uh-huh," Sin replied with an eye roll. "Anyway, now that we're all cool with shit, I'll let you all do your mission prep thingy." She took a seat next to Kevin, who seemed to considerably warm up to her when she pointed at his screen, saying, "Wow! Cool graphics."

With eyes spanning the team, I asked, "What's been done so far?"

Ram responded first. "I've done the radio communications in and around the warehouse perimeter, and snipers, Max and Rocco, will be positioned in the vulnerable areas."

"We're ready," Rocco and Max replied in unison before opening their arsenal supply, a weapons closet. High-tech weapons were anchored to the walls, and shelves were full of stacked cash.

Rocco smiled like a kid in a candy shop as he pulled out the weapons and quickly checked them before handing one to Zuri.

Sin stared, slack-jawed, as Zuri proficiently checked the gun.

Zuri was a gun expert even though you'd never know it by looking at her. She was graceful, beautiful, and feminine. People outside our circle thought she was just my pretty eye candy personal assistant, but she was way more. Zuri was an integral part of my team. She was tough as nails and could hang with the boys with ease. Once she'd joined the team, knowing how to handle a weapon was mandatory— as it would be for Sin after I warmed her up to the idea—because of the enemies we'd made over the years. So being ready to protect ourselves was top priority.

Kevin glanced up from his laptop. "I checked the perimeter with the drone," he disclosed. "We're good to go."

"I want this mission tight and everyone on their game," I added gruffly. "When Ram and I step into the warehouse to meet Bigsby, I'm expecting an ambush, but we'll be ready to handle it. But just in case something goes wrong, our body cameras will record everything."

This wasn't our first mission; my team was professional and specialists, and we all knew the drill. We might not make it out alive. But I'd never had something so precious at stake… Sin.

"Knowing Bigsby, there'll be plenty of firepower on both sides. Does anyone have any questions before we head out?"

Everyone responded in unison, "No."

Max and Rocco barked, "Hooah!"

I saw Sin's flushed expression. She was worried. I could see right through her anxieties.

We all marched out of the war room, silently getting into the elevator. Quiet prevailed on the ride down as we mentally prepared for our dangerous battle. Without pause, we quickly slid out of the elevator—private garage level—moving toward the waiting military-style vehicles.

I pulled Sin aside, brushing a few stray strands of hair off her forehead. "Don't leave Kevin's and Zuri's side, no matter what you see or hear on the live video feed to the surveillance van. Okay?" My chest constricted at the thought of ever losing her.

She nodded. "Got it. And you be safe, McKay. I need you back alive."

Lifting up on her toes, she kissed me hard on the lips. My fingers pushed through her hair as I devoured her mouth with sweeping strokes of my tongue, slow and deep, needing the comfort of her taste and touch. I kissed her neck, her chin, and her cheek as the recollections of Mom's and Maya's deaths echoed through my mind. Memories of fire engulfing my SUV, taking Maya with it… the moments frozen in time of the gun being pressed against Mom's head. Tragic events that had shattered my world into a million pieces, leaving me emotionally vacant until Sin came into my life, making me want to move on from the past and build a future with her.

My family—Max, Ram, Rocco, Zuri, and Kevin—and business gave me direction. But Sin… she gave me purpose. And I would fight tooth and nail to protect her and our future together.

I stepped back and then escorted her over to the van where Kevin and Zuri were waiting. Once she was safely inside, I slipped into killer mode. Ram, Rocco, Max, and I loaded the vehicles with black crates filled with weapons. When we were done, I pulled on my body armor, black baseball cap, and mirrored sunglasses.

I nodded as we all piled into the vehicles with grim faces.

"Let's roll," I snapped.

CHAPTER 17
CORE

I powered the military-style vehicle around the corner, gathering speed toward the warehouse. Rocco and Max had already driven off to secure their sniper positions. Kevin, Zuri, and Sin were parked on the perimeter of the warehouse but out of sight.

I dropped a gear and floored it right inside the large warehouse filled with forklifts, cranes, and various forms of heavy machinery.

After sharply hitting the brakes and throwing the truck into park, I grabbed the ledger and the thumb drive with the recording of Bigsby's confession and jumped out of the vehicle. With Ram following, I stalked toward the black SUV parked in the middle of the warehouse. We stopped midway, assessing as much as we could of the vehicle with tinted windows. We then panned the area with our eyes for any of Bigsby's people hiding in the wings.

"You seeing this, Kevin?" I asked, just checking that Ram's and my body cameras were sending the video and audio feed as they should.

"Yes." Kevin's answer echoed in the hidden earpiece receiver I was wearing. "Scanning for body heat signatures in the warehouse. I only see two at this time, and they're in that black vehicle in front of you."

I replied, "I need you to keep it tight and stay alert. This could be an ambush."

"I'll be scanning for any other radio transmissions or heat signatures," Kevin announced.

"You're on it," I answered. "Out."

The driver's door to the parked vehicle opened, and Bigsby hopped out, followed by what looked like his bodyguard.

"McKay," Bigsby greeted.

I deliberately said nothing, letting the cooling sound of silence speak volumes.

The chunky gold ring on Bigsby's middle finger glinted as he nervously adjusted his cuff. The ring was the stark reminder that this man standing before me was a cold-blooded killer… the man who had murdered my mother. I shoved down the rage that threatened to surge through my body. I needed to stay calm… collected… keep my emotions from spurring me to make fucked-up decisions that could jeopardize this mission and my team's lives.

"You're late," Bigsby snapped.

"I'm here." I countered, walking toward him and his bodyguard with Ram at my side. "So let's make this quick. I've got things to do." My lips flattened when we stopped mere inches from him.

Ram crossed his arms, widening his stance, as both he and the bodyguard silently sized each other up. Ram could easily take him—with or without having to use his weapon.

I studied Bigsby for a few minutes.

Bigsby shifted uneasily. "Before you pulled up, my men informed me that a van just parked on the edge of this property." He tilted his head. "More backup?" His eyes flicked to Ram.

I kept my face neutral, but I knew from his statement that he had eyes outside, watching our moves. Hopefully, the guys had picked up that detail on the audio.

"Are we going to do this exchange or what, Bigsby?" I replied in a sharp tone.

"You're one impatient fucker." Bigsby's jaw tightened.

"I'm just cutting to the chase." I countered tonelessly.

The vein along Bigsby's jaw pulsed rapidly. "Fine. Let's get this business done. Once I have what I came for, my dealings with you and Sin are finished."

I handed him the ledger and thumb drive. Bigsby accepted the items and then turned to walk away.

He skidded to a stop, turning to glare at me. "Did you make any copies of these items, McKay?"

"I won't need it," I replied. "Because our business is not finished." I pulled out the trophy gun I'd retrieved from Bigsby's safe after ransacking his home, looking for anything and everything to bring him down.

Bigsby's mouth flopped open and then closed. "What the hell are you doing with my gun?"

The bodyguard reached behind him, pulling out a 9mm handgun from his waistband, but Ram drew his weapon first, aiming at the man.

"Drop the gun or make my day," Ram hissed.

The bodyguard threw the gun to the ground.

"Kick it away," Ram ordered.

The bodyguard anxiously kicked the gun across the ground.

With eyes locked on Bigsby, I aimed the gun at his head. "Isn't it ironic?" I hissed. "You'll die by the same gun you used to murder my mother."

"That," Bigsby croaked, "was you? You little bastard!"

"Yes." My lips thinned. "That was me. Now I'm all grown up. And I bet you're wondering how I knew it was you," I spit.

Bigsby nodded, swallowing hard.

"You fucking idiot. You still have that same fucking ring. The same piece of jewelry you wore the night you killed my mother." I widened my stance. "Now I'm here to finish what you started... and I won't miss."

Bigsby laughed. "Do you actually think it's going to be so damn easy? That van that I mentioned to you?" He grinned. "I wonder if your sweet-ass bitch Sin is inside it."

"It's not going to make any difference to you," I finished and then pulled the trigger.

The bullet pierced Bigsby's head. He slumped to the floor—dead.

The bodyguard scrambled to the ground to retrieve his weapon, but before he could touch his gun, Ram pulled his trigger. The man was dead.

I seized the ledger and thumb drive from Bigsby.

Kevin shouted in my earpiece, "Here they come."

Outside the warehouse, gunfire erupted.

"Ram, let's get the hell out of here," I bellowed. I knew Kevin and Zuri could take care of themselves if attacked, but Sin, she had no weapon experience. "And make sure Sin's safe."

We jumped in our vehicle. Tires squealed upon our exit out of the warehouse.

"Core," Kevin called in my earpiece, "incoming. Several hostiles coming at you."

Bigsby's men shot at our SUV.

Ram launched a grenade out the window.

Boom!

Some of Bigsby's men fell to the ground. Ram raised his gun, shooting and taking the rest out. But more men streamed out from the buildings that encircled the warehouse.

"Fuck this." Ram grabbed a walkie-talkie, yelling into it, "Sniper A and B, take the bastards out."

I drove down the street, gathering speed. I saw bodies slumping to the ground from sniper gunshots. I dropped a gear and floored it away from the warehouse perimeter.

Looking into the rearview mirror, I could see Max slipping off the overlook of the warehouse like a ninja.

I grabbed the two-way radio receiver from Ram. "Kevin. Status?"

There was no response.

My heart raced.

Is Sin okay?

"Zuri?"

Nothing.

Shit! Are Kevin, Zuri, and Sin injured? Oh God… don't let them be shot or… dead.

CHAPTER 18
SINTHIA

Kevin, Zuri, and I watched and listened to Core's verbal exchange with Bigsby while sitting inside the back of the completely furbished van with plush seats and a bank of monitors tracking the activities going down inside and outside of the warehouse.

My fists unfurled and the tension disappeared when I heard the gunshot. Then I saw Bigsby fall to the ground. Core had finally gotten his revenge for his mother, for my dad, and for Greer.

It was finally over. Bigsby was no more.

It was as if the dark cloud that shrouded my past and threatened to consume my future had disappeared, and my future looked—

I blinked in confusion when I saw several dark-clad men creeping toward the adjacent building I'd seen Core and Ram drive into earlier for their meeting.

Jabbing a finger at the monitor, I asked, "Kevin? Do you see that?"

He gave me the side-eye. "Of course, Sin," he muttered with exasperation in his tone. "Sniper A," he barked into the intercom. "Sniper B. Hostiles approaching Alpha and Beta."

"Sniper B. Got it," Rocco replied.

"Sniper A. Engaged," Max relayed. "Shit!" he snapped when we saw on the monitors that more men were streaming from the buildings. "Too many hostiles. I'm going in closer. Sniper B, cover me."

We saw someone dressed in all black slip behind some packing crates.

"Who's that?" I asked.

"Max," Zuri answered before Max swung into action, squeezing off a series of shots, taking out a swarm of men.

More men converged to Max's left, turning in unison and firing their guns. Max dived for cover.

"Sniper B. Shoot!" Kevin ordered.

One body collapsed to the ground, then two more, and then the last two. Max looked up from behind cover. All five were dead.

My heart was in my throat. I'd only seen moves like those in action movies. "Who the hell are you people?" I muttered in amazement.

"Max and Rocco are former military," Zuri answered. "The elite of the elite—Special Forces."

"Well," I muttered, "I'm glad they're on our side." And I made a mental note to thank them for their service.

Max started to retreat when a hostile came out of nowhere. My stomach plummeted with fear. Max lunged, wrestling the man's rifle away and knocking it down. The man drew a knife and slashed at him, but Max grabbed his knife arm, twisting it at an awkward angle that caused the knife to drop, and then he seized the man in a two-handed neck-breaker.

"Jesus. He broke the man's fucking neck," I whispered, both terrified and awed by his badass but brutal display, "with his bare hands."

"That's what he gets paid for," Zuri stated, nonplussed.

Boom!

The sound echoed outside our van.

Startled, I swung my head to the side, wildly glancing around.

I gasped in a strained whisper when our vehicle tilted slightly to one side, followed by the sound of lots of pings against the metal shell of the van. All of the monitors flickered and then went black.

Silence pushed from seconds to minutes.

"Kevin?" Zuri hissed. "What the hell was that?"

"Bigsby's men," he replied. "Grenade." His fingers flew over the keyboard and then the console, pressing several buttons, as if trying to get the monitors online. "Then bullets." He sat back, frowning. All systems were down. "Fuck!" he hissed, standing up.

I backed up a bit, giving him space. He was a massive man who had to be at least six-seven and looked like he could bench-press a car despite his Clark Kent nerdy appearance.

Staring directly at us, Kevin simply explained, "Now it's our time."

"Dammit!" Zuri's lips drew into a straight line. "This is the last thing we need."

Without another word, Zuri and Kevin pulled out their weapons.

"I'm sorry." I blinked in confusion. "What are we doing?"

Zuri's eyes locked on to mine. "Sin, stay behind us. It's fixin' to get rowdy."

My eyes widened. "Rowdy?" I swallowed hard. "Holy shit! Please don't tell me they're going to try to get inside the van," I squeaked, heart racing like a rabbit as the panic started to take hold of me.

Zuri gripped my shoulders. "Take a deep breath," she ordered in a calm voice.

I nodded and did what I had been told.

Zuri spoke plainly. "Now get yourself together because shit's about to get real chaotic up in here."

What. The. Hell?

My limbs started shaking.

I'm going to die. In a van… out in Nowhereland. Fuck my life!

Kevin yelled into his handheld intercom, "Sniper A and B. Bigsby's goons are at our location. We're compromised and under attack." He stormed over to the solid metal partition erected behind the front seats of the van, locking the fixed door in the center and sealing us inside the cargo area.

"We're on our way," Rocco answered.

Kevin shrugged off his armored vest, handing it to me. "Sin, put this on," he spoke in an even tone once again.

There was a sour taste in my mouth when I asked, "But what about you?"

"Don't worry about me or Zuri. Our job is to protect you."

Zuri took a position in the rear, as if guarding the back door.

Scared out of my damn mind, I followed direction, putting on his vest.

"Sin," Zuri hissed, "brace yourself. They're going to try to get inside the cargo area to kill us."

"What?" I chewed my inner cheek so hard I tasted blood. "How do you even know that?" Sweat trickled between my breasts.

Kevin's face looked grim when he responded calmly, "Because that's what we would do."

My pulse raced as I tried to keep from peeing myself. I was so terrified that bladder control was almost nonexistent.

I marveled at how unruffled Kevin looked when he explained, "Sin, we have two choices. Stay where we are and possibly get blown up in the van by more explosives or shoot our way out of this clusterfuck. We choose the last option. So let's surprise the fuckers."

"Shoot our way out?" I sputtered. "Are you kidding me? I've never touched a gun in my life."

"You want to live, right?" Zuri asked, her voice just as tight as mine.

"Hell yes!" I clipped out with hands on my hips.

"You want to see Core again, right?" Zuri barked.

I screamed, "Fuck yes!" The thought of dying, of losing him, made my heart race with fear.

"Good," Kevin answered. "This is an automatic weapon." He handed me the gun. "All you have to do is point at the bad guys and pull the trigger, and don't stop fucking squeezing until the weapon has no more ammo."

My hands trembled while holding it. I took a deep, calming breath.

Sin, you have to do this.

I steadied the gun.

Kevin picked up another weapon and readied himself beside me. "Zuri? You ready to rock and roll?" he roared.

My head got a little lighter from holding my breath.

"I stay ready," Zuri shouted before grabbing the handle of the back door and swinging it open, which surprised the bad guys, dressed in all black, who were getting ready to place the explosive clutched in one of the men's hands on the back door.

Shit. Shit. Shit.

I heard Core's commanding voice through the two-way radio receiver. "Kevin. Status?" There was a slight pause. "Zuri?" Core hissed.

Shots rang out from inside the van. Kevin and Zuri were unloading their weapons in rapid succession, and all I could remember was Kevin's instruction to point at the bad guys and pull the trigger.

Sin, do it… or you'll die. You'll never see Core again.

I aimed the weapon at the bad guys and squeezed the trigger… surprisingly hitting the guy holding the explosive, which exploded in his hand.

"Damn, Sin!" Kevin yelled. "Boom shakalaka!"

I didn't stop shooting until my weapon clicked. It was out of bullets. Glancing over, I saw Kevin laid out on the floor, covered with blood. I went into reaction mode, picking up his weapon, and I continued to squeeze the trigger along with Zuri, who was holding her own.

I have to protect Kevin as he protected me.

Perspiration rolled down my forehead as I fired at the hostiles, taking out one.

Then, *blam!* The burst of bullets killed two more men. Then there was another burst, and two more went down.

Then there was silence.

I couldn't believe I could kill so effortlessly.

It is all surreal.

I killed at least five men.

Not in a million years had I thought I was remotely capable of doing something like taking a life. No, several people's lives. But I had. And I felt no remorse, just relief and gratefulness that I was here, alive.

Now I truly understood the primal survival drive that coursed through Core and his team. When it came down to it, if the only thing that stood between life and death was the will to survive, who wouldn't fight until their last breath?

My thoughts snapped back to the present when I heard wheels squealing outside and the sound of guns blazing. I wondered if someone was shooting at the bad guys.

And then there was utter silence again.

I crawled over to Kevin. His chest area was a bloody mess, but he was breathing. "Are you going to live?" I asked, cradling his head on my lap.

"Sin." Kevin glanced up at me with a grimace of pain. "You can be on our team anytime." He looked like he'd been through hell, but he still grinned at me.

Frantically, I glanced around for Zuri. She seemed fine. Her weapon was still pointed, at the ready.

"Sin!" I heard Core yell from outside the van.

"Shit!" Zuri's body relaxed. "About damn time. The cavalry is here."

It's over.

My shoulders sagged with relief.

Core's alive… and here.

Core appeared at the back of the van… and I'd never been so relieved to see his face.

In a rush of adrenaline, I scrambled to my feet to meet him. There was a soft thump behind me.

Kevin yelled, "Dammit, Sin!"

Looking over my shoulder, I saw that my sudden movement had caused Kevin's head to hit the van's floor. "Oops! My bad," I offered before hopping out of the van.

Leaping into Core's waiting arms, I wrapped my arms and legs around him. The man felt so good under my hands.

"Thank God," I whispered. "I didn't want to kill anyone else. Five is enough," I finished, burying my face against his beefy neck, inhaling his familiar masculine scent.

Core protectively wrapped his arms around me. "I'm sorry it took me so long to get here."

I slightly leaned back, feeling secure with his grip under my ass, pinning me to him. "But you're here. Alive. And that's all that matters."

His lips quickly took mine, claiming me. His tongue curled around mine, coaxing it to join in. We both groaned at the contact, and my eyes slid closed as his grip tightened, pulling me closer. He pulled his mouth away from me, allowing me to get to my feet but keeping me pinned to his side.

Core asked, "Zuri? Is everyone okay?"

Zuri shakily breathed out. "Yes. Kevin took a bullet, but it looks like it went in and out. He'll live," she finished with eyes assessing the dead bodies littering the ground outside the van.

Ram patted Zuri on the back before hopping into the van.

"Watch it, Ram," Kevin yelled from inside. "Bro! I'm fucking injured. Handle with damn care." There was a slight pause. "Zuri!" Kevin shouted. "Get in here. I need protection from this asshole."

"Jesus." Zuri rolled her eyes. "He's such a big baby." She moved out of sight and farther into the van.

Core and I watched as both Ram and Zuri got out of the van with Kevin in tow. He was walking between Ram and Zuri—one arm over Ram's shoulders and the other over Zuri's.

"He's good," Ram stated. "The bullet went straight through," he muttered while they carried Kevin toward the waiting vehicle.

Then they leaned him against the hood while they caught their breath. Kevin was a big man.

"I need a fucking drink," Zuri grumbled, bent over with hands on her knees. "No, several drinks," she tiredly huffed out. "And you"— she shot Kevin a dirty look—"weigh a ton. How many times do I have to warn you about the perils of using muscle-enhancing drugs?"

Kevin, who was slumped against the vehicle's hood, grunting as if in pain, abruptly popped straight up. "This is all natural," he growled while stripping off his T-shirt and then pointing to his six-pack abs. "It's called excellent DNA." His entire body was one sheet of pure, rippling muscle.

"Sure it is," Zuri grumped.

"Woman…" Kevin warned.

Core shook his head. "This is like kindergarten."

I laughed, enjoying the fun, sibling vibe. Frankly, it eased any tension that lingered from the danger we'd just lived through. "Give her hell, Kevin," I urged playfully.

Core pinched my ass. "Don't encourage them."

"Bro?" Ram shot Kevin an irritated glare. "Will you shut it?" Ram snatched Kevin's shirt out of his hand. "And no one wants to see this shit." He sneered at Kevin's bare chest while balling up the material in his hand and then slapping it against Kevin's wound.

Kevin yelped. "You fucker!" he yelled. "That hurts!"

Ram scowled. "Press it against your wound to stop the bleeding... and zip it, bro."

Max and Rocco pulled up and then got out of their vehicle.

"I took a bullet," Kevin directed at Max and Rocco.

"So what?" Max frowned. "You want a fucking medal for that shit?"

"Where's the fucking appreciation on this damn team?" Kevin grumbled.

"Kevin," I called, "I appreciate the hell out of you." And that was an understatement. I was damn grateful because both he and Zuri had saved my ass... big time.

"Ditto," Kevin grunted. "Because you're a badass. Shit. I can't believe you took out four men without blinking an eye. Damn, I like your style."

"Four? Oh, hell no," I sputtered, slightly stepping out of Core's embrace, eyeing Kevin. "I got five men in total."

"That's my woman," Core declared, pulling me closer and kissing the top of my head.

Wrapping an arm around his waist, I tenderly squeezed him.

"Well, you don't have to brag about it, Amazon warrior princess." Kevin grinned at me.

"I'm just saying. Do the math," I finished.

"But here's what I can't figure out," Kevin interjected. "Why were your eyes closed while shooting?"

"Oh, be quiet," I scolded and then burst out in laughter.

"Sin, the designer gunslinger," Ram retorted.

"That shit has a nice ring to it," Kevin quipped.

"Kevin!" Zuri snapped. "Will you shut the hell up? You're bleeding like a stuck pig, and we need to get you patched up."

They loaded him into the back of the SUV, and both Ram and Zuri hopped in and pulled away.

Core touched my cheek before saying, "Give me a minute. I need to make this call."

I nodded.

Core pulled out his cell and voice-dialed, "Doctor." There was a slight pause before the person answered, and Core said, "You need to get over to the penthouse. Kevin. No. Flesh wound. Yes. They're on the way. Yes. See you there." He ended the call.

I eyed Core. "You have a private doctor on call?"

"Yep. I keep him on payroll to take care of my team and me in case of emergency. He even has a private medical office in my building."

I blinked. "Your building?"

"I own the whole building where my penthouse is located. It just makes it easier to maintain our privacy. Ram, Max, Rocco, and Kevin have their own luxury apartments in the building. We call it Command Central because we all live there. Well, everyone except Zuri."

"So it's like a fraternity house?"

"Without the fucking parties," he returned. "The single security code elevator gives us unlimited access to each other's space." He frowned. "That means don't be surprised to see them hanging out in my penthouse or going through my refrigerator like I'm their personal grocery store." He touched my cheek. "Since you're going to be spending a lot of time at my place…"

"Am I now?" I grabbed his shirt, leaning into him.

He reached down, clutching my face. "You are." He kissed me, saying against my lips, "Every night, I want to go to sleep with you in my arms and wake up every morning with my face between your gorgeous legs."

I shivered deliciously. "Damn. That sounds like a plan, McKay."

I sensually licked his bottom lip. He roughly growled before kissing me.

Breaking off the kiss, he explained, "Seriously, there's no privacy. Is that going to be a problem?"

I cupped his cheek. "Core, I don't mind. I like your team. They're your family, so they're mine, too."

I already respected the hell out of Zuri, Ram, Kevin, Rocco, and Max because of their skills but more importantly because of how much they obviously loved, respected, and protected Core. And just that devotion was enough for me to hope they'd someday feel the same way about me.

He gave me an honest-to-goodness bad-boy smile that made my heart thump with joy. "Damn, I'm one lucky man."

"And don't you forget it, McKay." I smiled gently.

My attention was diverted when I heard Rocco mutter, "Fuck! Too many bodies."

Core grabbed my hand as he strode over to Max, taking me with him. My eyes panned over the open field. Rocco was right; there were a lot of dead bodies. I shivered at the reality of this faceoff. So many lives had been lost.

"Text the cleaner," Core directed at Max.

Max pulled out his cell and barked into the phone, "Cleanup requested," and then he clipped out the address to the warehouse and our current location.

Rocco walked up to us. "How are we going to handle Bigsby's body?" he asked Core. "Are we going to leave it for the authorities to find?"

Core nodded. "Yes. We'll have the cleaner dump his body in the Hudson so when it floats to the top in a couple of days, someone will find it, and the authorities will assume one of his rivals did him in."

Core's plan was cold and calculating but bloody smart.

"Got it," Rocco replied before he and Max moved over to the side and started talking in low voices.

Core turned me to face him. "Are you sure you're okay?"

I glanced up at him. His face was relaxed. He looked at peace. It had to have been hell for him, waiting all these years to finally put the past behind him. Now his mother could rest in peace, and he could move on… finally. And so could I. Now all was right in our world.

"Yes," I started and then bit my lower lip, fighting the urge to cry—both sad and happy tears.

It was finally over. Bigsby was dead. His death didn't fill the empty hole from the loss of my dad, but it was a start.

"But let's not do this shit again. Being a commando is not my style. I'd rather stick to designing clothes."

"You've got it, darling," he remarked before hungrily kissing my mouth, tilting my head back and deepening his kiss. He repeatedly swept his tongue through my mouth, pausing only to nibble at my lips before sinking into me again, the passion and heat in his kiss bringing every erogenous zone to life. He lightly kissed my lips before saying, "I'll ravish you later. Now it's time to finish business." He gestured toward the dead bodies.

CHAPTER 19
SINTHIA

Exhaustion consumed me as I sat in the passenger seat while Core drove.

We had stayed just long enough to see the cleaner and his crew pull up to the scene in large black vehicles with tinted windows. Then Core had ushered me into his vehicle, leaving Max and Rocco behind to ensure that everything was taken care of, and we had taken off.

"Forget what you just saw, okay, darling?" Core asked me.

I nodded because there was no way in hell I was built for going to jail, ending up as Big Bertha's prison yard bitch.

But now that the adrenaline had worn off, my mind slipped to thoughts of Dad—Ian. I hadn't visited his grave in years. Partly because I'd felt so guilty I had caused his death—though now I knew better—and partly because, frankly, I believed the body was just a shell for the soul, and upon death, it was freed.

Even though it was late at night, I longed to visit his grave at least one more time. So I asked Core to take me there before going back to his place.

"Are you sure?" he asked.

I stared at the skyline through the window and nodded. "Yes. It's time to say good-bye."

"Okay, darling," he responded simply.

After that, I was grateful that he respected my need for space, leaving me alone with my thoughts. Completely calm, I felt my eyelids slide closed even as I fought the need for sleep.

Core's cell echoed throughout the vehicle, startling me awake.

"Shit. Sorry, darling," he said in my direction before grabbing his earpiece and answering the call with, "McKay."

I couldn't hear the person on the other end, only Core's response.

"Hey, Mitch," he greeted. "Look, I'm kind of busy. Can we talk business tomorrow?"

The business conversation lost my interest. Mitch Fillion was Core's lawyer and Erika's husband.

"Now?" Core asked. There was a pause. "Why?" There was another beat of silence. "Okay, if you insist. I'm heading to a cemetery in New Jersey. The address is…" His hands tightened around the steering wheel. "How do you know the location?" He scowled. "Mitch, what the fuck is going on? Okay… but only because you've earned my trust. Don't make me regret this. See you there." He ended the call.

Glancing over at him, I asked, "What's wrong?"

Core frowned as he raced through traffic. "Mitch wants to meet me at the cemetery. He says it's important."

He looked worried.

"What's the problem?" I inquired.

"Maybe nothing. It's just…" He shrugged.

"Relax." I squeezed his leg. "While I'm visiting Ian's gravesite, you can wait for Mitch by the car and take care of whatever he wants from you."

"But that's just it." His eyes slipped to me and then back to the road. "He asked me to make sure you were there, too."

I raised my eyebrows.

What does Mitch want with me?

CHAPTER 20
SINTHIA

Leaving Core behind to wait for Mitch, I walked across the grass, not remembering the gravesite being this serene and beautiful. It had been so long since I was there that I fumbled along until I found Dad's plot.

There were fresh flowers lying on top, which was strange because Grace was dead so she couldn't have put the arrangement there. But truthfully, even if she were alive, I couldn't imagine her ever bringing flowers. She had just been too much of a selfish person to give a shit about doing something so sentimental, even for a man she'd shared years of her life with.

With my arms hanging slack at my sides, I stood, staring at his headstone, as the crisp fall air whirled around me. There was a tightness in my chest when I thought about his remains locked in a coffin in the stone-cold earth.

"Hi, Dad. I know it's been…" I croaked and then bit my bottom lip, fighting back the tears that prickled my eyelids. "Way too long. I'm so sorry about that."

Reaching down, I placed the flowers on his grave that I'd purchased after Core and I made a quick stop at a twenty-four-hour grocery store on the way to the cemetery. "I was a coward." My chin trembled. "I couldn't face the guilt I felt for getting you killed… but now I know the truth."

A tear slipped down my cheek. I dashed it away.

"I know now what you did to give me a place to call home and to make me happy." I swallowed around the lump of emotions clogging my throat. "And I want to thank you for that and for loving me as hard as you did." My voice broke. "And it doesn't matter that you're my uncle. You will always be the man I consider my dad."

Sniffing, I wiped at my nose before taking a seat on the cold grass, facing his headstone. Drawing my limbs close to my body, I whispered, "I love you." A long stretch of silence passed. The only sound was a jet in the distance. "And I want you to know that you can rest in peace because Bigsby's dead." I inhaled deeply, taking in a lungful of air and mentally shaking myself.

"Now we can both breathe easier because Bigsby's no longer in our lives," I heard Erika's husky voice say.

Startled, I looked over my shoulder to find her standing right behind me. I'd been so lost in my thoughts that I somehow tuned out the sound of her footsteps.

"Erika?" I stood up, wiping my hands against my legs. "What are you doing here?" I regarded her for a moment, noticing her face with no makeup, hollowed cheeks, and eyes red and puffy, like she'd been crying.

"Sin"—Erika's eyes locked with mine—"Core told me you know about the ledger and what happened to your dad—to Greer."

"Why would he tell you—"

"Sin." She interrupted me. She moved closer, her eyes searching my face. "It's time for closure for both of us. I'm Aubrey… your mother."

I blinked while teetering on the edge of losing my shit.

My lips parted because, for once, I was at a loss for words. After minutes of silence ticked by, I finally shouted, "This is bullshit, Erika!" I spit. "Or is it Jemma Kane?" I narrowed my eyes. "No. It's Aubrey Cruickshank, right?" I laughed without humor because my life had officially become some fucked-up reality show, starring me.

Erika frowned. "All of the above."

My heart hammered hard as her response sank in. "I guess that solves that mystery," I muttered.

"Sin." Erika reached for me.

I swatted her hand away.

Her hand dropped to her side. "You're not planning on making this easy for me, are you?"

I stared at her like she'd lost her ever-loving mind. "What do you think?" Heat flushed through my body.

Erika sighed heavily. "I get it. Not telling you sooner was wrong. I messed up." A look of regret crossed her face.

My nostrils flared as my anger began to boil. "No. More like fucked up," I retorted. My entire world felt ripped apart. Up was down, and down was up.

"You're angry with me," Erika accused before running a hand down her face. "I don't blame you." Taking a deep, pained breath, she briefly closed her eyes.

Erika is my mother? How did I not see this coming? But how could I have?

Nothing could have prepared me for this news. Nothing.

But it did explain Erika's interest in me.

"Why didn't you tell me? We've known each other forever." My heart thudded in my chest. I wanted to walk away from her, but I didn't—I couldn't—because I was done running away from the truth. Now I just wanted damn answers.

Erika clenched and unclenched her hands. "If Bigsby found out you were my daughter, he would have killed us both right then and there."

Given what I now know about Bigsby, that is true… but still…

"But Bigsby did find out," I snapped. "That's why he went after my business."

Erika's eyebrows drew together. "And that's why I had my husband, Mitch, get so close to Bigsby."

I arched my brows high. "Mitch knows everything?"

"Yes." She nodded. "Mitch knows about my past, and he also knows about you. We've both been keeping tabs on Bigsby while ensuring you were safe. We've even been feeding the Feds information about Bigsby's shady dealings, including the sex trafficking ring."

I snorted. "Ensuring I was safe?" I pursed my lips. "Well, that was an epic fail because he was plotting to kill me and Core. And the only person who stepped up to the plate to save my ass was Core."

Erika opened her mouth to say something and then stopped short and pinched her lips together.

My breaths quickened when something horrible occurred to me. "Wait. Is that why you hired Jade?" I narrowed my eyes. "To get close to me?" There was a knot in my belly.

Erika crossed her arms. "You know better than that shit." She countered with a sharp tone. "I hired Jade because she's a talented actor."

"You're damn right she is," I defended. "What about Ariana? Did you seek her out because of me?"

Erika didn't seem that cold and calculating.

But shit, what do I really know about her?

"Contrary to your belief, Jade and Ariana didn't have shit to do with you and me. It was fate that brought them both into my same social circle. Nothing more, nothing less. Six degrees of separation is damn real."

I eyed her, really wanting to believe her. "That'd better be the truth, Erika." Stepping forward, I jabbed a finger in her face. "Because they're my family. And no one fucks with my family. No one," I hissed.

Her eyes softened. "I love both of them, Sin. They mean the world to me." She paused. "You know that. Shit, you know me."

I arched a brow. "Do I?"

"You do."

I silently stared at her because the truth of the matter was I didn't know her at all.

"I know finding out that I'm your mother is shocking." Her voice was soft and measured.

I rolled my eyes skyward. "That's putting it mildly." Rubbing my brow to ward off a headache, I replied, "Maybe this is a bad idea. It's been a long damn day, and frankly, I can't deal with more drama right now."

"Please," Erika pleaded, "just let me say my piece. And if you still don't want anything to do with me…" Her voice broke. She cleared her throat. "I won't push it, okay? I'll leave you the hell alone if that's what you really want."

I hesitated but then let out a long and tired sigh. "Fine." My head barely moved into a nod, and I controlled the frown that was threatening to form. "Let's get this talk over with."

Erika's eyes darted around. "Don't you want to go someplace else to talk?"

"No." Irritation stormed through me, and I fisted my hands by my sides. "Right here. Right now."

The confident Erika that I knew fidgeted uncomfortably. "My real name is Erika Aubrey Watson. I never liked my first name, so my mother just called me either Aubrey or Brey."

She bit her bottom lip, and the familiar gesture—something I did when I was anxious—made me relax slightly because it proved that this conversation was important to her.

To ease the tension a little, I asked, "Is your mother still alive?"

She shook her head. "No. I was fourteen years old when she died from cancer. And since I didn't have any family, I bounced around from foster home to foster home until I was done being used by foster parents that were more interested in the monthly check they got for taking me in than giving a shit about me, the little girl who needed stability, love, and protection."

I arched a brow. "And your father?"

"He left my mother when she got pregnant with me." Her eyes hardened. "And he never looked back."

"Oh… I see." And I did.

The pieces to the puzzle of who Erika had been before becoming one of the most powerful women in television slowly started to come together.

She's a broken crayon just like me.

Feeling completely drained, especially after Erika had dropped a big bucket of emotion and a lot of expectations in a matter of minutes, I plopped down on the grass to sit.

Erika followed, crossing her legs, facing me.

"What about Greer?" I asked, uncomfortably shifting on the grass.

She studied me for a few minutes before she spoke. "I was involved with Greer way before I went into business with him and Bigsby."

"By 'involved'"—I made air quotes—"you mean having sex with him." It was a statement, not a question.

"Yes," Erika replied, and I nodded for her to continue. "I knew who Bigsby was, even before Greer gave me the lowdown about him. I'd heard the rumors on the streets that Bigsby was a backstabbing asshole who would cut a person down in a heartbeat, but my business deal with him and Greer was too good to pass up."

I snorted. "It was all about the money, huh?"

"Yes, it was. I'm not going to lie about it." She shrugged. "I was young, ambitious, and yes, greedy." She pursed her lips. "I wasn't thrilled about working with Bigsby, nor did I trust him, so I had Greer be the middleman between us, making sure Bigsby never saw my face. For that matter, none of my clients or girls ever saw my face. I was the puppet master behind the curtain."

I arched a brow. "That was cunningly smart."

She nodded. "I'd started out as an escort and worked for a woman who took me under her wing before she got busted. She ultimately pleaded guilty to arranging an encounter between two prostitutes and a man who turned out to be an undercover police officer. Her downfall was her clients and escorts who snitched her out to the police. I never wanted to be that vulnerable. So when I had taken over her business, I'd made sure never to reveal my identity to anyone.

"Anyway, I wasn't thrilled about working with Bigsby, but he had the right connections to get me the upscale clients I needed, and I had the women to make the engine work."

A big gust of wind blew, and I briefly stared up at the sky.

Erika sighed, an exhale that was one of the weariest sounds in the world. "Business was booming for a good while, but I was smart enough to know that our escort business wasn't my final destination in life. I wanted out, but the escort business was Bigsby's cash cow. He would never let me just walk away. And then there was this little issue. Greer and I had fallen in love, and I got pregnant. With you," Erika confessed, eyes still watching my expression.

Pulling my legs up, wrapping my arms around them, I rested my chin on my knees. "So your little black book was the ledger?" I asked.

"Yes. Greer and I got married secretly, and we needed a little insurance against Bigsby when we demanded release from our business arrangement." Her jaw tightened. "Bigsby was pissed that we wanted out, and that's when everything blew up between us. It was lucky that we'd given the ledger to Ian before..." Her voice broke, and she cleared her throat. "Once Greer was dead, Bigsby came after me. He snitched me out to the authorities as the ringleader of the escort business."

"But he didn't know your identity. How did the police even connect you to the ring?"

"My ex-boss." Her nostrils flared as she took a deep breath in through her nose. "She was the only person who knew my real identity. You see, when she was convicted of pandering, tax evasion, and money laundering, she got three years in prison. When she got out, she wanted her business back. I said hell no. So she got her revenge by hooking up with Bigsby to take me down."

"Wow." My eyes locked with hers. "Why didn't you just tell the authorities about Bigsby? You had enough evidence in the ledger."

Erika let out a sigh. "I was scared he'd come after me and you. I couldn't risk that. The best way to throw him off our trail was to let him believe that his plan to get rid of Greer and me had worked." She ran a shaky hand through her hair. "Anyway, I wasn't worried about serving time because I had a plan. I threatened to reveal the names of dozens of powerful, high-profile politicians, top law enforcement, influential lawyers, bankers, entertainment execs, and Fortune 500 businessmen listed in my little black book—the ledger. And I had every intention of doing that by splashing their names on the front page of every paper in New York." She jutted her chin out. "So the Manhattan prosecutors—who were also my clients—decided to make a secret deal with me. The arrangement allowed me to avoid jail time, but not before seizing all my assets, along with Greer's and Bigsby's."

I shook my head. "Well, I guess that explains what Bigsby was doing for all those years following my dad's death. He was broke and rebuilding his assets."

Erika cocked her head at my words. "Yes... and also plotting to wipe away any remnants of his sleazy pimp past." Her eyes hardened. "Anyway, after my secret deal with the prosecutors, they wanted me to just quietly go away—which, frankly, I had no problem doing. I wanted to get away from Bigsby. So after I had you, I got out of New York, pronto."

I whispered, "You mean you got out of town without me." My voice swam with emotion, the words spilling out around a rock-hard lump in my throat.

"Sin, I was young with no money," Erika whispered as tears began to pour from her eyes. "I couldn't take care of you. Besides, I was always on the run, and that was no type of life for a baby."

Disappointment churned through me even though I knew she was right.

"I wanted more for you. And I knew Ian would take care of you like his own," she replied, clasping her hands together in her lap. "I"— her voice croaked—"bounced around the country for a while before landing in California, but I've always been around, looking over you."

All my breath and defiance whooshed from my throat in a violent exhale as I sat silently, digesting all of this information.

Everything Erika had explained made sense. She had been young back then and made some fucked-up mistakes. Who knows? If I were in her shoes, I probably would have done the same. All in all, people weren't perfect. But still, I needed time to process everything and come to terms with the truth of Erika being my mother.

I took a deep breath, filling my lungs with air, and exhaled slowly. I wasn't sure if I'd ever have a mother-daughter relationship with Erika, but at least the door was now open.

CHAPTER 21
SINTHIA
THREE YEARS LATER

It was fall NYFW—New York Fashion Week—one of the busiest, most stressful, and most exciting times of the year for me and my team as we got ready to present my spring/summer collection.

I took a deep breath, glancing around backstage. *Damn! This is the calm before the storm.*

There was nothing but steamers, coffee, and loud music.

The Zen moment was gone fifteen minutes later when the swarm of people—dressed all in black, armed with shears, blow-dryers, and hair spray, ready to bring my vision to life—started to flood backstage. The area became a packed house with models running around and the hair and makeup team covered in the tools of their trade.

Shit. This is finally happening. I'm about to lose my NYFW virginity in three hours.

This was my first Sin Michaels fashion show, and it was happening today, coinciding with the opening of my fashion line's Manhattan flagship store on Madison Avenue.

I smoothed my hand across my stomach to calm my nerves. All of the pieces of my life's work were finally coming together, but I was nervous as hell.

Leading up to today's fashion show, my publicist wouldn't even tell me too much about who was attending because I was so busy with styling and getting everything ready. Plus, I hadn't wanted to have to deal with the possibly horrible news that no one was going to show up.

Because why would they? I'm a designer that only my Sin Michaels A-list following understands.

No fear, Sin! You've worked way too damn hard to get here.

I kept busy, finishing the last-minute details, methodically checking over my collection that was sectioned off on hangers along with snapshots of each model who would be wearing each outfit.

Despite the looks of disapproval and frowns I'd gotten when I announced during an interview that I was staying true to my design sensibilities and heritage by infusing diversity into my show with plus-size and non-white models walking my runway, I was sticking to my position. It was very important to me to pave the way and push acceptance of a more diverse assortment of races, ages, and body types to be represented in fashion.

So fuck anyone who thinks otherwise.

This was my business, and these were my designs. I wasn't going to compromise my ethics or myself for anyone.

And to push the *it's simply not done* envelope further, I had been steadfast in my quest to pay homage to everyone who had supported me along my fashion journey. I'd decided to change the game by opening the show to the general public, and I'd set aside free passes for fans, fashion students, and faculty at FIT, Parsons, Pratt Institute, and The High School of Fashion Industries on a first-come, first-serve basis. Ticket holders would sit separately from industry members and celebrities, who would be positioned in a raised viewing area.

After that, I'd picked an incredible riverside location in Tribeca that allowed for an unobstructed view of the One World Trade Center from every seat. The setting was perfect for my collection—grand but still intimate and the ideal platform to tell the story of my spring/summer collection.

Now just two hours before the show was set to begin, I was obsessively steaming my wrinkled pieces and fixing final details, jostling with hair and makeup teams as well as models and trying not to stress over the press that had started arriving backstage, clamoring to interview me.

I watched as one of the hairstylists, holding several tools in each hand, talked to a reporter while trying not to burn herself or the model. In the crush, everyone was fighting for space in the small backstage area that was our studio for the evening.

I beckoned Giselle, my right hand and creative director. "Status?" I asked.

"Everything's good," she stated with a forced smile.

I gave her a look, lifted an eyebrow, and waited. She knew better than to sugarcoat things for me.

Giselle's resolve faltered beneath my steady, authoritative regard. She sighed heavily. "Okay. Yes, there are a few hiccups with models arriving late, but we're on it."

I eyed the models making the most of their short prep time—eating sandwiches from the buffet, getting their hair, nails, and makeup done, being interviewed, practicing their poses, and looking good for candid backstage photos.

I blew out a breath. "Then why do I feel so damn nervous?" I was a hot mess of knotted nerves.

"Stop worrying, Sin. Everything is going great." A smile curved Giselle's lips.

I nodded because I trusted Giselle. She was a whiz at helping me be as organized as possible.

I'd planned everything in great detail. The venue would open just before sundown, and what awaited guests beyond the metal barricades was a well-planned, multisensory experience, beginning with a wooden and scrap-metal set constructed of only recycled materials and performance artists suspended on platforms against the skyline.

"So in other words, I need to chill the fuck out," I replied—a statement, not a question.

Giselle nodded. "Exactly."

"Okay. Got it," I responded, deciding to use my energy for last-minute adjustments when Jade burst onto the scene with a flock of eager reporters trailing behind her.

Jade grinned at me while waving her hand.

The paparazzi screamed questions, coming at her from all directions.

"Jade! Jade!"

"Jade! Can you pose for a photo?"

"Is that outfit you're wearing from the Sin Michaels collection?"

Jade stopped and preened for the cameras. She was beautiful and lithe with shocking apple-green eyes. Jade was undoubtedly one of Hollywood's most beautiful actresses, and the media was obsessed with her glam style and beauty. But I knew she was more than just good looks. She was funny, genuine, and smart.

"Everything that I'm wearing," Jade quipped clearly to the reporters, "is from the Sin Michaels line." She turned strategically, allowing photos to be taken of her outfit—one I'd designed just for her —a black asymmetrical ruffle crepe jacket featuring an exploded asymmetrical ruffle peplum with square, masculine padded shoulders and silk lapels and button fastenings. Her wide-leg black tuxedo trousers had a tonal satin stripe detail on the sides.

Damn. My bestie is the best commercial for my line. I love it.

A reporter shouted, "How do you describe Sin's style?"

Jade chirped, "Daring, fearless, and constantly evolving." She flipped her hair, playing up to the cameras. "Sin has an exuberant take on fashion that combines a willingness to experiment with a strong sense of self. Sin has fun with her clothes… which makes her clothing *everything*." Jade put dramatic emphasis on the last word. "Sin is the coolest, hottest, most talented, most impressive fashion designer today." Without another word, she sauntered away, toward me.

When she reached me, she pulled me into a tight hug, whispering in my ear, "I brought the paparazzi circus. You know, to whip up more social buzz for you."

"Love you, girlie," I whispered back.

I adored that Jade always had my back and was my bestie and my partner in crime. When she needed me, I would be there just like she'd been for me. It'd been that way from the first day we met as freshmen in high school, and it would always be that way.

We turned in unison, facing the rabid paparazzi. Cameras clicked. Microphones pressed forward.

Jade playfully batted her eyes and whispered, "Relax."

Despite the whirlwind of media coverage I'd gotten over my collection, I still wasn't comfortable in front of the paparazzi's cameras. It was sensory overload. The bright side of this current fiasco was the attention I would get from Jade wearing my couture design.

It had been quite a year for Jade. She was still on fire from starring in a smoking-hot television series. Not to mention she'd finally finished production on her first directorial feature. It had taken so much longer since she did it herself. I was so proud of her.

One reporter asked me, "How do you handle the pressure of being the costume designer for your mother, Erika Watson's, hot new television crime drama series starring Midori Petite?"

Mother… Erika…

Even years later, hearing those two words together… I still couldn't believe it.

Erika is my mother.

I remembered how angry I had been when she revealed she was my biological mother and why she'd left me with Ian. Her path had been complicated, and given what I knew about life now, I understood that sometimes decisions weren't so cut and dry. Life was short, and I didn't want to live it with bitterness and regret. I wanted her in my life… and I'd decided to forgive her, just like I'd forgiven Core.

Simply put, I'd come to terms with the fact that Erika did what she had to do to keep me safe. I had been angry about her decisions, but I hadn't rehashed the past. I'd just moved the fuck on.

Still, it hadn't been a smooth or immediate road to some sort of mother-daughter relationship. Every interaction had felt fraught with meaning. It had been similar to the most difficult dating relationship ever—where both of us were overanalyzing every little thing the other person did. After a few months of this painful tap dance, Erika and I'd decided something had to change. Instead of trying to force an instant bond as mother and daughter, we'd decided to just be friends and let it play out the way it played out.

I cleared my throat before responding. "Easy. Like me, my mother pulls no punches about what she wants. She had a vision, and I made it happen… of course, the Sin Michaels way. When you have a new show, there are so many ways to build it from the ground up," I told them. "Before we did the pilot two winters ago, we discussed the tone of the character, the tone of the clothes, the tone of the show, and what we didn't want the show to be."

Another reporter chimed in, "I've heard you talk about how important it is to have a range of designs for a very diverse group of people. How do you incorporate that mentality into your Sin Michaels line?"

I smiled before answering, "There needs to be inclusivity in the fashion industry. You know, something for a curvy woman and also options for a really petite woman. I want people to appreciate the clothes and not think, *Aw, that's hot, but it only looks good on her*," I told reporters.

Diversity was very important to me, especially given my heritage, and that was why I'd not only chosen the strikingly beautiful buzz-cut, gap-toothed famous black model to parade down the runway tonight, but also another famous hijab-wearing model.

I carried on. "I want to make things for all body types. With the Sin Michaels line, I have so much freedom. I'm curvy, but I don't just design for myself. I use my taste as the muse for everything. I like to play around with silhouettes. I like women to be comfortable in my designs."

Giselle, who was waiting in the wings, dramatically tapped on her watch.

"Okay. Thank you," I said. "I have a show to put on."

Giselle swept in, ushering the reporters away.

Jade bounced up and down. "I'm so fucking excited. My Sin is having her first fashion show," she squealed, pulling me in for a tight hug. "I always knew one day your hot collection would be parading down the runway during Fashion Week."

I hugged her back. "Well, thank you for being my living mannequin."

Since we had been in high school, I'd designed most of my clothes, using her as my sounding board. She was patient, enthusiastic, and always there for me.

She pulled back, beaming with pride. "I'd walk across coals for your ass, and you know it."

She was everything a best friend should be. I gave her a wobbly smile as we dashed away the tears of joy. "Oh hell, now you're getting all emotional on me."

"I can't help it. Look at you." Jade's eyes swept over me. "You're glowing with happiness."

"That ain't nothing but the afterglow from two rounds of sex this morning," I replied, shivering deliciously at the recollection of Core taking me in the shower and then in the kitchen.

"Morning sex…" Jade started. "I haven't had a good, hard pounding in…" She frowned. "Oh Lord, it's been so long I can't even remember."

"And whose fault is that?" I countered. "I can get you some of this if I can only hook you up with—"

"Don't say it." Jade cut me off. "I'm not interested in you hooking me up with Ram, Max, or Rocco."

"Hmm… that's weird." I gave her a mock perplexed stare, tapping my chin. "You didn't mention Kev—"

"Don't even mention that cunt tease's name," Jade warned playfully.

"Kevin!" I burst out laughing when Jade got flustered, and I loved it.

Jade had it bad for Kevin, the high-IQ genius who was the official geek of Core's team.

Jade pointed a finger at me. "You know, ever since you've been getting dick on the regular, you've become a mean woman."

I rolled my eyes. "All I'm saying is don't you think it's fucking funny that every time he sees you, he either hightails it away or stays to give you the mean-mug stare like you're some sort of evil vixen who needs to be doused with holy water to atone for your filthy sins?"

"What damn sins?" She pursed her lips.

"Come on, you know that everyone who watches your television show knows you're a down-for-anything, man-eating tigress." I swiped my hand at her like an animal, making a big cat sound.

Jade burst out laughing. "Don't make me shank you."

"I'm just saying…" I grinned. "Don't kill the messenger." I playfully batted my eyes.

"Well, you have one thing right. I am down for anything with that man. I refuse to chase him… but a bitch like me might power-walk her ass off to get him." She winked while mockingly pumping her arms like she was midstride.

I burst out laughing so hard that tears trickled from my eyes.

Finally catching my breath after doubling over with laughter, I said, "I mean, I love Kevin to death. But seriously, I don't get your weird attraction to him."

Jade could have any man she wanted with a flick of her finger, but she wanted Kevin. Yes, he was supermodel gorgeous. Essentially, he was the way hotter version of Superman's alter ego. But Jade's and Kevin's personalities were polar opposites.

"You're outgoing with a party-over-here vibe… and Kevin, well, he's reserved with an *I'd rather spend my Friday night scouring the Dark Web for intel* thing going on."

She threw her hands up in the air. "Damn if I can explain it. All I know is every time I see that fake Clark Kent, I want to snatch off his glasses and shove my hands down his pants just to see if he becomes" —she waggled her eyebrows—"the Man of Steel."

"Well, you know what they say… Nerds do it better." I grinned.

"Give me some time to snag him… and I'll let you know if that's really true."

I shook my head. "And on that note, I have a show to do." I kissed her on the cheek. "Now scoot your ass to your front row seat and let me dazzle you with my extravaganza of drool-worthy fashion."

"Yes, Queen Sin." Jade bowed dramatically. "See you on the runway, sweetie," she replied before strolling away.

Jade coming backstage was a welcome distraction from my frayed nerves about the debut of my collection.

"Well, back to the grind," I muttered under my breath before turning my focus to the last-minute details that needed my attention.

The final sixty minutes before showtime went by in a blur. In true Sin Michaels style, the hair and makeup teams put the final touches on the models' conceptual beauty looks that included sparkling, tribal facial jewelry, lace masks, floor-length fetish ponytails, and warrior-like metal headbands.

Finally, the group of dressers arrived. Models were outfitted in their looks and lined up backstage, ready for their turn on the runway.

Once the sun had fully set, it was runway time. The formerly deafening hum of workers backstage became so quiet that I could hear a pin drop.

Models lined up, and I double-checked the ensembles as they waited for their cue. The gong signaled the start of the twenty-five-looks show, which would wind around a runway the entire length of the pier.

My stomach fluttered with the excitement that I was about to turn the fashion world sideways.

Three, two, one, go time!

I positioned myself in front of the monitor backstage to watch my collection on the runway. It was equally as important to me to see the women exit the runway as it was to see them walk down the runway. I had to see how the clothes worked and moved from all angles.

Years ago, my life had gone into a tailspin after finding out the truth about my parents and who I really was, and the Bigsby drama had finally been put to rest. I wasn't the same after everything I'd experienced in such a short period of time.

So after much deliberation, I'd decided to take a mini sabbatical to get my head together. Core and I'd traveled the world together to places I'd only dreamed about—Italy, Australia, Singapore, Japan, France, Africa, Morocco, Egypt, to name a few—and I'd immersed myself in the different cultures and their fashion in a way that only heightened my design sensibilities. It didn't hurt that, along the way, I'd collected swatches and bought fabrics during our travels that became the foundation for my new collection.

After our expeditions, I'd come back to the United States refreshed, excited, and ready to take on the fashion world again. I'd scrapped my old designs and started anew by creating a mood board that captured the essence and vibe of my new collection. The process of creating the mood board had allowed the subconscious creative narrative to come out of my head. Then I'd used the swatches and fabrics I'd collected during my travels as inspiration for my sketches, illustrations, and pattern-making. But the creative process was not complete until I'd made patterns and handed it off to my friend and seamstress, Summer.

I liked to keep it local as opposed to sending it to the factories. It was important for me to have the human experience transferred to the garment. The creation process was exhilarating; sometimes I sewed until my fingers bled, and then I began to fit the garments on my foam mannequin that I'd named Jade.

For months, I had created over a hundred samples, but only twenty-five styles had made the show after my editing process. I smiled, remembering the hectic three weeks before the show when it had become intense. During that time, I'd had to firm up the guest list with the show producer I'd hired, which tremendously helped me. She'd not only assisted with producing the show, but she'd also handled the press and sales.

But it was the week leading up to the show that was the worst for many designers, including me. It had been filled with endless days of problem-solving all the things that could and would go wrong. I remembered all of the angst that I'd gone through as my show drew near. It was marathon time with no time to eat or sleep. Shit, I was lucky to get a damn shower in.

I couldn't believe that now it was almost time for curtains up. And after all this work, a typical show only lasted minutes.

But even with all the angst and drama I'd been through just to get here tonight, if anyone asked me, the fashion junkie, if it was worth it, they'd get a resounding, *Hell yes!*

Even despite the fact that, all day, I'd worried if the audience would understand the message—*fashion is for everyone*—of my entire collection based on these selected looks.

As the lights dimmed, the crowd hushed and the show began. I held my breath while self-doubt crept in.

I was scared to death to share my collection with the world even though I knew that my show was courageous.

Eager fashionistas perched in the front row and battled for photos as the models finally made their highly anticipated journey down the runway.

I bit my bottom lip, and I started to wonder if I'd made all the right choices.

The models were on the runway, showcasing the designs I'd worked on for so many months.

The crowd buzzed with anticipation.

The first model strutted down the runway, wearing a black dress featuring an open-knit mesh detail in metallic silver and holding up a black leather purse to her forehead that read *Sin Michaels* in gold letters to let the audience know I was a brand force to be reckoned with.

I could feel the collective sigh from my team. We just loved it so much.

The crowd buzzed with anticipation.

My favorite female R&B vocalist, Infinity, provided the soundtrack, followed by pop hits of the past half century that formed a medley on the Sin Michaels soundtrack—everything from Rihanna's "S&M" to Jay-Z's "Empire State of Mind." The lively sampling was the key to my collection. It was my love letter to diverse women and their individual style.

There was something electric in the room as the next model strutted down the runway with *Who the fuck is Sin Michaels?* etched on the back of an oversize shirt. It was these stolen moments during the show that felt the most special to me because it encapsulated the badass bad-girl DNA of my clothing line.

As the models completed their circuit of the runway and returned backstage, my team of ten dressers quickly changed them into the next look, and off they went again.

The audience pressed forward, applauded, and made sounds of oohing and aahing. I felt breathless from excitement.

The clothing was a celebration of my life. The models, clad in head wraps with jeweled detailing, represented New York in all of its organized chaos. The collection had beading, sequins, psychedelic prints, tinsel, and more, embodying New York City's essence.

A main focus was lingerie-like lace dresses. Many were draped or tied around the body, which had that edgy Gothic yet romantic feel I was known for. To toughen up the sheer, delicate looks, I incorporated plenty of menswear-inspired suiting pieces—some structured, others done up in fluid silk and heavily adorned with metal hoops and chains, hanging pearls, and textured leather, accessorized with Swarovski crystal lunch bags etched with the letters *SM*.

Palpable excitement buzzed through the charged air.

My team and I'd stitched every single bead, sequin, and rhinestone onto my elaborate clothing by hand.

Along with a selection of menswear, the drama really came out halfway through the show when a series of couture-like looks walked the runway. There were voluminous ballgowns, modern tie-dyed feathers, cascades of fringe, impeccably layered sequins, intricate embroidery, and patchwork—each the result of a painstaking attention to detail.

Jade was among the famous faces on a stylish front row, and she caught the attention of the cameras as she shouted out, leaning forward and cheering with a lot of enthusiasm, as the rest of the audience applauded the designs parading down the catwalk.

Sculptural organza danced around the models like whimsical waves, and then came my va-va-voom blood-red asymmetric halter gown that wrapped around the model's neck in a buckle and slinked down her body with a slit across one hip.

The next model wore a tiara that read *Boss Girl* and a diamond Swarovski crystal suit—silver, slinky, and ultra-sexy with a jacket cut very low to reveal as much cleavage and collarbone as possible.

The last model who took the runway sported a tiara that read *Bossy* as she wore a strapless mini frock that featured a nude underdress covered with embellished, chain-mail-inspired detail. It was sexy and seductive, and it was paired with my favorite fuck-me red-bottomed heels.

And then the show ended all too soon. I could feel the pride in the studio. The looks, the lighting, the hair, the makeup, the nails, the girls, the styling—it all came together to tell the story of female empowerment—love, strength, and inclusion in the world—and I loved it all.

As the models took their final walk, the empowering version of the song "Run the World (Girls)" rang out, allowing the audience to soak up the final moments before it was time for me to go out on the runway to say thank you to everyone for coming and to take my bow.

I swayed over to the mirror to check my appearance. My diamond engagement ring and wedding band glinted while I adjusted my see-through blouse, which was from my collection. It flaunted my very round tummy in all its glory and also showed off a hint of cleavage. I'd teamed the blouse that featured a sheer panel down the front with black jeans and a long silver chain as well as large black-and-silver hoop earrings.

Giselle glanced down at my stilettos. "You know you're going to have to stop wearing those things once you get further along."

I frowned. "Oh, hell no. I'm rocking stilettos until they wheel me into the delivery room, and even then, I'll demand to keep them on." I waggled my eyebrows. "It'll be a very kinky delivery indeed." I blew her an air kiss, swaying past her.

The song, which championed womankind's incredible ability to get shit done, still played as I showed my supermodel prowess, taking to the catwalk, strutting and waving at the crowd while flaunting my huge baby belly in the sheer lace blouse, which left nothing to do with my bump to the imagination.

I was overwhelmed by the thunderous applause and standing ovation from what turned out to be a large group of the most influential names in the New York fashion community. All of these incredible people whom I had so much respect for were there. I hadn't imagined that sort of generosity and support until I experienced it. It was obviously a turning point in my career and definitely a great NYFW moment for me.

But it wasn't until I looked at the front row seats and saw the people who meant everything in the world to me—Cisco, Jade, Ariana, Erika, Mitch, Zuri, and Core—clapping with huge smiles on their faces that the dam of happy tears burst, and they streamed down my cheeks.

There had been a lot of bumps in the road just to get here today, and I couldn't help thinking briefly about Tabitha and if she'd have been here, celebrating my success, had circumstances been different. Not that I missed her or felt any guilt about the way Core had booted Tabitha out of New York with a little cash and a stern warning never to contact me again or come back to the city, or he'd take pleasure in giving the authorities all the evidence he'd collected about her shady dealings with her ex Vargos. And that was enough information to land her in jail for a very long time.

My world was complete now. I had friends—Cisco, Jade, Ariana, and Zuri—who loved me. My mother, Erika—along with my stepdad, Mitch—and I had built a close relationship even though it had taken months of work. And last but not least, Core, the love of my life, who loved and supported me as unconditionally as I did him.

The crowd quieted down when I started talking. "Thank you all for coming tonight. This truly means the world to me. Hugs and Sin Michaels." I blew an air kiss to Cisco, Ariana, Jade, Erika, Mitch, and Zuri and then beckoned my sexy hubby Core over to the stage.

He stood up, kissing the precious bundle in his arms—our baby—before handing him over to Erika with a, "Go to Grandma," order.

Erika clutched her grandson with a wide smile on her face as Core walked over to stand by my side, clutching my hand.

I couldn't believe how much I'd grown emotionally. In the past, I'd decided relationships were too much trouble. It was the easy way out when every relationship had been a certifiable disaster. It was like quitting before I got fired. Up to the point when I'd met Core, however, each one had been too much work for not nearly enough in return. That was never the trouble with my husband, though. Even when it seemed impossible, the end game was always worth it. With Core, every bit of work was worthwhile.

I said to the crowd in a clear, loud voice, "Tonight was a dream come true, one that was made possible by the love and support of my friends, family, and my partner and husband, Core McKay. Together, this sexy man and I have created something strong, beautiful, and precious."

I protectively placed a hand over my belly while looking over at my son cradled in Erika's arms. With Core by my side, now I truly understood what it meant to unconditionally love and be loved. Now my world was complete because he had given me a reason to trust… and love.

I was almost close to tears, just thinking about how much he meant to me. In roughly three years' time, I'd been able to open myself up to him enough to fall for him. I loved him… and that used to scare the shit out of me. Not now.

He turned me around to face him. I stared, mesmerized, as those delicious lips of his came nearer, finally settling across my mouth. He tilted his head to the side and slipped his tongue into my mouth. As soon as his tongue touched mine, I was lost, even right there on the runway. The man had no damn idea what he did to me.

Even after all these years, it was still hard for me to believe the life I now had. Every morning, I woke up by his side, and every night, I went to bed in his arms. Our relationship wasn't perfect. It was perfectly imperfect.

Damn. I've finally found a man who loves me like he means it.

He pulled out of our kiss and drawled huskily, "I love you, Sinful."

"And I love you, Core." And I did with all of my heart because, every day, he showed me with actions and words just how much he loved me.

Even though the process of opening up to Core and love hadn't been easy, I wouldn't change a damn thing. Finding the love I deserved had proven to be the best thing to happen to me in a very long time.

He kissed my fingers before saying, "Now let's go home, Mrs. McKay."

Weaving his fingers through mine, he escorted me along the runway and toward the backstage as the cacophony of the crowd's clapping, cheering, and whistling surrounded us.

Thank you for reading my complete **DIRTY SECRETS SERIES BOX SET**! Want more heart throbbing romance? Check out my second chance romance **HEART OF FIRE!**

GET A FREE SEDONA VENEZ BOOK!

https://sedonavenez.com/free-book

SNEAK PEEK AT HEART OF FIRE
CHAPTER 1 / KENDRA

When I pulled up to my grandmother's house, I had to do a quick double check. Although I'd driven to her house probably a thousand times—maybe more—since I first learned to drive, it had been years since I'd seen the place.

I spotted the old pear tree next to my grandmother's battered old mailbox, shaped like a 1950s-era pickup truck. I'd never understood why Grandma insisted on keeping the mailbox—why she'd repaired and painted it again and again instead of ever replacing it, but it made it easy to find her house, set back a bit from the street. I maneuvered my SUV onto the driveway, feeling the cramp in my leg as I pressed harder on the brake. *Son of a bitch.*

I put the car in park and shut off the engine, taking a deep breath to steady myself. It had been weeks since my "officer-involved shooting incident." The wound was healed but had been severe. My bulletproof vest had caught the shot the perp had aimed at my chest, but my thigh still had a deep scar from the second shot he'd gotten off as my partner had knocked him down from behind. The physical therapist told me I could expect to get full function back, but I bet it would keep aching for the rest of my life, just a token of my service to the NYPD.

I got out of my vehicle and stretched my leg, hoping to ease the cramp along the scar tissue. I looked around me, and almost without thinking, my gaze went to a spot across the street. There was a house there, newer-looking than all the other ones on the block. Brick facade, little garden boxes in front of a bay window, stained-glass inset on the front door, white trim. I frowned, rubbing my leg, trying to work out the details of the house and why it looked so different from what my memory told me would be there.

It hit me all at once. The last time I'd seen the house on that plot, it was ablaze. Whoever had bought the property had just bulldozed the wreckage and built fresh, which was why it looked so out of place among the older homes on the block. The fire…

I stopped rubbing my leg, remembering that night and remembering the family that used to live in that house. More than the family, the kid they had. The first person to welcome me to the neighborhood when I'd been a sad, scared, thirteen-year-old who'd just lost her mom to cancer and never lived outside of the Bronx. The one who'd helped me navigate the suburban middle school Grandma enrolled me in, ripped out of the cramped, crowded, noisy New York Public School system. *Lukas.* I sighed and rubbed at my leg again.

I heard the screen door open with a creaky groan and turned to see Grandma coming out of the house.

"Hi, Grandma," I called out.

"Hey, baby girl," she returned with a huge smile.

Most people had mistaken Grandma for my mother when I was growing up, and even now, at seventy-five, she didn't look old enough to be a grandmother, much less the grandmother to a twenty-nine-year-old adult woman. Grandma only had a few strands of silver in her neatly braided hair, and while her ebony-hued skin had some wrinkles, they were what you'd expect on a woman of fifty-five, maybe sixty. Grandma had taught me her secret when I was a teenager —every day, she washed her face with black soap then smoothed on shea butter. She also drank eight glasses of water every single day, starting with a big glass first thing in the morning.

Grandma made her way down the walk to my SUV, pulling me in for a big hug. Clutching her back, I inhaled her familiar scent of lavender. *God, I missed her.*

Pulling away, Grandma pinched my cheek before stepping back and moving toward the rear of my SUV. "Open the back," Grandma ordered. I rolled my eyes before clicking it open, limping a bit as I tried to stop her from yanking out my luggage. I knew it wouldn't work—I would not talk her out of it, but I had to try.

"No, Grandma. I got it."

"You're a guest in this house, Kendra Powell," Grandma rebutted.

"And I'm your granddaughter. I used to live here," I countered, reaching for my suitcase.

"You haven't lived here in years," Grandma insisted. "That makes you a guest in my house."

"They're too heavy for you," I said, trying for another argument.

"And you with your injured leg—they're easy for you?" Grandma asked me, turning to pin me down with her gaze. I felt my cheeks warm up, and I sighed heavily.

"You take one, and I take one?" I suggested.

Grandma grinned. "That's fair."

I knew that although she looked like she was maybe sixty at most, Grandma wasn't as strong as she used to be. I let her grab the lighter of my two suitcases and took the heavier one for myself, balancing it against my bad leg for a second while I put my weight on my good leg before pressing the button to shut my liftgate.

"Are you going to get up the porch steps okay?" I asked, shoving my keys into my pocket and following behind her. Grandma nodded without so much as looking at me.

"The day I can't get up the steps is the day I get Martha Peters's son Jackson to come and install a ramp," Grandma said. "And I will probably die a week after it's built, at that."

I snorted, sparing one last look at the new, pretty house on the block where there had been a burned-out husk before. I shook my head and continued up the driveway and onto the stone walk toward the front porch, trying not to think of Lukas. I stepped up onto the stairs, and my bad leg cramped up again, making me stumble. In an instant, Grandma had my suitcase out of my hand and her arm under me, holding me up and helping me onto the porch.

"I'm fine," I said.

Grandma tsked, shaking her head and letting me into the house. "You should have let me take that one," Grandma said, steering me through the front door and setting down my suitcase.

"I said I'm fine," I protested. "It's just a cramp."

"Uh-huh," Grandma said dryly. "Did they even clear you for lifting?"

I sighed. "They cleared me for everyday tasks and light chores," I told her. "I'm just not cleared for duty yet."

"And if it weren't my birthday, you'd be back in New York, in that tiny Brooklyn apartment, chomping at the bit to at least be on desk duty," Grandma said, picking up the heavier of my two suitcases and gesturing for me to take the lighter one.

I didn't want to discuss this thorny topic further. "Happy birthday, Grandma."

"Well, thank you, baby girl," Grandma returned warmly while propping my suitcase against the couch. She took the moment to kiss and hug me quickly, before bustling off toward my old room. "Are you able to keep up with me, or should I make two trips?" she asked me, glancing worriedly over her shoulder.

I hefted the lighter suitcase and followed her down the hall, to the room I'd lived in from eighteen until college, when I'd moved out for good. I followed her into my room, setting down my suitcase near the door. Grandma had changed nothing, other than occasionally cleaning the room and changing the bed linens since I'd last been in there. Missy Elliott posters, pictures of my friends from high school, and I could even still—barely—smell the horrible perfume I'd spilled on the carpet.

Knowing that Grandma was concerned about my well-being and recovery, I mumbled, "Grandma, my job is competitive. With being one of the very few black women to make detective, I have to work hard, take as many cases as possible."

"I know, I know," Grandma said, wiping her hands dramatically on her pants. "You had to make a name for yourself. I know my ambitious granddaughter. But all work and no play is a recipe for disaster." She eyed me. "I just want you to slow down, enjoy life, and take some time for you. And for goodness' sake, visit me more. I ain't getting any younger, baby girl."

She was right. I'd been going full throttle at work for so long that I'd forgotten what was important to me—my health, happiness, and Grandma, my only family. "Forgive me?" I asked, giving her my best doe-eyed look.

Grandma laughed and kissed me again, cupping my face in her hands and peering up into my eyes. "It's about time you slowed down, baby girl," Grandma said. "Maybe you'll get a taste for it."

"Maybe," I said while moving over to the bed and sitting down. "But my commanding officer back in the precinct is staying on top of any updates on my condition, my potential readiness to come back." Reaching down, I pulled off my sneakers, sighing while wiggling my toes.

Grandma shook her head. "You're still not listening to what I'm saying." Marching over to me, she plopped down beside me. "I'm proud of you and how much you've accomplished, but I haven't heard shit about your personal life." She pinched my cheek. "Like, when's the last time you were on a date? Or had sex?"

Grandma and I had a very candid relationship, so talking about sex wasn't awkward. "Too long," I grunted.

She laughed huskily. "So, I'm getting more action than my twenty-nine-year-old granddaughter."

"Sadly, yes." I hadn't had sex in over a year, and that hookup was fast and unsatisfying. Frankly, I missed sex, but I wanted more than meaningless fucking with some random dude. I didn't have time for dating. Besides, I intimidated most men because of my job in law enforcement. "But finding Mr. Right isn't easy."

"You're beautiful and smart. It can't be that hard," Grandma returned.

"That's easier said than done." I rolled my eyes. "My occupation brings a boatload of challenges to a romantic relationship. The mere act of trying to date is difficult. It's hard to find someone who wants to go out on a date with me when I get off at six in the morning." And sorting through all the physical and emotional issues my job brought into a new relationship was difficult for any man to deal with. "The dating struggle is real." I pulled my hat off my head and fluffed out my thick, curly, shoulder-length hair. "And the stereotypes of women in law enforcement are fucking ridiculous. Most men think I'm carrying a gun all the time and always eating donuts. There's a real lack of understanding of what I do daily."

Grandma snorted. "I'm not talking about dating some asshole. I'm talking about all the good men out there who will understand and respect what you bring to the table, baby girl." She paused. "Maybe you need to look for the right man in a smaller pool, like right here. There are lots of hot men in small towns."

"Lots?" I narrowed my eyes. "Here? I doubt it. The dating pool here dwindled when all the young people, like me, got the hell out of here, either after graduating from high school or college."

"Many people of the younger generation are moving back here in droves. It's refreshing that they're coming back to their roots to settle down. They've come to their senses and realized that the big city ain't where the action's at." She winked at me.

"If you say so," I answered. Unlike most occupations, police work often defined a person in the mind of a potential mate. There was an odd fascination with women in law enforcement. I didn't have the time or the patience to wade through that cesspool of crazy. Besides, it could be very intimidating for a man dating a female cop who carried a gun and had a legal authority to take a life.

Grandma grinned at me. "I say so." She patted my leg. "Enough about that. My party is tomorrow night, and you're here at least a week. I'll get the chance to fatten you up and make sure you're resting."

"I'm guessing your party is a big deal around here."

Grandma laughed, throwing her head back. "Baby girl, it is *the* party of the year. Down at the country club, lots of food, good people… I hope you're ready to see your grandma treated like the queen bee of the town."

"You've always been that," I pointed out.

"You're damn right I have, and it's about time this town recognized it," Grandma said. "I hope you have something pretty to wear for it."

"I have something appropriate," I told her.

Grandma gave me a little look—the look I'd gotten more than a few times living with her as a teenager, the look that told me she had a juicy secret she wasn't about to tell me.

"Good," Grandma said. "Because you never know who you'll meet."

I rolled my eyes. "Grandma, there've never been more than fifty thousand people in town," I pointed out. "My entire high school was less than the graduating class at PS 111. I can't meet anyone I haven't already met."

Grandma shrugged. "Still," she said while getting to her feet. "People come and go. You never know if Mr. Right will come strolling back into your life."

I frowned, watching her bustle out of my room. *What is she up to?*

~

Devour this friends to lovers story **HEART OF FIRE!**

WANT FREE SEDONA VENEZ BOOKS?

Sign up for Sedona Venez's Newsletter and receive FREE BOOKS. In addition to the free stories, you will also get special pricing, exclusive previews and news of new releases.

GET A FREE SEDONA VENEZ BOOK!

Join Sedona's mailing list to be the first to know of new releases, free books, special prices and other author giveaways.

https://sedonavenez.com/free-book

ABOUT THE AUTHOR

USA TODAY BESTSELLING AUTHOR SEDONA VENEZ lives in New York City with her former military hubby—hooah—and their fur babies. She loves writing sizzling, sexy intricate stories about strong but broken characters who push limits, overcome their fears and risk it all for love.

Sedona loves to connect with readers!
www.sedonavenez.com